COLD
MALICE

COLD
MALICE

Toni Anderson

ALSO BY TONI ANDERSON

COLD JUSTICE – CROSSFIRE
Colder Than Sin (Book #2) Coming 2019
Cold & Deadly (Book #1)

COLD JUSTICE SERIES
Cold Blooded (Book #10)
A Cold Dark Promise (Book #9~A Wedding Novella)
Cold Malice (Book #8)
Cold Secrets (Book #7)
Cold Hearted (Book #6)
Cold in the Shadows (Book #5)
Cold Fear (Book #4)
Cold Light of Day (Book #3)
Cold Pursuit (Book #2)
A Cold Dark Place (Book #1)

THE BARKLEY SOUND SERIES
Dark Waters (Book #2)
Dangerous Waters (Book #1)

STAND-ALONE TITLES
The Killing Game
Edge of Survival
Storm Warning
Sea of Suspicion

'HER' ROMANTIC SUSPENSE SERIES
Her Risk to Take (Novella ~ Book #3)
Her Last Chance (Book #2)
Her Sanctuary (Book #1)

Dedicated to the brave members of the FBI.
Fidelity – Bravery – Integrity.

CHAPTER ONE

Nearly Twenty Years Earlier. August 22.

"CLEAR THE TABLE, Theresa Jane."

Theresa Jane sighed resignedly. Since her sister, Ellie, had left home two months earlier, it was always her turn to clear the dishes. Her mother sent her a pointed look when she didn't move fast enough and she hurriedly got to her feet and started scraping plates.

"What time did your father say he'd be home?" Her mom directed the question to Walt, one of Theresa Jane's two older brothers.

Walt was seventeen and had his own truck.

Theresa Jane didn't like Walt very much. Her other brother, Eddie, was a year older than Walt. He'd gone into town with her daddy that afternoon to pick up some supplies.

She didn't like Eddie much either.

"Don't rightly know." Walt wiped his mouth with the back of his hand and pushed his plate away.

Her mother's lips tightened and Theresa Jane ducked her gaze. An angry Francis Hines tended to lash out at the first thing that caught her attention. Theresa Jane had learned not to be that thing.

She moved around the table scraping plates and collecting cutlery, trying to be as invisible as possible. She worked her way around her mother, Walt, her mother's cousin, Jacob, and his girlfriend, Lisa.

Her daddy had a girlfriend, too, but she wasn't supposed to know.

Theresa Jane tapped her five-month-old baby brother's snub nose as he smushed mashed potatoes on the tray of his highchair. Bobby gurgled at her and she grinned back. He was the happiest baby in the world though no one ever paid him no mind.

Her arms trembled from the weight of the dishes, but she knew she'd get the belt if she dropped them.

A sharp screech of chair legs against hardwood floors shattered the silence as Kenny Travers climbed to his feet. Kenny had moved into the compound six months ago after getting into a fight with his boss. Her daddy liked Kenny because he was good with the horses. Her momma thought he was up to something. He took the heavy stack of plates from her grasp and put them on the table, adding his own to the pile before scooping them up. She sent him a shy smile and he winked. Kenny might be a "no-good cowboy" according to her momma, but he was the only person in Kodiak who was ever nice to her.

Walt had been nice to her last week—for about five-seconds. He'd offered to help collect eggs from the chicken coop. Should have known it was a trick. Soon as they'd gotten to the barn he'd trapped her in the horse stall and grabbed one of her hands, placing it against the front of his pants. Her stomach lurched from the memory and she glared at him as he sat at the table belching.

He was *disgusting.*

Boys were disgusting.

She was so glad she was a girl.

Thankfully, a rooster had flown up onto the side of the stall that day in the barn, startling Walt. That rooster had given her the chance to pull her hand away and escape. She'd run smack bang into Kenny outside and he'd caught her by the arm. Her expression must have told him something bad had happened even though she hadn't made a sound. Theresa Jane did most of her screaming on the inside.

Then Walt had walked outside adjusting his zipper and Kenny's eyes had gotten all glittery and mean. His voice had turned real quiet when he'd told her to go back to the cabin and that he'd fetch the eggs along shortly. Then he'd dragged Walt back into the barn by the scruff of his neck, and barred the door.

At dinner later that same night, Walt had shown up with a busted lip. He'd avoided looking at her and told everyone he'd walked into a door. He hadn't bothered her since then, but she still didn't trust him.

Kenny Travers was her Guardian Angel.

She collected the drinking glasses, avoiding Walt's foot when he tried to trip her. She followed Kenny into the kitchen where he dumped the stack of dishes on the draining board.

"Thanks." She craned her neck to look at him where he towered over her. She barely reached his waist.

"You're welcome, missy." He started running hot water into the bowl.

"I'll do it." She dragged over a chair so she could look out the window as she did her chores.

One side of his mouth curled up and his blue-green eyes twinkled as he studied her. "I don't mind helping, sweetheart."

They were nearly eye level when she clambered up onto

the chair. Her heart fairly burst from looking at him. Maybe when she was thirteen she could marry him, instead of one of Daddy's other friends.

She glanced over her shoulder into the dining room where her family was starting on one of their nightly rants about the cost of fuel and government taxes and the president and colored people. She'd never seen a black man, but from what her family said, black people would kill her as soon as look at her. It didn't make sense, but she was smart enough to be scared.

Most things didn't make sense even though she was ten now—like the fact they'd tattooed the number fourteen onto her left arm. She liked math, but she didn't like the number fourteen any more than she liked any other number. The skin was red and raised and itched like poison oak. She rubbed at the scab. Kenny's mouth tightened until his lips disappeared.

"Sorry." She cast her eyes downward.

"You've got nothing to be sorry for, Theresa Jane." His voice was low and funny sounding. Rough. Deep. Like her dog Sampson's warning growl.

She sighed as she squirted washing up liquid into the bowl along with the hot water, knowing she was gonna get told off for making too many bubbles, but doing it anyway. "Momma says if I paid more attention to my lessons I wouldn't be so darn stupid."

He swallowed so loud she thought he'd gotten something stuck in his gullet. "You all right?"

He nodded and cleared his throat. "You sure you don't want a hand with these dishes, missy?"

She let out a gusty sigh. "They'll just get mad with me and call me lazy if I don't do it all. An' I don't like being called

4

names."

Kenny's brow quirked and he leaned in close to murmur, "How can someone sitting on their butt doing nothin' call you lazy when you're the one doing all the work?"

Theresa Jane giggled because Kenny always said the things she was thinking. "Don't make no sense to me, either, but that's what they do."

Kenny shook his head and said in a low voice, "You're a good kid, Theresa Jane. Don't ever change." Then he hesitated, moved closer and whispered in her ear. "If there's ever trouble, will you promise me something?"

Her eyes locked on his as she nodded.

"Hide in your closet or under your bed. Don't come out for anything or anyone."

Theresa Jane stuck out her bottom lip and raised her own brows. "What kinda trouble?"

Kenny glanced into the dining room and his gaze darkened. "Any kind. And lock your door at night. Promise?"

"Okay. I promise." She nodded curiously, then his lips compressed and his expression closed down and he took a step back. He turned and walked out the back door.

Footsteps approached from behind her as she tested the temperature of the water with her fingertips.

"You used too much soap again, stupid girl."

Theresa Jane kept her eyes averted. "Sorry, Momma."

"What was he saying to you?"

"Nothin', Momma."

Francis Hines walked up to stand next to her at the sink. "He say where he was going?"

Theresa Jane tucked in her chin. "Nope. He just left."

Francis twitched the net curtain and they both watched

Kenny climb into his truck and drive down the winding dirt road, kicking up dust behind it before turning left on the main highway into town.

"Maybe he's going to find Daddy?" Theresa Jane suggested, hoping that would make her momma happy.

"Ha. Your daddy isn't *lost*, Theresa Jane. He's either drunk or…" Her mother trailed off when they heard the honk of a horn and saw her father's truck pull into the long driveway and start rumbling along the road.

Theresa Jane risked a glance at her mother's face. "He's home," she said brightly.

"So he is. So he is." Francis's lips pinched. Then she turned and got Daddy's and Eddie's dinners out of the oven.

Theresa Jane braced herself as her father came in. He frowned when he saw her standing on a chair over a sink full of white foam, but didn't yell at her. Eddie came in behind him and pushed past her to help himself to a glass of water from the tap.

"Hey!" She almost lost her balance and had to grab onto his arm to steady herself. He pried her fingers off him as if she had cooties. She grabbed onto the sink instead. "Watch it!"

God, he was annoying.

He leaned down until she went cross-eyed meeting his gaze. "Shut up, brat. Else I'll teach you some manners."

The pungent scent of beer hit her in the face and her stomach churned. A shiver of repulsion moved through her. He laughed, then walked away with a cocky swagger that made him look like he'd pooped his pants.

She stuck out her tongue at his retreating back.

Ever since her older sister, Ellie, had married Harlan Trimble in June her brothers had started treating her different.

Meaner.

She didn't like it.

She scrubbed the scourer over the first plate and placed it on the drainer. Bubbles drizzled over the stainless steel and into the sink.

"Get a move on, Theresa Jane. Sun will have gone down by the time you're done lollygagging," her mother berated her. "And make sure you rinse off those suds."

Theresa Jane scrubbed faster and wished she could have driven away into the sunset with no-good cowboy Kenny Travers.

SIX HOURS LATER, a hand clamped over Theresa Jane's mouth as she lay asleep in bed and a voice hissed in her ear. "Get up. The Feds are coming!"

The words shot terror into her heart as she lurched into consciousness. Her mother let go and ripped back the bedclothes. Despite it being summer, an icy draft pierced her thin nightclothes and made goosebumps dance over her skin.

"Get dressed," her mother commanded.

Theresa Jane dragged on yesterday's clothes that lay in a heap beside the bed.

"Why are they here? What are they going to do with us?" She'd grown up hearing about the evilness of the federal government, how the government wanted to control what they thought and did. Destroy their way of life. The Feds wanted to steal her daddy's hard-earned money, tax their land and take away their guns. Guns were the only way they could protect themselves from the bad people.

Theresa Jane wasn't exactly sure who the bad people were but they were everywhere according to her folks. And now the Feds were coming for them.

"We're not going to let them do a damned thing," her mother snapped.

Theresa Jane's heart pounded. Tears gathered in her eyes. "I'm scared, Momma."

Her mother's expression softened for the briefest of instants. "I won't let them hurt you. I'll shoot you myself before I let them take any of my babies."

Theresa Jane flinched.

"Keep down." Her mother pressed a heavy pistol into her grip. Then she ran, hunched over, into the hall. Theresa Jane followed, using both hands to carry the weapon. She knew how to handle a gun. She'd been having weekly shooting lessons since she was five years old, and regularly beat her brothers at target practice. But the idea of pointing this at a real person and pulling the trigger made her want to weep.

She ran awkwardly after her mother. A gunshot made her scream so loud her ears hurt.

"Shut the fuck up with that screeching," Eddie snarled at her. He was hunkered behind the refrigerator, a dark shadow despite the bright moonlight that shone through the open drapes. Walt was in the living room staring out of the north-facing window.

"They're not taking us alive," her mother stated, sending a sliver of dread coiling through Theresa Jane's gut.

Cries filled the darkness. Through the window Theresa Jane saw an orange glow lighting up the sky. The acrid smell of smoke drifted on the warm night air, coating the back of her throat.

"They're trying to burn us out." Her daddy walked into the kitchen from the back of the house.

Oh, God.

Her daddy exchanged a long look with his wife. "They've taken the compound and surrounded the cabin. Stan told me on the radio Kenny's dead. Saw him shot out near the barn."

A sharp pain stabbed Theresa Jane's chest. Kenny couldn't be dead. Not her Kenny.

"I hate them." Fury burned inside her chest even as her heart withered. "I hate them all."

Her father studied her and for the first time in her life she saw a small measure of respect reflected back in his eyes. "Go cover the window in your bedroom. Shoot anyone you don't recognize."

Theresa Jane nodded, scurrying back to her room. A baby's wail made her pause outside the door. Everyone had forgotten about baby Bobby who was sleeping in his crib beside her parents' bed.

She heard more gunshots from the direction of the kitchen but didn't know who fired. Bobby's cries were getting louder so she rushed and picked him up out of the crib and ran back into her room. The baby was warm against her body, but his diaper was saturated. Her dog Sampson followed her, whining unhappily.

She stripped the sodden sleep suit and diaper from Bobby's body and tossed them on the floor. Then she laid the baby on the bed and wrapped him in a towel that hung on the back of her door.

The gunshots were getting more frequent now and glass shattered. Kenny's words from earlier that evening came back to her in a rush.

"If there's ever trouble, promise me something? Hide in your closet or under your bed. Don't come out for anything or anyone."

How'd he known?

She had no idea, but somehow, she was sure he had.

She stared at the gun she'd laid on the bed, and then back at the baby smiling up at her, torn as to what to do.

Kenny was dead and she needed to avenge him, but she didn't want to get shot or die. Bobby gurgled and her heart twisted. She didn't want Bobby to die either.

She didn't allow herself to worry about the rest of her family. They never listened to her anyhow.

She ran to the bedroom door and closed it, turning the key quietly in case one of them heard and came running. Then she wedged a wooden chair under the handle. Next, she picked up the baby and cradled him against her chest. She grabbed the handgun, climbed inside her closet, shoving aside old shoes and toys, urging Sampson to join them. She pulled the door closed, lying on the cramped floor beside the infant. She put the gun behind her so Bobby wouldn't be able to reach it.

Gunshots sounded louder now and she shivered as the baby cried out in alarm. Vibrations of bullets slamming into her home reverberated through the wood and along her bones. She curled over the baby and hugged the dog, protecting them both as best she could.

The shooting seemed to go on for hours. Eventually, she heard her mother's voice, faint between the two closed wooden doors.

"Theresa Jane?" Her bedroom door rattled. "Theresa Jane, you in there? Open the door. Theresa Jane! Open the damned door!"

Theresa Jane's hand started to inch toward the closet door and then stopped. Her mother sounded angry enough to carry out her earlier threat. Theresa Jane was smart enough to be more terrified of Francis than of the bullets flying around.

"Theresa Jane, I'm warning you—" Her mother's threat was cut off by a scream of pain and a sob.

Theresa Jane sat up.

Oh, God. Had her mother been shot?

"Help. Help." Her mother's voice grew fainter.

Theresa Jane's heart twisted. Her mother was hurt. She started to go to her, then froze when her mother started yelling. "You always were a contrary little bitch. I should have drowned you at birth."

Hot tears filled Theresa Jane's eyes. The tightness in her throat made it impossible to breathe. Bobby started fussing and she gathered him closer as Sampson stuck his nose between them and whimpered. "It's okay, Bobby. I'm gonna take good care of you. I love you, baby." She kissed Sampson's wet nose. "I'm gonna protect you both, forever and ever."

CHAPTER TWO

T HE TIME HAD come. All the years of planning, plotting, pretending, had finally come to an end.

Now was the time to act.

The targets had been carefully chosen. Each one would send a message until it was time for the ultimate demonstration of power. Let the government scurry madly in mindless fear. Let them mobilize their resources and throw a thousand imbecilic drones at the issue, trying to hunt them down. They'd fail. It was already too late. They moved too slowly. She was too clever. The plan was in motion.

Now was the time for vengeance.

The morning was still dark. The late February air crisp and dry. She pulled her hat lower, the wool black scarf wrapped high around her neck, the heavy black winter coat done up to her chin against the chill, concealing her build, her shape, her femininity. She hunched her nose into her scarf and avoided meeting the gaze of a man wearing a business suit and woolen overcoat.

If she hoped to complete her mission, she couldn't afford for anyone to remember her face.

Her grip tightened on the pistol she concealed in her deep coat pocket. It was a generic gun, holding unexceptional bullets. They carried a clear message.

North Cleveland Park was one of the few areas of the city not covered with cameras. If people knew how much the government spied on their every move they'd have more members in their ranks. But theirs was a small and exclusive club. Restricted to those they could trust, those committed to *doing* something about their problems, rather than just mouthing off. She kept her head down as she turned right and walked up the hill, passing beautiful, century-old homes with leafy driveways, and gardens that were a dark, lush green, even in the dead of winter.

Three more houses.

She didn't glance around, or draw attention to herself as she turned into the driveway of number forty-four. She slipped around the side of the house to the back door, drew out her pistol. With her gloved left hand she rapped sharply using the small iron knocker. She looked around. The rear of the house was concealed by a tall privet hedge and a dense band of trees on either side, a heavily wooded ridge behind. She heard the tread of footsteps from inside, a voice calling out and another one muttering in response. The man opened the door, his bushy gray eyebrows rising up his wrinkled forehead. He opened his mouth to say something—probably some biting comment meant to put her in her place.

She didn't give him the chance.

She pulled the trigger twice. The suppressor made the gun heavier than normal but her aim was true. Then she stepped over the dead man and walked into the warmth of his home. A woman stood slack-mouthed beside the open refrigerator. She pulled the trigger again and the woman crumpled to the hardwood floor. Determinedly, the woman tried to drag herself forward. The messenger stepped closer and put a bullet

13

between terrified black eyes.

No witnesses.

She picked up the shell casings.

No evidence.

She stepped over the man's body, avoiding the dark pooling blood.

No remorse.

She walked away.

CHAPTER THREE

I T WAS ASSISTANT Special Agent in Charge Steve McKenzie's first day in his new position and he was early.

He'd just wrapped up being team leader of a Joint Terrorism Task Force investigating the November attack on a shopping mall in Minnesota. The carnage still gave him nightmares but that was the cost of the job. Stopping terrorists from hurting others made it worthwhile.

Prior to Minnesota, he'd spent two years at the Crisis Management Unit in Quantico. Now he was bringing those skills to do a stint at HQ—a necessary evil if you wanted to get promoted within the FBI. The only drawback was somehow the heart of FBI operations felt a whole hell of a lot like the sidelines, and he did his best work neck-deep in shit-storms.

But this was a plum job that utilized all his skills and messing it up wasn't on the agenda. His plan was to make Special Agent in Charge (SAC) and be put in charge of his own field office by the time he was forty. At the ripe old age of thirty-nine he was cutting it fine.

He got off the elevator on the fifth floor. A tall, burly man approached from an office on the left. Mac headed that way, passing a small, wooden desk, cordoned off with protective rope, a framed photograph of J. Edgar Hoover sitting pride of place on its shiny, mahogany surface.

"ASAC McKenzie?" the man approaching asked.

"Yes, sir." Mac nodded as he held out his hand. "Most people call me Mac."

"I've heard great things about you, Mac."

"All lies," Mac said straight-faced. "ASC Gerald, I presume?"

The man nodded. "Let me give you a quick tour of SIOC and help you get settled."

Gerald swiped his badge over an electronic panel and opened the door. SIOC—or the Strategic Information and Operations Center—in the depths of FBI headquarters was over forty-two thousand square feet of state-of-the-art facilities that looked like it had been ripped right out of a Jason Bourne movie.

They entered a large room filled with a big conference table and TV monitors mounted on the wall. Off to the side there was another smaller Executive Suite with coffee making equipment and en suite facilities.

"That's where the director and the attorney general meet every morning to talk through the most pressing issues of the day." The ASC checked a wristwatch that looked capable of launching rockets. He nodded to a woman setting up refreshments. "They'll be here any minute. The suite has everything except a Jacuzzi." Gerald laughed at his own joke and walked through to another larger conference room, swinging his arms out in an arc to encompass all the screens and clocks on the wall showing local times around the globe. "We have six crisis action team rooms, five large-scale operations areas, executive briefing areas and conference rooms. We operate around the clock, 365 days of the year, 24/7, with three watch units and one critical incident unit."

Mac's job was to act as liaison officer between the Crisis Management Unit here and the one in Quantico.

Gerald stopped in one of the Executive Operations rooms and stood with his hands on his hips looking around, the sense of pride obvious from the smile on his face and the confident angle of his chin. "This is where we manage special missions like the Somali pirates' operation."

"You ran that from here?" Mac was impressed.

The ASC's deep brown eyes glowed with satisfaction. "Every second of it."

Those were the sorts of cases Mac wanted to be involved with—a fix for his inner adrenaline junkie and a way of gaining valuable insight into the full capabilities of the Bureau. But he'd been working for the FBI long enough to understand it was ninety-five percent paperwork, five percent high-octane action. That proportion only increased the higher you climbed up the food chain.

Each FBI Field Office had their own Operation Centers, but SIOC made most of them look like high school media rooms. From this place, they could monitor the position of every aircraft in US airspace, access all street cameras in five states, and know the deployment of all national assets from bomb squads to surveillance units. This was important information to have on hand and CMU needed access to it. Excitement snaked up Mac's spine as he took everything in. This was where he was meant to be.

A commotion broke out and several agents came hurrying out of a media operations room across the hallway. One of them, a young woman with straight brown hair, searched around until her eyes found Gerald. She walked briskly toward them carrying a piece of paper. Clearly something big had happened.

"What have you got, Hernandez?" Gerald held out his hand.

"Just got word a federal judge has been found murdered in his DC home."

Gerald took the paper. "What do we know?"

"Judge Raine Thomas of the United States Court of Appeals for the Federal Circuit. Shot dead in North Cleveland Park this morning before he left for work. Wife was also shot dead."

"They catch anyone?"

The woman shook her head. "Local cops were first on the scene. But as soon as they discovered the identity of the victim, they called in the Feds. Washington Field Office has agents en route."

"ASAC Steve McKenzie." He indicated Mac with his right hand. "I want you to meet Libby Hernandez, a top analyst at SIOC. Mac just joined us from the Crisis Management Unit at Quantico."

Mac shook hands with the analyst and didn't bother to correct Gerald. It was close enough. "WFO has the lead on this?"

They were heading toward Gerald's office, the men's long strides forcing the woman to almost jog to keep up. Mac slowed down and indicated she go ahead of him.

"Correct." She nodded and smiled gratefully.

They walked into Gerald's office and the man went behind his desk to pick up the phone. "I need to update my boss."

"I'd like to visit the crime scene and talk to the case officer. See if they're going to need our services," Mac said.

Strictly speaking, the Assistant Section Chief wasn't his

boss—that was still the head of the Critical Incident Response Group, but Gerald was one in a long line of superiors within the Law Enforcement Services division.

Gerald appeared amused and tapped his fingers on the phone's handset. "You understand that's why we have all these monitors and computers here, right? Remote access."

"But there's nothing like being at the actual scene to get a feel for what happened and how it went down. That's how agents figured out there was a female terrorist involved in the Minnesota mall attack." Mac held Gerald's gaze. They all knew that same female terrorist had tried to assassinate the President of the United States. It wasn't something that could be overstated. He didn't know how long Gerald had been in administration or whether he still got that buzz from being in the field, but Mac did. That was the one thing he was going to miss as SAC. "With such a high-profile murder occurring on our doorstep, I think it's worth a quick field trip."

"Makes sense." Gerald conceded. "Let me find out who's on it from WFO and I'll tell them you're on your way." He covered the mouthpiece with his palm. "You have transportation?"

"I'll grab a cab."

Five minutes later, Mac was back on the streets of downtown DC, trying to hail a cab. Only a few top FBI officials were assigned parking spots beneath HQ and he wasn't on that list. It was a stark reminder that while he might think he was hot shit, around here, he was simply another cog in the wheel.

———————

TESS FALLON LET herself into her brother's house and dumped

her laptop case on top of the kitchen table.

"Cole?" She shouted. "You here?"

Silence met her greeting and her breath rushed out in frustration. She checked her wristwatch. They were supposed to meet at nine to go over his tax returns, but to say her brother had other priorities was an understatement.

"Zane, Andy, Dave?" She paused. "Joseph? Anyone?"

Cole had bought this house using money he'd inherited from their mother last year. He rented rooms to three of his friends, other members of the university soccer team, and his best friend, Joseph, spent more time here than in his own dorm.

No one answered her.

"Damn." She eased out of her coat and hung it over the back of a kitchen chair. She gave Cole's cell a try and cursed when it went straight to voicemail.

He'd obviously forgotten she'd arranged to come over this morning. She had a client meeting at ten-thirty, with an influential civil liberties group—her specialty—and she knew more-or-less where Cole kept his files. She could wait around, wasting her time, or she could get on with the job.

She headed through the messy living room with its polished hardwood floor, rumpled couch, and massive flat-screen TV. Two empty breakfast bowls sat on the coffee table, along with two half-full mugs of coffee which suggested someone had eaten a quick breakfast here this morning—or they hadn't cleaned up lately.

She headed to the den, which served as Cole's office. This was strictly his space and pretty much the only rule he had in the house was that the guys did not mess around in here. Two PCs and an iMac lined one wall and another flat-screen TV decorated the bare space above it. Her brother's paperwork was stacked haphazardly on his desk next to his laptop docking station.

She eyed the papers. She had him automatically copy her on electronic receipts every time he made a work purchase or got paid. Even so, this was a mess.

Cole had enrolled at American University on a soccer scholarship but had busted his knee at the end of the first season. During his recuperation, he'd started writing software apps. It turned out he was phenomenal at it.

Tess didn't have the first clue about writing code, but she did understand that if he didn't pay taxes, he'd go to jail. On a positive note, he now earned more than she did, which was a little demoralizing when she thought about all the years she'd put in to her CPA training, but at least she didn't need to worry about supporting him through college or paying off his student loans.

"So where d'you put the household bills, genius?" She leafed through the stack of papers on the desk, slowly grinding her teeth. Didn't matter how many times she'd asked him to pull those numbers he always forgot—and yet here she was, enabling him.

She glanced at the filing drawer where he kept most of his personal information. He didn't like people going through his stuff. He never had. She didn't like snooping, but she had a living to make and she was the one doing her brother a favor. The least he could do was allow her to enable him at her own convenience.

She opened the drawer and made short work of locating the files she needed: Internet, phone, heating, insurance, mortgage. She was just about to close the drawer when a shiny black folder caught her eye.

Her fingers plucked at it before she could stop herself. Apparently, she was compulsively nosey, but if her brother had turned up like he was supposed to she wouldn't have been forced to go digging through his belongings. Inside the folder was a printed photo of a man she didn't recognize, along with some personal details like his name, home address and phone number. There were pages on other people, too. Her eyebrows scrunched together as she quickly flicked through the pages. Weird. A bright purple data stick was also tucked inside the file.

Maybe they were professors, or people who'd hired Cole to create software for them. Or maybe they were potential investors. Cole had talked about opening his own company, but she'd insisted he get his degree first. It didn't mean he'd listened to her.

With a grumble, she slipped the file back into the drawer. He was twenty years old next month. An adult capable of making his own decisions. It wasn't her business.

Grabbing the bills, she headed into the kitchen where there was more space to spread out. She pushed the junk mail and cereal boxes to one side. Cole had probably gone to the library. Or maybe he hadn't come home at all…

Summer after he graduated high school he'd replaced glasses with contacts and started working out. By the time he'd left for college he'd turned from the slightly overweight, nerdy kid with bad skin into a lean, ripped hottie. The fact she'd always thought he was beautiful was irrelevant. Nowadays he had no problem getting dates and she kind of wished the girls who'd ignored him back in high school could see him now. But the thought of her baby brother having sex made her queasy so she pushed the idea out of her mind.

Irritably, she stabbed her finger at her calculator. She may as well be eighty considering her dating life. Most eighty-year-olds got out more than she did. Between getting dumped for her best friend and starting her own business, her love life had become more fiction than reality. Her lips compressed and she pushed away her self-pity. Tax season was just around the corner. This was her busiest time of year and she didn't have time to even think about a relationship.

So stop thinking about it.

She made herself a coffee and turned on the radio for background noise. Ed Sheeran was playing. No more tall, dark and handsome taekwondo instructors, she decided. What she needed was an adorable redhead who played guitar.

She'd barely sat down with her cup of coffee when the hourly news came on. A federal judge and his wife had been shot dead that morning only a few miles from here. An icy wave of horror stole over her as the announcer mentioned the judge's name. Raine Thomas—an unusual name. She'd just seen it in a file in her brother's desk.

Why did Cole have personal information on a judge? A judge who'd been killed? Her hands jerked, spilling the coffee, burning her fingers, making her curse.

She stood and sat back down again.

No way would Cole be involved in something as despicable as murder. There *had* to be a reasonable explanation. Should she ask him about it? And say what exactly? *Hey Cole, where were you this morning? Out committing double homicide?*

What if he lied? Worse—what if he told her he *was* involved? Then what would she do?

Dread took a tight hold of her innards and gave them a slow, painful twist.

She pressed her hand hard against her stomach. Could it be, despite all her efforts, he'd turned out like their father after all?

No. She refused to believe it. Cole was the one person in the world whom she believed in and she wasn't going to sacrifice that trust on the basis of a piece of paper.

There was no way Cole was capable of murder. Maybe the file belonged to one of his buddies?

Should she talk to the cops?

Hell, no. That was *not* an option. That would involve answering a lot of questions she didn't want to deal with.

One thing she did know. Her brother couldn't know she'd snooped through his stuff. She gathered up his paperwork, rushed back to the office, opened the filing drawer and slid each piece of paper back into its respective folder. With shaking hands, she pulled out the black file and debated whether or not she should take it with her.

And what? *Become an accessory?* That realization had fiery panic licking along her nerves. The last thing she needed was anyone connecting that file to her. She wiped the cover and the pages she'd touched with her sweater and eased it gingerly back into place using the sleeve of her cardigan.

Everything appeared like it had before. She shut the drawer and ran back into the kitchen and stood there, trying to catch her breath. Then she crammed her belongings into her laptop case, washed up her cup, dried it, put it away in the cupboard. Rearranged the kitchen table into its familiar mess. She stuffed her arms into her coat sleeves, searched around to make sure no trace of her visit remained.

She took a breath. It looked precisely like it had when she'd let herself in thirty minutes ago.

She left, locking the door behind her, and sat in her car for a moment, trembling, her heart racing as her carefully constructed world fell to pieces.

Then she remembered whom she was dealing with. Her brother, whom she'd watched take his first steps, whom she'd walked to kindergarten, whom she'd taught to stand up to bullies. Her *brother*, whom she knew and loved with every molecule of her being. Not some violent asshole who liked guns or fighting, but a registered Democrat who bought her flowers on Valentine's Day when she was single and called himself a feminist. For his birthday this year, he'd asked her to adopt an endangered species from the World Wildlife Fund in his name. No way would Cole commit murder, but she needed to know what was going on and how he was involved.

Blind trust was for the gullible and foolish. She'd rather put her faith in facts and empirical data. Unlike people, numbers never lied.

CHAPTER FOUR

MAC PUSHED THROUGH the throngs of gawkers gathered on the sidewalk and held up his gold shield before ducking under the yellow crime scene tape.

The victims' house was in North Cleveland Park a few miles northwest of the National Zoo. It was a beautiful older building, worth easily upward of a million bucks in today's market. Someone might kill for that alone.

There was a uniform from the Capitol Police at the corner of the house, taking names and handing out gloves and booties. Mac signed the log book and covered his shoes.

"You seen Agent Ross?" he asked the guy.

The uniform gave a sharp shake of his head. He was solidly built with gray at the temples. His mouth compressed, eyes pained.

"You first on scene?"

"Yeah," he acknowledged gruffly. "Knew the judge. He was a fine man. Didn't deserve this."

Mac didn't ask more questions. It shouldn't make a difference, but the mood shifted when someone had a relationship with the vic. Dark humor, used so often as a way for law enforcement and medical professionals to dissociate themselves from the daily grimness of their jobs, was shelved. The victims became more human. More deserving of respect. It was wrong, but it was natural.

"They're around the back." The uniform indicated with a jerk of his head. Mac headed that way. A black BMW sat gleaming in the garage. A tarp had been strung up over the entrance to shield the scene from prying eyes. Mac ducked behind the material and his stomach lurched.

Now he understood why the patrol officer looked like shit.

A man lay on the threshold. Gray suit, blood red tie falling in a wave over the stoop. No overcoat. No shoes. Mac moved closer and studied the body.

Two shots. One to the chest. One in the head. Point blank range.

An agent stepped into view. Late twenties. Average height. One seventy. Eager rather than weary, which was a promising sign. It was easy to let the job consume you.

"Agent Ross?" Mac asked.

"No, sir. Agent Atherton. You must be ASAC McKenzie?"

Mac nodded. At least they'd been informed he was coming. "Medical Examiner here yet?"

Atherton finished scribbling in his notebook and said distractedly, "On her way."

"What do you have?"

"Two victims." Atherton motioned for Mac to follow him inside.

Mac edged around the victim before stepping into a clean, well-kept home. The acrid scent of burnt coffee filled the air, along with the metallic taint of blood.

"Judge Raine Thomas and his wife of over thirty years, Kate," Atherton said. "Murder-suicide looks unlikely because both victims were shot twice, and no sign of a weapon, unless someone removed it before we got here. ME should be able to tell us for certain."

In Mac's experience when men killed themselves they didn't start with one to the chest and a second to the head. They stuck the gun in their mouth and blew out their brains.

Mac stepped into a high-ceilinged kitchen that belonged in a magazine except for the dark slick of blood pooled beside the body of a dead woman. She hadn't died quickly or painlessly. Now he wished he'd skipped breakfast.

She lay on her side. The chest wound was indicative of the bullet being fired from farther away, presumably the doorway. Powder burns on the victim's skin suggested the second shot had been taken at point-blank range. Part of her skull was obliterated. Blood streaks on the floor indicated at some point she'd tried to crawl toward her dead husband.

Gold and diamonds glittered on her ring finger.

"Signs of forced entry?" asked Mac.

"Nope."

"Security?"

"A basic alarm that was turned off. Bullet trajectory on the judge suggests the shooter was standing outside firing into the doorway. No signs of a struggle. No nine-one-one call. Neighbors didn't hear a thing."

"They used a suppressor?"

Atherton shrugged. "Looks that way."

Mac scanned the floor. No evidence markers for shell casings. "Shooter picked up their brass?"

"Yup." Atherton blew out a long breath. "Whoever did this didn't leave anything obvious behind except two bullets lodged in each victim. No signs of robbery, either. The UNSUB didn't take jewelry, laptops, wallets, phones or cash all of which are lying in plain sight. No obvious signs of sexual assault."

"Jesus." Mac expelled a breath. A full pot of coffee sat on the counter, two pieces of toast in the toaster, two plates beside it. An open butter dish and jar of marmalade sat nearby. These people had been going through the motions of a normal workday morning when someone had walked in and shot them dead.

It looked like a hit.

"*Any* idea as to motive?" asked Mac.

"Not yet."

"Could be personal? Or some sort of revenge attack? What do you know about the judge or his cases?"

Atherton seemed pained, as if Mac was slowing him down. He probably was.

"Federal Circuit Judge. Dealt mainly with patent cases and veterans' affairs."

Hardly the hotbed of passion or vengeance, although veterans knew guns and patents could be worth millions.

"Thomas ever receive death threats?"

"I'm in the process of checking it out." The man sighed and the eagerness dimmed a little. "It's early days."

Mac glanced around. "Who stands to gain from the couple's death?"

Atherton checked his notes. "There are two grown children. We have agents talking to them both. They heard the news on TV."

Christ. Mac didn't want to imagine how much that had sucked.

Atherton continued. "We haven't found a will yet, but there's a safe. We also need to find out the name of their lawyer."

Mac asked the obvious question. "Could this be a hate crime?"

The judge and his wife were both black.

"It's a little early to say." This comment came from a new voice.

Mac glanced up. The guy who stood in the doorway had dark hair longer than generally considered acceptable in the FBI, and sharp eyes that were the norm. "You're ASAC McKenzie? I'm Mark Ross. What can we do for you?"

Mac inclined his head as they shook hands. This guy did not like a superior being on his turf. "I started working in SIOC and wanted to see this crime scene for myself."

"I haven't seen you around. How long you been at HQ?" Ross questioned, watching him closely.

Mac checked his watch. "Two hours."

The other agents laughed, but then they all glanced uncomfortably at the dead woman lying on her kitchen floor.

"That's about as long as I'd last, too," Ross told him.

Mac put his hands on his hips. It wasn't that, but why blow a reason to bond? "I'm the new liaison for the Crisis Management Unit at SIOC. I wanted to offer any assistance we can provide."

"Appreciate it, but I don't think we need SIOC at this stage." The tone was just south of condescending. "If that changes, we'll let you know."

Dismissed.

Mac held Ross's gaze but their silent pissing contest was interrupted by voices outside.

"That's the ME," Atherton volunteered like a puppy trying to keep both owners happy. "Better watch where you step because she's fussy about her blood spatter and scares the crap out of me. I'll walk you out."

The last time Mac had felt this unwanted he'd been having an animated discussion about jurisdiction with a member of the US Marshals Service. But how would he feel if some bigwig from headquarters tried to insert himself into his investigation?

Like a dog guarding his bone.

"Don't worry. I'll show myself out."

Atherton and Ross nodded absently. They obviously didn't give a crap as long as he left them alone to get on with their job. He walked through the beautiful home, with its warm colors and plush furniture, paused near the front door and studied a portrait of the judge in his robes. Another photo hung beside it, more informal with the judge kissing his wife.

They appeared beyond content—they looked in love. Not a condition Mac ever wanted to suffer from again.

He pressed his lips together. The murder of a black federal judge would be celebrated in certain circles. Bigotry and antigovernment sentiment was alive and well despite the fact they lived in the twenty-first century.

Unfortunately, it wasn't a crime to hate people because of their job or the color of their skin. It *was* a crime to act on it. He pushed aside the old anger and disgust and let the agents do their job. There was more than enough crime to go around.

CHAPTER FIVE

"GREAT SHOW TODAY, Sonja."

The security guard in her radio station's downtown DC studio offered her a high-five as she strode toward the back door of the building.

"Thanks, Tommy." She smiled at him and slipped outside into the frigid February chill. He was a young, good-looking guy and she knew he'd had trouble accepting her when she'd first started working here. But she'd won him over.

She smiled smugly.

Her goal was to win everyone over, one scared, ignorant, uninformed fool at a time. She paused to button up her pea-green, boiled wool jacket. It was a lot warmer than it had been at four a.m. when she'd arrived for work that morning but, even after six years in the US, she still wasn't used to the cold. Delhi's heat was akin to being put on a spit and roasted alive. Her parents still got excited every time she told them it snowed.

Her smile dimmed. They wanted to visit, but she kept putting them off.

Although hers was primarily a music show, she'd made a name for herself by being very public about the fact she'd been born into the wrong body. It was no more complicated or perplexing than that. She'd always known she was female, but somehow the genes had gotten mixed up and she'd ended up with dangly bits. It had been confusing as hell as a kid but at some point, she'd read a magazine article about transgender people and transitioning. That article had saved her life. It had suddenly been clear what she needed to do.

Ironically, the main reason her parents were glad she lived in the US was because LGBT rights were more advanced here than in India. But if they ever found out the number of rape and death threats she got on a daily basis, they'd kidnap her and bring her back home.

Sonja didn't want them to worry.

She was used to the anonymous hatred and bigotry of the internet. It was the all-encompassing love that she cherished. When someone reached out and said her story had helped them figure out what was wrong with their lives—that made everything worthwhile.

She descended the steps, taking a quiet shortcut between two buildings to head to the nearest metro station. A late-night gig meant she'd had zero sleep. Still, it paid the rent.

This morning's show had been a lively one. She probably shouldn't have called the senator from North Carolina a douchebag with the intelligence of an amoeba live on air, but when he'd insisted on calling her by her birth name, not her legal one, she'd lost her temper.

Unprofessional, true. But her fans loved it. Haters were always gonna hate.

She hitched her *Michael Kors* handbag higher up her shoulder and passed a woman wrapped up like they were in the middle of an Arctic vortex.

"Morning," Sonja said sweetly. Her grandmother always said it cost nothing to be nice.

The person's expression didn't alter but her eyes flickered as they passed one another.

Sonja shivered. Those were the coldest eyes she'd ever seen.

A second later a bolt of fire burned through her back and Sonja stumbled to her knees. For a second she thought she'd been Tasered. Then she saw the blood blooming on the front of her new coat—the crimson turning the pretty green to an ugly black—and the pain started.

She couldn't breathe. She put her hand on the wound and tried to draw in air but nothing happened. Her lung had collapsed.

Footsteps crunched toward her, the sound ridiculously loud in the quiet of the morning. Pain made everything sharper. She bent her head back as the woman came around to stand in front of her, a large pistol in her grip. It looked like a gun out of the movie, fitted with one of those badass silencers.

"Why?" Sonja wheezed. Hot liquid bubbled up her throat. Blood. Not a good sign. Her attacker raised the gun and pointed it at her face. Sonja wanted to scream but no sound emerged. She was about to die, she realized. She tilted her chin. If the bitch was going to kill her, she wouldn't die cowering.

"Why?" she rasped.

But the woman didn't answer. Cold malice shone brightly in her eyes as she pulled the trigger.

CHAPTER SIX

THERE WAS ONE big downside to his new job. Mac was meeting her for lunch.

He exited the J. Edgar Hoover building and turned north along Tenth, walking past the hulking concrete monolith that housed headquarters. The building covered an entire city block and although he'd only worked there for a day and a half, he'd been lost three times. Not because of his crappy sense of direction. Whoever had built the place inexplicably placed brick walls, seemingly at random, right in the path of where he needed to go.

The building was Hoover's baby but the father of the FBI had died before construction finished. It took up two and a half million square feet and housed over seven and a half thousand staff. They even had their own Starbucks on the ground floor.

He crossed E. Street and walked up to the window of Lincoln's Waffle Shop opposite Ford's Theatre.

The place was packed but his wife was easy to pick out of the crowd.

Ex.

Ex-wife.

It had been two years and he still had trouble getting the terminology right. That was the problem with saying what you meant and meaning what you said.

What the hell was he doing here?

Heather Surrey was a short, bubbly blonde who had the sort of curves that made a man's palms itch. Not him though. Not anymore. She wore a bright crimson coat and matching hat. The color reminded him of how much she'd made him bleed during the divorce proceedings.

Looking at her now, he hardened his jaw along with his heart. He'd been curious as to why she wanted to talk to him, but now he didn't want to know. He was about to turn and run when she spotted him, stood, and waved.

Damn.

Reluctantly he went inside. The waiter, a squat, harried little man, asked him where he wanted to sit.

"Unfortunately, I'm meeting someone." Mac pointed to a smiling Heather who held out a chair for him—as if they hadn't parted bitter enemies.

He so did *not* want to be here.

Mac wound his way through the tourists and locals, all happily stuffing their faces in the cramped setting. It was noisy and overcrowded, and popular enough for there to be a line out the door during the breakfast rush.

This wasn't Heather's usual kind of haunt. She liked high-end, waiter service and linen napkins. He'd picked it for that exact reason. Plus, it was close to work.

She went to kiss his cheek but he avoided her by sliding into his seat. As hot as she undoubtedly was, Mac found it hard to believe the two of them had ever been a couple, let alone a married couple. He must have been temporarily insane.

"You made it," she said with a wide smile like they were

old friends. Technically speaking, he supposed they were.

Ex.

Ex-friends.

Maybe he wasn't the only one who hadn't fully come to terms with the altered status of their relationship.

The look in her eyes suggested she hadn't thought he'd come and was relieved he hadn't stood her up. Unlike some people, he always kept his promises.

"What do you want, Heather?" he asked without preamble.

Her expression tightened at his less than friendly tone. She drew in a breath and watched him through her lashes. "I wanted to touch base now you're in DC."

Geography hadn't been the problem. Her touching other people's bases had.

He leaned back in his chair, his long legs stuck out to the side of the small table to avoid any accidental contact with hers. "And how'd Lyle feel about that?"

She swallowed tightly and turned her attention to the flyers on the wall. "Lyle isn't in the picture anymore. I left him."

And everything became crystal clear. He should stand and walk out, but his inner sadist was obviously working overtime.

Before Quantico he'd been based in Philly, which was where Heather met Lyle when she'd taken a job as the asshole's PA. Lyle was a hotshot partner in a law firm with offices all over the country. After the divorce, she and Lyle had gotten hitched and settled in DC, which had suited Mac fine, until yesterday.

Mac said nothing. Anything he did say would be used against him.

The waiter came over. "What would you like to order?" the man demanded brusquely.

Mac picked up the menu, staring at it blindly before realizing he'd lost his appetite. "Coffee with milk, please."

"French toast for me." Heather gave the guy a bright smile as fake as her new breasts.

Mac frowned. What did she want from him? Money? He didn't have any. Blood? She'd already sucked him dry.

She filled his silence. "I thought that maybe…" Her fingers reached over the table, edging toward his. *Whoa!* He withdrew his hands into his lap as if she was a cobra about to strike.

No fucking way.

This was not happening.

Not when everything was going so well.

The only kind of woman he wanted in his personal life right now was the type who wanted to use his body for a few hours of sexual gratification, and only on the condition it didn't interfere with work. Names were optional. Numbers were off the table. No one was getting between him and his goals.

His coffee arrived, thank God. Mac added one sugar, stirred, took a sip and then put his cup back down on the table, hoping it would be enough of a barrier between him and whatever fucked up drama was about to come out of his ex-wife's mouth.

Heather plowed on and he must be a callous bastard because rather than shutting her down, he let her spell it out. "I thought that maybe we could, you know, give our relationship another chance?" She was looking at him with big blue eyes and another man's diamonds on her fingers.

"Are you insane?" He leaned forward so he didn't have to

raise his voice. "You dragged me through the courts, accused me of being abusive, attacked my reputation. Hell, you even took the fucking cat, and you don't even like cats. Now you want to get back together?"

Heather's lips pinched at his use of bad language but he was done pretending to be something he wasn't. He cursed. A lot. And he goddamned liked it.

"I loved that cat," she argued.

Loved? Past tense. So the cat was dead and she'd never bothered to tell him. The woman was a piece of work.

She reached out and finally placed her hand on the back of his. He forced himself not to flinch.

"I was hurt and lashing out. I said things I didn't mean."

"Heather." He slowly withdrew his hand, relieved there was no trace of the lustful insanity that had gotten him into trouble in the first place. "I found out that taking dictation in your boss's office involved you naked on his desk. What the hell did you think I'd do when I found out, join in for a threesome?"

Mac realized he was speaking too loudly when the woman at the table beside them glanced over with interest lighting her gaze.

"Lyle was a mistake," Heather said determinedly. "He used his position to seduce—"

"Heather," he growled.

Her eyes narrowed. "What?"

He didn't look away or back down. She'd gotten away with shit her whole life because she was a spoiled brat who knew her way around men's egos the way a Russian spy knew his way around a hidden camera. "Don't bullshit me. You liked the fact he was loaded—"

"I liked the fact he was there!" she raised her voice and then glanced around in consternation.

"Well, that hasn't changed, darlin'," he drawled and on cue his phone rang and he checked his messages. He smiled sharply. "Like the ladies, my job always comes first."

With a patience that was new, she gathered her temper rather than lash out at him the way she probably wanted to. She must be desperate.

"Look, Mac, honey, I still love you. I want to try again." Her fingers played with the sugar packet in front of her. "You have to admit we had something special. We were married for two years."

"During which I was faithful and you were not," he said coolly. "That's not what I consider a real marriage."

Heather glared at the woman beside them who was now openly eavesdropping. Mac winked at their spectator. She was easily sixty, possibly much older and appeared to be enjoying herself. At least someone was having fun.

"I made a mistake. It's you I love. *You* I want to be with."

He resisted rolling his eyes at the dramatic emphasis. After the way she'd hurt him he'd thought he'd enjoy seeing her crawl, but it turned out to be just as unsatisfying as the rest of their relationship. The real problem with their marriage was demonstrated by the fact she'd hurt his pride, not his heart. They'd never really been in love, just in lust and too stupid to appreciate the difference.

He finished his coffee, took a deep breath and said gently, "It's over, Heather. We are never gonna happen."

"Why not? We can make it good again—"

She was giving him a headache. He gritted his teeth. "Because I can't forget you went behind my back, fucked that asshole, and then flat-out lied about it."

Heather hissed back at him, "I made a mistake! Isn't that one of your mantras about criminals? 'Sometimes people make mistakes and poor choices, it doesn't mean they're bad people?'"

"Doesn't mean I want to be married to any of them." He was breathing heavily now. Trust Heather to use his empathy as a weapon against him.

He leaned farther across the table as more customers began to stare. All he wanted was to do his job and she was getting in his way. Time to make his position crystal clear. "You betrayed our marriage. You broke solemn vows. And then you dragged me through the courts, called me a bad husband, took my fucking cat, and you think I'd ever want to get back together with you?" And then he got it. "Lyle's the one who had an affair, isn't he?" He laughed though he shouldn't. This was karma. "Is he fucking his new PA? Maybe he thinks it's part of the job description?" He chuckled, knowing he was being an asshole now, but wanting to end this charade.

Heather picked up her bag and stood. "I should have known you'd never be able to forgive one little mistake."

"It wasn't 'one little mistake,' darlin'. It was a great, big, gigantic 'fuck you' to our marriage. And I got the message. Loud and clear. I may be a dumb cowboy, but I never make the same mistake twice."

Heather slapped him and his eyes popped. Fuck.

"This was your last chance, and you blew it," she spat.

Cheering would be wrong, right?

She headed to the door even though she hadn't paid a bill.

Classic Heather. Just like old times. He rolled his eyes,

threw down a twenty and followed her outside into the bleak winter chill. DC was having a cold snap but having grown up in Montana he'd experienced far worse.

It was too much to hope the woman had actually left. Where was the drama in that? She waited for him on the sidewalk, not yet satisfied with her pound of flesh.

"You think you're so important being a federal agent. You think you're so smart and dignified."

He almost snorted at that. It was hardly dignified to be fighting with his ex on the second day of his new job. He crossed his arms over his chest and waited her out. He wanted her to say her piece and leave.

"You're constantly trying to make up for being poor white trash, but you know what, Mac?" Heather stuck her hands on her hips and leaned toward him. "You'll always be poor white trash."

He narrowed his eyes and kept his mouth shut. She knew his weak spots. No way would he let her see her words had the power to affect him.

Pissed at not garnering a response, she turned and walked away.

Hallelujah.

A young man of about twenty whistled as he watched her go. "You were married to that?"

He eyed the guy who, in turn, was eyeing his ex-wife's heart-shaped ass.

"Trust me, pal, it isn't worth it."

The guy shook his head, "I don't know, man…" He looked tempted to go after her. Worse, Mac knew Heather would lap up the attention.

"Save yourself some heartache and find yourself a nice

Doberman." Mac put his hands on his hips and sighed. Men were inherently stupid when it came to chasing the wrong kind of woman. "Make sure you get your shots before you exchange bodily fluids."

The guy grinned at him and started walking. Poor kid.

A couple of suits came out the door and eyed him curiously. He recognized them from HQ. *Great.* He stared down at the pavement beneath his feet. A couple of days in DC and he was already making an impression. He also appreciated that just because Heather had walked away didn't mean she'd given up. He'd challenged both her femininity and her pride.

The good news was she didn't know where he lived. The bad news was he was going to have to change his cell number. It was either that or murder her in her bed—and that probably wouldn't be beneficial for his career aspirations either.

———————————

TESS WASN'T CUT out for the espionage business. After a sleepless night, she'd decided to follow her brother and see what Cole was up to, whom he met. Anything was better than sitting home worrying about what the heck he was mixed up in. He spotted her coming out of a Metro Center turnstile before she'd even left the station.

"Hey, sis, where you off to?" He waited for her to catch up with him and wrapped his arm around her shoulder, giving her a hard squeeze. She'd spent the morning working on her laptop in a coffee shop near his local Tenleytown metro station. Spotted him walking down the hill close to eleven-thirty. She'd gathered her things and thought she'd done an okay job of following him without being seen, until now.

"Cole." She forced lightness into her tone, kissed his cheek, noting the clean shave and spicy aftershave he was wearing. Part of her wanted to scream questions at him and shake him until he told her everything. Another part of her was sick with guilt for not trusting this boy whom she loved with her whole heart.

But he wasn't a boy any longer, she reminded herself. He was a tall, handsome adult—who had the image, name, and address of a murder victim in his desk drawer. She needed to understand what was going on.

"I have a client meeting at one. Thought I'd check out the new exhibit at the Natural History Museum beforehand," she lied.

"You always were a nerd," he teased.

"Says the kid who writes code."

"Nerds rule." Cole bumped her shoulder and she laughed.

No way was her brother involved in murdering a mouse, let alone a federal judge.

"Where are you off to?" She strove for casual, but her voice cracked a little at the end.

"Meeting a friend."

"Anyone I know?"

He avoided her gaze, suddenly evasive. "Someone from college."

He was lying. She could tell from the way his ears turned pink. Her mouth went dry. Why would he lie about that unless he had something to hide?

She looked away before he noticed she'd noticed. He'd never kept secrets before—not that she knew about. How many other signals had she missed?

They walked past Ford's Theatre. On the other side of the

44

road a woman in a scarlet coat and hat was berating a tall, handsome guy in a gray suit.

He seemed vaguely familiar.

She frowned. Who did he remind her of? She couldn't place him. Maybe it was the way he carried himself. Or the confident stance that reminded her of someone. Maybe it was the fact she'd watched *Jurassic World* last Saturday night and Chris Pratt star-featured in her recent fantasies.

"They're in the middle of a domestic, Tess. Don't embarrass them by staring," Cole chastised her and she let him propel her forward, almost giddy with relief.

"He looks familiar." How could she think a boy who worried over someone being *embarrassed* would cold-bloodedly murder two people in their own home?

Cole said something else and then snapped his fingers in front of her face. "You're still mad at me for forgetting you were coming over yesterday, aren't you?"

Duh. "No."

His lips curved. "I don't believe you."

"Fine. I *was* mad, but I'm not anymore. Is it a female friend you're meeting today? Maybe the one you blew me off for yesterday?" She winced at her lack of subtlety.

Cole laughed. "I didn't blow you off! I forgot, all right?"

"What's her name?" She was appalled with herself for needing him to give her an alibi, but she pressed on regardless.

His smile was forced. "I don't kiss and tell."

Tess made a wry face, knowing she needed to drop it before he got suspicious. "Well, at least one of us has a love life."

He grimaced. "I don't want to think about my sister having a love life."

"Your brotherly outrage is a moot point right now so don't worry about it."

He gave her a long look. "Jason was an asshole. You need to get over him. You'll find someone a thousand times better and he might be worthy enough to deserve you."

She smiled. This was another reason she loved her brother so much—he believed in her when she didn't believe in herself. She wanted to ask him straight out about the file in his desk. Surely there was a rational explanation. She opened her mouth but the words wouldn't come.

What if he lied?

It would kill her.

No matter how much she wanted to, she didn't do blind trust anymore. Six months ago, her boyfriend had eloped with her best friend in the worst kind of clichéd love triangle. Jason and Julie's betrayal had blindsided her, but had been a timely reminder of all the reasons not to take anyone at face value. Not even her brother. She needed proof, not words.

"What time are you finished with your client?" Cole asked.

She blinked stupidly for a moment and remembered her cover story for being here. "Not long. About two? Two-thirty."

He checked his phone. "How about you call me when you're done and we'll head back to my place together? I'll get the rest of those details you need for my taxes."

And she could accidentally on purpose find that file with the photo inside and confront him directly. Gauge his reaction.

"Sounds good. I'll text you and meet you at the metro."

"See you later." He tugged her hair lightly and walked away, getting lost in the crowd before she remembered she was supposed to be following him.

Darn.

She turned around and realized she stood at the southeast corner of the Hoover Building. Abruptly she was bombarded by a series of frightening memories and coincidences that seemed to be trying to tell her something. The FBI. A picture of a dead judge in her brother's desk. Cole refusing to tell her who he was meeting for lunch.

The nightmare was starting over again...

Or, she told herself in annoyance, she was just being paranoid.

"Ain't paranoia if they're really after you." Her father's words boomed in her brain with the force of a chainsaw revving to life. Sweat popped out of her skin. She swiveled on her heel and started walking fast. She jogged across the wide avenue and turned in the direction Cole had taken, determined to end the uncertainty.

She spotted him half-a-block ahead and ducked behind a giant potted shrub.

He wasn't looking her way. Cole was focused one hundred percent on the woman in his arms and sucking her in like she was his personal oxygen. Tess couldn't see the woman's face, but she was slender and dressed in a smart pant suit and a black woolen coat. And her brother's hands were getting mighty familiar for lunchtime on a busy city street.

Tess leaned back against unyielding terra-cotta, her heart thundering inside her ribcage, her breath sawing in and out of her chest.

"Thank you, thank you, thank you."

Icy cold seeped through her jacket and into the flesh across her shoulders, down the ridge of her spine, but she didn't move. Her brother was not meeting some wild-eyed bozo, plotting the next phase of the revolution. He was having a hot and heavy fling and wanted to keep it private.

She sighed in relief, rolled her shoulders and then peeked to see if they were still on the street.

It was empty.

Of course it was empty. They were having a nooner, not sightseeing.

Maybe the woman was married. That bothered her, but not close to how worried she'd been at the thought of Cole meeting with some antigovernment activists with a domestic terrorist agenda.

Been there. Done that.

She stood and raised her face to the sky, surprised by the icy track of tears on her cheeks. She swiped at them and pushed away from her hiding place, ignoring the odd stares of people walking by. Worst-case scenarios didn't seem so far-fetched when you'd lived through hell the way she had.

She had plenty of work to get on with, and decided to do it in one of her favorite places. She crossed the street and went up the steps and through security into the Natural History Museum. She still had questions about that photograph, but for now she could breathe again. Cole would have a rational explanation for that file being in his drawer, and she would feel like an idiot. She was the one who was going to have to lie and pretend she didn't know what he'd had for lunch.

CHAPTER SEVEN

M AC ENTERED SIOC and immediately knew from the high level of activity that something was up.

He slipped into the media room where agents simultaneously watched fifty different TV channels and monitored trends on social media. In today's world, stories were not broken by reporters from news organizations. They were broken by eyewitnesses with cell phones and service in a twenty-four-hour news cycle.

"What's going on?" he asked Libby Hernandez, the analyst ASC Gerald had introduced him to yesterday.

She looked up from her seat. "Local DJ was found murdered after she left her radio station around eleven-thirty this morning."

Mac checked out the monitors. Droves of reporters were camped out on a street about a five-minute drive away.

"What do we know?" Gerald appeared at his shoulder. The chatter from one of the sound feeds coming through the speakers had drowned out the noise of the other man coming into the room.

Hernandez typed furiously on her keyboard and the volume decreased. "Sonja Shiraz hosted 'Sunrise with Sonja' every weekday morning on Radio WDC. Nine-one-one call came in from a member of the public saying they found a body in an alley. A paramedic recognized the vic."

Mac's gaze scanned the monitors and the newsfeed, taking in the buzz. The murder of a public figure was shocking but it wasn't *this* shocking. "What am I missing?"

"Sonja Shiraz's former name was Sanjay Patel," Hernandez told him.

"Transgender?" A sinking feeling entered his gut.

Hernandez nodded. "She detailed the whole transition experience on her show and on her blog. Generated a huge following."

"And a lot of hate mail, I bet." Mac's gaze flicked over the screens. First a black federal judge, now a transgender DJ, all within two days? He didn't like it. "I'd like to go take a look—"

Gerald was shaking his head. "I know what you're thinking, but three murders in two days isn't that unusual."

"All high-profile potential hate targets?"

"No evidence to suggest either were hate crimes, let alone that the murders are connected."

"Was she shot?" Mac asked.

"Unfortunately, getting shot isn't that unusual either." Gerald pressed his lips together. "WFO weren't happy with you turning up at their crime scene yesterday. I got a call from their SAC telling us to butt out."

"I offered help. I didn't tread on any toes." Mac rolled his eyes. He hated politics.

"How would you have felt if some headquarters' suit insinuated himself into one of your inquiries?"

"Pissed, but I don't need a friendship badge from the Brownies. I can help solve these crimes. I know how these guys think."

"WFO?" Gerald queried.

Mac laughed. "Right wing extremists." At Gerald's doubtful expression Mac continued, "I spent a year undercover during the investigation into David Hines's Pioneers organization." At Gerald's surprised expression, he added, "It was before I joined the FBI."

Several people nearby were listening hard to their conversation but this wasn't a secret. It just wasn't common knowledge.

"That was back in the mid-nineties. What, were you in diapers?"

"It was my first undercover job." Mac scratched the back of his neck. "I was a little wet behind the ears, I'll admit. That's why they chose me. The Pioneers never imagined a goofy cowboy was also an undercover cop."

"You must have had a hell of a resume by the time you joined the FBI." There was grudging respect in Gerald's tone now.

"I was lucky I wasn't strung up by my balls," Mac told him honestly. "After the shootout, my identity was kept out of the reports because of fears of reprisals from the surviving members. The assholes all turned on one another anyway so they didn't need my testimony." Mac curbed his impatience as the media room danced around them. "The thing is, during my time with them David Hines often discussed his 'manifesto.' First thing on it was kill a federal judge. The next was kill a prominent black man." He tucked in his chin. "Obviously they used a more derogatory term than 'black.'"

ASC Gerald's mouth firmed. "Obviously."

"I forget the exact phrasing but I can find it in my notes. Next on the list were prominent figures who sympathized with homosexuals, Jews, Mexicans, Arabs, abortionists, followed by any cop, federal official or politician they could get their hands on. Last but not least, POTUS himself."

He let that sink in.

These assholes had been eager to kill their president regardless of his politics or ideology—just for being the man in the White House. There had already been one attempt on President Hague's life—Mac had been on scene for that and it had ripped out his insides. The idea of a second attempt pissed him off.

"The Pioneers were not alone in their antigovernment rhetoric in the nineties, and white nationalists and extremist groups have been on the rise for the last decade," Gerald said slowly.

"It would be wise to warn other agencies to increase their levels of alertness."

Gerald scanned the screens, then crossed his arms over his chest. "Agreed, but I can't sign off on your deeper involvement in this. If there's a connection between Judge Thomas and the DJ the ME will notify the field office and they'll deal with it. Until we have some viable indication it's a hate crime, we stay out of it."

Mac nodded and followed him out of the media room into the quieter hallway. He'd be lying if he said he wasn't disappointed but knew better than to show it.

"Hostage fusion cell wanted to talk to you about ways of increasing networking between negotiators across the county." Gerald seemed busy and distracted. Running SIOC must be complicated enough without some newbie stirring the pot.

"I'll get right on that." Which would take him a couple of hours tops. Mac reined in his frustration and tried to quash the eagerness to get involved in every case. He needed to focus on his career.

He headed off to where the small group of guys from HRT and the Crisis Negotiation Unit hung out in one of the breakout rooms at the back of the National Assets Command Room. This room was the place where all the experts would gather if there was ever a nuclear bomb on the ground in the US. Thankfully it was quiet. Hopefully it would stay that way.

The room itself was a reminder that SIOC brought together the best of the best in a small space. It was the waiting part that killed him and he missed the hands-on rush of running an investigation. *Special Agent in Charge by forty*, he reminded himself as he searched out Eban Winters, one of the best negotiators in the world and head of the hostage fusion cell at SIOC.

Mac's phone dinged and he looked down and saw Heather was now angry-texting him.

Nice.

He'd rather deal with a hundred white supremacists than deal with his ex, which said more about him than it did about her. She'd done him a favor by having an affair with her boss. He plainly wasn't cut out to be the romantic lead in someone else's *happily ever after*. He'd rather arrest the bad guys.

TESS PLACED HER laptop on the kitchen table and eased out of her coat. Cole was putting the trash out on the curb for garbage day. She started through to the den, determined to *accidentally* come across this file folder and get her questions answered so she could quit worrying.

She collided with a hard, male body that nearly knocked

her off her feet. Joseph, her brother's best friend, grabbed her by the upper arms and held her against him.

"Well, hello, beautiful." He smiled down at her. "I finally get my hands on the lovely Tess." Joseph leaned closer. "Cole's not here, but you're welcome to keep me company while you wait for him." His hands were large and warm and started to drift down her waist toward her ass.

She jerked out of his grip and took a step away. "I'm good. Thank you."

"Oh, you are better than good, Tess. *You* are perfect. You wanna come to my birthday party next weekend? I'll feed you chocolate cake. I know you like chocolate cake."

He flustered her and unsettled her but she realized a tiny part of her was flattered by the attention. That's what happened when you dated losers. She did not intend to encourage him. She crossed her arms. "Your *nineteenth* birthday party." She raised a knowing brow at him. She was thirty for heaven's sake.

He dropped his voice to a murmur. "But it's only cake, Tess." Except he said the word 'cake' like he was licking it off her naked skin.

The door opened behind her.

"There he is now." Joseph walked over to the refrigerator. "Want a beer, Cole? Tess?"

"Sure." Her brother threw his jacket on the back of a kitchen chair.

Tess checked the clock. It wasn't even four o'clock. "You guys remember you're underage, correct?"

"Seriously?" Joseph handed Cole a bottle, ignoring her protests. "We're old enough to go to war, and have sex," his eyes lingered on her chest, "but not drink a beer? Live a little,

Tess."

He held out a bottle to her in challenge, but she hadn't been peer-pressured since high school when she'd been caught taking her one and only puff of a cigarette by her favorite gym teacher.

"No. Thank you." She smiled tightly. "Those of us who work for a living have things to do."

"Ouch." Joseph gave a wince. "Your sister's killing me, dude."

Cole laughed. "She has your number. Did you go to class today?"

"Three classes *and* I finished an assignment. Where were you?"

"Had something important to do," Cole muttered evasively, flushing.

He'd skipped class? He never skipped class. She watched him anxiously as he avoided her gaze.

Joseph took a long pull of beer. "I'm supposed to have a date tonight but I might ditch it."

"You going to let the lady in question know you're bailing or should we expect angry texts?" Cole asked sardonically.

Joseph sent Tess an assessing look. "I haven't decided yet. What do you think, Tess?"

Tess tried to keep her face expressionless. "Treat her with respect. If you're not going to show up, at least tell her. No one wants to look stupid being stood up—especially if she actually likes you enough to go on a date with you."

"She asked me." His smile said this happened a lot.

Women would find him attractive. "How would you feel if she stood you up?"

He shrugged like it was no big deal. "I'd find someone else

to take home."

She blew out a gusty breath. The more she discovered about men the less she liked the species.

Footsteps thundered down the stairs as Zane and Dave joined the party.

"Hey, Tess." Zane gave her a sly grin and Dave blushed. Zane was all silky, black hair and long, lean muscle. He was the captain of the soccer team and had one of those faces that could easily transition into a modeling contract. Dave was a stocky redhead from Oklahoma who morphed into a demon defender on the pitch.

Their gazes went to where Cole stood in the kitchen. "Wanna play Medal of Honor?" Zane asked Cole. "We're gonna have a tournament."

Her brother looked like he was about to say yes.

"Nope," she interrupted. "Cole and I need to finish his taxes."

Joseph spluttered into his beer. "Kill me now."

"Tempting," Tess smiled sharply, "but I want to get this done first."

Her brother laughed. Zane and Joseph chuckled. The three young men vied for the best position on the couch while she and Cole went through into the den. Cole woke up his laptop and colored a little at the screensaver featuring a topless woman.

"Crap. Sorry." He quickly inputted his password. Tess tried to see what it was but he was way too fast.

Apparently, her nerdy little brother had discovered the opposite sex in a big way. His roommates weren't what you'd call shy. She dreaded to think the sort of trouble they could get Cole into.

As long as it wasn't enough to get them arrested, she'd deal.

"I just want the household bill totals for the year," she told him. "Utilities, internet, phone, insurance, mortgage, bank charges and interest. And any other expenses or income you might have forgotten to mention."

Cole opened the filing drawer and began a methodic search through the files. Her OCD brain itched as he haphazardly shoved things back into the wrong place. She leaned over the desk and peered into the drawer, silently urging him to pull out the black file with the judge's photo in it so she could ask what the hell it was.

Cole glanced up and eyed her quizzically. "You all right, sis?"

"Sure," she said, brightly. Too brightly.

He directed a glare toward the doorway and Tess turned her head to find Joseph standing there enjoying the view. Dammit. She straightened up from the desk.

"Spoilsport," Joseph joked.

"Go leer at someone else," Cole told him in disgust.

"Excellent idea. Maybe I'll call your girlfriend," Joseph said. "Give me her number."

Cole gave Joseph the finger.

"So you do have a girlfriend?" asked Tess.

Joseph chuckled and turned away.

"Nope." Cole didn't look up but she could tell he wasn't telling the truth from the way his ears started to glow.

"Do I know her?" she pressed, genuinely curious as to why he wouldn't tell her.

"No."

"Who is it?"

57

"Drop it, Tess," he snapped.

She flinched.

He carried on searching, his movements jerky, but missing the files she needed.

She drummed her fingers impatiently on his desk.

"Do you want to search for this stuff?" Cole stared pointedly, clearly irritated.

She ignored the fact he was being facetious and took the opportunity to come around to his side of the desk and start looking through the drawer herself.

He rolled his chair back as she quickly pulled out files. The tightness of his jaw told her he was mad with her, but when she caught his gaze his expression softened.

"Sorry. I shouldn't have snapped at you."

"But you don't want to talk about her," Tess said quietly.

"Exactly."

"I shouldn't have pried."

He raised his eyes to the ceiling, then scrubbed his face. He glanced at his roommates and friends drinking beer in front of the PlayStation and sighed.

"There's an age difference. She doesn't want anyone to know we're seeing each other."

"She's older?" Tess wondered if the woman was married but feared she'd be pushing it too far by asking.

He tucked in his chin and squinted at her. "You think I'd date a high school student?"

He was right. He'd be twenty next month. Younger would be an absolute nightmare and remind her too much of darker times. He wasn't the only one keeping secrets.

"How much older?" she tried to sound nonchalant.

He crossed his arms over his chest. "I'm not saying anything else. I already told you more than I should."

Tess studied him. "Just be careful, okay?"

"Are you giving me the 'safe sex' talk?" He cocked a brow.

She groaned. "Do I have to?"

He shook his head.

"Good. I meant be careful with your heart. And hers."

His eyes narrowed. "Jason was a complete jackass. You know that, right?"

A lump formed in her throat and she went back to the files to hide the fact he'd hit a nerve. "And I really do not want to waste another thought on him."

"We're not all dicks, you know." Cole opened up his email browser and let her finish what she needed to do. Her fingers moved fast and furious over the tabs, but the file with the photograph of the dead judge was gone.

Where the hell was it?

She re-examined all the folders and checked it hadn't gotten tucked inside another one. It wasn't there. What did that mean?

A flash of purple caught her eye at the bottom of the drawer. The data stick. Some unknown force made her reach down and palm the device. She sat back on her heels. "I think that's everything I need. Let's go into the kitchen and pull the final figures and I promise to leave you alone for another year."

Cole griped. "How long is it gonna take?"

"A couple of hours tops. You have a hot date?"

He grunted. "None of your business."

Her fingers tightened around the data stick.

Cole checked his watch and growled. "I hate taxes!"

She winced. "No one *likes* taxes, Cole."

"Except accountants like you. And the IRS." His good

humor returned. She got to her feet, grateful he was joking. When Cole moved to walk in front of her she slipped the data stick into her pants pocket. When she looked up Dave was watching her through suspicious eyes.

She picked up the armful of papers and followed her brother through the living room.

"Does this mean the rent is going up?" Dave eyed the pile of paperwork dubiously.

Zane laughed but didn't look away from the screen. "Cole's designing a new app that's gonna make him a freaking billionaire."

"What kind of app?" Tess observed her brother with interest.

"Nothing." Cole glared at his buddy. Obviously being secretive was becoming a thing. Then he went into the kitchen and started noisily clearing away dishes.

"Well, when he's a billionaire he'll still have to pay taxes," Tess said evenly.

"The only thing certain in life are death and taxes, am I right?" Joseph smiled, but there was a hard edge to his handsome face.

"Considering how many people try to cheat the IRS, I'd say the only certain thing in life is death and I'm hoping to avoid that for the next few decades at least."

"Make sure you enjoy the moment, Tess," Joseph advised. "You never know how long you've got." That little bit of wisdom coming from such a consummate player should have sounded flippant, but for once Joseph sounded remarkably somber.

She gave him a slight smile. "I'll enjoy the moment as soon as tax season is over."

His eyes moved back to the video game, but then he leered at her with his habitual smirk. "I'm available to help you out with that if you ever require a naked shoulder rub."

"I'm more than ten years older than you," she bit out with exasperation.

He grinned. "A woman approaching her prime."

She rolled her eyes.

He stood suddenly, looming over her. "You seriously have an issue with the age difference?"

She had an issue with a whole lot of things regarding this young man. "I simply think the idea of a thirty-year-old having a relationship with a college student is a little gross."

"You wouldn't even blink if it was the guy who was older."

She did blink, unable to believe she was being lectured on gender equality by Mr. One-night stand, but she would still find it a bit distasteful for a thirty-year-old guy to be dating a freshman. Shaking her head, she entered the kitchen, just in time to see her brother's angry scowl, a split second before he slammed out of the house.

Dammit.

She put the folders on the kitchen table and raised her eyes skywards. How could she be so insensitive? Now he'd never open up to her about his new girlfriend.

She glanced over her shoulder to see Joseph standing with his shoulder braced against the doorway. He gave her a "what can you do?" shrug, then went back to the TV when she glared at him.

Torn between going after her brother and just getting this over with, Tess sat down and put in her earbuds. The sooner she was done with Cole's taxes the sooner she'd be out of here and dealing with her fee-paying clients who didn't make it their life's mission to screw with her.

She didn't want to think about the photo of the dead judge or the thumb drive burning a hole in her pocket. Maybe she'd imagined the file? Maybe she was losing her mind? It happened to accountants around tax time.

She turned on her radio app to listen to the local news in the hopes they'd caught the killer of Judge Thomas and his wife. Instead, the presenter started talking about the murder of a prominent DJ that morning. There was speculation it was carried out by the same person who'd shot the judge.

Despite the fact another person was dead a huge wave of relief crashed over her. She'd been following Cole on the metro when the DJ had been shot. Not that she really believed her brother had been involved. Not really. But hoping and knowing were two different things.

She bit her lip as a fresh wave of guilt assaulted her. It was time to tell her brother the truth about so many things but maybe she'd wait until he was less pissed with her. Everything she'd done she'd done for him, but now the secrets and lies were piling up and, if she wasn't careful, they'd bury the love they'd always had for one another.

MAC BREATHED OUT slow and steady and squeezed the trigger like he was stroking a woman's G-spot, with just enough pressure to make her go bang. He hit the target dead center and then again, another fifteen times at twenty-five yards, firing until the magazine was empty.

He checked the target in satisfaction.

He'd gotten into the habit of coming to the shooting range

on a daily basis when he'd first joined the Bureau. Not only did it keep his skills sharp—agents were required to qualify with their Bureau-issued firearm at least four times a year and needed over eighty percent to qualify—it was also a time when his thoughts slowed and his mind cleared. Ironically, it was where he had most mental breakthroughs on cases.

Meditation via hot lead.

This time he reloaded his service weapon with frangible bullets that the firearms instructor wanted to use up as the Bureau was transitioning from the Glock-22 .40 caliber across to the 9mm. He forced himself to relax and not to think about investigations that weren't even his. The murders bothered him. They showed no mercy or compassion for the victims, and he'd seen this kind of blind hatred before. It took a special breed of sociopath to pull off that kind of calculated outrage.

The investigators had little to go on. No CCTV footage. No mode of transport or tire tracks. No eyewitnesses. No trace. No DNA.

Mac blanked his mind of everything except the target. He began firing rapidly, putting the bullet dead center in the target. Twelve rounds. Thirteen. And his mind suddenly flipped to a vision of a dark-haired young girl, blowing the barrel of her revolver seconds after wiping the floor with her brothers on their makeshift gun range.

His shot went wild. *Shit.* It had been a long time since he'd thought about that kid.

The instructor closest to him hitched a brow in surprise. Mac never missed the target. He put the last shot where it was supposed to be.

"What happened?" the guy asked as they removed their ear protectors.

Mac grimaced. "Sneezed."

The instructor jerked his chin in acknowledgement, but Mac felt like an idiot. He wasn't about to admit to his mind wandering while firing his weapon.

He bent down to clear the range. Other agents were doing the same thing, picking up their brass. He nodded to a couple of agents he'd seen around SIOC. One was a nice-looking brunette with blue eyes who sent him a smile that suggested she was single.

Even as he smiled back that little girl's impish grin flashed through his mind again. God, she'd been cute. Unspoiled despite her family's best efforts to take her with them on the crazy train. He wondered where she was now.

David Hines's ideology wasn't startling or unique. It was shared by thousands of others who feared they were diminished in some way by people they didn't understand. But the manifesto itself had been fairly specific, ending with an attack on the White House. The details of the manifesto had never been released to the public although it hadn't been a secret amongst the Pioneers' members. Law enforcement had never recovered Hines's original handwritten version. Some white supremacist was probably out there somewhere jacking off to it like porn.

These latest killings in DC didn't religiously follow Hines's outline. Instead they'd combined target groups and accelerated the process. Or maybe it was a coincidence.

These weren't his cases. He'd been told to keep out of it. But he understood more about the Pioneers than anyone outside the group. May as well do a little digging—at least find out where the main players were currently hanging out. And, yes, the idea of breaking this case wide open appealed to his ego. He'd be lying if he said it didn't.

A vision of young Ellie Hines's dead body flashed through his mind as it had so often through the years. Her "husband" had shot her in the back as she'd tried to run away from his cabin during the raid. Autopsy revealed she'd been sixteen weeks pregnant.

At least Theresa Jane and her baby brother had survived.

Hell, she'd be thirty now. Probably married with kids of her own. *That* made him feel old. And while the men had been evil personified, it had been the women who'd made his flesh crawl with more extreme beliefs and seemingly endless commitment to the cause. Francis Hines had reminded him of a serpent, with less warmth. She'd never fully trusted him and he was pretty sure part of the reason David Hines kept him around was to deflect some of her ire.

Had Theresa Jane grown up like her mother with hate in her heart, nurturing the desire for revenge? Had the baby, Bobby, grown up believing his family had been unlawfully gunned down by the big bad Feds?

It was possible.

He'd lost track of the kids once they'd gone into foster care. Rather than going home he'd go back to the office and start digging around. There were plenty of survivors. The only fatalities had been those in the main cabin who'd started a gunfight, and poor innocent Ellie. Harlan Trimble had set fire to his cabin in an effort to disguise her murder, but the State Police had figured it out.

Harlan was doing life, but telling anyone who'd listen he'd been set up by the cops.

Asshole.

Mac dumped the spent shells into the bins provided, then

reloaded his duty weapon with hollow points and headed to the elevator.

"Nice shooting." The pretty brunette caught up with him and smiled when he held the elevator for her. Another woman got in beside them. She was blonde and stiff looking, like if she smiled her face might crack. He held the door for two more agents and wished he could find the enthusiasm to return the brunette's interest.

"U can't touch this" by MC Hammer rang out through the elevator and one of the guys grinned. Mac took out his cell and turned off the ringer without answering. Dammit.

"I recognize that sentiment," the man said. "Ex-girlfriend?"

Mac grimaced. "Ex-wife." He didn't want his personal life to become a talking point.

"You new to HQ? I haven't seen you around." The man held out his hand in greeting. "I'm ASC Reece Jackson. Counterintelligence."

Mac introduced himself to the other agents in the elevator. The pretty brunette, Paula Rice, had smooth, warm skin and held his hand a fraction too long.

The blonde's eyes flickered over him nervously. Her name was Fiona Green and she was from Records Management Division. And looks were deceptive because he'd seen her shoot the balls off a fruit fly at twenty-five paces.

Jackson handed Mac his card. "If you wanna grab a beer sometime, give me a call." The guy exited on the third floor as did everyone except SA Paula Rice.

He felt her eyeing him as they continued up to five.

"I'm on the dayshift at SIOC so I've seen you around." Her eyes were a dark navy. "I mainly supervise computer techs."

Just before the elevator doors opened Paula handed him her card. "Ditto to what ASC Jackson said—if you ever need a coffee break with a friendly face give me a call." The way she held his gaze suggested she could be very friendly.

"Thanks." He slipped the card into his pocket and gave her his in return but had no intention of calling.

Getting involved with someone from work was a bad idea and, where women were concerned, he was no longer open to bad ideas. Nothing but good times and smooth sailing ahead.

Sure.

CHAPTER EIGHT

A FEW HOURS later, Tess was naked and wet when the insistent, repeated ringing of her doorbell had her stumbling out of the shower. She'd planned to put on her pajamas and spend the evening plowing through tax forms. The doorbell rang again and she hurriedly grabbed her robe and wrapped the soft material around her damp body, tying the belt firmly at the waist. She wasn't expecting anyone and people rarely knocked on the door without calling first. Her mind immediately shifted to an emergency.

Cole.

She ran down the stairs and yanked open the front door without checking the side window. Every drop of blood drained from her head when she saw a tall stranger lounging against the wall outside.

"Remember me?" he asked.

Hearing his voice clicked the memory into place. Twenty years ago, she'd barely reached his waist. Now her eyes were level with his chin. She gripped the door to stop herself swaying.

Kenny Travers.

Her hand went to her mouth and her knees sagged as she backed up a step. "Oh, God."

He was still lean, although there was a width to his shoulders that she hadn't been aware of all those years ago, a solidness to his jaw that spoke of stubbornness. Her eyes hooked on a dent in his chin she didn't remember, but then the last time she'd seen him she'd only been ten years old.

She met his gaze. She'd forgotten a lot of things, but not those green-blue irises, bright and changeable as the ocean.

"I thought you were dead," she managed.

He looked over his shoulder onto the quiet street, then back at her, taking in her damp hair and terry robe. "You alone?"

The question surprised her. "Yes."

"Mind if I come in?"

She hesitated and pulled her robe tighter. What did she actually know about this guy? He could be a rapist or a murderer for all she knew. Her intuition told her he was none of those things and she'd learned to trust her instincts a long time ago.

A car door slammed across the quiet street. It was a few minutes after seven p.m. and dark out. The houses in this quiet bay belonged mainly to people with young families. The last thing she wanted was anyone finding out who her parents had been.

He pulled back one side of his suit jacket and revealed a shiny gold shield attached to his belt and a sidearm in a shoulder holster. And all of a sudden things started to make sense.

He was a cop.

"We can do this down at FBI headquarters if you'd rather, Theresa Jane." His voice held a softness rather than a threat, but she flinched.

FBI headquarters? The hairs on her nape rose. Why was he

here? What did he want? Was this about Cole?

"No one's called me that name in a very long time." She stood back. He took that as an invitation and brushed past her to step into the hallway. A wave of awareness jolted through her from the slight touch of his elbow. She crossed her arms over her chest in a protective gesture that was as revealing as it was ineffectual. Thankfully he wasn't looking at her.

He walked through into her kitchen and stood peering over the papers spread out on her table. She had an office upstairs, but the kitchen table was her favorite place to work.

"You're what—an accountant?" He didn't bother to hide his skepticism.

"Why?" All those childhood putdowns were suddenly fresh in her mind. "You didn't think I could count?"

One side of his mouth tipped up and dimples she hadn't known existed appeared. "Oh, I always thought you were smart, sweetheart, but we both know how your daddy felt about taxes." He scrubbed his fingers through his short hair. "Can't say I blame him on that one."

Was this a test? Did he suspect her of sympathizing with her daddy's twisted philosophy? There could only be one reason why this man had turned up on her doorstep after twenty years of silence and it wasn't to talk about her job skills.

Was *she* a suspect?

"I'm not my daddy. I want no part of that world." She rubbed her upper arm, something she always did when she was nervous. His eyes followed the motion and something sparked in their depths. Damn. She dropped her hand. "And I'm a *big* believer in people paying their taxes. No matter how rich or poor they are."

He grinned like she amused him, which really pissed her

off.

"You work from home?" he asked.

She let out a big breath, realizing how tense she'd become—hardly surprising under the circumstances. He had the distinct advantage in this conversation, especially when she wasn't even properly dressed. "I tried working for one of the big corporations, but being stuck in a cubicle sucked out my soul."

"Something else we have in common. You have a lot of clients?" He pointed at all the neatly stacked paperwork.

"I just started my own business." She shrugged uneasily, wondering what he was getting at. Wondering if he was going to use her past to blackmail her in some way.

"But this is your busiest time of year, right? Building up to the tax deadline?"

"Yes. Why? Do you need an accountant?"

"Nah, I'm good." He tilted his head to one side like a cat toying with prey. "You said you thought I was dead, yet you don't look that surprised to see me."

She shrugged again and his eyes flicked down her body. She recognized the exact moment he realized she was a grown woman and not an ignorant little kid anymore. A surge of satisfaction moved through her though there was no way she'd ever get involved with a man like him. But they were both adults now, and that acknowledgment evened the playing field. Aside from the badge and the gun.

"I saw you downtown earlier today, but couldn't place you," she admitted. "I hate puzzles. I think my brain has been subconsciously trying to figure out where I recognized you from ever since." She had no reason to hide the information. She hadn't been following him. "You were arguing on the street with a woman in a red coat."

"You saw that?" He was looking at her funny now.

"She was hard to miss."

He groaned and swore colorfully. "It wouldn't surprise me if it appears on CNN tonight."

"So who was she? The woman in the red coat?" Tess didn't know why she felt compelled to ask such a personal question. Except this man had never asked permission to gatecrash her life. She wanted to know.

"Got any coffee?" he asked.

What?

"Coffee. It's a warm beverage that forms ninety percent of the blood of most law enforcement personnel." He was already filling the jug like he was an old friend, not a virtual stranger she hadn't seen in twenty years.

She pulled the ground beans out of the freezer and filled the dispenser, careful not to get too close as he filled the reservoir with water. Him being a cop made a weird kind of sense.

Kenny Travers had never truly fitted in with the rightwing extremists she'd grown up with. For starters, he'd always been kind to her. He'd never spouted hatred or spite. Sure, he'd attended the Pioneers' church and made all the right noises, but he hadn't seemed like the rest of the people in Kodiak Compound. She'd felt safe with him.

"That lady in the red coat is my ex-wife," he said finally, leaning casually against the counter as they waited for the coffee to brew.

She hadn't thought he was going to answer. "She didn't look that ex to me." She watched him warily, needing to judge his veracity. Needing to judge him.

His mouth tightened. "Her second husband just left her. She thinks she can get back at him by getting back with me."

"You're not interested?" Apparently, it was her day for prying.

He shot her a look. "I make it a habit not to make the same mistake twice."

She smiled at him and batted her eyelashes innocently. "Something else we have in common."

He laughed and the sound rolled over her body. He'd always had a voice that soothed nerves. She remembered him gentling a terrified colt once, not long after he'd started coming out to Kodiak. He'd talked the foaming creature into a quivering, but trusting wreck, and that horse had followed him everywhere until her daddy had sold the animal to a neighboring rancher. Thinking about it, she'd followed him everywhere, too.

Heat burned her cheeks. But this man had been one of the few bright spots of her childhood—why wouldn't she have gravitated toward him? Hell, she'd wanted to marry him...

"Well, your ex is very pretty." All blonde and perfectly made up. Tess didn't know why she was belaboring the point, except it told her his type was not lanky brunettes with frizzy hair.

"Heather hates being called *pretty*. You'd think it was an insult. She prefers elegant or beautiful." His gaze moved over Tess's features and landed on her mouth. "I've always been partial to pretty."

Those warm looks of his suggested interest, but she couldn't allow herself to forget why he was really here, and it wasn't to catch up over coffee. He was playing her. She knew it but it still had an effect on her pulse. She pulled two mugs from the cupboard as the coffeepot filled.

Time to bring them back to what separated them—the events of that long-ago night. "Did you really get shot during the raid? Daddy said you'd been killed."

His mouth tightened. "No, I wasn't shot. I made it look like I was so I could crawl through the back of the barn and get out before all hell broke loose." A muscle in his jaw clenched. "Those were my orders."

So he'd definitely been an undercover cop back then.

Most of the people in the compound had given up without a fight. Despite their fighting words the Pioneers had crumbled like sandcastles in the rain. All except Harlan Trimble and her parents.

"Did you know I almost joined the fighting when they told me you'd been killed?" Her lungs felt as if they'd iced over and every inhalation formed cracks in her chest. "Momma gave me a gun and Daddy told me to look out my window and shoot anyone I didn't recognize." Dense silence filled the kitchen at her admission. "It was only the warning you gave me before you left that night that stopped me. Instead I took Bobby and Sampson and hid inside my bedroom closet."

So he'd almost gotten her killed, but he'd also saved her life. The admission hung in the air between them like acrid smoke. It spoke of a trust that didn't exist anymore.

He took a half step toward her then stopped, grimaced. "I wanted to get you and your baby brother out before the raid, but my bosses wouldn't allow it. Said it might alert the Pioneers something was going on. I shouldn't have even said what I did."

"It saved my life."

"You saved yourself by hiding." He sounded angry.

She nodded. He was right. She'd been a ten-year-old girl and left in the firing line when hell had broken loose. It gutted her to have it spelled out quite so starkly.

Pity entered his eyes.

She hated pity. She raised her chin a notch and went for the kill. "What about Ellie?"

The coffeepot hissed. He turned to stare out of her kitchen window and she watched his Adam's apple bob up and down his throat.

"Harlan shot Ellie." He turned away from the window.

"In the back. I read about it in the newspaper." Her voice got gravelly. She never talked about her sister's murder. How could she without revealing who she truly was? "So if you were a cop back then the law must have realized she'd been married off despite only being thirteen and they did nothing, correct?"

His eyes flashed dark and stormy. "It wasn't illegal. Fuck, it's still not illegal."

"It's disgusting and you know it. And every day Harlan Trimble raped my sister—despite that ridiculous piece of paper it was *rape and pedophilia*—the cops knew all about it but did nothing to save her. They didn't think she was worth rescuing, did they? Just like me and Bobby. None of us were worth saving."

"They said it wasn't enough." He swallowed tightly and his eyes glistened. But she didn't trust him. He was obviously a talented actor. He'd pretended to care and then left innocents to take their chances with a bunch of sociopaths and a thousand rounds of live ammunition.

She didn't bother to hide her bitterness or disgust. He didn't give a damn about her or her wellbeing. It was too late to pull that bullcrap. This visit down memory lane was about him doing his job, no matter the cost.

"You're here because of the murders, aren't you?"

———————————

"WHAT DO YOU know about the murders?" he said, watching her carefully.

"I'm not an idiot—*Kenny*. We were both there in church every Sunday when my father preached about committing these exact sorts of atrocities." Her teeth bit into a lush lower lip. She was nervous and he didn't blame her one bit. "Don't you people usually travel in pairs?" A touch of nasty entered her tone, which beat hurt hands-down.

"I'm not here in an official capacity, Theresa Jane. I don't want to expose you to any trouble if you haven't done anything wrong. I just have some questions I need answered." He kept his voice low and gentle, but she flinched anyway.

Before tonight he'd always thought of Theresa Jane as that cheeky kid with the wavy hair and rampant freckles who'd regarded him with adulation wherever he went. The image of her standing on a chair by the kitchen sink, the setting sun making her glow like an angel was an endearing memory that snuck up on him occasionally and made a nice change from dead bodies that haunted him. The fact he'd left that same kid in the center of a gun battle was a permanent bruise on his conscience.

And she knew it.

Tess Fallon might have the same long dark hair as Theresa Jane Hines, but she was no kid anymore. Her eyes were the same hazel-green as her mother's. There the resemblance ended.

Whereas Francis Hines had turned his blood cold, the grown-up version of Theresa Jane…didn't.

That clear hazel gaze followed him, but it wasn't filled with adulation anymore. It was full of intelligent suspicion.

He took a half step toward her then stopped. Fuck. He'd been a good cop, and the op had been considered a success, but that didn't necessarily make him a good person. Tess Fallon was smart enough to appreciate the difference.

"I'll say one thing about your daddy. He did give one hell of a sermon." He stared at the coffeepot, willing the jug to fill faster. "It's not Kenny Travers. It's Assistant Special Agent in Charge Steve McKenzie of the Federal Bureau of Investigation."

Her brows rose at the information. "Sounds impressive." Her tone was decidedly unimpressed. "Scottish?"

"Great, great, great Granddaddy came over during the gold rush of '48 from the Highlands." The smile he gave her was supposed to charm. Her glower suggested he needed to keep working on it.

The coffee was finally done and he filled both mugs with strong Colombian roast while she grabbed milk from the fridge. It was unnerving how at ease he felt in her kitchen. More at ease here than having lunch with his ex.

"Sugar's in the jar near the stove."

He froze in the act of reaching for it and turned to stare at her. "You remember how I take my coffee?"

Her lips pinched for a moment, reminding him of her mother.

"Turns out I have a fantastic memory for absolutely meaningless trivia. Probably why I remembered your face," she said dryly.

77

Ouch. He wondered if he could use that in some way.

"It's one of the things that makes me a good accountant." Her chin lifted belligerently.

He recognized the chink in her armor, her battered pride, and remembered how her family had treated her. Like she was stupid for not going along with the party line. It was one of the many reasons he'd liked her so much.

Was she still that funny little girl? Or had what happened that awful night, and in the twenty years since, warped her?

He handed her a mug and raised his in a toast. The coffee was hot and strong and gave his system a kick. "Nothing wrong with having a good memory."

"Sometimes there is." She gave a humorless little laugh as she raised the mug to her lips.

Damn. His voice grew soft. "It was a long time ago."

She stared at him like he was crazy. "Some things you don't forget. Not ever."

He grimaced. She wasn't letting him off the hook that easily. His attention shifted lower, to the damp terrycloth robe clinging to a lean body that was curvy in all the places that mattered.

"You still have the tattoo?" he asked, nonchalantly sipping his drink.

She pulled the robe tighter, maybe not realizing that gave him a better view of the outline of her body. Or maybe she did realize it and was playing him like a guitar string ripe for plucking.

She chewed her lip in a nervous habit she'd had even as a kid. It jolted him back to that time and filled him with regrets.

But she was right to be nervous.

If she was innocent she'd be worried he'd upend this life

she'd built for herself. If she was guilty, and an FBI agent who'd been associated with her life at Kodiak Compound turned up out of the blue? Yup. He'd be nervous, too.

"Why do you want to know about the tattoo?" Those eyes of hers drilled into him.

"You know why." He wasn't letting her off the hook, either.

Her eyes flared wide. That tattoo would prove exactly how attached she was to her daddy's ideology. She put her coffee mug down on the counter and slipped the bathrobe over her shoulder. He found himself holding his breath. She slipped her sleeve lower, careful to hold the material in place with a hand between her breasts.

He put down his mug and crossed the room toward her. She tensed when he reached out and stroked the skin of her upper arm, smooth as velvet.

When she was nine, her father had taken it upon himself to have every member of the Pioneers tattooed with the number fourteen. It was less obvious than a swastika but meant basically the same thing—to white nationalists at least. Kenny had escaped by claiming he was allergic to the ink.

"Pi?" He shot her a grin.

She raised her brow in mock surprise. "You recognize it?"

His lips quirked. Touché. "My high school math teacher offered ten bucks to whoever memorized pi to the most decimal places."

"You won?"

He nodded.

"How many decimals did you memorize?"

"Fifty."

"Because you're competitive?"

His smile lost its humor. "Because I needed the money."

She tugged the robe back up her shoulder, firmly adjusting the belt. She smelled like strawberries, and his palms itched like a neon warning sign.

This was *not* how he'd imagined he'd react to this woman.

"Altering the tattoo was my adoptive mother's idea. I was already a math nerd." Up close there were thin streaks of gold amongst the browns and greens of her irises. "I'd been wanting to get it removed before any of the other kids at school spotted it and asked questions. She thought I might be able to reclaim what they'd done to me by making it my own. I was eleven when we got this done."

Mac stared at her intently, much too close in the cramped confines of her kitchen.

"Do you want to check me for others?" If she'd been aiming for sarcasm it came out wrong.

The flash of heat that crackled between took them both by surprise. He stepped away, picked up his coffee. The silence between them suddenly taut with a different kind of tension.

"Were you always a federal agent? Back then I mean?" she asked after a few awkward beats.

He said nothing for a moment, then tipped back his drink, draining the mug. Then he washed his cup in the sink, placing it upside down on the drainer. "I was an Idaho State Trooper back then. Kodiak was my first assignment. Joined the Bureau a couple years later."

"My parents would have been livid to discover you were a cop." She gave the appearance of being amused by the idea. Not many people had fooled David or Francis Hines.

He wandered into her living room without an invitation. On paper, she lived alone, a single woman with no live-in-lover or kids of her own. But that meant nothing in the real world. She might have a long-term boyfriend or rent out rooms on the side.

She followed him, cupping her mug in both hands. Not willing to let him out of her sight. Frankly he didn't blame her.

He'd been shocked to discover she lived so close to DC, in a quiet residential neighborhood of Bethesda. Close enough to pop into town for a quick triple homicide. He'd decided to check her out for himself.

He wasn't sure what he was looking for. Dog-eared copies of *The Turner Diaries* or other white nationalist hate literature? Maybe a confederate flag tacked to the wall?

There were two framed POOM certificates with fancy silver characters decorating them. He peered closer. Tess Fallon was a two dan black belt in taekwondo. Impressive.

"Who's this?" He pointed to a framed photograph on the mantel.

"My mom."

"Seriously?" He turned to her in surprise. "You realize she's black, right?"

"I did notice," she said drolly. She stared at him for a few moments as if gauging how much to say. "No one wanted me. People wanted Bobby, but they didn't want me. She was the only person who'd take us both."

Shit. A whole new dose of guilt hit him. There were all kinds of prejudice in the world and children from right-wing compounds were pretty low on the cute and fuzzy scale. He didn't like to think how she might have suffered. He couldn't afford to go easy on her.

"She fostered us for a year and then filed for adoption. I grew up in Leesburg."

"This Bobby?" A picture of the three of them was also on the mantel, showing an overweight teenager with dark hair and glasses.

She nodded.

There was a resemblance to David Hines in the boy. How deep that resemblance ran was what interested him most.

"You and your mom are close?" he asked cautiously.

Her expression closed down and she looked away. "We were. She died. Last year. Heart attack."

He deliberately adjusted the frame on the mantel, cleared his throat. "There's something I need to ask."

She tensed.

He made himself ignore her vulnerability and her pain and the guilt of all she'd endured simply because of who her parents had been. He had a job to do. A job he'd dedicated his life to. Instead he thought about the dead judge and his wife, murdered as they'd prepared for a normal day. "Where were you on Monday morning between seven and eight a.m.?"

CHAPTER NINE

ABEL ZINGEL LOCKED the doors to the synagogue and gave them a rattle just to be sure. There had been a series of break-ins recently and he didn't want any vandals getting inside because he'd failed to lock up. Rabbi Hirsch would never let him hear the end of it.

The corns on Abel's feet throbbed as he started the long trek home. His wife always took the car on Tuesdays to go grocery shopping. Usually he liked to walk, but he liked to walk less when the cold made his ears burn. He pulled his hat lower and dug his hands into the pockets of his overcoat, trying to keep out the bitter wind.

His wife was cooking lamb chops and roast potatoes for dinner tonight and his stomach was rumbling in anticipation. His daughter, Ruth, and her fiancé were coming over to discuss wedding plans.

He smacked his lips together. He could already smell the sizzling, succulent meat. Judith was the best cook he'd ever known. He'd have married her for that alone, but she was also beautiful, in mind and body and they'd produced four wonderful children together. All of whom had gone on to college and gotten respectable jobs.

They were great kids. He was proud of each one of them but, he could admit privately, Ruthie was his favorite.

He neared the deli on the corner and decided to go in and buy a bottle of fine red wine. He left the store with a nice bottle of kosher Merlot tucked under one arm and pushed on up the hill toward the house he'd called home for more than two decades. They were planning to downsize soon, but he and Judith both loved the place so much that neither of them had made any move to look for something smaller.

The wind howled and the branches of the trees clacked together like dry brittle bones. It was dark. One side of the road backed onto woods where he used to walk the dog. He missed that old dog. Maybe they'd get a puppy. Something to give him more exercise and his wife an increased sense of security when he was out.

He stopped for a moment to catch his breath, then continued onwards, crossed the road to reach the street he lived on. The streetlight halfway along the road was broken and he frowned in annoyance. He'd called the city twice and they'd told him they'd fixed it. He kept his gaze focused on the uneven sidewalk because he didn't want to trip and break his ankle in the dark.

"Rabbi Zingel?" A quiet voice called out and a shadow separated from between two parked cars on the side of the road.

He squinted at the person but couldn't make out their features. "Can I help you?"

"You are Rabbi Zingel, correct?"

"Yes. Do I—?"

The pain in his chest felt like fire. The wine bottle slipped from the crook of his arm and shattered on the sidewalk. He dropped to his knees and the figure came closer. A glint of light caught the circular barrel of a handgun as it loomed out of the darkness and Abel knew he was about to die.

"Why are you doing this? What have I ever done to you?" The gun came closer to his face and he thought of the suffering his wife and his children would endure from this mindless act of violence.

"My God and God of my people…" he began.

Pain flared for a brief instant before the darkness came.

CHAPTER TEN

"YOU WANT ME to provide an alibi?" The glow drained from her cheeks.

Tension sizzled through the air as Mac watched her body language to see if it matched her words. "You know I have to ask."

She crossed her arms, every line of her body defensive and resentful. "I don't remember exactly where I was on Monday morning." Her eyes moved up and right.

Shit. She was lying. People lied to cops and FBI agents all the time. The question was, what did she have to hide?

"But this morning, when the DJ was shot"—She'd already put together what the cops were officially refusing to admit— "I was in a coffee shop and then on the Metro."

"Got people who can verify that?"

She gave him the name of a coffee shop near Tenleytown and the metro stop where she'd got off the train.

"Don't tell them why you're asking," she said. "Please."

He grimaced.

She cradled her forehead in her hand and looked like she suddenly felt ill. Because, really, what were they going to think when the FBI started asking questions about her movements? He made himself push on. She wasn't his friend or his date. He had a job to do.

"Any idea who might be committing these murders?"

"I told you. I'm not in touch with anyone from that life anymore."

"What about your brother?"

"Eddie?" An ugly laugh escaped. "I don't have anything to do with that wacko."

Eddie Hines was still incarcerated in the Idaho State Correctional Center. They'd pulled a bullet matched to his gun out of a SWAT officer's vertebrae. The policeman had been lucky to not be paralyzed. To prove that point the officer turned up in a borrowed wheelchair and a "here but for the grace of God" sign every time Eddie came up for parole.

"I meant your *other* brother."

She reached out to hold on to the back of the couch. "He doesn't know about any of this."

Mac frowned. "You mean the murders?"

"No," she bit out sharply. "*Any* of it. Not the Pioneers. Not Kodiak Compound. Not who our family really is. Nothing." Her fists clenched and unclenched. "And I want it to stay that way."

What the hell? "Where does he think he comes from?"

"I told him we were the children of Trudy's second-cousin on her mom's side. I told him our parents died up in Oregon and Trudy took us in."

"You lied to him about his parents?" *Holy shit.*

She put her hand on her hip. "Don't use that judgmental tone with me, Assistant Special Agent in Charge *Steve McKenzie.*"

"Sorry, *Tess.*" He strode toward her until they were only a foot apart. "I didn't realize you had the monopoly on changing your identity."

She flinched and blinked rapidly as if fighting tears. "If anyone should understand why I wanted to leave that ugliness behind it should be you. You need to leave. Now."

When he didn't move she went to the front door and opened it, waiting for him to take the hint. Damn. He'd blown it. When he stood in front of her again he opened his mouth to speak.

She beat him to it. "Don't leave town, right?" Bitterness was rife in the lines around her mouth. In the bite of her tone.

"I was going to say that if anyone from Kodiak gets in touch—"

"They won't."

"But if they do—"

"They *won't!*" She appeared on the verge of crying, but fighting it.

He'd seen all sorts of tears during his time on the job. It was always the ones that didn't fall that affected him most.

He pulled a business card out of his pocket, took her hand and folded her fingers over it. The skin on skin contact made something unexpected spread through his body. Despite her anger she felt it too—he could tell by the way her pupils widened and her lips parted on a gasp. She tried to pull away but he didn't let go and he didn't back down.

Instead he pulled her toward him into a stiff embrace. His breath brushed her hair as he kissed the top of her head—like she was still that little girl he'd known all those years ago.

"I'm not the bad guy here, Tess," he murmured against her hair.

She kept her head bowed, and eyes closed, hand pressed like a fiery brand against his heart.

"Neither am I, but no one seems to care."

She pulled away, and he let her go. Then he walked away just like he had nearly twenty years ago.

He sat in his car, staring at the house, knowing she was inside watching him right back.

The unexpected attraction had caught him off guard. He'd forgotten what it felt like to actually want someone. But he couldn't afford to start something with the daughter of one of the most notorious white supremacist leaders in history. That would not look great on his résumé.

That stupid hug had knocked him off balance and made him sit here like a damn stalker. He'd hoped to neutralize some of the antagonism his turning up out of the blue had created and keep her onside should he need her help in the future.

But now the fresh scent of her shampoo invaded his nostrils, and the feel of her soft skin tantalized his senses. The sight of her in that damp robe—knowing that she was naked underneath—had distracted the hell out of him. And damned if that embrace hadn't felt like coming home.

Chances were she wasn't involved in the current murders. It didn't seem likely that an accountant, raised by a woman of color, would turn around and start killing people based on her daddy's evil doctrine. But who knew? He'd seen crazier things in his career. Tomorrow he'd check out her alibi and cross her off his to-do list.

More's the pity.

And so what if his mind turned dirty. It wasn't going to lead anywhere. She was off limits. And he was in control of his wants and needs.

He started the engine. What he undoubtedly needed was to find out more about the kid brother. His records were sealed but Mac had a friend in the DOJ working to get them unsealed. It might take some time, not to mention a warrant, but he would track the kid down if only to rule him out.

He could come back and talk to Tess again, but this wasn't his case. Plus, the idea of spending more time with her appealed a little too much, and he wasn't about to blow his chance of getting his dream job for a woman he barely knew.

Twenty years ago, Federal and State law enforcement in Idaho had been growing increasingly worried about the activities of David Hines's expanding group of white nationalists who hid under the cloak of a fervent whites-only Christian church.

Apparently, Jesus Christ was the only person in the Middle East to be born white.

Go figure.

He'd never blamed Tess for being part of something she had no control over. He didn't want her dragged into the public eye if she was innocent. That's why he'd come alone in an unofficial capacity. But she was definitely hiding something and he intended to find out what it was.

The Pioneers had been able to spot most informants before they ever got near the compound. Mac had been new to Idaho, fresh out of the police academy, and had grown up on ranches.

Cowboy Kenny Travers had started working on a cattle ranch near the town of Kodiak, Idaho, hanging out in a local bar in his spare time. He'd become friendly with Eddie Hines. Shooting pool, talking racist bullshit, chatting up girls. It had taken a few months to gain Eddie's trust, then the guy had invited Kenny out to the compound and into the fold.

The rest was history.

Did Eddie still have connections on the outside? Did white nationalists visit their buddies in prison? Did Eddie-the-asshole know who was involved in this new string of murders? And might he swap that information for his freedom?

Or was this killer a whole new ball of wax?

As far as Mac knew there was no evidence the Pioneers were involved in these new murders. So as appealing as the idea was to turn up and see Eddie's ugly face contort with rage when he found out Kenny Travers had in reality been an undercover cop, Mac was needed here. He'd send a lead to the office in Boise and ask for an agent to go question Eddie. Find out who he'd been communicating with.

Mac pressed his lips together. He remembered every detail of the year he'd spent undercover in that cesspit. Every flat handed salute, every racial slur his lips had been forced to utter.

It might have proven that a poor boy from Montana could make a difference, but it had stained his soul. He'd been forced to stand by and do nothing when he'd witnessed things that made him physically ill—like a girl forced into an early marriage with a man old enough to have been Mac's father.

His stomach knotted when he thought about the children. Theresa Jane—*Tess*—and the others had been treated like indentured servants, or worse. Most of them had been brainwashed minions, but she'd always had spunk and had laughed more than anyone else in that whole damned place.

He flashed to her standing in her kitchen in that white bathrobe. It didn't look like she laughed much anymore.

To this day he didn't know if Theresa Jane—*Tess, dammit*—had been sexually abused or not. He hadn't been privy to her psychological assessment although he'd contributed to the reports. The fact Walt had died during the shootout was not something that had troubled Mac's conscience one little bit, but Ellie...

He still woke up in a cold sweat some nights hearing Ellie scream. If Mac had married her like David Hines wanted, she would have survived. He needn't have slept with her. She'd be living her life somewhere, maybe doing people's taxes like her sister.

He'd begged his boss to go in when he found out she'd been married to Trimble, but they weren't ready and underage marriage wasn't illegal as long as the parents gave permission—it still wasn't in more states than most people in America realized. The evidence they'd had at that point wasn't enough to arrest the ring leaders and permanently shut down the compound. Two months after thirteen-year-old Ellie had been married off, dumber-than-a-rock Kenny Travers had come across the cache of stolen guns stored in a horse trailer in one of the barns. That had been the beginning of the end for the Pioneers. But it had been too late for poor sweet Ellie.

He put his car in drive and rolled slowly past Tess's house. Her silhouette was outlined by his headlights in the window, as she watched him leave. It was time to say goodbye to this part of his life. There was no going back.

A few seconds later his cell rang. Work—not Tess asking him to come back and start something they shouldn't.

"McKenzie," he answered impatiently.

"There's been another murder. A rabbi on Munroe Street," ASC Gerald told him brusquely.

Shit. "When?" Mac asked.

"Twenty minutes ago."

He blew out a big breath. Well, at least he knew for sure

Tess had an alibi for this murder.

"The director wants a task force assembled ASAP."

Mac's attention laser-focused on what the guy was saying.

"I mentioned your concerns about the judge and the DJ being victims of hate crimes to my boss yesterday."

He held his breath.

"They want you to head the task force and run it from HQ."

He fist pumped the air.

"McKenzie? You there?"

"Yes, sir. Thank you, sir." Excitement shimmered through him. Like the Minnesota mall attack, this was the sort of case that made careers and might leapfrog him straight to SAC. "Do I get to pick my own team?"

"Some of them," Gerald allowed. "Send me a list of agents you want. I'll start reaching out to DHS, the Capitol Police and WFO. I'll get everything they have on the murders so far."

"Ask the officers and agents involved in those investigations to join the task force. It'll give us additional boots on the ground and fast-track the information they've already gathered. Tell the ME not to move the rabbi's body until I get there." He checked his watch. Wrote down the address. "I'm thirty minutes out."

"Roger that." Gerald hung up.

Mac's heart pounded in anticipation and he started driving like he meant it.

Four murders in thirty-six hours. Someone was killing people of this fine city based on their beliefs and the color of their skin. That wasn't the kind of America he wanted to live in. He'd waged this war before but now they'd brought the battle to his turf and this time they were the ones cloaked in shadows. But he appreciated how these guys thought; he understood how they hated. They'd make a mistake at some point. Unfortunately, until they did there were thousands if not millions of potential targets in the DC area alone.

And every last one of them was at risk.

———————

TESS CLOSED THE door and locked it, leaning her forehead against the cool wood. She was never going to outrun her childhood, but she would not let it destroy the one person in the world she loved. She turned off the lights and went into the living room, stared into her quiet street long after Steve McKenzie had driven away.

Did he really suspect she was involved?

Well, why not? Her family had been a bunch of freaking lunatics.

She stared down at the card in her hand. The fancy embossed foil FBI symbol seemed to mock her attempts at making a new life for herself and her brother.

ASAC Steve McKenzie. She rubbed her thumb over his name.

Her ten-year-old self had loved him more than she'd loved her own parents but that did not make him her friend. Twenty years ago, McKenzie and his fellow officers had abandoned her to her fate. She'd saved herself and her brother and she wasn't about to rely on the cops for anything now she was an adult.

She closed her eyes at the realization she sounded just as paranoid as her parents had been. *Trust no one* must be the family motto.

McKenzie's visit brought it all back. The suffocating environment she'd grown up in. The gunfight that had ended her childhood. Her mother's poisonous last words.

The bullets had finally stopped pounding her childhood home in the hour before dawn. The silence had been more unnerving than the gunfight. Incredibly, at some point she must have fallen asleep. Only to be woken by a huge bang as the cops stormed the cabin. She hadn't cried out when two masked men had opened her closet door, leading with their big black guns, though she'd been terrified. They'd found her clutching Cole to her chest and hanging on to Sampson's neck when he growled at them.

She'd screamed when they'd eased her brother out of her arms. Another man came in and removed Sampson from her grasp. They'd searched her, gently but firmly. She'd thought the black masked men were going to kill her. Instead one of them had wrapped her in his arms, pushed her face against his chest and told her to keep her eyes closed as he carried her out of there.

She still remembered the smell of his uniform—smoke and sweat and gunpowder. She'd tried to keep her eyes closed, she truly had. He'd even placed a hand half over her face, but in her peripheral vision she'd spotted the body of her mother as the man had stepped over her outside the bedroom door. Francis Hines's eyes had been wide open. Tess still saw those dead eyes—the exact same color and shape as her own—in her nightmares. In the kitchen, the dawn's rays had reflected off the mother-of-pearl buttons on her daddy's favorite chambray shirt as he lay dead on the kitchen floor. A dark stain of blood had mottled the pale blue fabric.

Her stomach had churned and she'd pressed her nose tighter against the stranger's chest. He'd cupped the back of her head and squeezed, trying to give her comfort.

He was the enemy, but in that moment, he'd tried to soothe the pain and terror that ripped through her in a way her family never had. Instead of hurting her, the stranger had taken her to safety and made sure she was uninjured. It was then she'd realized her family had lied to her all those years. She'd started sobbing uncontrollably and he'd taken her in his arms and rocked her until she'd fallen asleep.

Looking back, she wondered why she'd cried at all. Her family had been monsters who'd tried to instill their twisted beliefs into her psyche. They'd belittled and mistreated her when she'd questioned them or disobeyed their rules. Walt had tried to sexually assault her and she was sure he would have succeeded eventually. At thirteen she'd probably have been married off to one of the many losers who came in a constant stream to her daddy's isolated compound. If she'd rebelled they would have killed her for spite and called it justice.

It wasn't justice. It was abuse.

The only person she missed was Ellie.

A knot formed in Tess's throat at the thought of her sister's death.

No, Kenny Travers had never really fit in. She wondered how he'd managed to hide his true essence for so long when surrounded by such all-encompassing hate.

The coffee she'd drunk churned in her stomach as the memories swirled. Part of her wished she could forget that time and where she came from, but another part was proud. She'd been strong enough to retain her compassion and humanity despite everything she'd endured. She'd been resilient enough to move on, to grow and thrive and blossom into a respectable and worthwhile human being.

Tess stared across the darkened room to the photograph of her mom. What would she have done?

Trudy Fallon had been the first genuinely good person she'd ever met. The daughter of a rich, white mother and poor, black father who'd met in college and fallen in love, gotten married against their families' wishes. The marriage hadn't lasted more than a couple of years and a young Trudy had been shuffled between two worlds never fitting into either. That's what had made her so perfect for Tess and Cole. She understood what it was like to be unloved and unwanted. She'd appreciated that where they came from didn't define who they were, it was what was inside that mattered. The three of them had made their own little family, one blessed with a deep abiding love. Losing her adoptive mother last year had hurt more than losing her entire family at Kodiak Compound.

She shook herself out of her melancholy and ran upstairs to throw on warm pjs.

She came back downstairs and decided to work. But the silence was oppressive so she switched on the TV and immediately wished she hadn't.

The news headlines proclaimed a rabbi had been murdered.

Cold washed over her.

She'd been able to retain a small degree of hope that the murder of the judge and his wife, and that of the transgender DJ, were unfortunate coincidences. This was a big city. They led prominent lives, which attracted the haters no matter your creed, politics, or sexuality.

But the rabbi…

He wasn't a celebrity. He wasn't high profile. According to

the news anchor he was just some sweet old guy, beloved by his family and the community, renowned for acts of inclusion and kindness.

Dread spread through her veins.

She called Cole, but he didn't pick up.

Was he honestly pissed with her, or was he hiding something?

Then she remembered something that made her knees give way. Monday—the day the judge and his wife had been gunned down in cold blood—had been February twenty-third.

If he'd lived, it would have been her father's sixty-fifth birthday.

She swallowed repeatedly as her stomach threatened to crawl up her throat.

Had one of his followers decided to make some sort of statement for the twentieth anniversary of the raid on the compound? Anniversaries were a big deal with these antigovernment types. Just ask Timothy McVeigh.

Or was it one of those horrible coincidences that cropped up sporadically to mess up the world like a cosmic joke?

She paced the room. This was *so* like the plan her daddy had preached over and over again. The language so heinous it had been seared into her mind with the indelible ink—like the tattoo they'd branded her with as a child. Even the memory of his voice in her head made her want to gag. How could he have preached that twisted message and thought it was okay? How could all the people she'd known back then have been so deviant and misguided?

She wasn't surprised at her mother.

Francis Hines had been a hard woman who'd only balked at the constraints of being female in a white nationalist enclave, not at their ideology. If anything, she'd taken a harder line.

Occasionally she saw her mother's face reflected back at her in the mirror, or in a photograph taken from the wrong angle.

It scared her.

To think she shared her mother's DNA made her want to scrape the skin off her bones.

There were others on the lunatic fringe who shared similar beliefs to the Pioneers. They weren't the only crazies out there, but the link to her father's birthday... The fact it was twenty years since the raid...

She contemplated Steve McKenzie's fancy business card. Should she call him with the information about her father's birthday? But he was FBI. Surely, he'd figured it out? Maybe that was why he'd turned up tonight.

More importantly she needed to know *why* Cole had a photograph of that judge in his file cabinet? And why had he removed it?

She sat on the edge of her sofa and watched the same TV footage repeat, over and over. A row of parked cars along a dark street with yellow tape strung across both ends to prevent reporters getting any closer. A tent had been constructed over the body. Police cruisers with their lights flashing created a weird futuristic atmosphere. Small pockets of uniformed cops stood around, looking angry and nervous.

A man in an FBI raid jacket entered the tent covering the body. Tess rewound the footage. McKenzie.

At least she had an alibi for this murder.

Did Cole? *Damn.*

Police weren't saying how the rabbi died, but the reporter

suggested a witness had heard muted gunshots—same as the other murders.

Tess looked at the photograph of her adoptive mother on the fireplace. What should she do?

"There are growing fears that a series of hate crimes have been occurring in metro-DC area," the reporter said. "We've just been informed the FBI is forming a joint task force to investigate. Spokesmen for the FBI have so far refused to comment, except to urge everyone to remain calm but vigilant, and for anyone with information to please come forward."

Tess walked into the kitchen, her gaze pulled toward her purse where she'd stashed the jump drive.

If she found evidence that Cole was involved in these murders would she give him up to the police? Would she give up the baby brother she'd vowed to love and protect with her own life when they were still both children? The idea stabbed like a serrated knife right through her chest.

He was sweet and kind and she loved him more than she'd ever loved anyone, but was it possible he was involved in a conspiracy to commit murder? What if there were other people targeted for death? People who could be saved? Her mouth went dry. It was an impossible choice, but it was really no choice at all. If Cole was guilty she'd tell McKenzie in a heartbeat to save innocents.

She snagged the small plastic stick from her purse. Sweat beaded on her brow as she slid the drive into the USB port.

The files took time to populate and she stood there nervously clenching her fists. Movie files. She clicked on one of the icons, her heart pounding in trepidation.

The sound of heavy breathing filled the room. She blinked and stared wide-eyed at the thrusting buttocks that filled the screen. Her mouth opened. Whoa. She didn't know people could even do that standing up.

She tried another file. A girl in a tight-fitting outfit filled the screen, bent over, washing a car. Tess knew where that was going so she turned it off. She raised her face to the ceiling, and blew out a big sigh of relief.

This was her brother's porn collection.

She ran her hands over her face and laughed. How the hell was she going to sneak this back into his desk without him knowing about it?

Who cared? She yanked it out of the slot and shut down the computer.

She still didn't understand the connection between her brother and the judge's picture, but at least this data stick didn't contain a murder list.

A heavy feeling settled inside her chest. No matter how badly she wanted to, she couldn't ignore the unanswered questions hanging over her head. There was only one person she knew who might have answers, but to get them she needed to do something she'd sworn she'd never do. She needed to confront her brother.

CHAPTER ELEVEN

C OLE EYED HIS lover as she got out of bed, naked, and walked to the bathroom, closing the door gently behind her.

The room was almost completely black now and he leaned against the pillows and listened to his cell buzz in his jeans. He knew it was Tess calling to apologize again, but he was still pissed so she could stew for a little longer.

Who the hell was she to tell him who to see? Her track record was nothing but whiners and losers.

He plumped the pillow and lay on his side, waiting for his lover to return. They'd met before Christmas but she was still reluctant for them to be seen together in public. Part of it was the age difference. Part was her job.

He didn't give a damn about either, but she was sensitive and he didn't want to upset her. His sister's comment had made him realize, as much as he thought Carolyn's worries were dumb, old-fashioned attitudes still prevailed. It was weird considering Tess was the most inclusive person he knew, but they'd never had to deal with an age difference before. Tess was gonna have to get used to it.

He loved Carolyn.

It was too early to say anything without freaking her out, but he was all-in with this relationship and he hoped she was, too.

He'd thought he'd been in love before, but he'd been fooling himself. He'd sat in high school chemistry classes mooning over girls just like any other adolescent male. But no one had wanted to date the zitty nerd with thick glasses and an IQ thirty points above their own.

When he'd gotten tight with Joseph, the guy had urged him to play the field. Cole had for a while, but now he was ready for a real relationship. Joseph chased anything in a skirt, taking pleasure from rubbing other guys' noses in it. The dude was a compulsive player and better be pretending to want to nail his sister else Cole would beat the guy to a pulp.

The door opened and Carolyn gave him a smile. There wasn't a wrinkle on her body nor a gray hair on her pretty head. She looked almost angelic and he couldn't believe she'd agreed to go out with him in the first place, let alone have sex.

She walked across the room without a stitch on and the sway of her hips had him hypnotized. She cursed as she stubbed her toe on a box.

"Ouch." She grabbed her foot and massaged the injury. "Can you still do me that favor on Friday I asked you about?"

Wait. What? He frowned. It was hard to concentrate when she didn't have any clothes on. What had she asked him to do again?

"I'm not supposed to move in until the first of the month, but the landlord told me I could have the keys early as the old tenants moved out. A friend of mine is lending me his van…"

Oh, yeah. Something about helping her move her stuff to a new apartment. This place was pretty cramped. "Sure." Her breasts swayed as she bent down to pick up her suit pants and drape them over a chair. He swallowed. "No problem."

"I can ask someone else if you're busy… Trent said—"

"I'm not busy." *Who the fuck was Trent?*

It didn't matter. He couldn't believe anybody looked as amazing as she did naked. And she was worried about her age?

"You should probably be in class." She bit her lip.

That got his back up. "Friday's class is just about the ethics of hacking. I can skip it."

She sighed as she came towards him, the light from the bathroom making her skin glow. "I should no doubt be worried about that statement."

"I've got it."

"I worry I'm going to affect your studies," she admitted. "And that's when I remember you're still in college—"

"Hey." He caught her hand. "There are *some* advantages to me being younger." He placed her palm directly over the advantage he had in mind.

Her eyes widened and her lips twitched. "Seriously? Again?"

He grinned. "Come back to bed and find out," he urged.

"Work called. I need to go in." She made her voice firm but he could feel her wavering and saw the hungry way she caught her bottom lip.

"Call in sick."

She rolled her eyes as he pulled her down beside him.

"We're not all in college, you know. My job is important." A frown touched her brow at another reminder about their different positions in life.

He leaned over to lick one perfect nipple.

She shuddered and threw back her head. She moaned and sank the fingers of one hand into his hair. "We don't have time." But she was squirming against him in a way that made his pulse accelerate.

"We'll be quick." His hand slid between her thighs.

She groaned and then pushed against his shoulders so he was on his back. "We'll have to be."

She straddled him, impaling herself, the sensation making his brain whiteout.

"You have no idea how incredible that feels." He skimmed his hands up to her breasts and pinched the delicate tissue.

She laughed and gasped. "I have a pretty good idea."

She started riding him, slowly, setting the pace and controlling the depth. She leaned over him and he found her nipple with his mouth. His hands slid over her ass, grinding her against him exactly how she liked it. Her fingernails bit into his shoulders.

"I've created a monster," she whispered.

She had. He was insatiable for her and didn't care who knew it.

She held his gaze as she reared up and fucked him harder. He found her clit and squeezed. She bucked uncontrollably against him and her muscles contracted around him like a vise. She grinned as she caught her breath, never breaking rhythm, and reached behind her to stroke the taut skin behind his balls. Despite trying to make it last longer she shot him over the edge like she'd lit a fuse. Then she curled over him, laughing as his tried to figure which way was up.

"I love you," he blurted as his heart galloped. He closed his eyes and swore to himself.

But she didn't protest the way he'd expected. She pulled him with her into the shower and kissed every inch of him, once again proving that a woman in her sexual peak beat a college girl in every way imaginable.

MAC STARED OUT across the crisis action team room they'd been assigned. A sea of faces from at least eight different agencies stared back, including ASAC Lincoln Frazer of the BAU via video-uplink from his home office. It was midnight, but night was indistinguishable from day inside the windowless, hermetically sealed SIOC.

Special Agent Mark Ross—the guy who'd been so pissed by Mac's visit to the crime scene on Monday—slumped in the nearest seat and watched him through red-rimmed eyes. The guy probably hadn't slept since Judge Thomas's murder. The WFO agent recapped everything they had so far: No witnesses. No definite evidence. No recent threats. No obvious skeletons in the closet. No clear motive outside the fact the man was a federal judge with dark skin.

The homicide detective from Capitol Police took her turn updating the briefing. Annabel Dunbar had glossy, black hair cut brutally short and wore pants so tight Mac was surprised she could breathe, let alone walk. "Unlike the judge and his wife, Sonja Shiraz had been inundated with threatening letters, email and tweets."

Mac was old enough to find the idea that they were investigating "tweets" stranger than the fact the DJ had undergone a sex change.

"I want all the letters sent to the questioned documents lab for analysis. I want all the authors traced and put into a database."

"That's a lot of people," the detective commented. "Mainly trolls."

"Trolls go in the database, too." The anonymity of the

internet brought out the worst in some folks. Maybe the hatred it nurtured had spawned a murder campaign. "I want it noted if they make a habit of harassing people—and see if any of those other people have ended up dead." Mac named Libby Hernandez to work on it. "Pay particular attention to Sonja's blog and other social media outlets where she posts about her transition. Also comments on news articles about her." Where the real trolls hung out.

A couple of agents shifted uncomfortably. One raised his hand. "What pronoun do we use in the reports. Birth or…reassigned?"

A couple of the guys giggled like children. Detective Dunbar put her fist on her hip and glared.

Mac gave them an easygoing smile but they better be paying attention to his eyes before they smiled back.

Faces straightened. A little color entered the cheeks of the agent who'd asked the question. Fact was, a lot of people struggled with the concept of gender reassignment. Mac had struggled for a time, too, and then figured that if people cared enough to willingly have their genitals altered with a scalpel, then it was a serious matter and it should be treated as such.

"Let's show Ms. Shiraz the same respect you'd want for your sister or mother, shall we?"

Detective Dunbar visibly relaxed. "Sonja's parents arrive from India today. When I spoke to them on the phone they were inconsolable. They'd thought she'd be safer here than back in India." She pressed her lips together and stared at the charcoal carpet. "I felt like I'd personally let them down, let Sonja down with this occurring in DC. I want to catch this bastard before he does this to anyone else."

Mac recognized that driving desire for justice. The need to

make the bad guys pay. It burned hot enough in some people that the long hours and crappy wages didn't seem to matter.

Taking these bastards down was his personal catnip and he could tell Dunbar felt the same.

After the detective finished Mac took over the briefing. "We have four victims. Two slugs in each vic and no stray bullets have been found at this time. Evidence Response Team techs are continuing their search of the crime scenes. No shell casings at the first two scenes, so this UNSUB is careful and meticulous, but," he grinned, "an ERT Team tech got lucky at the most recent scene. He found a casing that rolled under a car and down a storm drain."

A stirring of excitement ran through the assembled agents.

"Agent Gabriel Harm is the leading ballistics expert with the Bureau and he'll be examining the casing and spent bullets." Mac pointed to Gabe Harm, who sat at the back of the room. He'd traveled up from Quantico to collect the evidence and stayed on for the briefing while the ME did her thing. The bullets from the other scenes had already been examined for fibers, fingerprints and DNA and those samples had now been sent to the lab at Quantico to be further analyzed.

Mac had worked with Harm before. The guy was a genius when it came to guns and ammunition.

"Slugs recovered aren't in decent shape," Harm said quietly. "But I'll do what I can with them. Recovering that casing is helpful. I can run it through the National Integrated Ballistic Information Network (NIBIN) to see if the gun that fired it has been used in another crime. It's slow, time-consuming work. Don't expect miracles."

Mac nodded. "We need to know if we are dealing with one offender or multiple offenders, so narrowing down a murder weapon is key."

Mac's phone buzzed in his pocket. He checked the screen in case it was urgent, but it was Heather trying to call him, again. Apologizing for her angry texts and wanting to meet. Again.

He ignored it.

Forgiving and forgetting wasn't in his nature. If he had a flaw—and he had plenty—holding a grudge likely topped the list. He wasn't proud of it, but he'd deal.

He'd offended her pride and he knew from experience she would now be determined to bring him to heel. Which in her case meant inventive sex and lots of it. A small part of his brain was tempted just to prove she'd made a big mistake when she dumped him. The brain attached to his skull appreciated it was a bad idea.

Her affair with her boss had offended his manhood and he'd been busy proving how wrong she was with more than one woman over the last two years. He wasn't about to take a major step back for the sake of his ego.

He drew his attention back to the meeting.

"Agent Makimi." He'd worked with the agent in Minneapolis and appreciated her meticulous attention to detail almost as much as he enjoyed winding her up. She'd driven up from Quantico where she was doing a stint with the hostage negotiators. "I want you searching ViCAP and talking to other agencies looking for any other possible crimes that might be linked to these three incidents. This shooter didn't start assassinating people like a pro right off the bat. There has to be some build up. Somewhere he or she gained experience."

"Agent Carter." Elijah Carter was from the Washington Field Office and had a reputation for being an intellectual who could actually tie his own shoelaces. Made a change from some of the geniuses Mac had worked with. "Look for any connection between the vics. There has to be a reason these people were chosen."

"Walsh." Dylan Walsh had been his second in command in Minneapolis. They both came from similar backgrounds of broken homes and worked their way up via grassroots police work. Whereas Mac looked like a cowboy in a suit, Walsh looked like an MMA fighter, which was useful for undercover work but tended to scare the newbies. Walsh had flown down from New York. "I want you to work with the Hate Crimes Unit, looking at any potential links to known domestic terrorist groups or right-wing extremists."

The woman from the Hate Crimes Unit raised her pencil. Agent Harrison was an attractive woman. Her hair was blonde and pulled back in a severe bun. Her first name was Debbie and, according to Hernandez, everyone called her "Blondie." Mac was gonna stick to calling her Agent Harrison.

"Have we determined from a legal standpoint whether this is a *hate crime* or *domestic terrorism* offense?"

Now she was trying to show him up as an ignorant hick.

Mac put his hands on his hips. This was a sticky issue the press loved to jump all over and she doubtless wanted to put her stamp on the proceedings as the local expert, which she was. To a point.

"Until we determine *motivation* and *intent* the legal definitions will have to wait. Obviously, there's a big overlap between right-wing extremism, domestic terrorism and hate crimes." This he knew from personal experience. No one could be charged with committing a "hate crime" *per se*. But the term could be used to enhance existing charges and increase the severity of the punishment.

Domestic terrorism was a different beast, but the rules and criteria surrounding those charges were confusing even in law enforcement circles. So confusing the FBI and Bureau of Prisons couldn't agree on the number of people currently incarcerated for terrorism offenses.

"We're looking for a killer or killers of these four victims and it's likely that the primary reason they were targeted was either race, religion or sexuality." Mac surveyed the room. Everyone was paying close attention. "Terrorists target civilians to push an agenda that makes sense to them—doesn't have to make sense to anyone else. This killer has killed civilians and I suspect has some agenda in mind. That makes him a terrorist in my book, but the media relations people can fight it out in the press releases. That's not my battlefield." *Thank God.* "Hate crime offenders have been identified broadly as either thrill seekers, territory defenders, retaliatory offenders or mission offenders and I don't yet know what kind of suspect we are looking for. I'm hoping the BAU can help us with that."

The hate crimes agent glared at him as if he'd burst her bubble.

What could he say? He disappointed people a lot.

"Send me the files," Frazer told him. "I'll look at them ASAP."

"Get Brennan to do it," Mac said with a sharp grin. "He owes me a lot of lost sleep."

Mac had worked with Jed Brennan in Minnesota last November. The guy had squirreled away the main witnesses to the mall shooting and nearly got the three of them killed. Then the bastard had thrown himself in front of a bullet meant for the President of the United States which had made kicking his ass a little difficult. He must be recovered by now.

"Brennan's busy. You're stuck with me. What I *can* tell you," Frazer said, to the visible irritation of the hate crimes agent, "is that violent extremists are more likely to have suffered severe childhood sexual abuse and many of them will have faced serious neglect as children."

That made Mac think back to another time and place, but his sympathy was firmly with the current victims. Abused or not, everyone got to make choices about which direction they took.

"Around sixty percent of white supremacists studied re-ported having considered suicide at some point, and also have histories of mental health issues or a family history of mental health issues. Psychological issues appear to be even more prevalent in lone wolf offenders."

It helped to know a lot of these people suffered from some sort of mental illness although he had to wonder at the ones operating without that basic excuse for being Grade-A assholes.

"Typical far-right lone wolf offenders also," the hate crimes lady put in eagerly, "tend to be males who live alone, like guns, have military experience, select government targets, and generally die in the offense."

Mac nodded. "But this isn't typical and already breaks the pattern of a lone wolf terrorist. We can't afford to make assumptions, especially when we don't know how many suspects we have." He wasn't a big fan of inductive profiling— it was too easy to miss something vital. But quick and dirty was sometimes useful, and not just in the bedroom.

Naturally an image of Tess in that flimsy bathrobe chose

that moment to flicker through his brain.

"It's worth noting that when examining mass murderers," Frazer said, "the more indiscriminate the attack, the more indicative of serious mental illness."

"And these attacks are discreet, calculated and precise," said Mac thoughtfully.

Frazer nodded, looking way too serious for Mac's liking. "Which is why I think we're dealing with a coldly-calculating psychopath who is planning these attacks meticulously down to the last detail. Someone who thinks they're superior in every way to both victims and law enforcement. Someone who doesn't want to get caught—at least not until they're finished. I'm leaning toward a mission offender at this point."

"And the mission might only be getting started," Mac agreed. It was a sobering thought.

According to experts, psychopaths made up about one percent of the general population, and twenty-five percent of the prison population. It was one of the many reasons Mac and his colleagues enjoyed job security. Thankfully, not all of psychopaths turned to a life of crime.

"Agent Ross." He addressed the WFO agent who'd chased him off the murder scene on Monday. His grin held a sliver of victory. "I'd like you and Detective Dunbar to talk to the rabbi's family and members of his synagogue. See if Rabbi Zingel had any recent runs-ins or threats, or if he'd ever met Judge Thomas or Ms. Shiraz. Cross ref those findings with any threats against the judge, his wife and the DJ." He checked the time. "It might be worth concentrating on the rabbi first because there's less noise in his background." Zingel wasn't high profile. He wasn't even the chief rabbi for that synagogue. "Any other thoughts?" he asked the room at large.

"What about your work on the David Hines case? What's *your* perspective on these murders?" Frazer asked him out of nowhere.

Mac narrowed his eyes at the screen. He hadn't realized Frazer knew about that. "I wasn't planning on bringing that up."

Frazer's mouth quirked.

"You worked on the Kodiak Compound investigation?" The other hate crimes agent leaned forward in his seat. Blondie was now on her computer, presumably reading up on the case. Or playing Candy Crush.

Mac opened his mouth to play it down when Frazer continued. "He didn't just 'work' on it. He spent a year undercover and formed the entire basis for taking them down."

There were some surprised faces in the room, including people he'd worked with repeatedly over the years.

"It was before I joined the Bureau." Mac tried to downplay it, but apparently Frazer had a hard-on for him today.

"He managed to find the cache of stolen weapons the Pioneers were selling off to various other ring-wing extremists to fund their upcoming war. ASAC McKenzie's work shut down an entire network of white nationalists before they were able to enact their plans to bring about another revolutionary war."

"Were you there during the raid?" The hate crimes guy appeared excited by the prospect.

Mac nodded. He didn't like to remember it, but today it seemed people wouldn't let him forget. Unlike Waco and Ruby Ridge, it had been considered a tactical success that the state police liked to flaunt over the Feds.

Mac accidentally cut the video link with Frazer when he started saying something else. "I didn't mention it because it isn't necessarily relevant to this case."

Eyeballs watched him attentively now.

"I don't want to bias the investigation in any particular direction and I know you Hate Crimes people along with Agent Walsh will do a thorough job going through the current list of all the alt-right and alt-left wing nuts, correct?"

"What was it like?" Agent Ross stared at him intently, ignoring the back off signals. "Living in that kind of bigoted society?"

Mac flashed back to the Nazi and Confederate flags on the walls and the bust of Hitler that had held pride of place in the so-called church. He remembered every time he'd been forced to salute that megalomaniac Hines like a stab to his soul, like a betrayal of every value he held dear. He remembered them kicking the shit out of a guy for wearing a Chicago Bulls T-shirt and trying to mow down a black man with their truck. The guy had jumped clear and managed to get away, thank God.

What was it like? "Like drowning in tar. Like sucking in toxic smoke." He shrugged.

"Did anyone ever suspect?"

Mac stared at Ross. Why was he so interested? "David Hines's wife—Francis—never liked me, but I think that was more to do with my rough and ready manners than suspecting I was working undercover. The woman didn't mind sleeping with a lunatic, but God forbid you put your elbows on the table."

"What about the daughter who survived?" asked Ross.

"She was only ten at the time of the raid." Mac eyed him

115

narrowly. He'd hoped to keep Tess out of this investigation.

"Old enough to understand her family died in a shootout with the cops," the hate crimes lady put in. She was really starting to get on his nerves.

"I knew her. She wasn't like the others. She was a good kid."

"People change," said Ross.

"I spoke to her earlier today." Irritation eroded Mac's patience. Investigating Tess was a waste of FBI resources. "I found out she lives in Bethesda and decided to pay her a visit. Her home decor didn't incorporate any burning crosses or third Reich imagery." And her tattoo had been cute in a way the average white supremacist wouldn't understand. "I was talking to her at the time Rabbi Zingel was murdered. She isn't the killer."

"She could still be involved in the conspiracy or know who is," Hate crimes persisted.

"As far as I'm concerned she's as innocent now as she was then."

"So you don't think the Pioneers are involved in any of this?" Hate crimes lady glanced up from her computer screen with a smug expression he didn't trust.

"Most of the Hines family are dead or locked up. Were there others in the compound who might have carried out this sort of attack? Possibly." Mac scowled. "The ones who turned State's Evidence pretty much scattered after the trials. The ones who went to prison weren't smart enough to commit these sorts of murders without leaving a trail of evidence a mile wide. I'm not saying ignore them, but don't lose focus on the big picture."

"It's the twentieth anniversary of the raid."

He was aware. "The raid happened in August."

"Maybe they're building up to the anniversary?" Ross suggested.

"Did you realize last Monday, the day the judge and his wife were murdered, would have been David Hines's sixty-fifth birthday?"

Fuck.

"Did his daughter mention that during your private interview?" Hate crimes lady's eyes sparkled with spite.

Tension worked its way into every muscle in his body. Tess must have known but she hadn't said a fucking word.

It changed everything.

"She has a steel-clad alibi for the rabbi's murder and gave me information to check her whereabouts for the DJ's murder, but we can talk to her again."

Precisely what he'd hoped to avoid but it was her own fault. Goddamn it. Of course she'd realized this had all started on her father's birthday. Anger fused his jaw. He couldn't believe she hadn't told him—but why would she? Despite everything they'd shared, he was a virtual stranger. One who'd once left her to the capricious mercies of her family on the eve of their apocalypse.

"Walsh," he said to the agent he trusted the most. "Talk to her in the morning." He needed someone objective, someone who hadn't seen her running out of that barn twenty years ago looking like the devil himself was on her heels. "Get a warrant for her little brother's records, too. They're sealed and she said he isn't even aware of his parentage." Suddenly it was a priority.

"On it, boss."

Mac scrubbed his face. "Okay people. Lots of leads to

follow." He checked his watch. "Let's reconvene at nine a.m. I'll be on the video uplink."

"Video?" asked Walsh.

Mac smiled grimly. "Unfortunately, I have a plane to catch."

CHAPTER TWELVE

T ESS STOOD IN line at security. She'd been traveling for hours and waited in a queue of equally grim-faced people, waiting to be processed and searched.

When it was her turn she braced herself and walked up to the guard.

"Name?"

"Tess Fallon." She handed over her photo ID to the officer.

The corner of his lips moved into a small smile. "I haven't seen you here before."

"I haven't been here before," she acknowledged.

His assessing glance scanned from the top half of her head to her hips before returning to his screen. After a moment, he turned back to her. "You're not on the list." His eyes were cooler now. Irritated she was wasting his time.

"There's been an emergency. I put in the application last night but I'm hoping I can get special dispensation."

He pushed her documents back towards her. "You need to wait for official approval before you can see the offender. Next."

"You don't understand…" Her mouth went dry. What could she say? That she was worried her brother was involved in murder? On what evidence? Their father's date of birth? She glanced at the big wall clock—only fifteen minutes until visiting began. She didn't want to have to stay in Idaho overnight. "I've traveled all the way from DC." Ahead of an approaching winter storm that she hoped to beat back home.

The guard's lips compressed into a stern line. "Information is all on the website. You should have read it before you left."

She had read the website but she'd been desperate and hoping she could charm her way inside. She'd have better luck conjuring a demon.

A shiver of awareness raced up her spine and a second later someone reached over her shoulder.

"Actually, she's with me."

A gold badge appeared, but she'd already recognized that soft voice with the slight country drawl.

Steve McKenzie. FBI.

Dammit.

"*You* have approval from the warden?" The guard spoke with even less warmth than he'd shown her as he checked McKenzie's credentials.

She twisted to look over her shoulder and found McKenzie standing way too close. He was wearing a dark gray suit, white shirt, and a blood red tie that screamed federal authority and competence.

He gave her the side eye when the guard turned away to pick up the phone.

Tess avoided his gaze and her nails cut into her palms. She couldn't believe he was here. Couldn't believe he was trying to help her get inside. Something must have happened—did it involve Cole? Had someone else died? The idea made her stomach pitch.

After a moment, the guard returned and spoke to McKenzie. "Warden says you can come in, but no one else."

"Get us in to see the warden and I'll talk to him about Ms. Fallon. Then he can make the final decision." McKenzie and the guard seemed to be in a pissing contest. Tess had learned from a young age that when one dog lost face it usually took out its ire on the nearest potential victim. The guard indicated McKenzie walk through. She watched anxiously as the FBI agent handed his weapon into a side booth in a secure area and the bag he carried was searched.

When the guard waved Tess through, he stopped her just past the counter with a heavy hand on her shoulder. "I need to search you."

Her spine went rigid. It wasn't that she hadn't expected to be searched—contraband was clearly a problem in any prison. She'd stowed her belongings in one of the available lockers and wasn't carrying anything on her person. She raised her arms, and the guard slowly but firmly slid his hands all over her body, being a little bit too thorough. He was punishing her and she pushed down her instinctive desire to bolt. None of it was obvious to the casual observer, but the malicious gleam in his annoyed stare told her all she needed to know about how much he enjoyed his job. She felt violated from those few basic strokes of his hand, and was grateful to be wearing jeans.

Then he opened his mouth and she knew he was about to order an even more intimate search. Her knees wobbled and she fought the urge to scream. This was too important to run away from, but she wasn't sure she could endure a stranger seeing her naked and touching her intimately just to ask someone she detested a few questions he probably wouldn't answer. And now McKenzie was here, maybe she didn't need to. McKenzie could confront Eddie and she'd go home. A wasted trip but, hey, at least her dignity would remain intact.

"The warden doesn't have all day." McKenzie tapped his wristwatch impatiently. He'd observed the search with an impassive expression, but Tess could read the storm clouds in the tornado green of his eyes.

The guard's shoulders dropped and his chin raised. He stood back and let her through. "I'll see you on the way out, Ms. Fallon."

Great.

McKenzie took her elbow and steered her toward another guard. This guy was bigger and his eyes seemed kinder. He introduced himself as Officer Pennington.

He smiled at Tess, spoke to McKenzie. "Some of the guards are still pissed about the FBI investigating the prison a couple years back. Might not take too kindly to a federal agent poking his nose in."

Fantastic.

"That was here?" McKenzie said with a grimace.

"Sure was," the tall guard told him with a smile. "You want to talk to Prisoner Hines?"

Not really.

"That's right," McKenzie said in that easy way he had. People instinctively liked the guy. He no doubt used it to his advantage.

"You know him?" she asked the guard.

The flash of white teeth against dark skin almost blinded her. "I make it a point to know where the white supremacists are housed." Pennington laughed. "Plus, he's been here longer than I have—since this place opened." Those dark eyes turned hard. "Knock on wood he'll be here long after I'm gone."

"We can hope," she agreed.

The guard's eyes rested on her face as if weighing each of her features. Did he see the family resemblance? Eddie had always favored their mother. With the exception of Tess's hair and eyes and the occasional killer glare, she had her maternal granddaddy's features.

"What's your business with him?" Pennington asked as they ambled along.

"I'm afraid I can't discuss that until after I've spoken to the warden," Mac said with obvious regret.

The guard assessed them both with a cool nod before showing them into an office. Inside, a tall, wiry man turned to look at them over half-frame glasses. He held a sheaf of papers in his hand.

A secretary with a benign expression was busy at a PC.

"Warden Flowers, you've got visitors," said Pennington.

"Thanks, Hal," Flowers said to the guard. "I'll let you know when I need you again."

Hal Pennington nodded and sauntered slowly away.

"Thanks for seeing us at such short notice, Warden." McKenzie shook the man's hand. "And for giving permission for the interview."

Tess was surprised McKenzie needed permission. She'd thought the FBI would be able waltz in and do what they wanted. Apparently not.

"Can you tell me what it's regarding?" the warden asked.

"No. Sorry. It's part of an ongoing criminal investigation."

"And you also want to see Eddie Hines?" Warden Flowers regarded her thoughtfully.

Tess nodded.

One side of the warden's mouth pulled back. He examined the papers in his hand. Tess saw her photograph. He was reading the visitor's application form she'd filled in last night.

The man looked up and nailed her with a piercing stare. "This is the first time you've seen your brother in twenty years?"

She cleared her throat. "Yes, sir. I had no desire to be involved in Eddie's kind of lifestyle."

"He doesn't have a *lifestyle*, he's imprisoned." His curt tone seemed reprimanding.

Her spine stiffened to steel. Was he *judging* her?

"So he no longer holds white supremacist views?" Mac asked, which was not what the guard, Pennington, had insinuated.

The warden's eyebrows bobbed up. "I didn't say that. But he's been a model prisoner and has found God. He appears genuinely repentant about his crime. He was only eighteen at the time of the offenses. It's hard to change the core ideology we are raised with." The look he sent Tess suggested she must be full of hatred and prejudice. She opened her mouth to correct that impression but McKenzie beat her to it.

"Tess was only ten when her brother was arrested. She never shared his beliefs," he told the man. "You can't blame her for wanting to leave that part of her history behind."

She swallowed the unfamiliar sensation of someone defending her.

The warden's expression reserved judgment. "So why the sudden and urgent change of heart?"

Because she was worried Eddie had somehow influenced their little brother and got him involved in a murder plot? She didn't want McKenzie to hear about the file in Cole's drawer, not until she found the slightest proof Cole might have had something to do with the judge's murder. Then she'd go to the

Feds. Not before.

Tess looked at McKenzie but he raised a brow, not helping her with the warden's question.

"Did you hear about the murder of the federal judge in DC on Monday this week?" she asked.

The warden nodded.

She glanced at McKenzie—did he already realize this? "Monday would have been our father, David Hines's, birthday. I wanted to make sure my brother wasn't involved in something that might get him into trouble."

She didn't say which brother.

The warden glanced at her application forms again. "I suppose it couldn't hurt to allow you to talk to him for a few minutes, but if you're questioning him about a murder he should probably call his lawyer."

"He's not being questioned about a murder, Warden Flowers," McKenzie told him. "He's just talking to his sister who he hasn't seen for years and I'd like to listen in to what he has to say."

The warden drew his slight frame upright and narrowed his eyes. "You want to record their conversation?"

McKenzie nodded. "I have a warrant." He fished a piece of paper out of his bag.

Tess swallowed uneasily.

"I think Tess might be able to pry information out of him I can't. And if he has nothing to hide it might help at his next parole hearing if he's cooperative."

"You'd speak for him?" the warden said with a raised brow.

"If he's changed the way you're suggesting, yes, I would. First, I need to ascertain he had nothing to do with this latest crime so I can concentrate on other lines of investigation. Can you send me a list of everyone he's had contact with via either visitation or correspondence?" He pointed his last request toward the secretary who smiled as he handed her his card.

The guy had more charm than was legal, and evidently used it to get his own way.

Warden Flowers nodded his consent. Then he cupped his right hand over his left cheek and massaged his jaw with his thumb. "You can talk to him," he said to Tess. "Visitation just started so you only have five minutes to prepare. I'll send someone to bring Eddie up, but remember, he doesn't have to talk to you if he doesn't want to."

"Five minutes prep is all we need," McKenzie assured him.

Tess's mouth went so dry she could barely swallow. The idea of facing Eddie wearing a wire didn't seem so smart. What if he implicated Cole? Nerves rose up but she pushed them back down. If Cole was involved she couldn't shield him forever. She was done being held accountable for the actions of others. McKenzie took her arm and pulled her into a bathroom across the hall. It was the ladies but he didn't seem to care.

He whirled her around and pressed her up against the door. She stared at him in shock at this sudden change from good ol' boy to hard-ass. Her pulse skipped a few beats.

"You made me look like a damn fool in front of the task force for not realizing these murders started on your daddy's birthday." His expression was stern, but for some reason it wasn't fear she was feeling.

"And looking like a damn fool is unusual?"

Something sparked in his eyes. "Why the hell didn't you mention it last night?"

She tried to pull away but he wouldn't let go. She glared. "I only remembered after you left."

His lip curled. "Says the girl who remembers how I take my coffee after *two decades*."

She gritted her teeth. She didn't like the fact all her nerve endings had come alive now he was touching her. She wasn't about to tell him she'd memorized everything about him back then. Her childish heart had been in love.

"Look, ASAC McKenzie, I've spent most of my life actively pushing thoughts of my parents out of my head. I have made it my *mission* to forget everything I can about my family."

He was unconvinced. "You could have called me once you figured it out. Pretty sure I gave you my card in case you had any epiphanies." His voice held an edge of sarcasm. "Instead you got on a plane. Tell me why that doesn't look suspicious."

She stared pointedly at where his large hands gripped her upper arms. She had enough taekwondo training to make him let go if she had to, but she didn't want to be charged with assaulting a federal agent or something equally lame. With her background, she'd lose every time it came down to a case of he-said, she-said.

He relaxed his grip but didn't let go.

"Why did you come here today?" he demanded.

"Once I remembered it was Daddy's birthday I had to come. I needed to know if this is connected to my family. Eddie's the only one who can tell me that." She raised her chin, held his probing gaze as he assessed her for lies. "I've built a decent life, ASAC McKenzie. If the Pioneers are involved in these murders that could all be destroyed." She specialized in working for non-profits and civil liberty groups. If they found out who she really was they'd never trust her with their financial information again. Her fledgling business would be dead before it ever got started.

His fingers squeezed tighter and for a second his knuckle brushed the side of her breast. She jolted. His nostrils flared and he swallowed tightly. He released her but didn't step away.

"Look, call me Mac. Everyone does." He ran his fingers over his skull, making his short hair stand up on end. One silver strand of hair stood out amongst the warm brown. Up close, his face had more lines than she remembered. Faint creases fanning out from the corner of his eyes. His brows were short, dark slashes of personality. A small scar etched his right cheek.

She met his gaze.

"What do you want from me, *Mac*?" The short version of his name rolled too easily off her tongue. "An apology for existing? Or to grind me into the dirt along with the rest of my family?"

His hands rested on top of her shoulders and squeezed. "Just be the person I hope you are."

What did that even mean?

He pulled something out of his computer bag. A tiny microphone.

"Did you know I was going to be here?" she asked.

"First I knew about you being here was when I walked through the prison's front door," Mac told her. "But this works better. I was going to pretend to be Kenny Travers. Tell him I escaped after the raid and went off radar and wanted in on any new action against the government. If that didn't work then I was gonna confront him and tell him I was actually an undercover cop and that I single-handedly brought down the Pioneers. Pretty sure the resulting explosion might have revealed a few home truths. But this is better. He might trust you. Here." He handed her the short piece of wire. "Attach that to the inside of your bra."

"He'll figure something's up."

"Just act natural. Forget it's there. You'll be fine."

She took it and undid the top few buttons of her blouse, then slid the listening equipment up under her shirt and camisole, positioning it beneath the underwire of her bra, adjusting the position from the top. Thankfully she was wearing dark colors which helped hide the thing.

"What makes you think he'll talk to me?" She glanced up as she tucked her shirt back into her jeans.

His pupils were large and his nostrils flared as he drew in a breath. Damned if his cheeks didn't hold a touch of fire.

His hand closed over hers when she went to do up the top buttons. "Leave those undone. It might distract him. Sure as hell distracts me."

The fact her brother might be interested in her body was disgusting, but she knew Mac was right. Eddie had always been an animal. She couldn't imagine prison had improved him any.

"Can you see it?" she asked.

His fingers clenched as he took a step back. "Nope, you can't see it."

She frowned at him. "They're just boobs, Mac. Snap out of it."

He mumbled something unintelligible and turned away, watching her in the mirror.

"What if he won't talk to me?"

Annoyance hardened his features. "Why wouldn't he?"

"He is nearly nine years older than me. We didn't have

much in common even when we lived in the same house. He didn't know I existed except as someone who cleaned up his dishes."

He frowned at her. "I'm nine years older than you and I knew you existed."

She eyed him from under her lashes. "You were different."

His expression grew serious as he turned to face her again. "Be grateful Eddie didn't notice you."

She frowned, confused. "What do you mean?"

Mac's lips pressed together and his expression looked torn. "Did you know Ellie was pregnant when she died?"

All the blood drained from her head and she steadied herself against the wall. "No."

He observed her carefully, though she didn't understand why. "Ellie was *sixteen weeks* pregnant when she died." With that he left the restroom.

What? Sixteen weeks? Four *months* pregnant? That was impossible. It didn't make sense. Ellie was only married for two months and had never had a boyfriend. She hadn't even liked Harlan Trimble…

Oh, God.

Tess hugged her stomach as rage and grief competed for control of her body. That meant Ellie had gotten pregnant when she'd lived at home, and no one in the Pioneers would have been foolhardy enough to mess with David Hines's girl.

That bastard. That fucking bastard. Heat spread through her body like fire. She followed Mac into the hall.

"Did you know?" she asked.

His lips were a thin line. Eyes pained. "No. I didn't know. Did you?"

Her eyes widened and her throat closed. Mute, she shook

her head. After that day in the barn with Walt she *should* have realized, should have guessed he'd done the same to Ellie. How could she have been so naïve?

Because you were ten, Tess.

"Was it both of them, or just Walt?"

"I don't know for sure, but looking back I think they were both involved."

How she loathed them all. Eddie, Walt, her parents. They must have suspected and yet they'd done nothing?

"What do you want me to ask him?"

Mac shrugged. "Find out if he knows anything about what's going on in DC. Who's doing this. See if you can get a slice of the action."

She nodded. "I doubt he'll fall for it though. Me turning up like this for the first time?"

"Try your best, Tess. Lives might depend on it."

She gave him a look. She wasn't one of his lackeys. Then she caught Officer Pennington's eye and followed him down a long corridor. Mac stayed where he was, out of sight, reminding her she was on her own. Not exactly unusual, but the loneliness stung today. She was worried about Cole. The idea of losing him to this sort of hatred was almost too much to bear.

She was led to a large, open room with lots of small tables set up. Inmates wore orange jumpsuits and sat opposite their visitors. She searched around for her brother but didn't spot him anywhere. Then he walked through the holding area opposite and slouched into a seat at one of the empty tables. Did he know who was here to see him? Did he care?

Officer Pennington led the way between the tables. "You have a visitor, Hines."

Eddie's eyes were the exact shade of cobalt their father's had been, but there the resemblance ended. Eddie had always looked more like their mother, with her brows, nose and strong jawbone. He was nearly forty now and gaunt. His skin held a pallidness that detracted from what would otherwise be a handsome face. He didn't wear handcuffs or chains. This was a medium security facility. His fingernails were dirty. Even after all these years he repulsed her.

He eyed her from the top of her dark hair down to her black boots, gaze lingering on the swell of her breasts as Mac had predicted.

"Well, hello, darlin'. What can I help you with?" The insolence in his voice hadn't changed one iota.

He didn't recognize her. That gave her a jolt. As did the fact he was obviously used to receiving women visitors he didn't know.

She eased into the hard, plastic chair, keeping her distance. "You don't remember me?"

He regarded her more closely then and one side of his mouth curled up. The eyes didn't change though, her daddy's eyes, as cold as the deep ocean.

"Little Theresa Jane. All grown up and come to see me. To what do I owe the pleasure?" His words slicked down her spine like ice water.

"Figured it was time."

His head shifted sideways as did his smile. "Twenty years is beyond time."

Not long enough.

"Too long." She cleared her throat. "I should have come sooner."

Eddie grinned, flashing a broken canine that made him

look feral. "Why? You hated me. I treated you like shit."

"You're the only family I have left."

"What happened to Bobby?" he asked sharply, eyes narrowing.

"Bobby's fine," she amended. "But he doesn't remember anything about the old days." And she wanted to make sure it stayed that way.

She studied Eddie for any clue he'd been in touch with their baby brother, but she wouldn't be able to tell if he was lying or not. He'd perfected the art of survival in this place and lying to someone as naïve as she was would be child's play.

"Last I heard, you and Bobby got adopted by some rich bitch and changed your names. No one's heard from you in years." He was watching her avidly through narrowed eyes.

"We did what we had to do to stay together." She didn't want to talk about her adoptive mother or the amazing life they'd shared together. She wouldn't give him any information he could use against her. "So which one of you got Ellie pregnant?" She tried to sound casual.

He laughed and the sound tore a chunk out of her soul. "I'd forgotten about Ellie."

Forgotten? And he hadn't been shocked by her words or denied touching his own sister. He'd *forgotten* her. Her hands vibrated in her lap. She wanted to slap the smirk off his thin face. "I can't believe Daddy didn't skin you alive."

Their father had ruled with an iron fist.

Eddie tapped his fingers on the table. "Daddy didn't know. He'd have killed us both."

Us. Him and Walt. God. Nausea curled through her stomach. "Momma knew?"

Francis Hines must have been even more callous than Tess remembered.

"Momma persuaded Daddy some boys were sniffing around Ellie's skirts and it was time to marry her off. Harlan didn't know she was already used goods when he got hold of her."

Used goods? Rage burned like fire under her ribs.

Eddie laughed. "Momma was mad as hell when she found out Ellie skipped her monthlies. She slapped Ellie around until Ellie told her what happened. Then she slapped me and Walt, but she never told Daddy." He was leaning to one side and his shrug looked uncomfortable. "I was always her favorite."

Favorite? Was he really that heartless? To care more about being a favorite child than being concerned with the sister he'd raped? She looked at his pinched features. His eyes rested below her chin on the vee of her shirt, as unbothered by the sin of incest today as he had been back then.

She would have crossed her arms but didn't want to muffle the microphone. She took a breath, ignored his efforts to disconcert her. "I remember Momma belting you for being cheeky with her."

"Momma was not an easy woman, but she loved us in her own way."

Tess huffed out a snort. "She was going to shoot me that night of the raid."

His smile told her he didn't care. "Poor little Theresa Jane, always getting into trouble. You should have learned to keep your trap shut and do as you were told."

"Like Ellie you mean?"

"You're assuming Ellie wasn't a willing participant in our games. She liked it once she got used to it. We gave her money to keep her quiet."

"I don't believe you."

His eyes narrowed a little, enjoying her torment. "At first Walt told her we'd kill her if she told anyone. But eventually she liked it. We used rubbers so I don't know how she got pregnant. Maybe someone else had her, too." He shrugged like he didn't care.

Tess's insides turned inside out—how long had it been going on? Ellie had only been thirteen when she died.

"Were you planning on abusing me next?"

She got a whiff of his sour breath as he laughed. "I wasn't planning on touching you for another couple of years until you grew some nice titties." His smile didn't go near his eyes. "But Walt was begging me to help him, getting desperate after being cut off from his regular supply of pussy. Harlan wouldn't let Ellie out of his sight once they were hitched— probably the first time *he'd* gotten any in years. And Walt was too much of an asshole to find a real girlfriend."

The fact he spoke this way about their sister—someone he'd seemed to like—made Tess want to vomit. Something else about his words struck her.

"Walt tried to grab me in the stable. Did you know about that?" She wondered if he'd known about their brother's plan.

He ran his teeth over his tongue. "Like I said I had a girl-friend who gave me what I wanted. Walt was an impatient asshole." He raked her up and down with his gaze. "I didn't trust you to keep your trap shut. No pussy in the world would be worth Daddy finding out." He stretched out his neck first one way, then the other. "Your tits turned out great by the way. They're very…" He wiggled his brows as he smirked, "*Pert.*"

She stared at him. He was disgusting, but she couldn't afford to let the horror show. "I remember your girlfriend now. Sandy or Candy or—"

"Brandy." He sat up straight. "How the fuck do you remember that?"

She remembered her momma going off on her daddy when she'd smelled a woman's perfume on him. He'd said it was Eddie's girlfriend standing too close to him. Momma hadn't believed him.

Eddie's expression narrowed. Mad she'd remembered something that might be important, or pissed she wasn't rising to his bait?

She rested her hand on the table and stared at Eddie through her lashes. "You must miss it—sex."

His eyes crinkled at the edges as if amused. "You'd be surprised."

"You're gay?" She feigned shock. Being gay was as bad as being a person of color in the white supremacist world.

He gave her a long look and then stared at a female guard who was standing against one wall and licked his lips. "Nope."

Tess's eyes widened. It might be a bluff, but she wouldn't be surprised if he was in a physical relationship with someone who worked here. Like any sociopath, Eddie could be charming when he wanted to be. And sex was doubtless something he needed.

She hooked her hair behind her ears and forced herself to lie. "I'm glad. I'd hate to see you suffering."

A smile played around his mouth. He leaned forward and touched her hand. "Liar."

She froze and withdrew her hand, sending him a glare.

"You have her eyes," he said suddenly. Harshly.

She knew it. Hated it. "And you have Daddy's."

"Yeah." He let out a deep breath. "But hers were always

scarier." Eddie's mouth thinned and they almost shared a smile of childhood remembrance.

If only he hadn't raped Ellie, Tess might have sympathized with the guy. After all what chance had he had? But Ellie had been kind and thoughtful and sweet. And this asshole, their own flesh and blood, had treated her like a piece of meat.

Steve McKenzie had understood what he was doing when he'd loaded Tess with that information.

A jagged scar ran behind Eddie's right ear, as if someone had tried to cut it off. Eddie saw her gawking but didn't enlighten her. Just returned her stare with Momma's features and Daddy's eyes.

It was weird to think that the physical resemblance was all that remained of their parents. That, and a twisted legacy of hate.

"Someone got in touch with me about these murders going on in DC," she told him. Needing to say something to broach the subject as Eddie patently wasn't going to.

"Who?" He didn't ask what murders. The fact made a shiver travel from the base of her spine to her nape. She hoped McKenzie noticed, too.

"He didn't leave a name."

He laughed then leaned back with his hands folded across his stomach. "Is that so? And now you're here seeing if I know anything about it?"

"Do you?" She pushed.

"All I know is you promised our parents you'd go shoot some cops, but instead you took Bobby, locked the bedroom door and hid like a coward."

"I was ten," she snapped.

"You were better with a gun than any of us." Malevolence shone in his eyes. Something had changed. Danger radiated off him.

"I was a good shot. Didn't mean I was prepared to kill another human being."

"More fool you." He tapped his foot, looking at the clock on the wall. People were beginning to stand and say their goodbyes.

Tess felt sick. She'd blown it and hadn't gotten anything useful out of her brother. She felt dirty being in the same room as him, let alone carrying the same genes.

"If they find out you know anything about these murders and you don't tell them, you might never get out of here, you know that, right?" Not that she wanted him released.

"Who said I knew anything?" His eyes narrowed and he used his index finger to indicate she lean closer.

She did. Cautiously.

"But if I did know something…"

She held her breath and inched a little nearer.

"I wouldn't tell you, you conniving little bitch." His hot breath brushed over her neck. Eddie grabbed her by the hair and slammed her face into the table. She managed to protect herself with her hands before the second slam but she heard screams and saw people running away. He dragged her roughly over the table like a rag doll and held her by the neck with both hands.

"Why are you still alive?" he hissed in her ear.

Fear seared every cell in her body. She backpedaled as he dragged her up against the nearest wall.

"I'll snap her neck like a twig if anyone comes near us!" he yelled. One hand delved under her shirt and he gave a cry of rage when he found the wire. "You traitorous slut. You should have died back then like Momma wanted."

Tess's vision was wonky and her breathing was cut off by

his strong forearm. She turned her head into his chest to get more oxygen. He stank of sweat and hatred.

The guards edged closer but Eddie would never release her. He was going to kill her first.

She took a breath, fought her panic, ignored the pain and fear and centered her mind. With one hand, she struck his groin hard, then twisted inward and smashed her other palm against his face.

He screamed in agony and she danced out from under his arm. A rush of blood cascaded from his nose. She darted away as the guards closed in behind her.

"You bitch. You fucking little cunt. I'm going to find you. I'm going to come to your nice little house and I'm going to wait until you're asleep in your bed, and then I'm going to fuck you until you are battered and bloody and when you're lying there begging for mercy I'll shove my knife up you so deep you'll feel it in your gut."

Tess's entire body trembled. She had no doubt he'd do just that, and enjoy every second of it.

McKenzie was suddenly beside her. A guard tossed him the small black listening device, then Mac was dragging her out of the visiting area. Eddie went berserk, shouting about Kenny Travers being a backstabbing motherfucker and how he was gonna die, too.

Reaction set in and Tess's teeth chattered so hard she could hardly see let alone walk.

"Wait here." Mac retrieved his bag of tricks and then herded her toward the entrance. He stopped for his sidearm. The warden met them as he was replacing it in his holster.

"I need to talk to you." Warden Flower's demeanor screamed tension. "I need to know what happened in there."

Mac spoke in a low whisper. "You have the video surveillance tape from your cameras so you know what happened. I'll send you a copy of the audio as soon as it is cleared with HQ."

"Do you need medical attention, miss?" Officer Pennington stood in front of her and reached out to touch her neck.

Tess flinched, then shook her head. "Nothing's broken." She touched her nose and Pennington passed her a box of tissues. She took some gratefully. "I'm just sore." And humiliated. And angry. "Good thing he's rehabilitated."

The guard from earlier stepped forward and blocked her exit. "I need to search her before she leaves."

Mac got in his face. "She's been through enough."

Tess rolled her eyes and raised her shaking arms. Office Pennington stepped in and searched her clothing with much more efficiency and less insolence than the other guard had earlier.

Pennington stepped back. "She's clean."

"Fine. Let them go." The warden nodded. He pointed a finger at Mac. "I want that audio recording on my desk by the end of the day."

The pissed off guard shot them a glare but stood aside. Tess stopped to pick up her belongings from the locker, then she and Mac hurried out the front exit.

It was snowing heavily, which was an unwelcome surprise. Mac threw his arm around her shoulders as she shivered uncontrollably. So much for beating that winter storm out of here.

He shepherded her to his car and popped the locks. "Get in."

She slid into the front seat and sat numbly with her belongings on her lap. She was too freaked to do anything except shake.

Mac got in the driver's seat and started the car, staring out the windscreen. "Holy fucking shit, Tess, I thought you were dead. Where'd you learn a move like that?"

Seeing she was incapable of normal behavior he grabbed her luggage and tossed it on the backseat. Then he leaned around her and grabbed the seat belt, dragging it across her body and punching it into the clip.

She raised a hand to touch her nose, which was sore and swollen. "Taekwondo, remember?" And if she hadn't been a black belt, she'd probably be dead back in the visitor lounge, awaiting the ME with Steve McKenzie staring down at her body.

Would he have cared? She doubted it. Not really. Except for the information he'd never gain and the trouble it might cause his career.

"You all right?" he asked.

She gaped, incredulous. The bridge of her nose throbbed, her scalp burned and her throat was scorched as if someone had poured bleach down it. She was not okay. She turned to tell him so and noticed how white his lips were, noticed the strained tendons standing out in his neck. Stark fear shone bright in his eyes. Fear for her. Maybe he did care. More than she'd appreciated.

"I'll live." She touched her nose again and winced. "I'm sore. But grateful it wasn't worse." Much worse.

"Fuck. Tess. I never imagined he'd touch you. I'm so sorry."

"Model prisoner and all." She tried to make a joke of it. "I guess family brings out the worst in us Hineses."

"You're not a Hines. You're a Fallon." He put his hand on her thigh and squeezed. She felt the imprint of each finger like a brand through her jeans. "You were incredible."

He quickly removed his hand as if he'd just remembered

exactly who he was touching. A Hines, not a Fallon.

"Yeah. Incredible." Her head started to spin and she rifled through her purse to find some more tissues and an Advil.

"What time's your flight?" he asked as he drove out of the prison lot.

"Five." In the meantime, she wanted to curl into a pathetic ball and nurse her wounds.

"Mine's in forty minutes." He leaned forward and peered up at the sky. "With luck, we'll both get out of here before the blizzard really hits."

"Fingers crossed." Her throat constricted and tears burned her eyes, but she refused to let them fall. Eddie was a repellant monster and it was one of her many shames to be related to him. Now all she wanted was to go home and forget she'd ever had any family beside Cole.

The FBI could figure out what was going on without any help from her. She'd talk to Cole and explain about their past. Hopefully he'd be able to tell her why he'd had that file in his drawer and it would be an innocent coincidence—if it wasn't, she'd get him to turn himself in. She didn't believe he was involved in murder. He wasn't like Eddie or Walt or Francis or David. He was like her.

Hopefully he'd forgive her for all the lies she'd told him. But it was time for the truth. She was done with lies.

RoguePawn75: We have a problem.

They were in a secure "Members Only" chatroom on the dark web. Chance of anyone seeing this conversation was limited but not impossible. Chance of anyone tracking their location or real identities? Practically zero. By the time they did, the revolution would already be in motion.

MustangGuardian: What problem?

RoguePawn75: Discovered an undercover cop infiltrated Kodiak Compound the year before the raid and that cop is now the federal agent in charge of the task force investigating murders. Name is Steve McKenzie. Went by "Kenny Travers" back then. I never met him.

The blank screen was full of such menace unease crept up her spine and she found herself nervously filling the emptiness.

RoguePawn75: He's responsible for the whole thing—finding the guns, the raid, killing David—

MustangGuardian: How did you not know this?

RoguePawn75: I told you I thought someone inside the compound had ratted them out. I didn't realize it had been a cop all along.

MustangGuardian: You should have known. Have you made any other mistakes?

God, she hated the power this man had over her. She thought of all her careful planning, all her years of sacrifice, working to execute their plan faultlessly and still he treated her like a child. Like he was in charge. Some days she hated him more than she loved him.

RoguePawn75: No. Everything else has been flawless.

A third person joined the conversation.

EagleScreamr: He must have read the manifesto. He's gonna figure out what we plan to do before we get the chance.

RoguePawn75: No, he won't. We are leaving the clues they are supposed to find. Everything is going as planned.

MustangGuardian: What if this agent figures out who you are before you have a chance to finish?

RoguePawn75: He won't.

MustangGuardian: How are you going to stop him?

The empty screen was like a hungry animal waiting to be fed.

RoguePawn75: McKenzie needs to be taught a lesson as to what happens to people who betray us. I have an idea that will take care of him.

She quickly explained her plan. It was off script, but there was a good chance it would work. If it did it would be a brilliant display of cunning. If it didn't, it would still form the starting point of their revenge against this bastard. The man who'd destroyed her life.

RoguePawn75: But *I* can't do it. I have other messages to send and a schedule to keep.

No response.
All her sacrifice and no one else was willing to step up?

EagleScreamr: I'll do it.

A tremor of unease vibrated over her skin.

MustangGuardian: You're sure?

EagleScreamr: Yes. When?

She pondered for a moment. Was it wrong to involve him in such a dangerous mission? What if he messed up? What if he got caught? What if he couldn't go through with it?

She generally felt nothing when she took a life, but the people she killed weren't human. They were vermin that needed to be eradicated. She forced the unexpected worry out of her mind. They all needed to make sacrifices in this war.

RoguePawn75: It requires precise timing. I'll contact you. Be ready to move at a moment's notice and be sure to leave nothing behind.

She logged off and stared into space. All these years of hard work and careful planning and everything came down to what happened in the next few days. But justice wasn't going to wait forever. The FBI had better be ready to reap what it sowed. The government couldn't hang on to power forever, and only those prepared for armed resistance would survive.

She'd been born ready.

These murders were for David, and formed the opening salvo of the revolution. Their names would go down in history, irrevocably entwined.

Once she finished the first phase of the operation, thousands would rise up and join the fight. These people might not know her name yet, but it wouldn't be long until she was synonymous with the most daring act in history. She'd save the republic for those it was meant for, and drive the others from its shores.

CHAPTER THIRTEEN

A LL THE CHARM in the world and a federal badge weren't getting him any play at the airline check-in desk. Apparently, no one was getting in or out of Boise by air for the next fifteen hours—and maybe then some.

"There has to be something available?" Tess said plaintively to the attendant.

The woman at the ticket counter took in Tess's swollen nose and bruised neck, and shot Mac a nervous glance. He didn't think it would do any good to deny he had anything to do with Tess's injuries. It *was* his fault she'd been assaulted.

Eddie's attack had come out of nowhere. Mac had stood paralyzed in that observation room, not knowing what it might do to Eddie if he saw Kenny Travers suddenly rise from the dead. Would it have tipped the balance and made the sonofabitch snap Tess's slender neck? It wasn't a risk Mac had been willing to take. So, he'd stayed put, wishing he'd never put the woman in danger.

Had something given her away? Or had Eddie always intended to attack her and bided his time, toying with her until visiting time ended? Was that how psychopaths entertained themselves in prison? And why attack Tess when his sentence was almost up?

Maybe the guy liked prison. Maybe the asshole genuinely

hated Tess for not dying that night of the raid. Ironic, as Eddie was the only member of the family over the age of ten to have survived. Or maybe he knew something about what was going on with these murders and thought Tess might somehow give them away… That was a tantalizing proposition.

What might she remember that could help Mac with this investigation?

He wondered what Eddie's old girlfriend was up to these days. Mac texted Dylan Walsh on a secure line urging him to check up on that lead.

Mac needed to re-listen to the recordings of Tess and Eddie's conversation to see if there were any other clues. He had the list of visitors and copies of Eddie's correspondence and details of his internet activity which he'd also forwarded to Walsh. If Eddie was communicating with someone about these murders, they'd find out. It was only a matter of time. Unfortunately, time wasn't on their side. By their nature, investigations moved at glacial speed, and they needed to stop these murders fast.

Eddie-the-asshole was going to enjoy a few years added to his sentence, but maybe when someone had been inside their whole life that was a good thing. How would the guy survive in the real world?

The airline clerk had been typing furiously but finally looked up at Tess with a palpable expression of regret. "I'm really sorry, ma'am, there's nothing I can do out of Boise today. It's not just the snow. One of our de-icing machines broke down. We have technicians working on it, but a new part needs to be brought in from Utah by road."

"Roads are open?" Mac raised his chin and ignored her disapproval.

She nodded. "Storm's coming down from the north. Roads to the south are still open."

Mac checked his watch. The idea of being away from the office overnight because of something as unpredictable as a blizzard drove him nuts, but having grown up in Montana he recognized the futility of arguing with the weather. Mother Nature did not consider anyone's plans. He checked the weather app on his phone and sauntered over to the rental company.

"Got any SUVs?"

The guy nodded.

"I need to be able to drop it at Salt Lake City."

The guy filled in the paperwork as Tess trailed slowly across the concourse toward him, wheeling her carry-on luggage like a kid dragging a teddy bear.

He tossed the keys in his hand, nodded to the clerk in thanks.

Tess's hazel eyes widened when she spotted the keys. "You're driving?"

"This is the southern edge of the storm and the forecast is for it to move north in the next hour. Salt Lake City is south east and on a good day it's only a five-hour drive. The airport there is a lot bigger. I'd rather take a chance on getting a flight outta there than waiting in Boise."

She gnawed her bottom lip. Aside from dabbing away the blood from beneath her nose she hadn't cleaned up and her hair had escaped the pony she'd tied it in. And while her genes might have been warped, she was still one of the prettiest women he'd ever met.

"You wanna ride to Utah?" he offered.

Her eyes went huge. "You don't mind?"

Mac suppressed a smile. Seriously? He'd jump at the chance to ply her with questions for endless hours, to fill in the blank details he'd forgotten about. The fact he found her attractive was inconvenient, but he could deal with it.

"But I'm leaving now." There was something he wanted to see along the way.

She nodded eagerly.

He grabbed some coffees while she used the restroom. Soon they were loading their carry-on bags and laptops into the rear compartment and climbing into a brand-new Jeep Cherokee.

Tess was shivering and he couldn't tell if it was a reaction to what happened with Eddie or the fierce heaping of winter they were getting. He turned up the heater and thrust a brown paper bag at her.

"Supplies." He caught her gaze and grinned.

She peeked inside. "Donuts?"

"You used to have a sweet tooth." She wasn't the only one with a good memory.

"That was before the word 'calorie' entered my vocabulary." She gingerly pulled one out and passed the bag back. She ate slowly with her coffee. Her color improved, but the red welts on her neck and swelling on the bridge of her nose were still neon bright.

It had been a mistake to use her. He'd underestimated how dangerous Eddie was.

The snow was coming down in thick cotton balls the wipers struggled to deal with. Despite the forecast it didn't seem to be letting up, but Mac was familiar with this area and driving in these kinds of conditions. He actually missed Montana winters. There was a raw beauty in their ferocity. An elemental challenge in day-to-day living.

After thirty minutes, the amount accumulating on the road started to lessen. The handling got better and Mac drove faster.

"Did you notice he didn't ask what murders?" Tess broke the easy silence.

He nodded. He'd noticed. The sonofabitch definitely knew something about what was going on in DC.

A look of revulsion crossed her features. "At least I can stop feeling guilty about not getting in touch with him for the last two decades. He's repugnant. Did you hear what he said to me? About waiting for me to grow?" She hugged her coat tighter to her chest. "What an animal."

"I heard." The words hadn't surprised him. Eddie had always been a nasty fucker and prison hadn't softened him any. Mac's fingers tightened on the wheel. There had been times he'd gone along with that kind of perverted sexist language to get on the guy's good side. The memory made him feel ill.

"Did you know Ellie was being abused?"

"No, I told you. God, no." He turned to look at her, out-raged. Then his outrage died. "Except for the part where she was forced into marriage and, trust me, I'll never forgive myself for that."

Her next words made him wince. "Trust isn't something I do anymore. Too many hard life lessons."

She wasn't trying to wheedle into his good side. She was stating a fact.

She slipped off her shoes and raised her knees to her chest, drawing her shoulders in. Her socks had math symbols on them and she wiggled her toes as if trying to warm them up.

"Walt had a bedroom next to mine. Ellie's was the farthest away from our parents' room. I don't remember hearing noises and she never said anything to me about what was going on." Grief etched lines of remorse around her mouth as if what had happened was her fault. It wasn't.

"You didn't live in a place that encouraged girls to stand up for themselves. Ellie was probably too confused or scared to fight back. Even so, I doubt they abused her under your parents' roof. Your brothers were excellent at manipulating and threatening people but they weren't brave."

"No kidding," she agreed. "Attacking children."

Francis Hines's behavior was more shocking. If what Eddie said was true she'd pawned her daughter off to a disgusting old man to hide the fact her sons had gotten her daughter pregnant.

Mac could have saved Ellie but he hadn't. That guilt never got old.

"Did you know he had a girlfriend?" Tess asked. "Eddie?"

Mac frowned. "There were a couple of women I remember him dating. Eddie wasn't exactly the sort of guy to show a woman a fun time. He treated them like crap once he got what he wanted, but some women gravitate toward that kind of relationship."

"I remember Brandy. She wore skimpy clothes and too much makeup. Used to ride around on a motorcycle." A smile touched the bow of her mouth. "I thought she was cool. Momma said she was a slut."

Mac had a vague recollection of the young woman. It was a valuable potential lead they only had because Tess had agreed to wear the wire.

"What about you?" Tess said. "Were you 'dating' anyone?"

"Nah. I was too worried about letting my identity slip to get involved with anyone, although," he grinned, "it's possible a little 'dating' happened once in a while. I was nineteen and trying to fit in."

"And the girls liked you. Yeah, I remember that, too." She laughed and Mac watched her cheeks turn pink.

"It's funny, the age difference was like a thousand years back then. Now we're older it doesn't seem relevant," she said faintly. "Time changes everything."

He shifted uncomfortably. He didn't think she was trying to flirt with him. She seemed to be in a state of shock.

He certainly didn't think of her as a child anymore. When she'd put the wire into her bra he'd been locked into place as surely as if someone had poured concrete over his feet. She hadn't flashed any real skin but the idea she might have had held him transfixed.

Idiot.

He must be more deprived than he realized. Come to think about it, he hadn't had sex since before the Minneapolis case. He'd have to learn to deal with it because nothing was gonna change until this new case was wrapped up and that could take months.

"I think Daddy was cheating on Momma, too."

"What?" That was news to him. "What makes you say that?"

"I went into town with him once. Eddie was off somewhere, butchering a pig I think—probably with you now I come to think about it. Momma sent me to buy some groceries though Daddy didn't want me to go with him. He bought me an ice-cream and made me wait in the truck for over an hour before we went to the store. I saw a woman looking down at me from the bedroom above the bar. Someone kissed her, but whoever it was stood in the shadows so I didn't see his face. Might not have been Daddy at all, might have been my imagination, but I remember Momma complaining about smelling perfume on Daddy's shirts sometimes. He got pissed and denied it."

There had been a room above the bar that regulars sometimes used to hook up if they got lucky. Tess wouldn't have known about the room and come to think about it there were times when David Hines had disappeared when they'd gone to the bar as a group. Mac had never figured out where the guy went, always assumed it was on Pioneer business. He'd wanted to follow, but if he'd been caught he'd have blown his cover.

But maybe David Hines was just your average adulterer, trying to keep his sins secret. Having an affair behind Francis's back would have taken some balls, even for a man of David Hines's stature.

"I have the names of Eddie's girlfriends in my notes. I'll check them as soon as I get back to DC. See if they can be traced." They were buried somewhere in his new apartment.

"You kept notes?"

"Yeah." He tapped the brakes as he came up behind a semi climbing an incline. "I had to write them in secret and hide them in a special compartment in my truck. The Pioneers would have lynched me if they'd found out I was a cop."

Her hazel eyes studied him intently. "What you did was incredibly brave."

He shrugged, uncomfortable with her praise. He'd have done things differently now. "I just lived the same way you did for twelve months. Hardly brave when a ten-year-old could do it."

"I didn't have any choice and I didn't know any better." Her mind seemed to go somewhere else for a moment and a frown crinkled the skin between her brows. "It was all we knew."

"Do you know how your parents met?" He was curious.

"I have no idea. I remember them saying they bought the land in Kodiak after they got married. Momma came from money. She showed me the shack where they first lived while they were building the cabin." Her eyes grew huge. "The place always gave me the creeps…"

He remembered the shack. On the edge of the woods over the hill from the main compound, it sat with an endless view of the plains. But road access had been limited which was why David Hines had chosen another site for the main buildings. Mac had searched the shack once. It was deserted but had been structurally sound. The place was empty aside from some blankets in a cedar chest and some logs to make a fire in the winter.

"You think that's where Eddie and Walt took Ellie?"

"Either there or the barn where Walt attacked you that time." The guilt rose inside him. "I never asked that day if Walt…" Christ, he couldn't say the words.

She shook her head quickly. "He grabbed my hand and made me touch him, but I ran." A gleam entered her eyes. "He's part of the reason I took up taekwondo. I told Trudy about what had happened and she suggested martial arts training."

Which had probably saved her life today. His fingers tightened their grip on wheel. "She sounds like an amazing woman."

She swallowed noisily as if holding back emotion. "Yes,

she was. She taught me everything I'd missed out on growing up in isolation. She was the smartest person I ever met." Tess turned in her seat to face him. "Thank you for what you did to Walt that day."

"I didn't do enough."

"Whatever you did kept him away from me for those last few weeks."

He kept his gaze fixed on the road, the ghost of her sister drifting between them. "It wasn't enough."

"Ellie would have forgiven you, you know that, right? She never held a grudge."

And all of a sudden he couldn't speak, overwhelmed by the memory of a sweet little girl with red-gold hair and freckles.

He let the silence settle as he drove another few miles.

When he glanced at her again he noticed a dusting of icing sugar coated her cheek. Keeping one eye on the road, he used a thumb to gently brush it off. Her skin felt like silk.

He cleared his throat. "You have donut on your face."

She pushed his hand away, wiping at the sugar. "It was worth it. Remind me I said that when I can no longer fit in my pants."

"I don't know how you turned out so normal," he said honestly.

"I'll take that as a compliment." One side of her lips tilted. "If it wasn't for the fact I have her eyes I'd think I was swapped at birth."

"You can dream." Mac cleared his throat.

Her gaze grew pensive. "You think these murders are related to the Pioneers in some way, don't you?"

He shrugged. He couldn't comment on an ongoing criminal investigation. And he was reminded what his number one priority was. His job. Not Tess's wellbeing. "I've been put in charge of the task force investigating the murders. Someone else on the team will need to question you further."

Her expression turned wary. "You still think I could be involved?"

He shook his head. "I don't, which is why someone else is asking the hard questions."

"You're abandoning me to the wolves again." She seemed unimpressed and unsurprised and he felt like shit. "Feels like a habit when it comes to you and your law enforcement pals."

Mac gritted his teeth, but he couldn't ignore the fact he wasn't objective when it came to Tess Fallon. She didn't need to know that though. He glanced at the clock and swore.

"What?"

"I'm missing a task force meeting."

"Can't you call in?" she asked. "I'll drive." She dug out some earbuds from her bag and dangled them in the air. "I'll lend you these so the evil daughter of the dead white nationalist leader doesn't hear any damning evidence she can feed to…. Christ, *someone*, equally nasty."

With a resigned sigh, he pulled to the shoulder and climbed out, walking around the hood, grateful that the storm was abating though snow covered the surrounding fields and hills. Tess slid behind the wheel, adjusting the seat as he climbed in.

He dialed the number and plugged the buds into his ears. "Don't say anything. Okay? I'm hoping to be in charge of my own field office one day and I'm pretty sure I already broke fifty FBI guidelines this trip."

She gave him a cheeky salute and pulled out onto the

highway. He paid attention to the road signs because she didn't realize it yet but they were going on a detour. One that might rekindle all sorts of memories neither one of them wanted to deal with, but might jog something useful loose. Guilt eased through him but he pushed it away. He had a killer to catch and the sooner that happened the faster Tess could go back to her quiet life in the 'burbs.

––––––––––––

THE HOUSE WAS empty. He had his hand on his dick sprawled on the couch, watching an NHL game contemplating whether or not he could be bothered to jack off. He'd had sex earlier but was still feeling horny.

His cell rang. Anticipation made his nerves spark as he checked the number. He'd been waiting for her call. "Is it time?"

"Not yet," she said briskly. "Something came up."

He knew better than to ask questions, but he was weirdly disappointed. He wasn't sure he could do what she asked— part of him was terrified of messing up and the other part couldn't wait to prove himself.

"Things are about to get intense. You're sure everything's in place?"

"I'm sure." Although it wouldn't hurt to double-check. He got up off the couch and headed upstairs.

He heard her swallow and a familiar pang of longing shot through him. Pathetic. He lifted the mattress and used the sheet to pull out the file and flicked it open. The information on all the potential targets was right where he'd hidden it. He frowned. Shit. Where the hell was the thumb drive?

"Are you sending another message tonight?" he asked, prolonging their conversation while trying not to freak. He checked under the bed. Nothing. Maybe it had fallen out in the filing cabinet. He jogged back down to the den.

"Yes." Her voice was flat.

"Is it…"

"Is it what?" she bit out sharply.

"Is it easy?" he snapped back. God. Why was she always such a bitch?

A few seconds of surprised silence filled the space between them.

"It gets easier with practice. You'll be fine. Just think of it the same way as bagging your first buck."

That was an analogy he could relate to.

"I think it'll be tomorrow, but don't do it until I tell you. The timing has to be exact." She sounded like she was distracted. Maybe she was already on the next job? "You remember everything I told you?"

"I remember." Wear dark clothes with no insignia, a ball cap, avoid the street and surveillance cameras she'd marked on a map for him. Don't be seen. Don't get caught. Figure out the exit route before he went in.

"I'll call you tomorrow."

"Take care," he said, but she'd already hung up.

He dug down to the bottom of the drawer and felt around. Nothing. Where the hell was that thing?

He went to the kitchen and fetched rubber gloves from under the sink. Then he pulled out a chunk of files and felt around some more. The jump drive wasn't there. Taking a deep breath to stop himself from freaking out, he withdrew the rest of the files and checked inside the drawer and underneath.

Then he checked all the other drawers.

He started to sweat. Encrypted on that thumb drive was the master copy of their plans and potential victims. In the wrong hands, it could ruin everything. Where the hell was it?

He scrubbed his face. He couldn't afford to make a stupid mistake. He carefully put the files back, checking inside each one before sliding it in. Then he went through every drawer in the den, every pot and jar where someone might stash a data stick, including all the computer bags and backpacks in the house.

Panic bubbled in his heart, making it hard to catch his breath. She'd kill him if someone else got their hands on that information before the time was right.

An image of Tess going through the filing cabinet stopped his heart.

She must have taken it.

But why? Did she suspect? Or had she simply needed a thumb drive and borrowed it?

Something about the way she'd been watching him lately made him nervous.

He wiped his brow and stood, making sure the room looked like it had before. The hockey was still playing but he didn't care anymore. He took off the gloves, pulled on a plain black hoodie and a navy ball cap.

He lifted her keys off the rack. He didn't want to hurt Tess, but one way or another he needed to find that thumb drive.

His sister wasn't getting in the way of his revenge.

CHAPTER FOURTEEN

A N HOUR LATER Tess jerked awake, having briefly dozed off.

Mac was driving again. The snow had stopped falling. A thin, white blanket covered the entire area, and pale clouds hung heavy over the nearby hills. Mac's conference call had been one-sided and unrevealing. The take-home message had been they hadn't caught anyone, but no one else had been murdered. Yet.

They passed through Twin Falls. She'd seen signs for Crater of the Moon National Monument and Preserve.

As the miles sped by, a measure of foreboding stirred inside her that she couldn't explain. Tess got out her cell phone to look at a map, but there was no signal. She found a printed map in the glove compartment and spread the paper awkwardly over her lap. She found the road, tracked their position with her finger. The compound itself wasn't marked on the map but the town of Kodiak to the southwest was. Her pulse gave a little burst of acceleration. "We're not far from the compound."

Mac inclined his head, but didn't comment.

"I've never been back." She whirled to face him. "Have you?"

"Not since the days after the raid." He tapped the side of

his hand against the wheel to some internal beat.

She stared up at the darkening sky. It was only mid-afternoon, but seemed more like dusk. She shivered. She'd never wanted to return to this part of the world, but now she was so close the pull was magnetic. Something was drawing her. Some unanticipated compulsion. Or maybe it was the desire to lay her ghosts to rest. To know that that part of her life was well and truly history. "Can we go? Do we have time?"

There was an eight o'clock flight they were both hoping to catch, but Mac looked like he was debating with himself, too. Eventually he nodded and took the next right off the highway.

Much of the state was covered in desert, mountains, and forests, but this part of southern Idaho was fertile farmland. Wide open fields butted up to more hills and forest.

He took another turn and they were climbing, the shape of the hills familiar in the dim, distant memories of her child-hood. She flashed to sitting in the back of the truck eating ice cream, chasing the melting drips with her tongue and giggling like a banshee as Ellie did the same.

God, she missed her sister.

She closed her eyes. If the police hadn't shown up she would likely have endured the same fate as that beautiful soul. The idea of Walt or Eddie touching her made her want to gag. Instead she'd been rescued and raised with love and kindness by the sort of person her parents had feared and despised. A nice person. A wise person. A woman of color who saw the world in all its different shades.

Tess opened her eyes. "I always loved the landscape around here."

Her breath misted the glass and she wiped her sleeve against the condensation. McKenzie turned up the heat again.

She wanted to ask him if a visit to the compound had been on his agenda all along, but he'd hardly planned on her being at the prison, or that a winter storm would shut down the local airport.

"It's pretty," he conceded. "Not as pretty as Montana though."

"That's really where you're from?" she said, surprised.

"Born and raised." One side of his mouth tipped up and she spotted dimples she hadn't known existed.

She ignored the effect his looks had on her heart rate and settled back to stare out the window. "You still have family there?"

"Nope." He shook his head. "My dad raised me, but that was more by accident than choice. My mom died of cancer when I was a kid."

"I'm sorry for your loss." She worried at a hangnail. She gave in to the desire to find out more about him. "You miss her?"

He nodded, but his expression closed down.

It wasn't her business but there were no real rules as to their relationship. It was unchartered territory—or maybe she was kidding herself. Maybe she was legitimately a suspect and he understood the rules. It didn't matter. The little sparks of attraction that kept flaring up were nothing compared to the history that doused it. She may as well just enjoy his company. She hadn't done anything wrong.

But Cole might have... She pushed the thought out of her mind. He'd been with her when the DJ had been shot.

Could someone be trying to set him up? That seemed as unlikely as Cole pulling a trigger on another human being.

"I don't miss Francis," she said abruptly. She shuddered.

"Eddie reminded me I have her eyes."

Mac nodded again, confirming what she already knew.

You always were a worthless little bitch. I should have drowned you at birth.

Her birth mother's last words rang out in her mind. No wonder Tess didn't mourn her passing.

"If ever there was someone who shouldn't have had kids it was Francis Hines. And to have five?" she said. "Insanity."

"The Pioneers weren't big on birth control as I recall," Mac noted wryly. "Too busy trying to found their republic."

Tess huddled deeper into her jacket. She hadn't been able to get warm since Eddie had jammed his forearm across her throat.

"I don't think I'm going to have any kids."

He glanced at her. "Why not?"

"What if I turn out like my parents?"

"You won't."

"What if my kids turn out like them?" she pushed. However irrational it might sound, it was a genuine worry.

"Nature versus nurture, Tess. How'd your little brother turn out?"

Emotions tangled her in knots. "He's a sweet kid." But something was going on. And he still hadn't called her back.

"There you go, then. For what it's worth, I think you'd make a wonderful mom." He sent her a smile, and those changeable eyes of his eased into a dirty blue.

"I never thanked you, not properly. For the work you did undercover." She faced him, determined to get out what she needed to say. "Without you I'd either be dead, raped, or a white nationalist nutcase."

"You were never like the rest of them." He grinned and

physical awareness danced over her body like a feather drifting over naked skin. That stupid crush of hers was alive and well and making a full come back. But he didn't have to know about it. It didn't mean anything. He was a good-looking guy and there was no reason not to admire the view. As long as she didn't do anything stupid like trust those smiling eyes or those cute dimples.

She could feel him watching her out of the corner of his eye.

"I never felt like them," she said. "I never fitted in with them. I've never fitted in anywhere."

Mac nodded. "I know how that feels. You don't have to make any big decisions yet, you know. You're still young—"

She huffed out a laugh. "Thirty isn't young."

"Compared to thirty-nine it is," he said dryly.

She snorted. "Thirty-nine isn't old either. And I bet you fit in just fine with those other agents in the Bureau. In fact, I bet the female agents fall all over that easy charm of yours. I'm surprised you don't already have a wife and a passel of kids—" She cut herself off and winced. "Sorry, I shouldn't have said that. I forgot about your divorce."

He shrugged one shoulder. "Heather never wanted kids."

"But you married her anyway?"

"Who said I wanted kids?" he asked in surprise.

"I remember you at nineteen. You hung out with the kids more than the adults."

"The kids were nicer."

They both grimaced.

He turned his attention back to the curves in the road. "Heather was all wrong for me. I don't even know why I married her." Then a hint of red hit his cheeks.

It was amazing a man his age could still blush.

"I guess you just remembered," Tess said dryly.

"The sex was good," he admitted. "No reason to wear a ball and chain though."

"Especially if it feels like a ball and chain." She wasn't about to tell him she hadn't had good sex in so long she could hardly remember what it was like. She didn't want *that* to end up in some FBI report.

College, probably. With a boy she'd been in love with, but who'd gone off to follow his dreams when she'd been helping Trudy raise Cole. Her little brother had only been eleven and she'd refused to leave him. She'd gone to school in Georgetown to stay close.

She thought about her last boyfriend who'd ruined so many things in her life. "Relationships are overrated."

"Sounds like I'm not the only one who's been burned."

She pulled a face. "Vibrators are a lot less hassle than men."

His lips twitched. "Not as much fun, though."

"Fun?" She huffed out a laugh.

He shot her a look. "Sex is supposed to be fun, right?"

"I've obviously been dating the wrong type of guy, but then I knew that." Her own cheeks burned a little. While she couldn't believe they were having this conversation, she could far too easily imagine having sex with Mac. She eyed the five o'clock shadow roughening up his cheeks, imagined it scraping her skin.

She'd just bet sex with him was fun, but it wouldn't be worth the price she'd end up paying.

"What?" His voice deepened.

Catching his gaze, she realized he had one eye on the road

and one eye on her lips.

"Nothing." She knew this banter wasn't real and wouldn't lead anywhere and that made it safe. She was a pariah in law enforcement circles. Career kryptonite. She made a joke of it. "I can't believe I'm discussing my sex life with a Fed. I didn't think FBI agents even had sex."

He started choking. "Are you kidding me? FBI agents are considered *hot* in law enforcement circles. Now DEA or ATF...those guys struggle with image."

Her attention shifted to the scenery around them. And there, on the left, was the jagged peak that had loomed over her every day of her young life.

Her heart gave a terrified squeeze.

Mac had been keeping her engaged in conversation to distract her from this traumatic homecoming. She reached out and gripped his forearm, hoping he realized she was silently thanking him. Words were impossible.

He turned right again and she shifted in her seat as her old home came into view. The rusted barbwire fence had been replaced, but the shape of the fields was achingly familiar. Even the cows looked the same.

McKenzie pulled up on the side of the road, careful not to slide into the ditch. He left the engine running. A seven-bar gate barred entry to the old driveway.

They stared at the compound, each lost in their own thoughts. The signpost that used to stretch proudly across the top of two tall, wooden pillars had been painted over in dark gray, possibly to stop this site from becoming a mecca for white nationalists.

Three of the cottages had been demolished, as had some of the older outbuildings. The barn where Walt had tried to assault her still stood though. That barn signified both the good and the bad of her childhood.

Growing up on a farm, doing chores and taking care of the animals hadn't been a bad thing. Having a sister whom she'd loved with every ounce of her being hadn't hurt either. And whether she liked to admit it or not, Kenny Travers had also made life bearable.

But the beatings whenever she didn't do exactly as she was told, the incessant chores, the lack of formal education, the lack of friends, the constant barrage of hatred and bile and force-fed propaganda as they tried to destroy her ability to think critically or develop her own opinion.

At the time, it had been all she'd known, but looking back? A nightmare.

God, what had they been thinking?

Her parents' ashes had been scattered somewhere over these fields as per their last will and testament, but there was no grave marker or tombstone to worship.

Were their spirits still here? Had they finally found peace?

Tess pushed out of her door and jumped down to the snow that rose to her knees.

"Tess," McKenzie warned. "You can't go in there."

The cabin she'd grown up in was about two-hundred and fifty yards away down the winding, recently plowed driveway. She'd assumed the place would have fallen into ruin by now, but all the buildings were freshly painted and the main cabin had a new roof.

Someone had restored it.

Was someone living here?

That wasn't possible. But who'd plowed the drive? And why?

Her heart thumped crazily under her ribs. She climbed the gate, ignoring the "No Trespassing" sign and Mac's urgent shouts.

What was he going to do? Arrest her?

Needles of ice cold air took her breath and reminded her of all those frigid winters she'd spent right here on this hill. All the times she'd had to break the ice in the animals' water troughs to allow them to drink.

On the driveway, the snow only came up to her ankles and she moved quickly toward the house, watching carefully for signs of life. A car door slammed behind her, Mac's inventive cursing echoing through the valley.

The wind rattled the branches of the nearby cottonwoods and drew tears from her eyes. She walked onward, passing the spot where Harlan Trimble had lived, and where her sister had died. Her throat squeezed painfully.

The cabin drew her. It was single-story, deceptively small from the front, with five bedrooms—although hers and Ellie's rooms had been no bigger than some people's shoe closets—and a dining room. Her parents had wanted more kids, but Francis had suffered several miscarriages and two stillbirths before Bobby had arrived. Tess spotted the kitchen window where she'd often stood and watched the sun go down.

She stood quietly for a moment as the ghosts from her past whirled around her. This was where most of her family had died and though she might not have liked them very much, there was a bond between them, something invisible, unbreakable, unwanted. Blood.

She took a step onto the side porch that led to the kitchen.

Mac grabbed her arm. "Tess, you can't walk into some-one's home."

She shook him off and threw open the door. It wasn't locked. Someone must live here… But who?

She flicked on the light switch. "Anyone here?" she called out.

No one answered.

The kitchen was the same but different. New appliances, a warm terra-cotta color on the walls, refinished hardwood floors. A picture on the wall showed flowers rather than the old black and white western prints her mother had favored.

"Tess," Mac insisted. "We can't be in here."

Memories assailed her. Broken glass. Bullets flying. The noise so loud she pressed her hands over her ears even at the memory. She stared at the pretty furnishings. The bullet holes in the walls had been fixed and it was obvious someone either lived here or the cabin was rented out to vacationers.

Anger filled her.

She pointed to a spot on the floor near where the old refrigerator had stood. "Walt died there." She pointed to the spot beneath the kitchen sink. "Daddy. I remember him lying in a pool of blood." She headed through the dining room to another side corridor where the bedrooms were.

Tess pointed at the floor outside the room that had been hers. "That's where Momma died." Her mother's eyes had been open. Her face strained and bitter even in death. "I'm pretty sure if the cops hadn't shot her, I wouldn't be alive today."

She stepped into the room as if she were stepping over a corpse and shuddered at the reminder. The bed had been replaced, a small dressing table tucked into one corner where before there had been only a hardback chair. She went to the closet and opened the door. Inside was a row of empty wire, coat hangers. She considered the small, cramped space and then turned to Mac, who was shadowing her every move with a worried expression on his face.

She should put him out of his misery.

"I hid in here with Bobby and Sampson." Her throat was sore from the effort of suppressing emotion. "It looks so small now and yet for that entire night it was the only place in the world that felt safe."

Tears formed but she wouldn't let them fall. The time for tears was over.

Someone was using her family's sick ideals to wage a new war and she refused to let them drag her down with them. Someone had restored this cabin when in her mind it had ceased to exist. She needed to know who it was, and why.

She stepped up to the bedroom window and looked out at the view that had been hers for all those years. So much had changed, but not that. A field, some trees, the mountain behind them. She let out a pent-up breath, wishing for something she couldn't name—maybe just normalcy. Just the sort of childhood you could look back on and miss.

"I don't even know what happened to my dog." She hugged herself tightly. The cops had taken Sampson away and the people at social services had refused to tell her where. The more noise she'd made the more they'd stared down their pious noses at her.

"I took him."

She turned in surprise. "What?"

Mac shrugged and looked shame-faced. "I took him with me. I tried to get child services to let him go with you, but they told me they weren't the pound and didn't take pets. He was a great dog." He shrugged. "I looked after him."

She inhaled through an open mouth and observed him through the reflections in the glass. "All these years I wondered about him. I worried." She swallowed hard. "Something else to thank you for."

He scratched the back of his neck. "He lived another four years and died peacefully in his sleep. Never gave me a moment's trouble, but whenever a truck pulled up outside the house his ears would perk up and he'd wag his tail so hard I was worried he was gonna fall over. I used to think he was waiting for his best pal to come get him to go play ball."

But she'd never come.

Her throat was now so tight she could barely breathe. Her vision grew blurry. Still she didn't let the tears fall. She'd adored that dog, and had missed him terribly, but at least he'd had a loving home.

Unspoken messages passed between them and Tess felt connected to this man in a way she'd never experienced with anyone else. Maybe it was the fact he knew every secret she'd kept hidden all these years—things she'd never told anyone. Maybe it was the attraction that seemed more than skin deep. She didn't trust him, but hell if she didn't like him. A lot.

They were so busy looking into one another's eyes that she didn't hear the creak of the floorboard until it was too late.

CHAPTER FIFTEEN

T HE COCKING OF a gun made Mac freeze for a split second before stepping in front of Tess.

The man had a face full of wrinkles surrounding a red, bulbous nose, a grizzled jaw and a pair of small, beady eyes. The little hair that was left on his head was stringy and gray as the overcast sky.

"You people can't read? Sign says, No Trespassin'."

Mac slowly raised his hands and eyed the weapon—a Smith and Wesson revolver probably as old as the man holding it. Mac knew better than to declare his FBI status while someone held a gun on him in this part of the world. The old man might decide shooting him for trespassing was his chance at a free pass for getting rid of a Fed. Antigovernment sentiment ran deep in certain quarters of the States.

"Easy there. We didn't mean no harm." Mac let his accent thicken.

Tess planted her hands on her hips. "It would be hard to trespass on my own property now, wouldn't it? You best put that gun away before you hurt someone."

Her brows rose imperiously and Mac had to work to keep his lower jaw from dropping.

"I guess that's something you forgot to mention, sweetheart," he told her under his breath. That explained why she'd ignored his warnings earlier. Mac had never imagined Tess would have been able to hold on to the property. Her adoptive mother must have arranged it on her behalf. The question was, why?

The old man squinted and let the barrel of the pistol drop. "Well, I'll be darned. Francis and David's little girl?"

A chill worked its way down Mac's spine. He hadn't heard that tone used in reaction to the Hines family in nearly twenty years.

He shot Tess a look and wished he could take her aside and tell her how to play this guy. He wanted to know more but the man wasn't likely to talk to a Fed. But she didn't need him to tell her anything. She'd grown up in an environment that revered her father, and punished those who didn't follow the herd.

"Theresa Jane." She nodded and frowned as she held out her hand. "I'm sorry I don't remember you…"

"You wouldn't. You were just a little girl the last time I saw you. Jessop. Henry Jessop."

"Ah…now I remember you. You're the farmer who leases the land?"

He nodded. "Keep hoping you'll sell it to me…" He tucked the gun into a holster attached to his waist.

Mac knew the man's name. His ranch neighbored this one to the northwest. Jessop hadn't appeared to be directly involved with the Pioneers' plot to bring down the government, but David Hines had spent quite a lot of time there. Law enforcement had run Jessop through the system, but nothing suspicious had popped. The old guy had been considered a bit of a hard-ass to work for by the other cowboys who'd frequented the local bar. Mac doubted Jessop would remember a no-account cowpoke like Kenny Travers.

"I'm waiting to talk to my brother before we decide whether or not to sell," Tess told Jessop.

Mac noticed she was careful not to mention which brother.

She was gonna have to tell Bobby about his real parents soon, which she was obviously reluctant to do. Those tangled webs and all that. But what if someone else had already told him? What if her kid brother was busy avenging parents he didn't even remember? Would Tess flip on him or become complicit in his guilt? Mac didn't know. Hoped he didn't have to find out.

There'd been no real developments in the last few hours, but at least no one else had died. Labs were running evidence as fast as they could, and everyone was doing their damnedest to narrow down the killer, including him, even if this wasn't the most traditional way to run a task force.

The old man scratched his grizzled pate. "Eddie? Eddie doesn't want to sell."

"Not Eddie." Tess smiled coldly and the old man appeared startled for a moment. In that instant, she resembled her mother. "My baby brother, Bobby."

Eddie had forfeited his right to the property when he'd shot that cop.

The old man squinted and nodded. "Of course. Bobby."

"I never gave permission for you to rent this place out." Her tone was mild but Mac eased his hand toward his holster to unclip it just in case the old man got offended.

Jessop had the grace to look ashamed. "I couldn't stand by and watch the place fall apart. Thought it might be a good spot for Eddie to live once he got out of prison—assuming they ever let him out. There are serial killers who get less time than that," he said bitterly. "I don't make no money off the rental," he assured her. "Just use the income to pay for upkeep and put the rest in a savings account for him so he can get by."

So Jessop was close enough to want to look out for Eddie Hines. What else might he be involved in? Mac wanted to find out.

"I appreciate you thinking of Eddie, Mr. Jessop. I'm a little ashamed of the fact it's taken me so long to return to Idaho, but the memories of that time were difficult to face."

Mac eyed her still swollen nose. If someone didn't know better they might mistake the redness for cold. Her other bruises were hidden by a velvet blue and black scarf she'd wrapped around her neck. "I should have reached out to him years ago but I wasn't able to do that safely. That's why I'm here now. To see Eddie."

She wasn't lying, and she was being vague enough to suit all their needs.

He appreciated from his time living in this community that important things didn't come up in the first conversation—bigotry, conspiracy, treason, these things usually took time.

Jessop turned his attention to Mac and his eyes hardened. "And who might you be?"

Mac made a split-second decision and held out his hand. He took a step forward shaking the other man's heartily. "Mac Stevens. Theresa Jane did me the very great honor of agreeing to become my wife and you're the first to know. We don't even have a ring yet. Nice to meet you, Mr. Jessop."

The man didn't look impressed by his impromptu proposal.

"So, what are you people doing out this way?"

"Driving to Boise from Salt Lake City," Mac improvised. "Theresa Jane told me she had something to show me. I guess this was it."

Mac spotted a dark wad of chewing tobacco in the man's mouth. He'd chewed it for a time too, to fit in with the other cowboys. The memory of bitter tobacco sat on his tongue like oil and he fought the urge to spit.

"I wanted to see the place again," Tess said quietly. "It seemed like the right time to come home."

"Can't believe it's been nearly twenty years already." Jessop shook his head.

Mac tensed.

"Time doesn't dull the memories," said Tess.

Mac wondered how many nightmares she'd had about the shootout over the years. He eyed the closet and saw a stray bullet hole about three feet off the ground. If Theresa Jane had been sitting up at the time of that shot, that bullet could have passed straight through her. It hit him all over again how lucky she'd been. It was pure chance she'd survived that night. He'd do well to remember that the next time she thanked him for saving her.

"You were close to my parents?" she asked Jessop intently.

The man backed out of the cramped bedroom. He was almost as tall as Mac, but had rounded shoulders and a paunch. Mac didn't underestimate him though. Ranch work built muscles gyms had never heard of. He followed Jessop into the kitchen, Tess trailing him.

"They were fine people. Wonderful neighbors."

As long as you were white and straight and bigoted, Mac thought, bile rising in his throat.

Tess smiled sympathetically, rubbing her tattoo like it had started to itch. She did that when she was nervous. "I guess I should have called ahead and told you we were coming. I just didn't expect to find the cabin still standing, let alone still being used. It shocked me."

"Most people avoid the place." Jessop leaned against the sink.

Mac remembered Tess standing in that same spot doing dishes, the day of the raid.

"Some say it's haunted."

Considering the hairs that had raised on Mac's nape when they'd walked through the door he could believe it. And if anyone would turn into a ghoul, it'd be Francis Hines.

Tess checked her watch and frowned. "As much as I'd like to talk, we need to be going."

"Why don't you come to the ranch house for supper before you go on your way?" Jessop offered abruptly.

Tess started to shake her head, but Mac cut in eagerly, "I could eat."

Her eyes flicked over him. "I didn't think we had time."

He checked his own watch and on cue his stomach grumbled. Chances were they'd miss the eight o'clock flight if they stayed, but there was another flight after that. It might be worth the detour, to see what this guy had to say.

Jessop waved aside Tess's concern. "There's stew on the hob and bread in the oven. It would be faster than stopping at a restaurant and a man has to eat." His jovial concern for Mac's welfare put Mac on edge. He didn't trust the guy.

"You sure that's no trouble?" Tess asked again.

The reluctance was obvious in her tone.

Jessop's beady eyes got narrower. "I have a few things you

may want to have. Belongings of your parents..."

And Mac was absolutely all-in.

Could this guy know something relevant to his current investigation? Could he be involved? Tess met his gaze. She looked uncertain and he knew it was wrong but he did it anyway.

"My fiancée and I would be honored to join you for dinner, Mr. Jessop."

Tess shot him a dirty look, but the old timer didn't pay her any mind. Her man had spoken and that's all that mattered around here. As they followed Jessop outside, Mac rested his hand low on her back. She stiffened but didn't pull away.

"Should we follow you?" Mac suggested. He wasn't supposed to know where Jessop lived.

"We can cut across the ranch. I'll unlock the gate." Jessop nodded and walked to an old beat up truck that had probably been going since before Tess had been born. The truck had a snow plow attached to the front. Mac ignored the frigid moisture seeping into his shoes and followed the now silent woman down the driveway.

"Thank you for going along with me back there," he said to her stiff back.

A cloud of vapor erupted as she exhaled. "I didn't have much choice." She wrapped her arms tight across her chest and whispered. "You think this guy might be involved in the murders?"

Mac took her elbow as they negotiated a drift. "Makes sense that any plan to avenge your parents' deaths or carry out their agenda might originate from a former Pioneer or someone close to them. Jessop came up on the radar, but was never at any meetings and had no link to the stolen weapons we were tracking, that we knew about anyhow. If he's not involved, he could still have vital information about someone who is."

He opened the passenger door and helped Tess into her seat. He tried to ignore how soft she felt beneath his hands. How easy and natural it felt to be in her company.

She sat and her eyes searched his face nervously. "If he figures out you're a Fed we're in deep trouble."

He tipped his head to the side. "Let's make sure he doesn't figure it out."

"Can they trace the plates on this vehicle to Steve McKenzie or the FBI?" she asked.

He nodded. "Sure, if they have contacts in the rental place or if they know a cop who'll ask for them."

Her eyes went huge. "You think they have cops on their side?"

Mac huffed out a laugh. "Wasn't that one of your daddy's dreams? Getting a ghost skin working on the inside?"

Tess closed her eyes and shuddered. He caught her by the shoulders and leaned down to kiss the top of her head, but she looked up suddenly and they both froze. If he didn't kiss her now it would look weird. She seemed to realize the same thing at the exact same moment he did. So he brushed his lips quickly over hers, caught off-guard by the electricity that zapped at his blood with a wave of molten heat.

She bit her lower lip and he felt a punch of lust in his groin.

He jolted when a truck started honking behind them. What the hell just happened?

Jessop had opened the gate and was impatiently waiting for them to follow. Mac closed Tess's door, walking around to climb into the driver's seat and ignoring the fact he hadn't reacted to a woman like that in *years*. Maybe ever.

He started the engine and drove down a driveway he thought he'd left behind twenty years ago. Chills ran down his spine as ghosts bristled, and the memory of Tess's kiss buzzed on his lips, but he concentrated on the task ahead. Getting distracted at this point could get them both killed.

———————

TESS STARED AS they drove past old familiar fields. She spotted the hill where they'd tobogganed during some of the rare fun moments of her childhood. And a small copse of trees where they'd built a secret fort when she was barely able to toddle. Even Eddie had been fun back then.

She didn't want to think about Eddie.

Twenty years in prison had hardened what little heart he'd had. But this old man, Jessop, wanted to look out for him like he was some poor lost soul. Her sore throat ached. Poor Eddie. Poor violent, twisted, sadistic Eddie.

She didn't realize how tense she was until Mac reached over and untangled her fingers from the fists she'd made in her lap.

"It'll be fine."

"You said that earlier when you talked me into wearing the wire." She made a very unladylike huff. "Good thing I learned self-defense else I'd be dead." She rubbed her throat and adjusted her scarf so the bruises remained hidden.

"I'm sorry he grabbed you. I should have positioned a guard closer." A muscle rippled in his jaw. "Look, we don't have to stay at Jessop's long. We eat, take whatever memorabilia he saved from the compound for you—"

"I hope to God it isn't the Hitler bust."

"I hated that fucking thing. Still gives me nightmares," Mac agreed, and they shared a look of mutual horror. "Hopefully I can get a quick read on this guy, maybe take a quick look around his house without his knowledge and we can leave in time to catch the last flight out."

"Is that why you came to my house yesterday,"—had it only been yesterday?—"to get a 'quick read' on me?" She couldn't help the bitterness that infiltrated her tone. She didn't blame him, but it sucked to never be totally trusted. Although she was one to talk. She hadn't told her ex, Jason, or her best friend, Julie, about her real identity. Their subsequent betrayal proved it had been the right decision.

Mac pressed his lips together. "I came alone to reaffirm what I thought I already knew about you." He flashed her a narrow-eyed stare. "Unfortunately, because you failed to mention your daddy's birthday, there will be more agents with more questions."

She gave a harsh laugh. "So, it's *my* fault the FBI didn't figure that out?"

His glare dissolved and he glanced away. "No, I should have seen it, but I was busy investigating four murders and that piece of the puzzle slipped past me."

Guilt made her feel small for blaming him. He was right. People were dying. Her sensitive nature didn't matter anymore. "I honestly didn't remember the significance of the date until after you'd left. I am sorry I didn't call you."

She touched her lips, which still hummed from the insubstantial kiss Mac had laid on her when she'd climbed in the SUV. It had shot a bolt of longing deep into her core.

She was truly pathetic. The guy was playing a role.

She still hadn't gotten hold of Cole. Had he genuinely not forgiven her stupid comment about older women and younger men? Her double standards were screaming at her every second with being stuck in this car with a man she'd been crushing on since she was ten years old. The nine-year age difference had been insurmountable back then. Now, at thirty, the age difference seemed irrelevant.

Dangerous thoughts, but right now she was stuck with him. Perhaps that was for the best. The more willing she was to help the FBI, surely the better it was for her reputation? It was worth a shot. "What do you want me to do with Jessop?"

"Try and get him talking about your parents but don't be too obvious. You know how paranoid these people are."

"Ain't paranoia if they're really out to getcha." She deepened her daddy's twang and quirked her brows.

Mac's eyes widened. "That's a little scary."

She laughed. "Daddy was a scary guy. What else?"

"We both do our best to look around while appearing to not give a damn. I'm a…" He peered down at his suit and tie. "What the fuck do I do for a living if I wear a suit on my downtime?"

"Oilman. Pretty much the only men in suits these guys will talk to. Oil and gas folks, or a preacher."

"No way would I pass for a preacher." His mouth tightened. "I guess I can work for an oil company."

"Okay." She was amused at his lack of enthusiasm but hid it. They needed to be serious. "Let's keep the details to the bare minimum. Being secretive can go both ways."

Those eyes of his crinkled at the corners. "You're good at this."

"Lying?" she scoffed.

He groaned loudly. "I hope not, else I'm going to look like a damn fool when I get back to headquarters."

She glanced at him sharply. Did that mean he'd vouched for her? Or that someone else thought she was a suspect?

"You're good at thinking on your feet. Adapting."

"I've had to be. I've hidden my real identity my whole life, Mac. That tends to make a person cautious with information."

Mac held her gaze for a long moment then fiddled with his phone. "Shit. No signal." He shoved the cell back in his pocket. "Looks like it's just you and me."

She raised one brow. "You okay with that?"

He sent her a lazy grin. "I've had worse partners."

But she hadn't lied earlier. She didn't trust easily. In fact, she didn't trust at all. Maybe she really was as paranoid as her folks had been, but she didn't want to be. She wanted to be part of a team. She wanted to be one of the good guys.

Jessop's farmhouse appeared in the distance.

She squinted at it against its pretty backdrop of pearly white. "I don't remember ever visiting this place before."

"I did once." He turned to look at her. "I rode out here leading a young colt your daddy had gotten hold of from somewhere." Horses dotted across the fields and reminded him of another lifetime. "This guy, Jessop, has a weakness for horseflesh."

She found herself watching Mac's hands curl around the steering wheel. Big hands. Strong hands. Broad with long fingers that looked more suited to soothing beasts than taming bad guys. It was his eyes that attracted her most, she realized with a start. Not just the tantalizing color which shifted from green to blue like the sunlight on a shallow sea. It was the intelligence she saw there, combined with compassion. Intelligence was an aphrodisiac for any smart woman, but compassion was vastly underrated. It was worth more than money, power, even truth. It gave morality to strength and comfort to suffering. She could fall for him for that reason alone.

She suppressed her thoughts. She could deal with the idea of a childish crush. She couldn't deal with the idea of more.

She eyed the house. It was a pale river rock affair with a white-painted porch. There were stables and a bunk house across the paddock. A couple of thoroughbreds stood near the fence, lit up in the headlights. Both animals wore heavy-duty coats to help protect them from the weather.

Jessop parked near the front steps and motion-sensitive lights flooded the area.

Mac shaded his eyes. "It's like a goddamned prison break."

She snorted.

He drove the car in a circle so they were facing out. All the better for making a fast getaway.

Her heart thumped and her mouth went dry. "I'm not happy about being here, McKenzie," she murmured under her breath.

"We'll be fine. Let him do most of the talking."

Jessop headed up the front steps and waited for them. The trickle of fear that crawled all over her skin as she got out of the car did nothing to reassure her.

CHAPTER SIXTEEN

UNEASE STIRRED BENEATH Mac's skin. On the surface, Jessop was a perfect host, but something about this guy was making his senses twitch. There was a disturbance in the Force.

Mac hadn't planned this. Should be in DC running the task force. But this opportunity was too serendipitous to step away from, especially with the added bonus of having Tess by his side. As a Fed, he wouldn't get in the door. But as Theresa Jane Hines's fiancé he was almost part of the family.

There was nothing in the law to say an FBI agent couldn't lie to obtain the information he needed for a case, but he knew the best lies were the ones that stuck closest to the truth. He'd be lying if he said he wasn't enjoying himself.

He'd certainly never imagined he'd work undercover in any capacity in this part of the world again, yet here he was, here *they* were, working as allies.

He wanted to trust Tess.

He considered her as she sat with a fragrant bowl of beef stew in front of her. She hadn't eaten much. Her scarf was coiled high over her tight-fitted, black shirt, presumably to hide the marks her own brother had put on her skin. Her dark, wavy hair was pulled back in a messy knot and though she was pale and didn't wear a stitch of makeup she was ridiculously attractive.

Everything, from her quiet life as an accountant to the fact Eddie had tried to kill her, screamed her innocence. But she was smart. If she was involved, it was entirely possible they'd plan everything down to the last detail—including Eddie's attack if she thought the Feds were onto them.

Even though he was convinced they were on the same team she was definitely hiding *something*. He needed to know what that something was.

She felt his stare and sent him a curious smile.

He smiled back, but as much as he wanted to trust her he couldn't stake his career on it.

Mac reached for another slice of freshly baked bread. "You cooked all this yourself?" Mac asked Jessop. He was impressed despite himself. He could cook, but he rarely had time, and there was no fun when he was the only one eating.

Jessop nodded and chewed his food before answering. "My wife died a couple years ago, God rest her soul." He crossed himself. "Got a daughter, but she lives out east."

Henry pointed to a photo on the refrigerator of a small boy holding the hand of an older woman who was presumably Jessop's late wife. "When my Mary died it was learn to cook or starve." He patted his round stomach. "Thankfully, cooking ain't rocket science. Just takes a bit of patience, like everything else." A smile lifted the wrinkles on his face, like a concertina.

"The food is delicious. We appreciate it," Tess said warmly, though she hadn't eaten much.

She sipped her red wine. Mac ignored the glass in front of him. He wanted a clear head to deal with anything that might present itself.

Jessop didn't pepper them with questions. In Mac's mind,

the less people asked questions, the more they probably had to hide.

Mac cleaned his bowl and sat back, his stomach satisfied even as his mind hungered. Still he waited while Tess and Jessop exchanged a few more memories about her parents. Tess smiled but Mac could see the strain keeping any real happiness out of her eyes. She didn't try and hide it from Jessop. Why would she? As far as Jessop was concerned the Hines family had been brutally slain by the cops—why wouldn't that cause stress in their one remaining daughter?

"Your little brother—how old is he now?" asked Jessop.

"He'll be twenty next month." Tess smiled. "At six feet two, he's not so little anymore."

"Tall like his daddy."

Tess smiled tightly. "My daddy always seemed like a giant to me. I guess they're about the same height."

"What's he do?" Jessop wiped his mouth with the back of his hand. Something in the action propelled Mac back to his own childhood, his own father, eating, drinking, lashing out.

His jaw clenched.

Tess dabbed her lips with the napkin and Mac noticed the old man watching her with a gleam in his eye. It was close enough to lust to make something possessive rear up inside Mac.

Great. He was jealous of a woman who was posing as his fake fiancée.

"We better hit the road." Mac needed to get moving and he could tell Tess didn't want to discuss her brother. "Would you mind if I used the restroom before we head off?"

"Not at all. Go on through to the living room while you wait, Theresa Jane. I'll track down those things I mentioned earlier."

"Would you like help clearing up?" she offered.

A knot formed in Mac's throat. It reminded him of all the times Tess had been taken advantage of as a child. Not because she was weak—but because she was *good*.

Jessop shook his head decisively. "Guests don't help clean up. My wife might be dead but she'd still throw a fit if she found out."

Jessop led him to the downstairs washroom that also housed a small shower stall. The decor was folky Americana. Not a hooded robe in sight. Mac checked the medicine cabinet. There were razors and deodorant. No medication though.

Mac washed up and came out of the room as quietly as possible. Jessop was just coming out of a downstairs bedroom carrying a small cardboard box. Mac got a quick glance inside the room before the man shut the door firmly behind him. It looked like a teen's room with posters on the wall and a computer desk set up against one wall. The computer screen was dark but there'd been a light under the table, suggesting it was plugged in.

He wanted to get his hands on that machine.

"Can I help?" He offered to carry the box.

"I got this. You go on ahead." Jessop indicated with one hand.

Reluctantly Mac walked into the living room to see Tess standing in front of the fireplace holding her hands out for warmth.

There was an overstuffed floral couch and a couple of photographs in silver frames on a sideboard against the far wall. Hardly a den of iniquity, but Mac had learned a long time ago that the veneer of civility was sometimes just that.

Jessop placed the box on the coffee table and smiled at Tess, but she didn't come any closer.

"Wouldn't swap this part of the world for all the money in the world, but it doesn't mean I wouldn't change a few things if I could—like the weather," Jessop said.

"World's a long way from perfect," Mac agreed. "Weather's the least of our problems."

Jessop chuckled, but didn't take the bait.

She leaned against the wooden mantel and covered a yawn. "Sorry. I'm suddenly bone tired."

Mac doubted she'd got any sleep last night either.

"What did you say you do?" Jessop asked Tess abruptly.

Mac froze. They hadn't come up with an alternative career for her. She smiled sweetly. "I'm an egg farmer down in Mississippi. Free range. I run it with a friend of mine, although I might sell my share when Mac and I get married." She batted her lashes at him.

Mac's eyes widened. What the hell happened to keeping lies close to the truth?

Jessop's brows rose. "Nothing wrong with farming."

Did he suspect them? Or was Mac reading too much into the situation? Being undercover had always been lonely work, but having a partner to worry about was worse.

"What do you have in there?" Tess stared at the box like it might be full of spiders. She didn't come any closer. He didn't blame her.

"The cops took most things after they murdered your kin."

Mac winced inwardly.

"But they didn't take everything."

Mac leaned over as the old man opened the box. What the

hell had they missed?

Jessop pulled out a dog-eared copy of *The Turner Diaries*.

Mac wanted to roll his eyes.

Tess took a few steps forward to take the battered paperback. She pursed her lips as she flicked through the racist garbage. "I must have read this book a hundred times as a kid." She flipped through the pages and one came loose and fluttered to the floor. She bent down to pick it up. "I drew pictures in this one."

She turned to show him flowers in the margin, drawn in crude black biro. She sounded nostalgic but Mac heard the irony layered beneath. That piece of bullshit and the Holy Bible were the only two books allowed in Kodiak Compound, so of course she'd read it a hundred times.

Eddie and Walt had also kept a stash of *Playboys* under their mattress, and he doubted they were the only sinners in the compound. Disgust for the brothers and for himself fermented inside. He should have protected the girls better. But he still didn't know how he could have done that and shut down the group. He'd been a rookie cop still finding his place in the world. Trying to prove he was worthy of the faith his bosses had placed in him. Looking back with twenty years' law enforcement experience, none of the choices had been easy.

On cue, Jessop hauled out an old family Bible and handed it to Tess.

Her mouth opened slightly, as if she were pleasantly surprised, but Mac saw her eyes flinch.

"Momma's Bible." She smoothed her hand over the front. "God rest her soul." Her eyebrows quirked at him cynically when Jessop turned away. Tess obviously shared his opinion that Francis's soul had withered and died long before she had.

"Had your daddy's Bible, too, but I've misplaced it."

Mac frowned. How did you misplace something like that? Maybe the guy had sold it on Ebay, or was secretly saving it for Eddie's release. Tess moved to the box and put the books down. She reached inside and pulled out a bookmark made of pressed daisies. "Ellie made this."

Tess's hands trembled. Mac realized it was the first tangible object she'd touched of her sister's since she'd lost Ellie. He wrapped an arm around her waist and pulled her to him as she fought tears.

"Murdering bastards," Jessop muttered.

"Yes." Tess blinked rapidly and raised her chin.

Mac ignored Jessop's lies. He'd figured long ago that some people existed in their own reality, a reality that didn't always make sense. No amount of arguing got them to change their minds. They were happy in their fantasy world and as long as they didn't hurt others he left them there to live out their illusions in willful ignorance.

But if they crossed a line…

He drew Tess against him, and she laid her head on his chest and closed her eyes. His heart gave a little twist that she trusted him enough to let him comfort her even this much.

"I didn't mean to upset you." Jessop frowned at her. "Thought you might be interested in having something from your past."

"I do. I am. Thank you." Her hair stroked Mac's jaw as she nodded. It was silky and smelled faintly of lavender. She pulled away, as if suddenly aware of how he held her—as if they really were in love.

"It's so unexpected to find all these things after I thought they were lost forever." She put the bookmark reverently inside the box next to the books. "Thank you. I am really very grateful."

Jessop nodded and sent her a smile. "You going to see Eddie tomorrow?"

Tess drew her chin up and her eyes glittered. "Of course."

"You two are welcome to stay the night… Save you driving further in the snow tonight if you're not used to it."

Mac had pretty much learned to drive in snow and ice, but he was tempted to stay anyway. It would give him the chance to do more snooping.

"Thank you, but no." Tess put an end to that notion. "We need to hit the road. Don't we, honey?"

He heard the steely command in her tone though she disguised it with sweetness. But the pleading in her eyes was the deciding factor, that and the fact he needed to get back to DC.

"We appreciate the offer, Mr. Jessop—"

A phone started ringing in the kitchen.

Jessop held up his hand. "Excuse me a moment. Let me make sure it isn't an emergency with the stock. I'll be right back." He disappeared before either of them had the opportunity to say another word.

This was Mac's one and only chance. "Stay here."

He didn't give Tess time to argue just strode swiftly to the bedroom where Jessop had stored the box. He walked inside and took a quick look around. A claw of repulsion raked him. Behind the door, the distinctive stars and bars was draped on the wall above the bed. A Bible that Mac recognized as David Hines's own sat on the bedside table.

Why had Jessop lied about that?

Mac strode to the computer and moved the mouse, praying it was turned on.

The screen came alive to a chatroom on the Tor server with a green background. The site was called One-Drop-2-Many and Mac didn't need a Ph.D. to figure out what that was in reference to. It was a white supremacist chatroom. Unfortunately, the chat had timed out and it needed a password to re-access the site.

A noise behind him had him straightening. Tess pushed the door open, white-faced and wild-eyed. He opened his mouth to tell her to go distract Jessop when he saw the old man behind her. Jessop pressed a revolver to her temple.

Shit. "What's going on?" Mac demanded.

Jessop's smile grew ugly and Mac knew his secret was out. Well. Fuck.

"I don't take kindly to being lied to. Especially by people accepting my hospitality."

Mac didn't bother denying it. The million-dollar question was how'd he figure it out?

"I wasn't sure I'd be welcome if you knew the truth." What had the guy learned? "Sorry for the lack of transparency. We appreciate dinner, but we'll be on our way now…"

Jessop spat on the floor. Tess pulled a disgusted face which made Mac smile even though his heart was pounding.

"You think this is funny?"

"No, sir. You holding a gun on an innocent, unarmed woman is anything but amusing." He put his hands on his hips, making himself a bigger target but Jessop didn't take the bait and didn't move that firearm a millimeter away from Tess's skull.

Shit.

Tess's eyes were worried now. No way could she risk a

move like the one she'd made at the prison with that barrel pointed at her head.

"We'll leave and forget this ever happened—"

"I don't think so." The old man's hand moved up into Tess's hair, taking a firm grip and making her cry out in pain.

Rage surged through Mac. This was the second time today Tess had been manhandled.

Her chin angled back, no doubt trying to ease the pain of having her hair yanked out. "Mac thinks like we do," she cried out. "I recruited him the way Daddy wanted us."

"If you believe that then you're a bigger fool than I thought." Jessop sneered. "You," he indicated to Mac. "Take out your weapon real slow and toss it on the bed."

Mac slowly drew out his Glock. The weight felt beautifully familiar in his hand. He raised it and pointed it straight at Jessop. The man's eyes widened and he shifted Tess in front of him—typical coward, hiding behind a woman.

Mac tilted his head to one side and lined up his shot. "One of the first things they teach us at the Academy is never surrender your weapon."

"Then she's dead," Jessop declared boldly.

"You'll be dead, too." Mac's smile was cold. If he threw down his weapon, he and Tess were both goners.

They were at a stalemate and the old man knew it. Mac moved toward the computer and clicked the mouse. "Who've you been talking to, Henry? You involved in these murders in DC? Talk to us and I can cut you a deal that may keep you out of federal prison for the rest of your life." Mac pulled his phone from his pocket and started dialing even though he had no signal. Jessop didn't know that for sure. These people believed the power of the federal government went way beyond what it actually did. "Can't wait for the experts at the lab to start taking this computer apart, figure out who you're working with."

Jessop's gun came up and swung toward Mac. Mac dodged right as Tess elbowed the man in the face. She twisted out of his grip. Mac tried to get a shot off, but Jessop was already gone. He reached down to haul Tess to her feet, pulling her behind him. "You okay?"

"Fine," she replied. "Where'd he go?"

Mac frowned, listening hard. "Kitchen, I think."

"Think he'll make a run for it?" she asked. What sounded like the back door banged open and the two of them edged into the hallway and through the living room. Tess went to grab the box.

"Leave it."

"I just want the bookmark."

"No. This whole place is about to become a crime scene. Don't touch anything." He took her hand and tugged her into the kitchen, clearing the room before urging her to follow.

"You think Jessop is involved with this thing?"

"Oh, yeah."

"He could simply be an old coot who hates Feds. You know how many of them there are around here and how crazy they all are?"

"You don't know how much those words worry me." He made her crouch behind the stove before picking up the landline. No dial tone. He followed the line. Jessop had ripped the wire out of the wall. "Dammit."

He gave Tess a once-over. "Put your coat on in case we have to make a run for it across country." He nodded toward the chair. She passed him his jacket and he pulled it on, too.

TONI ANDERSON

"He could be waiting in ambush or he might have run to get reinforcements from the bunkhouse. I'll go out first and head right." He tossed her the keys to the Jeep. "I want you to head straight for the SUV, fast and low. Start the engine and keep it running. If bullets start to fly I want you out of here."

"What about you?"

He shot her a look. "I'll be fine."

She rolled her eyes. "You have a backup weapon?"

He nodded.

"Give it to me."

"I'm not giving you a gun."

"You don't trust me?" she sounded shocked.

"I don't know yet." Honesty went both ways.

She reared back like he'd struck her.

Dammit. "Look, fine, I trust you, but I don't want you to become a target."

"But being an unarmed pawn is okay?"

Shit.

He wasn't foolish enough to fall for emotional bribery but hell if his gut didn't scream at him that they were on the same side. He pulled the Glock-17 from his ankle holster. If he was wrong he was about to lose more than his career. Her eyes widened as he handed it over.

"Remember how to use it?"

She nodded. "I still go to the range regularly."

"Good." It was a risk but he didn't want her to be defenseless if anything happened to him. "It's for self-defense only. No getting involved in a shootout unless you have to. You don't want to end up like Eddie."

She swallowed loudly, eyes huge.

"I'll go out first. You don't wait more than half a second

196

before you follow and run to the Jeep as fast as you can. Got it?"

"Got it."

He touched her cheek. "It's gonna be okay."

A shot rang out and shattered the kitchen window. Tess ducked and shrieked as glass shards flew through the air. The memory of that long-ago raid on her childhood home flashed across her features as clearly as if she'd screamed the words.

Damn. Going out the front door was suicide and the idea of Tess getting shot did not sit well. He grabbed her hand and tugged. "Change of plan."

TESS COULDN'T BELIEVE that in the last twenty-four hours she'd gone from being a boring accountant in the 'burbs to ending up in the middle of *another* armed showdown in the wilds of southern Idaho.

"Come on." Mac dragged her along.

She pointed the handgun he'd given her at the floor and crouched low as she followed him back into the living room. He turned off the lights as he went and the world became a mass of confusing shadows. The fire glowed in the stone hearth and she eyed the box of things Jessop had given her and swerved towards it as another shot rang out in the kitchen.

"What the hell are you doing?" Mac said, sliding to a stop.

It was too dark to see inside the box but her fingers searched and found that bookmark that Ellie had given her for her ninth birthday. Tess didn't care if it was supposed to be "evidence." It was her one and only physical link to her dead sister and no one was taking it away from her. She slipped it into her pocket.

"Come on," Mac told her impatiently.

She sniffed something on the air.

Mac swore.

"What is that?" she asked.

"Gasoline." His voice sounded funny. "Sonofabitch is gonna burn us out."

She crouch-ran towards him. "That's crazy. He'll lose his whole house."

"If we escape he'll lose more than that. Assault and attempted murder of a civilian *and* a federal agent? A man his age. He'll die in a prison cell."

She followed on Mac's heels, tempted to grab his shirt so he didn't leave her behind.

"If he's involved in the murders maybe the evidence is here and he's trying to destroy it?" she suggested. "He doesn't want the Feds combing the place and identifying his accomplices?"

Mac cursed again, then ran into the downstairs bedroom where he'd been snooping earlier.

"Jessop came back from his phone call with his revolver drawn," she told him. "Someone must have told him that we weren't mourning the loss of my family the way we should have been."

Mac started ripping out the cords from the back of a PC tower. She went to the window. Thick snow lay beneath the eight foot drop to the ground. There were footprints at the base and the strong odor of noxious fumes. She opened the latch and forced the window up, getting blasted by a frigid wind and the pungent odor of gasoline.

If that vapor ignited they were all screwed and considering

an open fire burned merrily in the other room it was only a matter of time before this place went up in flames. Her stomach turned over at the thought of burning alive.

"I'll go first," Mac told her. "You pass me the computer."

"Hurry."

Mac holstered his weapon and slid over the ledge and dropped to the ground. She wrestled the heavy metal box through the same gap and leaned down as far as she could so Mac could grab it.

A sound made her look over her shoulder a moment before something grabbed her leg.

She screamed and let go of the PC. Mac caught it. She dropped Mac's pistol as she grabbed onto the sill. Jessop had her leg, but Mac reached up and caught her wrist. She felt like she was being torn in two, but with a fierce yank Mac pulled her through the window and she fell in a heap on top of him. He immediately rolled them over and over until they were out of sight.

A loud bang made her flinch and a patch of snow spurted upwards a few yards away from where they lay in the snow.

"You'll torch the whole goddamned place, you maniac," Mac shouted at Jessop. Then a *whoosh* of flame rushed over their bodies and ignited a weak trail through the snow.

Mac grabbed her by the hand and dragged her to her feet. A piercing scream came from inside and Tess stared in horror up at the open window. Why didn't Jessop throw himself out the way they had? A second gunshot reverberated through the night and she gaped in horror, trying to figure out what just happened, but unable to make sense of it.

Flames swept hungrily over the dry timber and up the drapes, getting louder and fiercer as they consumed the old house.

Mac fought the heat to grab the computer. She spotted his Glock in the snow and scooped it up. He hooked a hand around her shoulders as they staggered away from the burning building. They reached the Jeep and he tossed the PC on the back seat. "Get in."

"What about Jessop?"

"He's dead."

Tess stumbled in the snow. The stink of smoke and gasoline clung to her clothes. "How do you know?"

Lines cut down the sides of his mouth. "That's what the second bullet was. Him taking the easy way out."

She put her hand on her stomach to stem the queasiness. She crawled into the passenger seat and dragged on her seat belt. He got in and started the engine, shoving the transmission into drive. She handed him the weapon he'd lent her, glad she hadn't had to use it.

Silently Mac placed the Glock back into his ankle holster.

Tess looked back at the flames which now engulfed the entire ground floor and were working their way up to the second floor. Henry Jessop had fed them dinner and tried to kill them within the space of an hour.

"Are you going to call nine-one-one?" she asked.

Mac shook his head. "The ranch hands will spot the flames any moment and use the well water to stop it spreading to any of the outbuildings. By the time the fire trucks arrive the house will be burnt to the ground. Until I know how Jessop found out I'm a Fed I'm not gonna trust any local cops." He threw her a look. "I'm hoping that hard drive contains enough information to lead us straight to the killer in DC."

She stared at the house in horror. "A man just died. You

aren't going to stop and report that?"

"I'll file a report as soon as we get to Salt Lake City." Mac lurched off the long driveway and onto the main road.

She glanced behind them again. Orange flames lit up the snow with a devil's palette.

Horror swept over her as everything that had happened penetrated. "He was going to kill us." She covered her mouth to hold back the sobs that wanted to escape.

"Yep. And bury us in the woods probably. No one would have ever known." He glanced at her shocked expression and gave a full-body wince. "Sorry, Tess. It's my fault you got hurt again. You didn't want to go to Jessop's. I should have respected your instincts."

Reaction set in and her teeth chattered uncontrollably. If she'd died she'd never have had the chance to tell Cole the truth, the real truth, not the surreal fabricated versions constructed by the media. Her family's past wasn't pretty but her version was accurate and spoke of people, not monsters. She had to tell him everything. Before it was too late.

Strong warm fingers wrapped around her clenched hands and squeezed. "You all right?"

"No. It might be scenic, but Idaho doesn't seem to agree with me."

"We seem to have stepped on the hornets' nest," Mac agreed. "I think we pissed someone off—we need to figure out who that someone is."

"These people have got to be stopped." She could barely utter the words.

His fingers squeezed hers harder. "That's why I go to work every day."

Her hands turned and her fingers entwined with his. He

201

was a brave man and she knew he took his job very seriously. Could she trust him to do the right thing by her brother? Or would he automatically assume the worst about Cole?

"My little brother's name is Cole. Cole Fallon." She closed her eyes, maybe trying to hide from her own betrayal. "He's a student in DC."

She could just see him between slitted lids.

Mac pressed his lips together. "I know. But thank you for telling me."

Tess drew in a sharp breath at that. Were they investigating her brother because he'd done something specific, or was he also guilty by association?

Should she mention the file with the picture of the murdered judge inside? She was starting to think she'd imagined that thing. All she knew for sure was her brain was too exhausted to make an effective decision right now.

"He's a nice kid. A good person," she insisted.

"Then he shouldn't have any problems, should he?" Mac said, carefully. Too carefully.

God.

He blasted the heat.

Her past was trying to engulf her present in its ugliness. No matter how fast she ran, she never seemed to quite escape its grasp. Maybe it was time to turn and make a stand.

CHAPTER SEVENTEEN

MAC DROVE STEADILY, weighing his options. Tess was asleep or pretending to be. Her eyes were closed and the dark shadows underneath and in the hollows below her cheekbones indicated exhaustion. What a shitty day. Two people had tried to kill her today and it was his fault. Both times he'd asked her to lie for him and then failed to protect her. He still felt nauseous from seeing Jessop hold that revolver to her head. The cloying scent of gasoline didn't help.

Maybe Tess was right not to trust people. Trusting him had almost got her killed twice.

His first plan had been to go into the Field Office in Salt Lake City, but what he absolutely needed was to secure the scene at Jessop's farmhouse and take this hard drive to Quantico as fast as possible.

He dialed the number for the closest resident agency in Pocatello a few miles away. He used Tess's earbuds so she couldn't overhear the other half of the conversation, just in case someone said something classified. Despite the hour, he got straight through to the senior agent there.

He introduced himself. "I need you to take over an investigation of a fire and self-inflicted gunshot fatality near Kodiak." He explained what had happened and told the guy the investigation it was in relation to.

The agent listened carefully, then said, "I really need to question you and the other witness."

"We'll both make full statements at Salt Lake City. I need to get this evidence to the lab in Quantico ASAP. Lives may depend on it."

The agent backed off. Probably didn't want to waste time arguing with an ASAC. The guy was going to need all his patience to deal with the locals.

"Any known white supremacist sympathizers amongst the local LEOs?" The FBI tried to keep tabs, but with over eighteen thousand law enforcement agencies in the US it was up to local forces to maintain their own checks on whom they employed. A 2006 internal FBI report had warned about increasing incidences of white supremacist groups infiltrating law enforcement—ghost skins, people who avoided overt displays of their true beliefs in order to be hired into positions of power, and to influence investigations and proceedings from the inside.

Some days Mac was freaked by the direction the country was taking. It made him more determined than ever to fight for what he believed the American dream stood for. It sure as hell didn't involve the KKK or their ilk.

"Sheriff out there has a reputation for being tough but fair. Some of his deputies are less...discerning, shall we say. But aside from the usual reports of excessive force"—which, whether true or false, pretty much came with the job—"we haven't heard of anyone in particular being a problem. Why?"

"Someone tipped Jessop off that I worked for the Bureau. Talk to the Field Office about sending Evidence Recovery Teams. I want that place locked down and gone over inch by inch. HQ will okay any extra help you require."

"If you're in charge of the task force looking into the murders in DC you're a long way from home. You think there's a connection to that case and the Pioneers?"

Mac didn't want that information leaked either. "All I know is when Jessop found out who I was he pulled a gun on me and my companion. Then when we got away from him he poured gasoline around his home and it went up in flames. Then he shot himself. We were damned lucky to get out alive."

The agent swore.

"I don't want anyone outside the Bureau knowing what happened and making any leaps. We need to keep what we discover quiet so we can round up these people before anyone else gets hurt."

Dylan Walsh was his next call. "Any developments?" he asked.

The guy yawned. "Other than me catching a couple of hours of sleep? Nope. Nothing."

Mac checked the clock. Seven-thirty p.m., nine-thirty back east. Sleep was always sparse on these big investigations. He didn't bother to apologize. "Any new murders?"

"Not yet."

Well, that was positive news. Mission focused criminals rarely stopped on their own, but if the killer discovered Jessop was dead perhaps they'd go to ground and give the FBI time to figure out their identities.

"I need to know who Henry Jessop late of Kodiak Falls, Idaho, spoke with on the phone tonight, and how he found out I was FBI."

"Don't I need a warrant for his phone records?"

"Yep. But the guy tried to kill me and then set his home on fire with him inside. Pretty sure it was to destroy evidence, possibly pertaining to these DC murders although it isn't fully established if he's involved yet. I think you'll be able to obtain a warrant." He shifted uncomfortably and glanced at Tess. She appeared to be asleep.

"Did Eddie Hines give you this lead?"

There was a note in Walsh's tone that alerted him that something had happened.

"Nope. We drove past Kodiak Compound on the way to Salt Lake City and stopped. We met this guy Jessop at the compound and he invited us to dinner at his neighboring ranch. He was sympathetic to the Pioneers so I figured it was worth the time to accept his invite. Why?"

"We?" Walsh asked instead of answering.

"I bumped into Eddie's sister at the prison. She agreed to wear a wire for us. Somehow he knew she was working with us. He attacked her."

"Same sister you went to see last night?" Walsh said casually.

"Yup."

"She with you now?"

"Uh huh."

"I see."

What the fuck did that mean?

"Can she hear this?"

"Nope."

"Look, boss, something *just* came in on the wire courtesy of the US Marshals Service—whom I seem to remember are not your biggest fans."

One of them might have tried to deck him during the Minneapolis terrorist investigation, but tempers had been frayed after terrorists had killed two marshals.

"Eddie Hines escaped about an hour ago," Walsh told him. "The prison thinks he had outside help."

Crap. Mac thought hard. *Could* Eddie's attack on Tess have been a setup? Could she have slipped Eddie something that had enabled him to escape? And at the farmhouse she'd been alone with Jessop when Mac had gone to search the bathroom…the thought flitted reluctantly through his mind. Except it didn't make sense. The prison guard had searched her thoroughly—Mac had watched and wanted to punch out the asshole. And Mac had given her his backup weapon at Jessop's farm. If she was in league with Jessop she could have put a bullet in Mac's brain and gotten rid of his body and the rental vehicle, and disappeared. No one would have ever known what happened to his foolish ass.

"The sister isn't the leak, Dylan."

"If you're sure." His fellow agent sounded doubtful.

Dammit. Once again Tess was coming under fire just for being part of the Hines family. Or was he being blinded by the pretty looks and sweet smile? Maybe she was outsmarting him every step of the way and he was too stupid to know it.

"Well, if anything happens to me," he told his buddy, "you know who to question first."

He glanced across at his passenger and she was no longer asleep. Her eyes were fixed on his in a penetrating stare full of betrayal. He hung up.

"It's not what you think, Tess."

Her lip curled a little.

"Eddie escaped." He watched a wave of fear wash over her features and wished he didn't have to be the one to break the bad news. "The prison thinks you might have slipped him something to help make that happen."

Her eyes widened in understanding, then narrowed in anger. "After what he did to Ellie I want him to rot in hell and never be released." She hugged her arms around herself. "He attacked me." Her hand rose to her throat. "He threatened to come after me and do horrible things. He's the last person I want to see out of jail."

"He won't get anywhere near you, Tess. Hell, look, we can't even get to DC and we're flying commercial. Eddie has no chance." He reached over to take her hand, but she pulled away.

Her smile was bitter. "You don't know that."

"I won't let anything bad happen to you—"

"Like you protected me at the prison? And again at Jessop's? Forgive me for not believing you're going to protect me when twice you've put me in the line of fire, and twice I was almost killed."

Mac stiffened though it was true. "Marshals will catch him long before he gets to DC."

"I'm not some clueless young thing you can sweet-talk into thinking everything is going to be okay, Mac. You are aware what I've lived through. So, if I want to be worried what my deviant brother might do to me, I will. If I want to be worried that the authorities will somehow try to accuse me of helping him escape despite it being bullshit, I will. I've seen how the system works. I know innocent people get caught in the crossfire. Literally and figuratively." She crossed her arms over her chest and set her jaw. She stared out the window and he saw her reflection in the glass. Scared. Vulnerable. Resigned.

Dammit.

He should call his boss with an update, but he'd rather go

to him with a bunch of answers than a bunch of questions. As head of the task force Mac had a lot of autonomy. It was time to call in some favors.

He dialed Lincoln Frazer who was more connected than anyone else he knew. The man answered at home. "Know anyone with a private jet who can pick me up in Salt Lake City and fly me to Quantico, ASAP?"

A dog barked in the background and Mac thought he heard a woman's laughter.

"Did I call at a bad time?" he asked curiously.

"No." Frazer cleared his throat. "There are people I can ask about a jet, but why are you in Utah when you're supposed to be running a task force out of DC?"

"I am running a task force out of DC. But I decided to pay Eddie Hines a visit in prison this morning—after which he decided to escape."

Fraser swore.

Mac went through today's escapades again, ignoring Tess's tense silence whenever he mentioned her involvement, keeping a careful eye on the road for deer. Totaling this car would top the day off nicely.

"You have the computer hard drive?"

Mac flicked a glance in the backseat. "Yup. Jessop was communicating with someone on a website called One-Drop-2-Many on the Tor server, but I couldn't see the conversation. Could have been innocuous." As innocuous as any hate site.

"Let me make a few phone calls. I'll see if Alex Parker or Ashley Chen can give us some help with that site. It's possible if we move fast, whomever Jessop was communicating with won't realize it's been compromised. What's your plan?"

"To go into the Field Office in Salt Lake and make a statement. Catch the first flight I can back to Quantico and then drive to DC. Tonight, if possible."

"You sure the sister isn't involved?"

"As sure as I can be."

Frazer was silent for a long moment, maybe hearing all the things he couldn't or wouldn't say. "Call me again after you make your statements and I'll update you on the flight situation. One thing, don't let that hard drive out of your sight for *any* reason."

Chain of evidence was vital, as was getting this thing back to the lab. "I don't intend to." He hung up and rubbed his hand over his face.

"Want me to drive for a while?" Tess offered.

"I'm fine."

Dark circles shadowed her eyes, but the day was far from over.

"We need to stop at the Field Office to make statements about what happened at Jessop's."

She huddled deeper into her jacket. "Won't I get in trouble for leaving the scene?"

"You followed the instructions of the senior lawman on the scene." He reached over and gave her arm a squeeze, trying to ignore the fact that touching her eased something inside him. "Just tell them what happened. I'm working on getting us out of Salt Lake City as soon as possible after that."

She swallowed and shifted away from him. She was tired and she was pissed and, frankly, he didn't blame her. "I just want to go home."

So did he. Before this asshole killed anyone else.

IT WAS TESS'S first time inside an FBI office and she hoped it was the last. She'd been there for several hours, going over and over the same details. The agents questioning her had maintained surly, unconvinced demeanors throughout. They didn't like the fact she'd left the scene, they didn't like the fact she'd visited her brother the same day he'd escaped from prison, they didn't like the fact her last name used to be Hines.

She didn't like it either.

They seemed convinced she had something to do with Eddie's escape but the idea of him being out there, hunting her, was terrifying.

"When was the last time you visited the Idaho property?" asked the agent whose expression suggested she had a permanent bad smell stuck in her nostrils.

"I told you. I never went back there until today and that was a spur-of-the-moment decision because of the snow storm." Tess's mouth was parched and she was in desperate need of a drink of water. She refused to ask for anything from these people.

The woman leaned back in her chair and tapped her pen on the pad of paper. Tess had already signed a written statement. "Why'd you hold onto the property?"

"My adoptive mother bought it."

"She have alt-right tendencies, too?"

Fire seared her bones. Tess leaned over the table. "Do not insinuate anything sinister or evil about Trudy Fallon. She was the best of people—better than you with your ingrained prejudice and lack of empathy."

The other agent in the room tapped his partner on the arm and the female glanced at the screen of his laptop. Her eyes widened. Tess assumed they'd found a picture of Trudy.

What would it have taken to persuade them she wasn't a bigoted extremist if Trudy hadn't been black? Had her mom known how much adopting them would change the narrative of Tess's and Cole's lives? Probably. Trudy wasn't just smart, she was wise.

"My mom was all about facing the past and changing it into something better rather than letting it beat you down. I didn't realize she'd kept the land until after she died." Trudy's will declared Tess manage the property until Cole was twenty-one. Then it became both of theirs to do with as they wished. Tess assumed the provision was so that she'd eventually be forced to tell him the truth about their parentage.

It was past time.

A swell of emotion expanded in her throat and made it impossible to speak. She missed her mom. It hadn't been a year yet and the ache of loss still cut deep.

The throbbing in her head had started an hour ago, intensified, and wasn't going away. It felt like there was little person inside her head, stabbing a knife into the back of her eye. She cradled her skull and closed her eyes.

"Are we done yet?"

The woman harrumphed and checked her notes.

"I'm a witness, not a suspect, right?" She pushed her chair back. "So, I can go, correct?" Tess stood, trying to project confidence not cowardice. Obviously, they were trying to delay her for some reason, but she was pretty sure that unless they arrested her she was free to go. "Where's ASAC McKenzie?"

The woman gave her another sour look, but the guy relented. "Let me escort you out and I'll try and find him for you."

Tess nodded, but then held her skull and squinted through

one eye.

What a day.

Following the one agent with the other on her heels she almost bumped into Mac who was walking along the corridor joking with another couple of agents. He seemed so perfectly at home in this environment, she would have rolled her eyes if she hadn't been in so much pain. There was no way he struggled to fit in anywhere.

He caught her by the shoulders and gave the other Feds a stern look. "You okay?"

"No. I have a raging headache," she said between gritted teeth. "And I've had enough of being interrogated. I want to leave. Now."

"You were questioning her this whole time?" His voice was sharp as he turned to the two agents who'd interviewed her.

"She's part of the white nationalist movement that might be involved in—"

"Tess is not part of any white nationalist movement." He sounded exasperated.

"She was a member of the Pioneers—"

"She was goddamned ten years old at the time of the raid." Mac didn't raise his voice, but his anger was obvious.

Despite the fatigue and pain something inside her melted.

"She left the scene of a crime—"

"She was with me. Was I supposed to leave her behind?" Mac planted his hands on his hips. "If she hadn't come with me she'd have been disobeying a federal law enforcement officer. You ever heard of being stuck between a rock and a hard place, Agent Coats?"

Coats, whose name Tess hadn't known, wasn't done. "It was important to make sure we had as many answers as possible if we're going to run this part of the investigation effectively." The woman wasn't backing down even though she sounded defensive.

"So why aren't you on your way to the farmhouse, interviewing people who might actually know some of the answers to your questions?" Mac asked.

"Because they were having more fun torturing me instead," Tess bit out. She was feeling snippy and irritable.

Mac examined her closely and then moved her until she stood beside a bench. "Sit down while I find you something for the headache."

She could fall in love with him for that alone. She nodded, keeping her eyes closed as she leaned her head back against the cool wall.

She could hear him talking heatedly with his colleagues, but she zoned out. She didn't care anymore. She was done.

"Here."

She looked down as he slipped two red tablets into her palm and handed her a cup of water from the dispenser.

"Thank you." She swallowed them and got a refill before tossing the cup in the trash.

"Let's go."

She followed him out to the Jeep and he opened the door for her. It was close to midnight, and the night was as cold and miserable as she was.

"Are we going to the airport?" She wanted to go home, wanted to sleep, wanted to forget she'd ever had the stupid idea to come to Idaho.

He grimaced. "We have tickets on the first flight out in the morning. Turns out all the people I know with private jets are busy." His eyes crinkled. "So much for contacts."

She didn't like the way her heart did a little dance of joy when he smiled like that so she looked away. Going into an FBI field office had been a big reminder of who Mac really was.

"I vote for finding a motel near the airport and grabbing a few hours' sleep," he said easily.

"I agree." Sleep hadn't come last night or the night before. She'd dozed for maybe an hour. The pounding in her skull was starting to lighten up in response to the painkillers and she breathed deeper. Storm clouds hung heavy overhead and she figured it was likely a weather headache. Her skull was her own personal barometer. The stress and lingering stink of smoke and gasoline didn't help.

Mac headed toward the airport but most of the signs showed "No Vacancies."

Her headache receded enough for her to open her eyes without pain. Mac went to change lanes and they both jolted when a horn blasted from behind.

"Shit," Mac exclaimed. "Sorry."

She glanced at him anxiously. His eyes were red-rimmed and his mouth was grim. Despite his indefatigable attitude exhaustion dragged at his features, but he was too stubborn to admit it. He'd been driving for hours and presumably hadn't slept much lately either. After ten minutes of driving around they finally spotted a place with a vacancy. He turned into the parking lot and pulled up outside the dingy looking office.

The place was a basic motel, backing on to the highway. Not the Ritz but not a total dive either. There was a bar across adjoining concrete parking lots. A row of trucks filled one. SUVs and minivans filled the other.

Mac went inside while she waited in the vehicle. When he

came back his lips were pinched into a thin line and she noticed the pallor of his skin.

"They have one room left, but it has twin beds. There are three conventions going on in town. Comic-Con, some science gig and a writers' thing. We can carry on driving around on the off-chance of finding something more upmarket, but frankly…I'm beat."

"Let's just take the room. It's not like we're going to jump each other." Despite the fact she found him attractive, there was no way she was dumb enough to become involved with a federal agent.

He grinned despite the fatigue, and one of those dimples came out to play. "You say that now, but this body has been known to drive women insane." He paused for effect. "Or maybe that was just my ex." He was grabbing his cell out of the console, "and maybe it wasn't my body, maybe it was my mouth—"

"Can it, McKenzie." She smothered a yawn and grabbed her purse and small case. "Even if you were one of the Chippendales I'm too tired to care." She was so tired she was five seconds away from falling over.

"You sure?" He was serious now.

"You keep to your side of the room. I'll keep to mine. We'll survive."

CHAPTER EIGHTEEN

MAC STARED AT the double bed with its limp pillows and ugly brown covers, then at Tess.

"I swear the clerk said it had two twins." The lying sack of shit.

"In that case, someone stole one of them." Rather than turning tail, she dragged her carryon luggage into the room and parked it on a chair.

"I can sleep on the floor," he offered.

Tess shuddered visibly as she eyed the carpet. "You'll catch something and die. I'll end up in prison because they'll assume I did it. Look, we've both had a shitty day." She sounded resigned. "I'm going to shower, change and sleep. You keep to your side of the bed and I'll keep to mine. This is no more intimate than us sleeping together in the car."

She had a point.

She'd had a harrowing day, although he'd be lying if he said he hadn't enjoyed the adrenaline rush—not of seeing her in danger—but of ferreting out clues pertinent to his investigation. The information justified his coming to Idaho at such a crucial time.

His phone rang and MC Hammer's "Can't Touch This" blared out. He swore.

Tess laughed and the tension on her face eased. "You

never struck me as a rap fan."

He turned it off without answering the call. "My ex. Once again proving she has terrible timing."

"She's persistent."

Mac rolled his shoulders. "She doesn't like to be told 'no.'"

"You playing hard to get?"

He narrowed his gaze. "I'm not playing."

"Maybe she still loves you."

"If she loved me she wouldn't have fucked her boss." Mac stopped speaking. This wasn't something he wanted to discuss with Tess.

"You sure it isn't pride that stops you calling her back?"

Everything got very quiet inside his head. "You think I don't know the difference between pride and love?"

"It's not that—"

"It's exactly that. Would you forgive someone who cheated on you?"

Her eyes flashed to his. "No. I wouldn't. But I've never loved anyone enough to marry them, have I?"

With that she opened her case, took out a toiletries bag and something to wear and walked into the bathroom and closed the door, locking it behind her.

Christ.

He scrubbed his face again, trying to wake up his tired brain. He shouldn't have snapped at her, but he didn't like being made to feel guilty for ditching a bad marriage, although maybe it was just Tess. Everything about Tess made him feel guilty, especially the thoughts he was keeping strictly to himself.

He checked the message from Heather—more nonsense asking if they could go for coffee. He shook his head in frustration. Why? Was she hoping Lyle saw them together? Why would she even want Lyle back after the guy cheated on her? Was Mac naïve to believe fidelity should be integral to a loving relationship? He thought of the people he knew in healthy relationships. No, he wasn't naïve. Heather was selfish and greedy. Lyle was the same.

Looking back now, he realized he'd married Heather partly out of lust, partly because she'd seemed like the kind of woman who'd make him look good to his bosses. She was social—too social, evidently—and knew how to suck up to the right people. He didn't want to think about what a disaster it would have been if she'd focused on one of his co-workers rather than one of her own. And Heather wasn't really a bad person. She was a liar and a cheat, but her main fault was being needy. She needed attention. She needed to be the center of people's attention and didn't mind causing a scene to make it happen.

He shrugged out of his jacket and draped it over the nearest chair. He should get a few hours' sleep while he had the chance. He eyed the narrow confines of the bed. It should be okay as long as neither of them crossed that invisible line.

He was a professional. He could do this.

If his bosses found out he spent the night in the same bed as David and Francis Hines's only remaining daughter when there was even the slightest possibility she might be involved in these murders—say goodbye to running his own field office any time in the near future. Except, sticking close to Tess made it easier to do his job. He might be able to gain her trust, which was something she obviously didn't give easily.

She was probably innocent, in which case there was no issue with this situation. Finding out her brother wrote computer code raised alarm bells what with the whole chatroom on the dark web thing. The average citizen wouldn't know how to mask their online identity, but Cole Fallon would.

The pipes rattled as the water turned on.

Even in his sleep-deprived state he had no trouble imagining Tess naked.

The light flickered, snapping him out of his base thoughts.

Use the enforced proximity to forward the case.

Mac casually lifted the lid of Tess's baggage and peered inside. There was nothing more damning than a change of clothes, including some rather sexy lingerie, and an ereader. He turned it on and checked out the books she liked. His eyebrows stretched high at the titles and covers: *The Devil's Doorbell, Taking Turns, The Dom's Dungeon.* She evidently enjoyed erotic novels. He made a mental note to check out some of the books—for research purposes.

She had a laptop, but he didn't have permission and wasn't proficient enough to bypass her password—which he assumed she had—before she got out of the shower.

He dumped his duffle on top of the drawers beside the bed. At least this way he kept an eye on the woman. A very close eye... Keep your friends close and your enemies closer, and all that. Not that he thought of Tess as his enemy. Never had.

That was the real problem.

When it came to Tess Fallon he wasn't objective.

He sat down on the edge of the mattress and the springs squeaked. *Great.* He kicked off his shoes and lay back, staring at the brown water stains on the ceiling. They'd removed the hard drive from Jessop's PC at the FBI field office and the hardware now resided in an evidence bag inside his duffle. That evidence wasn't leaving his side.

He yawned. To hell with it. He'd close his eyes until she came out of the bathroom.

Next thing he knew he woke up with a start in a pitch-black room to the sound of a mattress squeaking in the next room.

Where was he?

Then the moaning began.

"You have got to be kidding me," he muttered irritably.

A voice murmured in the darkness. "At least they seem to be having a fun."

Tess.

Mac let out a long breath. He'd forgotten where he was and who he was with. He glanced at the digital alarm clock. One fucking a.m.

Shit.

"If my experiences are anything to go by the whole thing will be over soon." Her voice was a velvet whisper.

At least she had a sense of humor. He turned toward her. His eyes were gritty, but light from the parking lot shone through the skinny drapes making it relatively easy to see. He made out her outline buried up to her nose under the covers. He was fully dressed on top of the bedding. Definitely a good thing.

"How long do you think it'll take?" His voice was husky. He shouldn't be talking to Tess about sex again, but he was curious. And until the guy in the next room got off no one was getting any sleep.

"Three minutes?" She sounded warm and languorous. "Four tops."

"Three minutes? Who the hell have you been dating?"

She snorted in a decidedly unladylike manner. "Apparently, I'm so incredibly sexy it's *my* fault."

He grinned. "There are pills for that."

Her smile flashed in the shadows.

"So I've heard. It's kind of hard to introduce that into the general conversation before you get naked with someone. Maybe I should have sprinkled some in his salad." She was silent for a moment as they listened to the wallbanger next door. "He cheated on me with my best friend even after I told her the sex was lousy," she said quietly. "They actually eloped to Vegas."

"Bastards."

"I haven't been able to forgive either of them, so I do understand your feelings for your ex. Sorry if I made you feel bad earlier. It was none of my business." Her voice was small, as if she'd worried about his hurt feelings.

"I shouldn't have snapped at you."

Their mattress creaked as she turned to face him. The rusty springs made them sink toward each other. All the saliva in his mouth evaporated, though sheets and two layers of clothing separated them. Everything about this felt intimate. More intimate than he'd been with anyone in years. Maybe ever.

"Julie always said she was a sex goddess so it probably *was* me." Tess sniffed.

"Your best friend declared herself a sex goddess?" Mac asked. He felt her nod. "You can do that?"

"Evidently," she mumbled.

"Does that mean I can declare myself a sex god?" He kept his voice low although there was no way the neighbors would be disturbed if the rhythmic knocking of the headboard was any indication.

Tess laughed. "Only if you're any good at it."

"I can last more than four minutes—"

"Sex god." Laughter echoed around the room. He hadn't heard much laughter from Tess. It was a nice sound.

"And the woman always comes first," he added, unable to resist even though he should know better. He closed his eyes, determined to try and get back to sleep.

"Super sex god." She sighed.

There was a crescendo of noise and screams—the good kind—from the adjoining room. Then blessed silence. The show was over. *Thank God.* He closed his eyes. The room was warm and he began to drift into that half-doze state.

"Not that it's always possible," she murmured.

"What?"

"Nothing," she said quickly. Too quickly.

"Yeah, baby. Get on your knees." A third voice joined in next-door and the sound of a slap came clear through the wall.

"You have got to be fucking kidding me," Mac growled.

"Are there *three* of them?" Tess said, aghast.

Mac smothered his frustration and squeezed his eyes shut. *Fuck.* "Apparently so."

"Oh, my God." She scooted up the bed and stuck her ear against the paper-thin barrier.

He grabbed her hand and pulled her back down. "Tess, you can't do that!" *Christ.*

"Why not?" She tried to tug out of his grip but he didn't let go.

"You can't spy on people having sex."

"But they're invading my privacy with their antics. How

can it be my fault if I listen?"

He kept up the pressure on her arm until she reluctantly lay back down.

"Lying in bed and listening is one thing. Pressing your ear to the wall is something else entirely."

"You're no fun," she complained.

Some sex obsessed thoughts entered his brain at that. He could be fun. They could be having a whole heap of fun right now if it wasn't for the fact Tess was a former, if unwitting, member of the Pioneers. He swallowed and reminded himself to let go of Tess's hand.

"How long ago did you break up with the guy who cheated on you with your best friend?" Keep it casual. Dig for information. Don't think about what they might be doing in the next room, or what the two of them could be doing in this one if only circumstances were a little different.

"Last summer," she said glumly. "When they got back from Vegas they were hitched. That was the first I heard about it. They were both *very sorry*." Her voice got quiet and he could barely hear her over the rhythmic banging next door. Hell, the combination of listening to someone else having sex and lying in bed next to an attractive woman was having an unwanted effect on his man parts.

Great. Just what I need.

"Jason and I were both instructors at a taekwondo club. I'd persuaded Julie to start taking some self-defense classes."

"At least you found out before you got too serious." But betrayal always hurt.

"True love seems to be a vicious myth."

"No kidding," he agreed. "You haven't dated since?"

The bed moved as she shook her head.

"The only male attention I've been getting is from my brother's college buddies who seem to think they'll get a credit for seducing anyone with a vagina."

Mac could imagine exactly what the frat boy type would think when they looked at Tess. His jaw clenched.

"My little brother is mad at me," she confessed quietly. "He overheard me saying that I thought an older woman being with a younger guy was gross, and then discovered he's serious about an older woman. Tact was never my strong suit."

Mac filed the information away for when his brain woke up. They were still banging next door and he was considering going in there with his gun.

"I received a lecture on equality from him and his buddies. It was humbling because they are so young and naïve and yet they were right. I was being sexist."

He grunted. "I guess it all depends on the age difference. Once people are adults who gives a damn as long as no one is being exploited."

Some days he was impressed by how mature he sounded.

"When was your last relationship?" When he didn't say anything, she added, "Sorry. I guess that's too personal for our relationship. It's just you know pretty much everything about me—"

"I didn't know your ex was a limp dick asshole."

She laughed but she sounded sad now. His silence had made her feel like an outsider, again, but there was no way he was discussing his dubious list of nameless hookups. The reminder of his "relationships" over the last two years made him a little ashamed.

"Well, it's nice to know I have some secrets left," she told him.

"You always this chatty in bed?" he asked. Amused.

"No." She sounded horrified. "I'm not chatty at all. I'm quiet. *Too* quiet." That statement seemed to hover between them like a challenge he was doing his best to ignore. The idea of making her scream…of touching her, of taking that peck on the lips they'd shared earlier and investigating the fuck out of it? It was killing him.

Her hands covered her cheeks as if they burned. "I'm mortified by the fact someone, well *three* someones, are having kinky sex about two feet away from where we're lying in bed like a couple of corpses. *Not*," her voice rose, "that I think we should be having sex. God." Her chest rose and fell rapidly as she seemed to hyperventilate.

She might deny it, but he knew she was attracted to him. He'd seen the way she watched him. He knew that even though she didn't want to, she had a thing for him. She always had.

And now she was all grown up, that attraction wasn't one-sided.

He could use that.

Even as he considered it he pushed the idea away. If Tess was as innocent as he believed she was, she'd already been used enough. He would do his job but he would not hurt her. Still, no harm in pushing things a little. "You said earlier that sometimes it wasn't possible. What did you mean?"

The pounding was getting louder and louder. If he hadn't been running on fumes he'd have been cheering them on.

"Nothing," Tess mumbled.

"Did you mean orgasms?"

She buried her head under the sheets. "Can we not talk about this?"

"Are you saying your ex never gave you an orgasm?"

She muttered incoherently.

"You know that makes him an asshole, right?"

"Sex is overrated."

The woman in the neighboring room started screaming.

Whoa. "I don't think she got the memo." Heat poured off his skin. "I've had enough." He sat up. "I'm gonna knock on the door, show them my badge, and scare the crap outta them."

She shoved the covers off from over her head. "Careful they don't drag you in for a kinky foursome."

He blinked. "What?" Then he remembered the covers of the books she had on her kindle.

"You know—a sexy cop comes to the door and they invite him in to play with his handcuffs?"

"Sexy cop?"

She slapped him on the stomach.

He laughed. "Do you have group sex fantasies, Tess?"

"What?" She gave a strangled cry. "No!"

"I'm FBI." He reminded her with mock seriousness. "I'll find out if you're lying to me…"

She slapped him on the stomach again and he grabbed her hand just in case she accidentally made contact a little lower and got more than she bargained for.

He lay back down and rolled onto his side. "BDSM? Emphasis on the 'S' for slapping?"

She growled. "I just like hitting you." She pulled her hand away, and he let go before he did something really stupid like move it lower. He was playing with fire, but he didn't intend to take this further than teasing.

"I'm not into anything. The idea of some guy blindfolding

me and smacking my ass makes me want to punch someone."

"But you like reading about it?" he guessed. He could feel the heat coming off her face in waves.

"How on earth do you know that? Did you have my reading habits investigated? Is that gonna turn up in some case file somewhere? Tess Fallon likes to read Lexi Blake and Beth Kery—put her on a goddamn watch list?" She was getting angry and he caught her hand when she went to smack him again.

He leaned up on his elbows, edged closer and smoothed the hair off her face. She was getting upset and no wonder. He wouldn't want someone prying into his life in such detail. "It's okay, Tess. It isn't in any report. I'm joking with you. I snuck a look at your ereader earlier," he admitted.

"Because you thought I might be reading what? Some Neo Nazi crap?"

"I was curious. That's all," he soothed. He held fast to fingers that fought him with all her strength, but he didn't threaten. He didn't want her to break his nose with a ninja trick.

"I was just curious," he whispered again. He lay back down, their shoulders touching, still holding her hand as the *ménage-à-trois* did the bump and grind close by.

"When I was a little girl they tried to control everything about me. What I did, what I learned, what I thought, what I read." Her words crashed down on him like a hammer.

Ah, shit. He remained quiet. He hadn't thought about that when he'd been prying into her life. They'd tried to control everyone with their authoritarian system. Mac had always admired how strong Tess had been to resist the ideology of hate when that was all she'd ever been shown.

"No one is going to shame me into not reading whatever the hell I want."

"I wouldn't dream of it."

"I read all sorts of books from erotica to fantasy," she said fiercely. "Now I'm pissed that I don't even get to keep that kind of secret."

He squeezed her hand. "I shouldn't have pried. I'm not gonna put it in any report."

Her shoulder shoved him but he gripped her hand tighter.

"But it's *my* business, Mac. Not the FBI's."

"I won't tell the FBI, sweetheart."

"You *are* the FBI," she gritted out.

"Not tonight." For once he wished that were true. "Tonight, I'm plain old Steve McKenzie discovering new things about a woman he likes and is getting to know better."

Which unfortunately was true.

And there was a weird silence that filled the space between them. After everything they'd been through together there was no denying they shared a bond, something that usually took years to establish. It made him a little sad that this attraction between them was so forbidden. Or maybe that's why it was so compelling.

"How long can they last?" She sounded anguished as the pounding started up again next-door.

He laughed. "If it was one guy then maybe an hour if he paced himself."

"That's a damned lie."

God, she was funny. And the idea of proving how long a guy could last was becoming mighty tempting.

He squeezed her fingers.

"If it's two guys and one girl, which it sounds like, then

this shitshow might go on all night."

"I'm so tired I might go sleep in the bathtub." She pulled the pillow over her head.

He remembered something he should have thought of ten minutes ago. He dug into his duffle, fingers searching in the darkness.

"Here." He had ear plugs he used for the gun range. She took them from him and put them in. They both stared at the ceiling for a few minutes before fatigue gripped him again and smothered him like a pillow. Just before he fell asleep her hand slipped into his again and she gave his fingers another gentle squeeze.

His heart gave a jolt. For one terrifying moment, he considered tasting her lips again, letting his hands roam that body and play out a few of her favorite scenes. Then she let go of his hand and turned away.

The sense of loneliness that engulfed him took him by surprise. *FBI agent. SAC by forty*, he reminded himself.

He wrapped the words around him and tried to make them matter.

His daddy's bitter smile flashed through his mind, a reminder of what happened to people who didn't follow some sort of moral compass. Tess was not for him, not even for a one night stand, assuming she'd be interested in something that shallow and brief. It wasn't her fault. It was a matter of optics and didn't that make him feel like a sonofabitch.

But even if she was interested he couldn't afford to be. Didn't matter how tempted he was, the only thing that mattered was proving he knew how to do his job. Proving he was worthy of his vow and honorable enough to protect the American people, one unimpressed soul at a time.

TESS OPENED HER eyes. Sound was muted as if she was underwater. A heavy weight pressed down on her, crushing her lungs. Thick darkness surrounded her. She couldn't inhale enough oxygen and the air she did breathe was cloying and stale. She was hot, suffocating, buried alive. Fear drumrolled in her chest and she cried out, bucking, trying to get free.

"It's okay. Tess. *Jesus*, Tess!"

Strong hands ripped away the blanket that covered her face and grabbed her shoulders.

It was still dark, but there were shadows now, shades of gray. She could move. She could breathe. Sound was muted and she finally remembered she had ear plugs in. She pulled them out as she kicked off the remaining covers, her lungs pumping, sweat making her skin clammy.

Steve McKenzie stared down at her, a dark silhouette of a man. Her heart beat sped up for a different reason.

"I couldn't breathe. I panicked."

"I gathered." His voice was soft. Deep but not gruff.

She had always loved his voice. It soothed her, made the fear lessen its grip on her body that was as tense as stone.

"Sorry," she said.

He smiled.

She reached up and stroked her hand over his jaw. Sandpaper roughness grazed her palm. She loved it.

"Tess."

She put her finger against his full lips, feeling the heat of his mouth burn her skin. "When I was a little girl I was completely head over heels in love with you."

The quiet of the room pressed around them.

"I know."

She inhaled the warm scent of him. Wondered what it would be like to wake up with him every morning. Emotions squeezed her throat. Pain. Bitterness. Acceptance. "But you left me anyway."

"Yes."

Something glittered in his eyes as he smoothed the hair off her forehead before he leaned down to brush his lips against hers.

"I'm sorry," he whispered.

She let the silence stretch. Let their shared history settle.

"I know." She leaned up and returned his brief butterfly kiss. Tasted him. He stiffened against her and she thought he'd retreat from her now. He didn't. His hands still gripped her shoulders and he shifted his weight until he was lying on top of her, settling between her legs as he eased her lips apart with his.

She opened for him. Touched, tangled, explored his mouth with her lips, tongue, teeth as he did the same. Her hand slid over his shoulder and up into his short hair.

"We can't do this," he told her, but at the same time his hand cupped her breast and found her nipple through the soft cotton.

She ran her hands over his shoulders, down his back, feeling the ridges of muscle that flanked his spine. Her fingers found the groove in his back as he pulled her pajama top up and exposed her breast. Then he dipped his head and took the sensitive tip into his mouth and pleasure shuddered through her body, making her toes curl.

Impatiently, he dragged the top over her head and stared down at her nakedness.

Heat expanded in her chest as the cold air licked her skin. And then he was kissing her again, her nipples abrading against the cotton of his shirt, hot sparks of desire shooting right through her. She kissed him back, gripping his hair as his fingers slid down her body, pressing against her clitoris, gently stroking her. Lazily. Steadily. Like there was no need to rush. No need for haste.

Her hips rose, her body yearning for a release that was just out of reach. And still he drove her gently, refusing to change his pace until she was frantic with want and need. She held her breath as he slipped those clever fingers under the material of her pajama bottoms, but didn't dive inside. He teased the sensitive flesh of her labia, stimulating her leisurely, keeping up a gentle motion when part of her wanted hard and fast. But hard and fast with a man had never given her an orgasm.

How did he know how to drive her crazy? How did he comprehend her body needed this when her mind wanted something else entirely?

She'd climaxed on her own but never with a partner. She could feel him hot and hard against her thigh and wanted him inside her, but what he was doing... What he was doing made every cell in her body unwind and rewind, over and over again until she couldn't take it anymore. But she never wanted this feeling to stop.

Her body started to shake and she lost the ability to think, to process. Every sense focused on the coaxing touch between her legs.

She parted her thighs, silently begging him for what she thought she needed, but he kept on stroking her, slowly, lightly, inexorably pushing her toward that pinnacle, until she wavered on a shallow ledge.

He pressed one fingertip barely inside her as he pressed his palm against her mound and pinched her nipple harder than she expected at the exact same moment. She crashed over that edge, going into freefall as she shuddered and shook all the way to the bottom of the cliff, smashing onto the rocks in an avalanche of pleasure that made every particle of her being shatter.

As she lay there gasping he withdrew his hand and leaned down to kiss her tenderly on the lips.

He eased up into a sitting position and went to climb off the bed.

She grabbed his wrist. "Don't you want to…"

His lips turned into a frustrated smile. "I can't."

Then he stood, gathering his duffle bag and heading into the bathroom, leaving her to the cold, stale air and the quiet anger of not being quite good enough.

CHAPTER NINETEEN

HER BURNER PHONE dinged with an incoming message as she headed along Whitehaven Trail in Dumbarton Oaks Park. It was still dark. She hadn't gotten much sleep lately and the strain of living a double life was beginning to tell.

She couldn't wait for the subterfuge to be over, to deliver her final message and openly begin the fight. She couldn't wait to reveal who she was and revel in her achievements with the thousands of people who thought the way she did. This was a call to action that her people would recognize. The federal government had stolen the republic from the people. The people were stealing it back.

She slowed to read the text message in case it was relevant to this morning's mission.

A weblink appeared. An image slowly downloaded. She stumbled to a halt, panting in the cold air as a photograph of a burned-out farmhouse revealed itself. Her heartbeat reverberated in her ears like an echo chamber. Nothing remained of the building except two unstable-looking chimney stacks, the embers still smoking under bright klieg lights. The snow was blackened with soot and torn up dirt.

But she recognized it.

She quickly read the article. *"One man, Henry Jessop, believed dead. Arson suspected. Feds investigating."*

She squatted, resting one hand on the ground. *No!* He couldn't be dead.

She covered her mouth with her hand. Why was his death being investigated by the Feds? Had they connected him to the DC killings? Had they connected him to her? She stared around, looking for signs that this was a setup and that agents were hidden in the bushes ready to pounce. But it was too dark to make out much.

Rage filled her.

She needed to destroy the phone and figure out what the Feds might have found out. The old man wouldn't have given them away. That's no doubt why he was dead and the house destroyed. He'd sacrificed himself rather than give away the cause. He was a martyr. Another hero who'd dedicated his life to the revolution. She wouldn't let him down.

The faint sound of footsteps approached from around a bend in the path, masked by the noise of the nearby creek rushing toward downtown at full spate. She was in a secluded section of the trail, along a narrow gorge, hidden from the road by the heavy shadows and a thick stand of trees. Even though the branches were bare of leaves she couldn't see anybody hiding. If Feds were there she wouldn't go down without taking a few of them with her. She pulled her ball cap lower, then reached up to grip the weapon that nestled in a holster in the small of her back. She didn't have a suppressor this time. It wouldn't fit.

She started jogging, slowly, as if she was in this for the long haul—which she was.

Congressman Adam Trettorri came into view in keeping with his winter pre-dawn routine. He was one of the youngest politicians in DC. Handsome. An Army vet. Openly gay.

He was an abomination. The worst kind of monster because the outer package was so perfect.

She waited for him to pass before she drew the pistol. She turned and aimed for center mass. The noise was deafening and reverberated off the ravine walls.

He stumbled and crashed to his knees.

She approached, moving fast. She needed to get out of here ASAP. The Naval Observatory wasn't far away, and the home of the new Vice President, along with all the Secret Service that entailed.

Trettorri lay on his front now, not moving. Blood bloomed on his right side. She used her foot to try to roll him over onto his back, but he was a heavy sonofabitch.

She leaned down to wrestle him over, surprised when he grabbed her foot and yanked. She fell on her ass and scrambled backwards, Nikes slipping in the wet leaves. He reared over her despite the gunshot wound and tried to snatch the weapon out of her hand.

Even wounded he was stronger than she was. She twisted and fought within his grasp. She looked into his determined blue eyes and felt a spurt of fear.

"The Taliban didn't get the better of me." His voice was hoarse, but he kept right on talking. "I'll be damned if some hate-filled little bitch back home will."

"This isn't your *home*," she spat. "Your filth should be drowned at birth."

"I was thinking the same thing about you." He laughed despite the fact he was bathed in sweat and blood and in obvious pain.

She dug her fingers into the wound on his back and he reared away in agony. She jumped to her feet. She was covered in his blood and it wouldn't be long before the cops came to investigate the gunshot. She had to get out of here.

Without another word, she pointed the gun at where the freak lay panting in the dirt and pulled the trigger.

Blood spurted and she nodded in satisfaction and smiled. Seemed this hate-filled little bitch had gotten the better of him after all.

She ran down to the creek and washed the blood off her hands and face. Her clothes were black so bloodstains wouldn't show. She sloshed her sneakers in the icy shallows and decided to cross the stream then cut through the woods into the nearby Rock Creek Park Trails system. She needed to scrub every centimeter of her skin to eliminate that bastard's vile residue from her body. His scent was acrid in her nostrils.

Another message sent.

Shivers wracked her body and her teeth hammered against each other until she started running again. After a few hundred feet, her blood heated as her muscles burned. Half a kilometer south of where she'd shot the congressman she removed the SIM card and tossed it in the creek. The cell followed ten seconds later.

She grinned and picked up the pace on the race home.

The Feds didn't know a damned thing and they wouldn't figure any of this out until it was too late. Henry Jessop's death marked the start of the revolution. It wouldn't be long before the whole world knew what a hero he was. What heroes they both were. She was ready to lead this war. Hell, she'd already started. Soon others would follow and this charade would be over.

MAC CLASPED HANDS with Alex Parker who was a cybersecurity consultant for BAU-4. He'd worked with the guy during the Minneapolis mall investigation, but they'd never actually met. Now they, along with Lincoln Frazer, were in some sort of specially shielded room in the laboratory complex at Quantico where experts examined the effects of viruses and trojans on different computer systems. They'd had to leave all electronics outside and they were effectively cut off from the world.

"Thanks for the use of your jet." Mac smiled though part of him felt grim. "I enjoyed meeting your business partner."

"Haley's one of a kind," Parker agreed.

Mac had gotten a call around five a.m. to say he could hitch a ride straight to Quantico on Parker's company jet if he wanted. Tess had opted to wait for the commercial flight they'd booked, saying she needed to be in DC by noon. She was trying to put a little distance between them.

Yeah, after their not so innocent encounter, she was definitely trying to put some distance between them.

He'd let her.

He forced Tess out of his head. Maybe he'd call her when this was over, just to say goodbye. They were both better off pretending they'd never spent the night together listening to other people have sex and then, finally, giving into temptation.

Sonofabitch.

"Haley's a talker." Parker eyed him. "Don't believe half of what she tells you unless it's about the cost of her shoes. You could arm a third world nation with what she spends on shoes."

"I saw the shoes."

Parker grunted. Mac knew some of his history from friends at the Bureau. Alex Parker had once been incarcerated in a Moroccan jail and rumors were he'd got there by working for the CIA though they'd always denied any connection.

They'd never admit anything else.

Haley had filled in a few gaps. She, Alex Parker, and another friend from their days at MIT had started their own private security business from scratch and were now in such high demand they could barely keep up. She dealt with the management side, recruiting the muscle, handling logistics and basically telling everyone what to do.

"You have the hard drive?" Parker asked.

Mac handed over the evidence bag containing Jessop's computer. Wearing gloves, Parker signed and dated it and removed the item from the bag. Mac tried to concentrate on what Parker was doing as he plugged the drive into something that looked more like a complicated circuit board than any actual PC.

What Mac hadn't known was that he and Parker had more in common than he'd realized. Both of them had lost their mothers to cancer at a young age, and Parker's father had been a professional gambler who'd gotten his ass murdered in a back alley in Carson City. The guy sounded as much of a loser as Mac's own father had been.

Parker's friendship with Lincoln Frazer, who was notoriously distant and aloof, was the subject of much internal gossip inside the Bureau, but Haley didn't know any more about that than he did. Mac had first met Frazer during a posting to LA. Frazer had a reputation for being critical and cynical. A perfectionist who didn't tolerate fools. Mac and Frazer hadn't really spoken much until they'd been assigned together on a task force looking for a serial killer hunting street prostitutes in Hollywood. They'd caught the guy and he'd been executed in record time for California.

Happy days.

Mac and Frazer had gradually become good friends when they'd both worked out of Quantico, but it had taken a lot of years to establish that relationship. Frazer and Parker had hit it off almost straight away. There was something intriguing about Parker—the way he seemed capable on so many different levels. Mac had a feeling the guy had more secrets than the *politburo.*

Lincoln Frazer could have climbed as high as he wanted inside the FBI, but he'd chosen to stick with the Behavioral Analysis Unit. His focus was on catching criminals, not shaping policy, even though the guy liked power.

When the silence became oppressive Mac asked Frazer, "Was that a woman I heard at your house last night?"

Frazer eyed him narrowly.

"He has two of them now. And a dog," Parker interrupted without looking up. "And despite his sour expression he loves every minute of it."

Frazer's lips twitched. "You and Rooney set a date yet?"

Parker grunted. "She didn't tell you?"

"What?"

Parker eyed him grimly. "After telling me for months that she wanted to wait until after the baby was born, Mal suddenly decided she wants to get married in *April.*"

"Is that a problem?" Frazer asked.

"Nothing is a problem if it gets her down the aisle, but her mother wants a big fancy wedding, and I just want Mal and a preacher. Guess which one of us is getting their way?"

"Senator Tremont is a formidable mother-in-law to take on."

"Don't I know it."

Frazer was clearly holding back a grin. "So you have six weeks to plan a wedding?"

"About that. Which is why, despite female objections, I hired a wedding planner out of DC. Hopefully all I need to do is show up and say 'I do.'"

Mac and Frazer snorted at the same time. They'd both been through the grind of a wedding and a divorce. Frazer had obviously moved on though, something Mac had never expected to see.

The memory of sleeping beside Tess flitted through his mind. There'd been something unique about sleeping with a woman and not having sex. Which had been fine until she'd woken him up with her nightmare. And they'd had sex.

It was only natural he'd been turned on—an attractive woman beside him, an enthusiastic threesome next-door. Her sweet scent and lax warmth invading his senses. It would have been more worrying if he hadn't woken up with a cast iron dick. But to act on it? Monumentally stupid. He had no idea how he'd found the strength to stop at third base when a home run had been screaming his name.

Thankfully he'd been able to prevent himself crossing that last line of self-destruction, but it was more a technicality than a save should anyone in the Bureau ever find out what had gone on in that motel room.

Fuuuck.

"What about you?" Frazer asked unexpectedly as Parker booted up the drive and bypassed the password.

Mac gave him a patented blank stare.

"I heard your ex split with her new husband."

How the hell had Frazer heard that?

"She is the bane of my life," he conceded.

"What's the deal with the daughter, Tess Fallon?" Frazer asked.

Mac crossed his arms. "There is nothing going on with the daughter."

"Never said there was anything going on." Those blue eyes were amused now. "Just asked what the deal was. Think she's telling the truth about her lack of involvement in these murders?"

Mac thought about the question objectively. "She has an alibi for the rabbi's and the DJ's murder. She was raised by a black woman and does taxes for a bunch of non-profit civil liberty groups. As far as I can tell she's a model citizen." He fucking hoped she was a model citizen after making her quiver and tremble and cry out in the darkness. Otherwise his career really was toast. "It could all be a cover," he conceded. "She's very protective of the little brother which raises a few questions about his possible involvement. She hadn't contacted Eddie-the-asshole in all the years he's been incarcerated." He stared through the glass windows at the other FBI personnel going about their work. "When she was a kid she wasn't like the other Pioneers. She was quirky and kind. She couldn't exactly change her circumstances back then. I liked her," he admitted reluctantly. "I still like her. She's a nice person."

"Nice?" Frazer's voice held a bit of a sneer.

"What's wrong with 'nice'?" he challenged. Although *nice* wasn't the most pertinent word he'd use to describe Tess.

Frazer raised his brow.

"Fine. She's whip-smart and hard-working and, despite the crappy relations, is funny as hell." Sexy, too. He kept that thought to himself. He desired Tess Fallon in a way he hadn't allowed himself to desire anyone, not since he'd discovered his wife's favorite dictation position was over her boss's desk.

One side of Frazer's lips curled but whatever he'd been about to say was interrupted when the machine Parker was working on gave a sharp beep.

Mac watched as Parker scrolled through lines of gibberish code. The guy wrote down a series of long numbers.

"I checked her out," Parker told him. "Frazer contacted me last night and I spent time getting into the One-Drop-2-Many site on the Darknet. I ran Tess's IP address and usernames while I was waiting on some hacking tools to do their thing. I found no evidence of her trying to cover her tracks, or visiting anything more dubious than Tumblr."

A sense of relief washed over Mac.

Parker looked up. "Couldn't get a handle on the brother, mainly because I didn't have enough time to dig around his VPN."

The machine beeped and Parker switched his attention back to the task at hand.

"Find anything on the One-Drop site?" Mac asked.

Parker twisted his lips. "Plenty, but it's all encrypted unless you're signed in as a verified user and whoever set up the site knows their stuff. There's no money exchanging hands so that makes tracing people harder. One of my more dubious online aliases applied for membership but I have a feeling these people have a more referral based membership than volunteers." He shrugged. "I copied everything and sent it to the hate crimes people at HQ, but it'll take time. I also gave the task of cracking anonymous IDs to one of my newest recruits. He's just out of high school. Google and I fought to hire him."

"Why'd he choose you?" Mac asked, intrigued.

Parker gave a sharp grin. "I challenged him to a contest as to which of us could hack a specific internal phone number from the NSA database."

Mac's eyes bugged. "You hacked the NSA?"

"I have an ongoing contract to conduct pen tests—penetration tests—at regular intervals. The contest was a setup. I let the kid win and had him call the number, which just happened to be the line in the office where we did the hack. As soon as I answered the phone all his systems crashed with ransomware." A cool smile played around Parker's eyes. "He wanted to know how I did it. I told him if he worked for me for six months I'd tell him."

"But you'd trust him with information important to a federal investigation?"

Parker regarded him calmly. "These are identities the investigation won't figure out without his help. You don't learn to hack by signing into Facebook and saving your passwords in the keychain."

"How do you know if you can trust him?" Mac wasn't convinced.

"You look at what people do with secrets or zeros they uncover. If they auction them off to the highest bidder on the dark web, regardless of who the buyer is or what they intend to do with the information, then you probably don't want that person working for you. If they offer it on the gray market to pay their mother's medical expenses and carefully vet those they intend to sell it to, you've potentially got a keeper."

Mac nodded. He didn't understand much about computers beyond email and the internet, but he did understand the veracity of people's actions. If they were honorable when they thought no one was looking, they were likely good guys. But good guys sometimes went bad.

"Anything on Jessop's machine?" He nodded at the screen.

Parker grimaced. "You want the good news or the bad news?"

Mac groaned.

Frazer said, "Bad news."

"I always knew you were a pessimist. Someone cleaned off this hard disk and reformatted the drive in the not too distant past."

"The good news," Mac pressed. He'd been banking on them getting something concrete out of this machine.

"Some of the people who work for me can recover a lot of information that hasn't been written over, but it's going to take a little time."

"FBI can't do it here?"

Parker shared a look with Frazer. "Chen might have a shot."

Frazer frowned. "She's in New Orleans until tomorrow night."

"It's up to you guys. The FBI will be able to crack it eventually, but I employ the people the FBI turns to when they get stuck." Parker shrugged with an air of relaxed confidence. "I'm offering a free service but if you want to keep it in-house..."

Mac drew in a deep breath. "We'll take all the help we can get."

Parker grinned. "More good news is, Jessop has been using the machine since it was wiped." He typed in some instructions and downloaded information to a blank thumb drive. "Here's a list of his contacts and email addresses. Copies of his emails. I pulled his phone records last night and figured out he was regularly calling a burner in DC. Could be our shooter. I have a trap set so that the next time that burner hooks up to a cell tower it alerts me, but something tells me as soon as the owner of that burner realizes Jessop is dead they'll ditch the phone and dump as many things as they can that link them. I do have historical information on where that phone connected to cell towers that I will send to you."

"You were busy."

"Didn't get much sleep."

Mac didn't either. For different reasons. "That's a big help. Thanks. Any idea who told Jessop I was a Fed?"

Frazer spoke up. "Yep. Jessop called a local deputy, but that deputy claims Jessop was asking about a couple of trespassers on his land so the guy tracked down your rental car information for him. When he realized you were an agent he told Jessop not to do anything stupid. Obviously, Jessop didn't listen."

Mac nodded. "We need to keep an eye on that cop. Just in case."

Frazer nodded. "I already spoke to ViCAP. I'm on it." There was a system in place to cloak investigations of law enforcement personnel so they couldn't discover for themselves that they were under the microscope.

"Any sign of David Hines's manifesto?" asked Mac.

"Is that what he called it?" said Parker.

"Nah. He called it something like The Pioneers' Pathway, or some such bullshit," Mac said.

Parker typed that in but got nothing.

"Can you get me any of the actual wording? They might have buried it under a layer of crap. Techs can search for hidden content."

Mac tipped his chin. "I need to go to my apartment but I'm pretty sure I wrote notes on it. There was one paper copy but we never found it at the compound."

Was Tess right? Had Hines had a girlfriend? Might she have kept the original?

"I'm done here." Parker stood. "You can turn this over to the other analysts to see if they can find anything useful in the documents."

Frazer nodded and they put the drive back into the evidence bag and Frazer signed off on it.

Mac checked the time. Almost ten. "I need to check in with the US Marshals Regional Fugitive Task Force. See if they picked up Eddie yet."

Frazer grimaced. "The fact he escaped now when something is going down disturbs me."

"I think he thinks the revolution is about to start and doesn't want to miss it." Mac was pissed. "He threatened Tess."

"Think he meant it?" Parker asked.

Mac pressed his lips together and felt the pressure build up inside his chest. "Yeah. He meant it. But he isn't smart enough to outwit the marshals."

"Unless he has outside help."

And there Mac was, thinking about Tess again.

They left the shielded room and his and Frazer's and Parker's cells all started dinging like slot machines.

Mac swore as he checked the messages. "There's been another shooting. A congressman."

"Burner pinged off a cell tower near the Naval Observatory," Parker told him.

"That's close to where Trettorri was shot."

"So we have a likely connection between Jessop and the shooter," said Frazer.

Mac's teeth clenched together hard enough to shoot pain through his jaw. "I need to get back to DC." They started walking towards the main entrance. Mac got another text that stopped him in his tracks. "Sonofabitch."

"What is it?"

"Ballistics came back on the shell casing found at the rabbi's murder. Harm traced it to a gun that was used in a robbery twenty-two years ago." He looked up. "A pistol believed to be part of the cache stolen by David Hines and the Pioneers."

The links to a group he'd thought eliminated years ago kept multiplying. This wasn't over.

"I thought we recovered all those weapons?" Frazer said.

Mac nodded. "Most of them, but we were never sure exactly how many were sold before the raid or how many were stolen from the dealer. He wasn't the most reputable witness."

"What make is the gun?" Parker asked.

"Smith & Wesson Sigma Semi-Automatic Pistol, .40 cal."

"They started making those in 1993, so it was a new weapon at the time of the robbery," Parker told him.

"The fact it turned up now for these murders has to be symbolic. Maybe David Hines gave it to Jessop who gave it to the killer?" Mac shrugged. "I'm going to go have a quick chat with Harm as I'm here. See if he has anything else to tell me."

Parker checked his watch. "I can give you a ride to DC in about an hour. I have to get fitted for a new tux." His expression suggested he'd rather jump out of an airplane without a chute.

"You already have a tux," said Frazer.

Parker's lips pinched. "Apparently, I need another one to

get married in."

"Mal's worth it." Frazer suppressed a smile and slapped Parker on the back.

"Glad you think that way because you're my best man. You're gonna need one, too."

Frazer squeezed his eyes closed. "Damn."

Parker nodded. "You're welcome."

Mac's cell buzzed with another text. "Can you drop me off at the George Washington University Hospital in DC?"

"Sure," Parker said.

"What's at the hospital?" Frazer asked.

Mac showed them the latest text from Walsh.

Trettorri was alive.

CHAPTER TWENTY

I T WASN'T THAT late as the cab pulled up outside Tess's Bethesda home, but night already crept over the sky. She'd spent most of the day stuck in the Denver airport, waiting for a connection that had been delayed due to mechanical failure. She should have taken Mac up on his offer of a ride in a private jet to Quantico, but she'd needed to distance herself from him after their eventful night together.

She was humiliated by what they'd done. Or rather, by what he hadn't done. It had driven home the divide between them.

At what moment had he switched from being all-in to being only prepared to give her a pity orgasm? When had he gone from being consumed-by-the-moment to clear-headed enough to bring her to climax and let her down gently, as if he was somehow bestowing some gift on her?

Or maybe he'd never been consumed-by-the-moment. Maybe that had been all her.

God, she was furious, and mortified, and goddamned fucking furious.

She'd enjoyed his company way more than was healthy for her heart. She'd had no plans to become involved with a man who pried her deepest, darkest secrets wide open, even though he already knew most of them in excruciating detail.

Then he'd kissed her and she'd reacted like a frantic virgin. She wasn't.

She didn't need a man.

She fished around for her wallet and handed the cabby her credit card. She touched the thumb drive in her purse. Should she throw it away and pretend she'd never seen it? Or give it back to Cole at the same time she told him about their parents?

Why not get all her confessions over in one go? While she was at it she'd ask him about that paper file, too. Maybe someone had planted it in his drawer? Maybe he had a perfectly innocent explanation for having it.

Or maybe she'd imagined it.

The way her brain buzzed right now that was completely possible. She pursed her lips. Nope, that was plain old denial. She retrieved her receipt from the cab driver and climbed out, dragging her carry-on, shouldering her laptop.

She was a wreck. Fitful sleep for the last three nights. Getting involved with a man she couldn't trust. Worried for one brother, scared of the other. Terrified of her name being released to the press and her reputation shredded.

With the flight delay, she'd had to postpone a meeting with her biggest client and they hadn't been happy. It would take a miracle to make it through this mess with her business intact.

The idea of a bath and bed was beyond appealing. She needed to get inside her home and close out the world's ugliness. She'd seen on the news an openly gay congressman had been shot in an incident similar to the attacks on the judge and his wife, the DJ, and the rabbi. The congressman was in critical condition in the hospital. She prayed he survived and told the police who was committing these vicious acts.

Eddie was still at large. She shivered as she glanced around her quiet street.

The only advantage of having to hang out in a coffee shop in Denver airport all day was no one had a clue where to find her. The disadvantage of being home was Eddie's violent threats reverberated inside her head like a hammer hitting a gong.

Be brave, Tess.

Eddie didn't know where she lived. She wasn't listed in the phone book and she hadn't even registered to vote at her new address yet. She was blessedly anonymous.

McKenzie had found her…but he was FBI.

She went to her front door and unlocked it. The sight of her familiar space sent relief rushing through her. Her home wasn't fancy but it was hers. She locked the door behind her and threw the deadbolt.

Setting her purse and laptop on the kitchen table, she trudged upstairs with her small suitcase, dumped it on the bed and started filling the tub. She tossed dirty laundry in the hamper and unpacked the few toiletries she'd taken with her in their travel sized bottles. The bookmark Ellie had made her all those years ago sat inside the zippered pocket of her case. The pressed flowers were held in place with brittle tape and the whole thing was so fragile Tess was terrified it was going to disintegrate. She placed it reverently on her bedside table. Tomorrow she'd arrange to have it framed.

She walked around the house, nervous, on edge, and not sure why. She closed the drapes and made sure the back door was locked. The idea of Eddie being free freaked her out. Perhaps that was what was giving her this unshakable sense of unease. Or maybe it was just that achy feeling you got when you met someone you were attracted to, but learned the feeling wasn't mutual. Sure, he might find her a little bit attractive, but it would never come close to how he felt about his job, which was fine. He shouldn't have to pick one or the other.

But there lay the obvious conflict. A woman like her would kill a career like his, and she didn't want that. It was obvious he was born to be a special agent. She applauded him and all his colleagues. They kept people safe. Rescued people.

But…they'd rescued her and she felt as if she'd been tried and convicted at the ripe old age of ten.

She shook off her self-pity. The ache would go away eventually. It always did. Give it a few days, or weeks, and she'd forget everything about ASAC Steve McKenzie, from his dented chin to his elusive dimples.

Which would be way better than picturing those changeable eyes, or remembering the sense of security she'd experienced sleeping beside him last night. Or the fierce desire that had overwhelmed her when he'd put his mouth and hands on her. She sighed tiredly and stripped off her clothes as she walked from the bedroom to the master bath. She pinned up her unruly hair then added cold water and a healthy dose of bubble bath to the tub. She needed to relax.

Slowly, she eased her body into the steaming liquid and lay back to stare at the ceiling. Hot water seeped into her tense, tired muscles.

Where was Mac now?

Probably investigating this latest shooting.

The congressman was lucky to be alive, but he was in a coma and the doctors had no idea if he'd recover.

She prayed he did. Hopefully the congressman would

wake up tomorrow morning with nothing worse than a headache and give them an idea of the shooter's appearance.

Her gaze caught on the toilet and the vague unease she'd been experiencing exploded into a rush of fear. The seat was up. She never left the seat up. She stood, grabbed her robe and wrapped it around her body, fingers fumbling and making it hard to move quickly. Water sloshed onto the floor as she hurriedly climbed out.

Yesterday morning she'd left in a hurry, but there was no reason to leave the toilet seat up.

She hurried into the bedroom and grabbed the key to her gun safe from her jewelry box and retrieved her Ruger LC9s. Her heart thumped crazily as she checked the chamber and the magazine. Locked and loaded.

Her fingers hovered over the 911 buttons on her cell, but she hesitated.

Had Cole been over and simply used the bathroom? He was the only person who had a key to her house.

She dialed his number. Once again, the call went to voice mail, but this time she was pissed. "Look, Cole, this is getting old. I need to talk to you. Did you come to my house when I wasn't here? I know it sounds stupid but the toilet seat is up and I didn't leave it like that. Call me, okay? I'm about to search the house with my gun drawn, so I'm dead serious about you telling me if I'm worrying over nothing."

She shoved the cell into her pocket. Was it Eddie? Was he working with this killer in DC and had they figured out where she lived? Another horrible thought occurred to her. What if Cole *hadn't* been ignoring her calls? What if he'd been hurt or kidnapped?

Her mouth lost every drop of moisture.

Should she call the cops? And say what? That the toilet seat was up? That she'd had a row with her brother and he was ignoring her calls? He was a grown man not a kid. They'd laugh at her. She looked down at her damp robe. And no way did she want another confrontation with law enforcement dressed in nothing but damp cotton, but she wasn't putting the gun down long enough to get dressed.

She calmed her heart. She could do this. She could search her house for someone hiding. She started by looking carefully under the bed and in the wardrobe, but there wasn't anyone there.

Her grip tightened. What if Eddie jumped her and over-powered her...the idea made her heart tie a knot in itself. With her martial arts training she could protect herself from most threats but his size and the intensity of his hatred might give him the advantage if she lost the gun.

So don't lose the gun, girl.

She flinched as her daddy's voice echoed in her head. But then she remembered she'd always been a better shot than Eddie and she hadn't spent the last twenty years rotting behind bars. She'd spent those same years learning how to defend herself.

She concentrated hard, trying to sense another human presence over the deafening rush of blood through her veins. Nothing. Maybe her sixth sense was nonexistent. She thought about calling Mac in case this was Eddie, but she didn't want him to think she was pursuing him, especially after the way he appeared to despise his ex-wife for chasing after him.

Plus, he was investigating a series of *murders*.

Sure, he'd want to be informed if Eddie turned up here, but if her only clue was a toilet seat she didn't think he'd have much patience with her. She didn't want to look any more foolish than she already did in front of ASAC Steve McKenzie. She edged out of the bedroom and opened the door to the spare room which served as the office she rarely used.

At first glance, everything appeared normal. But one of the drawers wasn't closed properly and Tess wouldn't have left it like that. She was a little OCD. She moved into the room and opened the top drawer using the edge of her robe. The small supply of cash she kept in the house was still there.

She gritted her teeth and checked the rest of the house, but no one was hiding, nothing else was disturbed and the doors were locked.

Was it possible she was imagining these things? The file? The toilet seat? Was she going mad?

What sort of burglar would leave cash but use the bathroom? *The sort who broke in to commit rape and murder.* Or, the imaginary kind conjured by nervous women who lived alone.

Deflated and unsure whether or not someone had actually been in her house, or if she was just starting to lose her mind, she went back upstairs. The bath had lost its appeal. The scent of lavender failed to calm her nerves.

She pulled on clean pajamas and turned off all the lights except for the one in the foyer that shone up the stairs. The light gave her a sense of security, however false. She lay down on her bed, welcoming its familiar embrace. She was exhausted and needed a decent night's sleep.

She toyed with the idea of calling Mac to let him know she was back in DC, but it sounded like a pathetic come on. He already knew she was attracted to him—*duh*—and she hated that. The desire to hear his voice almost overwhelmed her good sense and told her more than she wanted to know about her feelings for the guy.

He's only interested in you because of who your relatives are.

Sadness pressed down on her. The camaraderie of last night, before they'd messed it up by messing around, was like a glimpse into how other people lived. Happy people. Normal people. People in loving relationships. Which was crazy as they were virtual strangers trapped in a relationship anchored in murder, hatred and bigotry.

But...

She sighed tiredly and slipped her Ruger onto the bedside table next to Mac's business card and Ellie's bookmark.

The idea of having Steve McKenzie in her life was a dream, not a reality. Her reality was fighting for survival and protecting her little brother as best she was able. If Eddie came for her, she'd be ready for him.

She thought of her beautiful sister and what Ellie had endured. She'd shoot the bastard for that alone.

But she couldn't afford to shoot first and ask questions later. If she made a mistake they'd lock her up and throw away the key. Innocent until proven guilty was not for the likes of David Hines's only surviving daughter and she had no desire to end up in prison.

She closed her eyes, her heart still pounding in her chest. At this rate, she'd never get any sleep.

Think of something else.

Mac's dimples flashed through her mind, along with that irreverent grin that made his eyes sparkle devilishly. And the way his voice flowed over her in that slight country drawl he tried so hard to tone down. And the way he'd touched her, relentlessly pushing her to a place no man had ever taken her before.

She smiled at her inner Star Trek nerd.

Gradually her heart rate calmed and her breathing deepened. Seconds later she was fast asleep.

MAC STRODE INTO the crisis action room in SIOC where the task force had set up and felt as if he'd been away for months rather than thirty-eight hours.

Media was going nuts talking about this string of hate killings in the heart of DC. Last time people had been this scared the Beltway Snipers had been picking off innocents going about their daily business. Ten people had died. Three injured. One of the shooters had been seventeen years old. The other one had received the ultimate punishment and Mac hoped this current killer joined him in hell sooner rather than later.

But the media attention wasn't getting them any leads. Instead it was raising the level of hysteria to white hot, which wasn't helping anyone.

"Trettorri gonna make it?" Walsh intercepted him on the way to the breakout room Mac had taken as his office.

"He's alive," Mac told him.

The brunette he'd met at the firing range caught his eye and sent him a smile. He nodded back and Walsh's gaze locked on her with interest.

"Friend of yours?" Walsh inquired.

Mac's love life was already complicated enough. "Knock yourself out."

Only a few agents were scattered around the place. Mac checked his watch. Dinner time. He'd grabbed a sandwich at the hospital and eaten on the hoof. Then he'd visited the crime scene, driven by his apartment and picked up his old notebooks, some clean clothes and repacked his go-bag before updating the Executive Assistant Director of Criminal Investigations on what had gone down in Idaho. He'd worked with the EAD before during the Minneapolis investigation. The guy was fine as long as you followed the rules. Apparently, Mac was in danger of falling off that particular bandwagon.

Now he was starving again. If he was lucky he might persuade one of the other agents to pick him up a burger and fries. And then hopefully he could ask someone else to go work out at the gym for him afterwards.

He rolled his shoulders.

"Second bullet skimmed his skull but didn't penetrate. Probably knocked Trettorri out cold," Mac told Walsh. "Wound bled everywhere. Shooter must have been in a hurry or they might have noticed the guy was still breathing. First bullet did a lot more damage. Straight through the left lung, and a fragment ricocheted inside his body and nicked a vein. Guy lost a *lot* of blood." Mac was a universal donor and the nurse had allowed him to donate blood while he was waiting to talk to the doc. "Surgeon is optimistic they've fixed the damage from the bullets, but worried about a possible brain injury from the concussion. They are keeping him in intensive care until they think he's stabilized. We have agents on his door to make sure no one finishes the job." When he'd gotten to the scene the evidence had already been collected to protect it from the rain that had started to fall. The area had been decimated for trace by first responders doing everything they needed to save the congressman's life.

"I had an agent drive two .40 caliber casings to the lab," Walsh told him, "so Harm could get to work straight away."

"Any other evidence?"

"No witnesses, no camera surveillance. It's like the shooter knows exactly where all the cameras are and chooses kill locations based on that."

Mac had been thinking the same thing.

"But looks like Trettorri grappled with someone and their DNA is potentially under his fingernails and on his clothes. An agent helped a nurse collect clothes and nail scrapings while Trettorri was prepped for surgery. It all went to the lab with the casings."

"Nice work."

Hernandez brought him a coffee and put the mug on his desk.

His brows quirked at the personal service. "Thanks, Libby."

"Figured you'd need it. You can't have gotten much sleep last night," she said by way of explanation.

He kept his expression blank.

"ASC Gerald wants to be informed when the next team meeting is so he can either go home or attend," she told him.

Mac booted up his computer. "Tell him ten minutes. I want everyone caught up on the latest. I'm about to email everyone." Supposedly he had an assistant somewhere, but she was nine-to-five and he hadn't met her yet.

Hernandez nodded and left. Mac sent out a general email notice for everyone in the vicinity to get there ASAP. This was a rapidly evolving case and he wanted to know if he'd missed anything. He checked his texts. Nothing from Tess about whether or not she'd made it home to DC safely.

He told himself she'd be fine, but he was worried about her.

Friends watched out for each other, right? Except, after crossing the line from friend to lover last night he'd decided to distance himself, remember? And she'd obviously decided the same thing, so calling her to make sure she made it home blurred those edges of their relationship again and confused things. The whole thing was confused enough.

Dammit.

"What you got there?" asked Walsh, nodding toward the heavy, plastic bag.

Mac grinned evilly. "My notes from the Pioneer investigation. I want you and Carter to go through them looking for anything you can find on Hines's manifesto. He also called it the "Pioneers' Pathway" and the "Road To Revolution" depending on who he was talking to and how much liquor he'd drunk." Mac searched his drawer for the tablet he used to take notes on. "From memory, Hines said they'd do a series of symbolic murders allowing their enemies to be marked and their 'army' to be put on notice for the upcoming war. After the murders, he called upon his followers to bomb either the White House or Capitol Hill—the target varied depending on whatever stuck in Hines's craw that day. I've urged increased security and vigilance at all potential sites." The callous disregard for human life, the law and the Constitution this country was based upon had always chilled him. The idea some of his fellow Americans might want to follow this bullshit agenda made him want to hit something, preferably something that was capable of hitting back.

Walsh took the notebooks from him. "Great. Can't wait to

try and decipher your scrawl." Mac's handwriting wasn't pretty. "I'm not going to find a book of love poetry in this lot, am I?"

Mac leaned back in his chair and grinned. "Shall I compare thee to a summer's day? Thou art more ugly and—"

"Shut the fuck up." Walsh snorted.

"I wonder what would have pissed off the Pioneers more," Mac said wryly. "Me being an undercover cop or the fact I could quote Shakespeare. Pretty sure they'd have shot me either way."

"I still can't believe I didn't know you worked undercover on that case. Did it seriously suck?"

Mac thought back to the year spent at the compound. "That's the scariest thing, sometimes it didn't suck. Sometimes it felt good to be part of a close community that seemed to care about each other. And then the hatred would spew out of nowhere, against blacks, Jews, abortionists—basically anyone who didn't look and act and think like they did. One minute they'd be offering you freshly baked rolls dripping with homemade butter, next they'd be hissing about how ZOG were taking over the world and needed to be stopped."

Walsh grimaced.

"It was like living in Satan's version of Little House on the Prairie."

"You did good work, Mac," Walsh told him.

"Clearly not good enough." Mac sighed and leaned back in his chair, wondering what the hell he could have done different. "I need to call the marshals for an update."

"Still no sign of Eddie?"

"Not that I've heard. I'm personally hoping he became a Popsicle somewhere in Idaho. You track down the girlfriend from before he was incarcerated?"

Walsh nodded. "I think so. Woman named Brandy Jordan visited him regularly during the first year he was inside. She visited a few more times over the years but much less frequently. I sent a lead to the resident agency in Coeur d'Alene to check out her last known address pulled from the DMV."

"I want her brought in for questioning and I want to talk to the agent doing the questioning. She might know where Eddie is or who his friends are."

"You sure Eddie's sister isn't hiding anything?" Walsh was watching him guardedly.

Mac held the man's stare, understanding what the guy was really asking. "She didn't help him escape, Dylan. He almost broke her neck when he grabbed her yesterday."

"That could have been a setup."

"Maybe if there'd been any love lost between them as kids, but there wasn't. The two older brothers were sexually assaulting the older girl and I witnessed Tess running out of the barn when Walt tried to do the same to her. Tess hated them both. They were both swine—and that's an insult to pigs."

"We a hundred percent certain Walt is dead?" Dylan Walsh asked.

"Unless the guy at the morgue lied." Mac pulled a face.

Walsh still didn't look convinced about Tess's innocence. The worst thing was Mac wouldn't have been either, but he'd been there. He'd lived it.

CHAPTER TWENTY-ONE

T EN MINUTES LATER Mac sat at the front of the room and scanned the crowd to see who was still missing. A couple of the analysts who worked fixed shifts. Ross, Atherton and Dunbar. Yesterday they'd started talking to the families about threats the victims had received and today they were chasing down more leads.

Mac started with Elijah Carter who sat on his left with the hate crimes duo. "Any connection between vics?"

"We have some basic crossover, like they all subscribed to the *Washington Post* online, shared the same cell service provider and occasionally shopped for groceries in some of the same stores, used the same metro line, etc., but nothing startling considering they all lived on the northwest side of the city. No indications they were ever in the same place at the same time. No record of any communication between them, but I'm still looking at their social media posts and credit card histories to see if they attended any of the same events. Ms. Shiraz was all over blogs and social media with her personal opinion, the others barely had Facebook profiles—except the judge's wife. She posted a lot of pictures of their grandkids." Carter scratched between his eyes, making the hate crimes lady lean away from him like he was contagious. "I started to add Trettorri into the mix and I'm coming up with the same kind of general things. I'm going to look for other commonalities next, determine if they were friends with any of the same people. I have a couple of analysts working on it."

Ross, Atherton and Dunbar entered the room with a muted apology for being late. The female detective was wearing skintight leather pants today and Agent Ross had trouble keeping his eyes off her ass. Nice to see Mac wasn't the only one with women issues.

His ex. Not Tess, he assured himself. He was going to have to deal with Heather as soon as he had an hour to himself. She was beginning to piss him off and interfere with his job. Tess, he was just going to have to let go. It wasn't like he hadn't walked away before.

Yeah, when she was ten.

Asshole.

Hell, he was really starting to hate himself when it came to his dealings with Tess Fallon.

"What did you find out?" he asked the latecomers.

Dunbar took the lead which seemed to annoy her colleagues but she grinned at Ross while she did it. Mac suspected they were both competitive individuals and that worked as long as they got results. "The rabbi and DJ both reported some threats to the police and the FBI. About a year ago someone painted a swastika on the synagogue where the rabbi worked and he filed a report. Sonja Shiraz had literally thousands of vicious emails and hand-mailed letters all promising to do vile things to her for switching sides. The judge never reported any threats and I spoke to some of his colleagues on the Federal Circuit and they weren't aware of the Thomases having any issues with haters. He was a well-liked, well-respected guy who didn't suffer fools. Then we spoke to Trettorri's husband."

Ross crossed his arms and seemed resigned to playing second string to Annabel Dunbar's fiddle.

"The husband promised to have an aide locate all their hate mail and deliver it to us ASAP." She stuck her hands on her hips. "Way he spoke suggested they had lots of it, but the congressman kept it at work so as to not sully—his word, not mine—their home. That's all we have so far." She gave an exaggerated shrug and went and leaned against the wall off to one side. Aside from the tight pants and hot bod she reminded Mac a lot of himself. Hungry to prove herself. Confident she could do the job. Determined never to show weakness. It hadn't taken her long to settle into SIOC. Mac figured give it a week and she'd be ready to take over.

"Miki?" Mac prompted Agent Makimi.

The agent delicately rubbed her brow. Only a fool would underestimate the woman or the agent. "I searched ViCAP for similar crimes." Her cheeks bunched as she pressed her lips together. "Lots of potential connections, but nothing solid. None using the same weapon Agent Harm identified, which would have been flagged by NIBIN."

"How similar are the crimes?" Mac asked.

"Potential hate targets as determined by race, religion or sexuality. Shot in quiet locations with no real fanfare. No witnesses. The casings weren't always picked up, but there were a couple of incidents where the brass was removed. One double homicide suggests the killer did not want any witnesses. Looks as if a young guy stumbled upon the shooting of an Arab male and got a bullet in the head for his trouble."

"Any vics in DC?"

She smiled. "That would be too easy. Memphis. Phoenix. Seattle. New Haven."

"Check with the local FBI or police stations. Find out if they can tell you anything about the crimes that might provide linkage. Any clue, specifically DNA or witness statements not listed on ViCAP."

"It's unusual to have a lone offender who doesn't want to revel in the glory of what they've done," the hate crimes lady said.

Mac agreed. "Usually they are so vainglorious they turn themselves in if the police don't catch them fast enough, but this killer doesn't look like he or she is going to stop. They're on a mission." He locked eyes with the woman, for once not in dispute. "Any other hate groups pop up on the radar?"

She and her partner exchanged a look. "Everything is pointing to this being related to David Hines's Pioneers group formerly out of Kodiak Compound, Idaho. We are looking deeper at people who were there or suspected of being affiliated or sympathetic to them."

"Could someone be deliberately misleading us to make us think it's the Pioneers?" Mac asked. And he'd be lying if he wasn't hoping he could spare Tess the scrutiny this would get her when the press made the connection, which would be any minute now.

Hate crimes lady smiled. "You're the one who was at the compound yesterday with David Hines's daughter. What do you think?"

That reminded him. He dug in his jacket pocket, tossed Walsh the recording from the meeting between Tess and Eddie. "Tess Fallon hadn't visited her brother in twenty years but agreed to talk to him and wear a wire once I informed her that her sister, Ellie, was four months pregnant at the time of her death." So what if he was being a little ambiguous about the timeline to make Tess look better? Tess was not the killer. "The pregnancy meant someone in the compound was having sex with Ellie Hines."

"Duh," said Walsh.

"And," he sent a quelling look to the peanut gallery, "as she was David Hines's daughter, and the Pioneers revered the guy and were even more terrified of his wife, I was pretty sure back then that Ellie was a victim of incest. I asked the ME to run tests during the autopsy and they confirmed a sibling fathered Ellie's baby. That information was never released to the media or the courts. DA didn't press charges. Walt was dead. Eddie was already doing a long stretch."

"The younger sister didn't know the older one was being sexually abused?" Hate crimes guy pushed.

Mac remembered the pain he'd seen in Tess's eyes when she'd figured it out. "No, she didn't. Eddie went for her at the end of visiting. She was lucky to escape relatively unscathed." His mouth went dry again at the reminder of how close she'd come to dying.

"You sure she's not playing you, boss?" Walsh said.

Mac forced a shrug. Knew if Walsh voiced it, others must be thinking it. "I'm just telling you what I know from my undercover days at the compound and what I saw at the prison yesterday. I believe her, but we'll do this by the book. I want someone investigating her activities so everything is on record. You," he pointed at Walsh because he trusted the guy. Tess would hate him if she knew. He thought of the books on her ereader. Her desire for privacy. "Listen to that recording of the prison interview carefully. I'm pretty sure there are clues on it, but I got distracted when Eddie attacked her. Also," he pointed to Carter. "Tess thinks both Eddie and her father had a girlfriend. Eddie's girlfriend was a girl called Brandy who I suspect he's been in touch with. Agents from Coeur d'Alene are trying to track her down. I want you and Walsh going through my old case notes for possible suspect names. Also search for clues regarding any potential females in David Hines's life."

"You think our killer could be a woman?" Carter asked.

"Why not?" Agent Makimi said angrily. "Any idiot can fire a handgun."

Miki was a firm believer in equality.

"That's cold," Carter responded, not dropping her gaze.

"It's cold no matter who pulls the trigger," Mac agreed.

Mac thought back to Tess's meeting with Eddie and what she might have said to the guy that had given her away. "Listen to the interview. Tell me what you think. And see how the marshals are doing catching that asshole." Mac remembered something else. "Eddie suggested he was nailing one of the prison guards during his chat with Tess, but that might have been bravado. Make sure you give that info to the marshals, too. He also threatened to track Tess down and kill her." His gut clenched at the exact phrasing. "Probably jailhouse bragging, but you never know with psychopaths, especially stupid ones." Especially when they then escaped from prison.

Walsh made a note of it. "Want protection on her?"

Mac nodded. "Get a patrol car on her street." He wanted Tess safe and although he didn't believe Eddie would make it this far he couldn't afford to discount the danger she faced. Tess would hate the extra attention a security detail would bring her, but she probably already hated him anyway. So be it.

"For the record, I don't think Tess Fallon is involved in the murders but she is connected somehow. We appear to have a conspiracy going with the involvement of Henry Jessop and links to the Pioneers. A computer consultant at BAU examined Tess's online activity and didn't find anything suspicious. Same consultant put some *wunderkind* on identifying the users of the One-Drop-2-Many chatroom on the dark web."

Hernandez dropped her pen on her notepad with a flourish. "Impossible."

Mac allowed himself a small smile. "Apparently, the kid is a genius and we have nothing to lose by giving it a go. I want someone here doing in-depth background on the younger brother, Cole. Tess claims he doesn't know who his parents are, but someone else might have told him without her knowledge. Atherton." The agent looked up from perusing his notes. "You go interview his college professors. I want warrants for his phones, email and all internet activity. Let's keep it on the down low. These people deserve to be treated with respect until we find evidence that suggests they are involved. Cole was just an infant at the time of his parents' death, but Tess definitely suffered enough when she was growing up." He forced the image of her running out of that damn barn from his mind. His knuckles throbbed in memory. Walt hadn't accepted his education lightly. Mac had enjoyed every fucking moment of teaching the guy to keep his hands off his own kid sister.

"Next. Henry Jessop. Who's working on him?"

A row of hands went up. An agent confirmed the calls to the burner Parker had mentioned. "I want you tracking the purchase of those two cell phones and figure out if the same buyer bought more. Maybe we can track SIM cards. Where, when, who and how did they pay for them, these people must have messed up somehow."

Right now, they were making law enforcement run in circles pecking at crumbs.

The agents provided more background on Jessop, but the guy had never been in trouble with the law and unlike most antigovernment types always paid his taxes on time.

"What about his family?" Mac asked.

Hernandez answered. "Wife died five years ago. Daughter was killed in a car accident almost twenty years ago."

Mac frowned and shook his head. "Jessop made it sound like she was alive and well. What about the grandson?"

She blinked. "What grandson?"

Mac paced. This didn't add up. "At dinner last night, he mentioned a daughter who lived out east. He had a photograph stuck to his fridge of a little boy holding a woman's hand."

"Maybe their deaths pushed him over the edge into delusion?" the analyst suggested.

Mac frowned. "It's possible he lost his mind. He did set fire to his house twenty minutes after serving the best beef stew I've ever tasted." He smoothed his tie as he pictured the inside of that house and all the things bothering him. "The downstairs bedroom, where I found the computer belonged to a teen. I'd say a male from the color scheme and bedding. I saw razors in the bathroom and Jessop had a beard older and uglier than I am."

"Could the razors have belonged to the wife when she was alive?"

"Nah, they were guy razors."

"Not wimpy girl razors," Miki grouched under her breath.

He hid his grin. Making Makimi mad was one of the many

things he liked about working with her. The woman had come over from Japan as a child and totally embraced the feminist movement.

"Exactly. Now I'm not saying male razors are better than female razors, they're just different."

She leveled him with a glare.

"It's hinky." He pointed a finger at Hernandez. "I want you digging deeper into Jessop's background, much deeper. Check local school enrollment, ask the local cops and Feds for information. Ask if the agent out of Pocatello will interview the ranch hands about the rest of Jessop's family members. Find out what the Feds managed to salvage from the house after the fire. I don't believe his daughter and grandson died twenty years ago. They could be involved in these murders. I want them found."

"What made you go to the compound?" hate crimes guy asked.

"I was literally driving within ten miles of the place and figured it couldn't hurt. I assumed it would have been torn down. Some of the buildings were gone, but the main cabin and barn are still there. Jessop told us he'd fixed up the cabin and rented it out—without the owner's permission. Jessop said he hoped Eddie would move in after he was released." Which would now be a long time coming, assuming they ever recaptured the guy.

Why escape now, near the end of his prison term?

Mac didn't believe seeing Tess had driven him over the edge. But maybe seeing Kenny Travers had... The guy knew something about what was going on and Mac wanted to know what it was. "See if there are any records for the people who stayed at Kodiak Compound. Seems to me it would be a nice va-cay destination for your average white supremacist family."

273

One side of Walsh's mouth curved up. At least someone besides Tess got his sense of humor.

"Cross check with Eddie's visitors."

"Who owns the land now?" asked Walsh.

Mac took a sip of cold coffee, feeling as if he was about to hammer nails into an innocent woman's coffin. "Tess and Cole Fallon still own the land. Their adoptive mother, who in an interesting twist was a wealthy woman of color, bought it and paid the taxes until she died. Again, Tess says Cole doesn't know about owning the land. I got the impression she doesn't want to sell the land until she's told him about their family history, but she's not ready to tell him about their past, so she's still got the land." A conundrum.

"Something tells *me* he's gonna discover the truth in the very near future," Walsh commented dryly.

Mac nodded. Either when the FBI questioned him, or when a member of the press figured it out. His stomach grumbled with hunger. He'd kill for a slice of pizza. "Okay, people, let's move on this. I want this murderer identified before he, or she, hurts anyone else."

He was itching to head back out into the field, but made himself walk into his office and start going through reports. Time to let others do the legwork. Time to delegate the good stuff.

A NOISE HAD Tess cracking open a heavy eyelid. It was dark and it took a few seconds to figure out why it shouldn't be.

She froze, listening intently for whatever it was that had woken her. She grabbed her weapon from the nightstand, moving the covers aside as stealthily as possible then sliding her feet onto the floor.

She cocked her head.

Someone was in her house, in her kitchen. They were being quiet but the sound of a zipper and then Velcro fastenings tearing apart were loud in the silence of the night.

What were they doing?

She picked up her cell, dialed 911 but immediately hung up. No way could she speak to an operator without alerting whoever was downstairs. And if it was Eddie, she didn't want him to run. She wanted him back in prison paying for the things he'd done.

She used her cell phone flashlight to see Mac's business card and dialed his number. She heard him pick up and she whispered softly, "Send help."

She slipped the phone into her pocket without listening to his response. She braced herself to do what needed to be done and hoped Mac trusted her enough to stay on the line. After a few moments, the creak of wood beneath stealthy footsteps made the hair on her nape rise.

Someone was creeping up her stairs.

She moved tentatively over the carpeted floor of her bedroom until she reached the open doorway. Below her, a shadow moved in the darkness.

Her heart pounded as she ducked back behind the wall. There was no lock on her bedroom door. No chair she could wedge under the handle if she wanted to barricade herself inside. Her grip tightened on her Ruger. It felt heavy in her hands, the idea of using it even heavier in her heart.

She steadied her heartbeat, stretched her neck to one side and calmly breathed out. This asshole was about to receive the fright of his life.

She stepped into the hallway and switched on the light. The figure on the stairs froze in shock as she aimed the weapon at him. Eyes glittered from behind a black woolen balaclava, too far away to make out their color. The guy was lean but fit looking in black pants and a plain dark hoodie. Eddie? She couldn't tell. He eyed the gun in her hand as if weighing the chance of her using it.

"Take off your mask and move down the stairs. Lie on the living room floor with your hands stretched out over your head. Do as I tell you and I might not pull the trigger."

Her intruder sniffed loudly and wiped his nose on the sleeve of his jersey. Then he slipped his hand in his hoodie pocket.

"Stop! Put your hands up where I can see them!"

But it was too late. He pulled a gun and got off a shot which hit the wall only a few inches from her face. Dammit. She jerked back behind the wall, heart pounding like a panicked jackrabbit.

The sound of his footsteps told her he was running away. Too late to return fire.

Damn.

She didn't want to live in constant fear. She wanted this over. She took a quick glance around the doorway and then moved fast across to the top of the banister, easing to look over into the hall below. Empty.

She heard him open the back door and it slam against the counter as he fled. Damn. She needed him caught. She needed this over. She ran quickly downstairs and noted the open kitchen door and the sound of trashcans being knocked over as the guy escaped.

The intruder had gone through her laptop case and purse. Her wallet was on the floor.

Another sound registered, a weird tinny sound like music through earbuds. She suddenly realized what it was and lowered her gun. She fished her cell out of her pocket and put it to her ear. Mac was yelling her name over and over.

"I'm all right."

He blew out a big breath. "Why the fuck didn't you talk to me? First responders are on the way. I'm twenty minutes out. What the hell happened?"

"An intruder was in my house." Her teeth chattered in reaction. So much for being brave.

"Who?"

"I don't know. He wore a balaclava. I didn't see his face."

"It was definitely a guy?"

"Yes. I think so."

"Eddie?"

"I don't know. Maybe? I really don't know." Who else would it have been? She went to the front door and opened it wide. Sat heavily on the front step when her knees gave out. "Y-you don't need to come. Cops are on their way. I wasn't sure what to do."

"I'll be there shortly." The words were curt.

She nodded and hung up when a fire truck arrived and a man from across the street started jogging toward her to make sure she was okay. Realizing she still had her gun in her hand, she released the clip and then emptied the chamber. Laid the bullets and the weapon at her side so the cops could do their thing. Covered her face to combat the overwhelming sense of stress and relief that wanted to pound her into the ground.

She'd thought she'd left the danger behind in Idaho. Instead it had followed her home.

CHAPTER TWENTY-TWO

T HAT'S HOW MAC found her.

A patrol officer was crouched down beside her as she sat on the steps. She wore soft-looking pink pajamas, different from the ones she'd worn last night—the ones he'd stripped off her just before dawn. All day, he'd tried to push aside the memory of what they'd done, but being confronted by Tess looking shaken and scared left him with a raw ache in his chest. Not for what they'd done, but for what he couldn't do. He couldn't pursue a relationship with her. He couldn't risk letting her into his heart. He was too close to achieving his goals to abandon them now. But the idea of never seeing Tess again except in an official capacity hurt like a punch in the gut.

It didn't matter. His job was what defined him. It had given him purpose and made a dirt-poor kid from the wrong side of the Montana tracks believe he could make a difference.

Police officers moved around inside Tess's house.

Fuck. He stood for a minute on the sidewalk next to his truck, his heart still spinning out of control after getting her call earlier. He'd been in his office, and at first thought she'd accidentally pocket dialed him and had been curious as to what he might overhear. Then he'd heard her say, so quietly he was worried he might have imagined it, "Send help."

He'd told Walsh to do just that and reeled off her address.

As he'd sprinted toward the underground garage where he now had a parking spot, he'd listened as she told someone to remove a mask and lie down on the floor.

He'd never felt so powerless.

He'd known she was in trouble, but until he'd heard the gunshot it hadn't hit him exactly how much danger she was in. And he hadn't realized how crazed with worry that would make him feel. She could have died. Again.

They were organizing a team to watch her but the agents wouldn't be available until tomorrow at the earliest. Unless Tess agreed to go into protective custody—which his boss wasn't ready to sign off on yet. Either way, she was going to have to get used to being shadowed by the Feds.

Was it Eddie? The idea that psycho was in town pissed him off. Why hadn't the goddamned USMS picked him up yet?

Motherfucker.

And if not him then whom? Why was Tess a target? What wasn't she telling him? What was he missing?

She glanced up from her position on the step and spotted him. The relief in her eyes was followed by a flood of tears and it seemed the most natural thing in the world to walk up to her, open his arms and let her hang onto him as she cried.

At least she wasn't mad at him anymore.

And in that moment, he realized something else—how isolated she was. How the events of twenty years ago continued to shape her existence.

"They find anyone yet?" Mac asked the uniform who eyed his badge with interest.

The guy rested his hands on his equipment belt. "Lady here swears she didn't see his face and didn't fire her gun. It's cold so I believe her." The uniform handed him the weapon, a nice little Ruger 9mm, which Mac slipped into his pocket along with the ammo.

"We found a bullet hole in the wall outside the bedroom door and neighbors report hearing a single gunshot and seeing a figure fleeing the house. No sign of forced entry."

Mac frowned.

Tess pulled away and seemed to realize what the officer said. "So how did he get in?"

"You sure you locked up?" Mac asked.

A look of incredulity passed over her features. "With Eddie on the run? Are you serious?"

"Eddie?" the patrolman queried.

Mac took pity on Tess as her eyes widened with dismay. "An escaped felon threatened Ms. Fallon's life if he ever got out. Feds are gonna be taking over this scene."

"Eddie Hines? The guy who escaped prison after serving nearly twenty years? Guy's got a screw loose."

"You're not wrong," Mac agreed. "Thanks for your help."

Tess was shivering in his arms. She thanked the cop through chattering teeth, and all the uniforms who started to leave as people from his task force rolled up.

Walsh, Carter, and Makimi turned up in one car. Agents Ross and Atherton piled out of another. Detective Dunbar pulled up in a Crown Vic that had a dent in the front fender. They eyed Tess like a pride of lions eyed fresh meat.

"Let's go inside," he said quietly.

She nodded mutely and headed back into her house. She seemed subdued, zoned out, in shock. He followed and the other members of the task force filed in behind him.

Carter thanked the last patrolman and closed the door

with a quiet snick that echoed through the house. Tess sat on the couch, dragging a blanket off the back of it and wrapping it tight around her shoulders. Her hair was tied up on top of her head, dark curls falling in unruly waves around her face. Her skin had lost all vestige of color.

Mac stood by the window, looking out onto the street. Turned to face her, strangely uncomfortable with his role as task force leader when questioning this woman who'd gone through so much and whom he was starting to think of as much more than a mere acquaintance.

He crossed his arms over his chest. Probably had something to do with sleeping with her last night and knowing what she looked like when she came.

"Why don't you talk us through what happened here tonight. What time did you arrive back at the house?"

She reached for a tissue from a box on the table and wiped her eyes, blew her nose. "I was stuck in Denver until early afternoon due to mechanical failure so didn't get home until after five."

She told them about coming home, and the unease she'd experienced. Then how she'd realized the toilet seat was up when she'd been relaxing in the bath.

Anger settled in his jaw. Why the hell hadn't she called him?

But he knew. She'd told him she didn't trust easily. When he'd walked away from having sex with her earlier she'd consider it a rejection and had retreated back behind her walls. He got it. She thought he hadn't wanted what she'd offered when the truth was he'd wanted it so much it had ripped out his guts to walk away.

He ignored the weight of the guilt. He could live with his

mistakes. But he wouldn't compound them by getting involved with another woman who didn't value his commitment to his career. He gritted his teeth. If he got involved with Tess he wouldn't have a career worth preserving.

He turned to Walsh. "Get an evidence response team in here."

"What? You're going to dust my toilet for prints?" Tess appeared horrified.

"Why not?"

"I hope they receive hazard pay. Tell them to dust my office desk drawers, too. I swear someone went through them though nothing was taken."

"So you thought someone had been in your house but you went to bed without calling the cops?" Walsh asked.

"I grabbed my gun, searched the house from top to bottom. Found exactly zero evidence besides my ever-increasing paranoia. I was exhausted." Her hazel eyes held his then glanced away. "I decided I must be imagining things and overreacting so I made sure the house was locked up and went to bed."

"What woke you up?"

"A noise." Her pale cheeks gained a little color. Probably remembering the noise that had woken them both last night. "I opened my eyes and realized someone had turned off the hall light. There's a switch at the top and the bottom of the stairs," she explained. "Someone was going through my bags." Her hand rose to her mouth and the blanket fell off her shoulders. "My laptop! My work."

She raced between Ross and Dunbar into the kitchen. Mac followed on her heels, the others crowding after them.

"It's still here. Thank goodness."

Mac grabbed her arm when she went to touch the machine. "We need to brush it for prints."

Her eyes flashed. "I need it for work."

"Evidence tech will be here in half an hour, tops. We'll get him to dust the laptop first as a priority."

"Or her," Miki said under her breath.

"Or her," he agreed. "Can you tell without touching if anything is missing?"

Tess bit her lip nervously. "I'd have to look in my wallet."

He averted his eyes from her beaded nipples. He tried not to think about the lack of underwear beneath her thin pajamas or the fact the house was cold thanks to the police searching the place earlier and leaving the doors wide open. No wonder the cop had interviewed her outside.

He told himself not to be an idiot as he fished out a pair of nitrile gloves and pulled them on. He took some photographs and then carefully lifted her wallet off the floor. Pens, notebooks, tissues, tampons were scatted amongst the papers on the table. He opened the wallet using the very edges and showed her the inside. Several bills were visible as were a bunch of credit cards and her driver's license.

She crossed her arms over her chest, maybe aware of the fact her nipples were poking against the thin fabric. He wanted to offer her his jacket but was aware of everyone watching their interaction, judging his ability to do the job. Judging the effect she had on him. And her ability to spin a tale.

"Is it all there?" This time his voice came out sharply and her chin came up.

"As far as I can tell."

"Is it possible the intruder got inside the house when you went to Idaho? Maybe you left in a hurry and left the front door open?"

"No."

"No? Are you certain?"

Her eyes flashed belligerently. "I locked up before I left for the airport. I told you before, I'm not an idiot."

"But rather than call the cops when you thought someone might be in your house, you searched it yourself and then went to bed with a gun by your bed?" This from Agent Ross.

"I figured the cops would dismiss me as a scared female living alone. Or maybe someone who wanted attention." She snorted. "Trust me, I do not want attention."

"So any idea how they got in?"

Her mouth opened and closed. Then she shook her head.

"Who has a key?" Mac's phone went off with the goddamn MC Hammer tune and he was ready to run the thing through the garbage disposal.

She swallowed. "Myself, obviously, and my brother, Cole."

"Any reason to suspect your brother might want to hurt you, Ms. Hines?" Ross asked.

"Fallon," she snapped at him. "And no way would Cole want to hurt me."

Ross nodded as if satisfied. Mac didn't believe it one bit.

Mac studied his team. They were waiting for instructions, unsure as to whether or not they were needed here. "They didn't take cash, jewelry or anything of value. It looks more like they were looking for something. Can you think of anything you might have that someone might be interested in, Tess?"

"If you're referring to things from my parents' compound then the answer is no." She clenched her fists and brought one to her lips. "I don't even have any photographs." She looked away.

Was there something she wasn't telling them?

The front door banged open and Mac found himself face-to-face with a young man wearing dark jeans and a green t-shirt. Easily identifiable as Tess's kid brother because he was so like David Hines Mac had to do a double-take. Gone was the pimply kid with thick glasses he'd seen in the photograph on Tess's mantel. This guy was younger and leaner than the man Mac had once known, but overall the resemblance was a little unnerving. Why hadn't Tess mentioned it?

"Tess?" The kid moved through the assembled agents and took his sister in his arms. Everyone watched like hungry vultures, wondering what he knew.

"What's going on? I got your message. I called back but you didn't answer your phone."

Her fingers curled around her little brother's upper arms and she drew him in tight as if she realized the moment of reckoning was finally here.

"I'm fine," she said. "There was an intruder." After a few beats of silence, she let him go and took a step back. "Cole, these people are from the FBI." She bit her lip. "There's something I haven't told you."

———

ANGRY TEARS STREAMED down Cole's cheeks as he slammed out of Tess's house. He was so furious he could barely see where he was going. He stood for a moment trying to get his breathing under control.

"I take it that was unexpected news?" The comment came from a slender brunette who was leaning against the wall of

Tess's house. She looked as if she was sneaking a smoke except he didn't see a cigarette, just skintight leather pants, a black tee and a biker jacket that failed to conceal her sidearm.

"The fact my sister has been lying to me my whole life? Yeah, you could say it was unexpected."

She huffed out a disbelieving laugh. "You're seriously telling me you didn't know?"

He looked her up and down. A sneer touched his lips. "Who the hell are you? Lara Croft?"

The tolerant smile she gave him spoke of sheathed claws. "Careful kid, I'm one of the people you need on your side."

Kid? "You mean now that I'm being accused of murder?"

"No one accused you of murder."

But he'd seen the insinuation in their eyes when he'd been questioned about his movements this week. "My sister tells me our family were Idaho's answer to the Klan, and the prick standing guard over her asks where I was on certain dates this week that I happen to know coincide with a rash of hate crimes happening in DC. But I'm not being accused of murder?"

"Tell us your alibi and end this thing."

He set his teeth. Why the hell should he? "Let me consult with my attorney—"

"Innocent people don't need attorneys," she touted.

"Bullshit." Cole called her on it.

Her eyes hardened. "If you have nothing to hide tell us the truth."

He narrowed his eyes at her. "When the DJ was shot I was with Tess."

Her finely plucked brows quirked. "It might be nice if you guys could provide a third-party witness to verify, preferably one who isn't related by blood."

The side of his mouth tugged. "Bite me."

She raked his body with her gaze and a small smile curved her lips. She walked toward him and put her finger in the middle of his chest. "Tempting, but you're a little young for me."

He raised his chin. Little did she know. But he needed to be careful about what he said. He wasn't about to draw Carolyn into a scandal. Her reputation was everything to her. She was skittish enough about the age difference. If he brought trouble to her doorstep he'd be history.

"I'll check my calendar and get back to you with my movements, Officer…?"

Black eyes twinkled at him but he wasn't fooled. She wasn't amused. She was hungry to nail someone for these murders.

"Detective. Detective Dunbar." She brushed past him to walk back into the house and he was aware she was playing with him, using her blatant sexuality to get him to lower his guard. Wasn't gonna happen. He was more mature than that. Another Fed spied on them from the living room window. Cole shook his head and walked away, climbing into his Prius and wishing he could rewind the entire night.

Tess had been obviously upset when he'd walked out. He was so angry with her he wasn't sure they'd ever get back to where they used to be. He loved her, but he'd never forgive her for this. When the hell was she going to realize he wasn't a little kid anymore? He was old enough to make his own choices.

What would people do when they found out he was related to the Pioneers from Kodiak Compound? His mouth went dry. What would his girlfriend do?

He wasn't sure. He needed to get his shit together before he saw her again.

His hands trembled as he turned the key in the ignition. As much as he wanted to be honest in their relationship he wouldn't risk Carolyn turning away from him. He needed more time to figure out how to make the FBI look somewhere else for their killer.

He looked up. Tess was watching him from the living room window. The worry on her face pissed him off all over again. He backed out of the driveway and drove off, wishing like hell he'd never listened to her message.

CHAPTER TWENTY-THREE

T ESS SHIVERED AS the last evidence tech stomped out the front door in his heavy boots. "Thanks," she called out, but he was already gone.

She stood in the middle of her living room absorbing the silence of her empty house.

Earlier, when it had become apparent the FBI wasn't going anywhere for a while, she'd grabbed a hoodie to wear over her pajamas so she didn't give a cold nipple display to every person on the DC law enforcement graveyard shift. Even now she couldn't shake the chills that engulfed her in the aftermath of confronting that intruder and, worse, the look on Cole's face when she'd told him she'd lied about their parents.

He'd been horrified and betrayed, and had turned that shock and anger on her. She deserved it, but she'd had solid reasons to shield him from the truth. Theirs was not a bloodline to brag about.

Now her emotions were stripped raw and bleeding and she wanted to run away and hide. But it turned out you couldn't run from your past. It always found a way to track you down.

So what did she do now?

Dark smudges of fingerprint powder decorated her house like patches of black mold. The cable box by the TV said 1:15 AM and she should be exhausted, but the few hours of sleep she'd snatched had revived her and she felt wired rather than sleepy. Mac had left with his posse of avengers ten minutes ago, and hadn't said goodbye. She'd overheard him tell them to head back to get some rest before the team meeting at eight.

It didn't sound like they'd made much progress in finding Eddie or this killer.

She tried not to let Mac's lack of goodbye bother her. He had better things to do and she was a job—she got that. A job who'd made him compromise his principles once already. Not that she intended to reveal that to anyone. There was a limit as to how much humiliation she could take and having to recount details of her sex life to the FBI crossed it.

But Mac didn't know that.

His aloof tone and the way he'd withdrawn once the others had turned up had upset her. He was ashamed of what they'd done in that darkened motel room. She didn't blame him, but she'd be lying if she said it didn't hurt.

When her secrets exploded—and it wouldn't be long until the media cottoned on to the links to the Pioneers and ferreted out hers and Cole's new identities—she would be a public pariah. Mac wouldn't come near her. Either her clients would stand by her as an innocent victim of circumstance, or they wouldn't. She had no idea how high-minded principles and standing up for others against oppression translated when it came to the daughter of a white supremacist who'd promoted hate over love. Revolution over democracy.

She swallowed her unease. She'd move. Start afresh somewhere no one cared what her second name had once been.

Running away again.

Or she'd write a book about her experiences. Get her version of the truth out there, regardless of whether or not anyone actually believed it.

She might leave out her feelings for a certain federal official.

Cole now knew the worst. She still needed to ask him about that file with the judge's photo in it but no way would she do that in front of the Feds—she owed him that much trust and loyalty. She *knew* her brother. Even the sulky, angry version she'd seen tonight. And she loved him.

That wasn't blind trust. That was years of personal experience. Cole wasn't a killer, nor would he help anyone with that much evil in their hearts.

She'd talk to him tomorrow, when he'd had time to calm down. If the Feds found some reason to search his house and they found that file—no matter the explanation—it would be game over for freedom until he could absolutely prove his innocence. That might take months.

She locked the back door and flicked off the kitchen lights. At the same time Mac stepped through the front door and she jolted in surprise.

"I thought you'd left already." Her voice came out scratchy with suppressed emotion.

"I stayed back to make sure the evidence guy got everything he needed."

She turned her head away, fighting tears, feeling ungrateful and immature and bitter. "Of course you did."

He took a step toward her. "Hey, I didn't mean it like that."

"Like what?" Anger sparked like magnesium in water. Explosive and hot. She snapped her spine straight and raised her chin. "Like I'm nothing more than a suspect to be interrogated and picked apart and detailed like a science experiment? Do you have enough information for your report yet or would you like to break out the polygraph machine?" She advanced on him and started pushing him in the direction of the door. Every nerve was a fuse that had just been lit.

He let her back him all the way to the front door. God help her she wanted to lash out at someone, but he grabbed her arms, turned them both so she was the one pressed into the cold, hard wood. Her chest heaved as if she'd been running.

Light from the living room lamp shone behind him and allowed her to see his eyes—blue now like the shirt he wore. Dark in the shadows. The intensity there captivated her.

"I didn't mean to make it sound as if what *you* needed didn't matter," he said patiently. "There will be an unmarked car out front by morning, and I'm talking to my boss about protective custody."

A sudden prick of tears had her blinking rapidly, then swallowing the sharp ache of want. The touch of his hands on her arms, the musky scent of his skin made her wish for things she couldn't have. She knew it was crazy, she knew logically that desiring this man would bring her nothing but heartache, but she wanted him anyway. She had a horrible feeling she'd never outgrow this version of her childhood crush.

"It's fine. I'm sorry for snapping at you." She tried to squirm out of his grip but he obviously didn't trust her not to shove him again so he didn't let go.

"Thanks for coming over. I'm okay now. You can go." Her hands were trembling.

He lifted a finger and moved a tress of hair off her forehead. His expression changed, his eyes going warm. He pressed his lips together as if he didn't quite know what to say to bridge all the things that stood between them.

She didn't want his apology. She didn't want his pity.

He took a half step closer and lowered his head toward hers. Her heart kicked against her ribs as she glanced up, startled. She held still, not daring to breathe.

He paused with his lips about a millimeter from her mouth, restraint evident in the tense lines around his eyes. "You scared the shit out of me with that phone call earlier."

His breath brushed her lips. Her heart tried to escape the bars of its cage.

His grip tightened. "I thought you were going to die."

She swallowed, never taking her eyes from his lips. Her blood fluttered in her veins like a thousand humming birds taking flight.

"I'm going to kiss you now," he told her. "You have a problem with that?"

She gave the slightest shake of her head—permission or acknowledgement, she wasn't sure which. Then waited as he took forever to close that tiny gap.

For some strange reason, she'd imagined it would be a gentle kiss, a restrained, polite peck, like the one they'd shared outside the cabin when Henry Jessop had been watching. A light caress like the glancing stroke of a feather. But there was nothing tentative about this kiss.

When his lips finally met hers, his tongue slipped along the seam of her mouth like he owned her. It was as if he was done thinking, done waiting. Her hands were trapped between their bodies as he stepped between her legs, pressing ever closer. Her mouth dropped open on a shocked gasp at the feel of his hardness pressing against her core. His tongue explored the texture and taste of her mouth, as if he was imprinting on her flavor.

He tasted like coffee and strength and sin.

The fire in her veins ignited and made her forget why she'd been so angry with him just moments earlier. He kept kissing her, urging her to kiss him back with such determined focus she finally let go and melted against him. He shifted her hands to either side of her body and moved closer so his large powerful body was flush against hers, his arousal rigid against her stomach.

He angled her chin, taking the kiss deeper, tangling his tongue with hers. His fingers held her mouth still when she tried to move away, to pull back and breathe. Those strong fingers told her no way was he ready to break this kiss yet.

Who needed air?

His other hand worked its way under the layers of her clothes to find her hip, then he hesitated as if deciding which direction to explore next. He chose up, stroking his thumb over her stomach, fingers skimming her waist, then tracing the bumps of her ribs, until gently cradling the soft weight of her breast. Her toes curled and, after being so cold earlier, heat now poured off her skin.

She rose to tiptoes, pressing against him in a way that revealed exactly how hungry she was for him. His touch gentled, calloused fingers reverently caressing her sensitive flesh.

It reminded her that long before he'd been a rough, tough FBI agent, he'd been a cowboy who'd soothed a terrified colt with infinite patience and compassionate determination. No wonder all the girls in the compound had been in love with him.

His thumb and forefinger found her nipple and rolled the tip, pinching just hard enough to bring her back to the moment and make her moan. Need filled her. Desire exploded as she moved against him, creating a delicious friction that reminded her he'd already demonstrated sex wouldn't be all promise and no payoff.

She wanted him. She didn't care about the million reasons they shouldn't be doing this. She was sick of always trying to stay in the background and not stand out, of being the nice girl, the pitied girl, the one who got ignored or screwed over and dumped for a best friend who declared herself a sex goddess.

This time she wanted to be the goddamned sex goddess.

She knew what this was. Physical. Temporary. There were no illusions about love or Happily Ever After with her Prince Charming. A small part of her heart had always belonged to Steve McKenzie and his alter ego who'd saved her all those years ago. She didn't kid herself he'd ever love her back. She wasn't that much of a masochist.

But she didn't want to regret not having the nerve to go after what she wanted while she had the chance. She wanted Steve McKenzie. All of him. And if he was going to bail on her halfway through she wanted to know now, before she was humiliated and shamed by the power of her desire for him.

She reached for his belt and he went tense even as his fingers tortured her aching nipple and his mouth devoured hers. She ran her palm over the front of his pants and wrapped her hand around his thick length and moaned her approval. Then he let go of her jaw to ease down her pajama bottoms and she kicked them aside. Then she unzipped her hoodie, dragging it off and tugging the top over her head so she stood there completely naked except for the numerical tattoo that wrapped around her arm in a symbolic blue snake.

"You're beautiful." His eyes went dark, a muscle bouncing

in his jaw. He started to say something else but she leaned up and took his mouth with hers.

She'd loved this man as a child. Now she desired him as a woman. For once his badge and gun didn't matter. She wanted him, and he wanted her, too.

He leaned back, dragging in a deep breath, cupped her breast as he teased one pink peak with his thumb, watching it contract and bead as if begging for attention. He stared fascinated, his fingers dark against her pale skin. "Pretty."

Watching the desire on his face as he touched her was almost as arousing as the contact itself. He switched sides, playing with her as if he had all the time in the world to strum her body into a fine pitch of desire. The pleasure he evoked from her breasts tugged sharply between her legs.

As if suddenly hot he shrugged out of his suit jacket, dropping it to the floor, and then flipping the deadbolt on the door behind her with a flick of his wrist. The sound echoed through the house like a gunshot. They weren't stopping. There was no going back.

She eased down his zipper and his erection jutted out of his boxers. She caressed the long, thick length of him, wrapping her fingers around the velvet skin that covered steel beneath. He closed his eyes, bracing his hands on the door behind her.

She undid his tie and slid the smooth silk out of his collar before letting it fall to the floor. She undid the buttons of his shirt, revealing broad shoulders and a thickly muscled chest, lightly sprinkled with brown hair. He took a moment to undo the shirt cuffs, his gaze never leaving hers as he tossed the garment aside. He kicked off his shoes and socks, and stepped out of his pants. He nudged her legs apart and skimmed the short hair nestled at the apex of her thighs. She tensed as he slowly ran a finger over her clit, and down, easing between folds to the wet slit at her center, before sliding inside her moist heat in a long, firm stroke.

She went up on her toes as he curled a finger inside her. She clutched at his shoulders as he withdrew and followed the same route over and over again until her hips unconsciously followed his hand and she whimpered with need.

Her skin was sensitized and her arousal growing and expanding until all she could think of was the need to have him inside her.

His tongue stroked the hollow of her collar bone. One hand pressed inside her, the palm putting pressure on her clit with every inward stroke, he kept a languorous rhythm that made her whole-body shake. His mouth moved lower, seeking out her nipple and sucking hard when he found it. Her knees trembled.

She sank her fingers into his hair. "Please tell me you have a condom."

He stepped back, drew in a deep breath and leaned down to scoop up his pants and pull his wallet out of his back pocket. He handed it to her and went back to teasing her body, searching out all the places that made her quiver and ache. She found a square package next to the dollar bills and let the wallet drop from her fingers.

She sheathed him carefully, caressing his hot length as she protected them both.

He grabbed her wrists. His jaw was tense, eyes narrow as they met hers. They both knew they shouldn't be doing this. It was bad for his career. Dangerous to her heart. But no one would ever have to know. She could be his dirty, little secret.

She wanted him so badly, her body was throbbing with

need. She had the horrible feeling she'd beg if he changed his mind this time.

Instead of backing away, he lifted her up until both her legs wrapped around his waist and he positioned himself against her entrance. Then he held both her hands against the door and stared deep into her eyes as he pushed slowly inside. Her head went back as she cried out and her back arched.

She went blind as pleasure rushed through her.

He dropped her hands and grabbed her ass. She gripped his shoulders as he eased farther inside. Sweat beaded on his brow and ran down his temple. She tasted it on her tongue.

With one last push, he was imbedded and Tess sucked in air as she got used to the sensation. He was big and she had never had sex against a wall before.

He seemed to realize she needed a moment, or maybe he did, too. It took a few seconds to get used to being so full and her muscles rippled around him. Not that she was complaining. Her body quivered at the wonderful feeling. Sex had always been plain vanilla. Horizontal and quick. After a few seconds, she deliberately clenched her muscles around him again and he growled his approval. He started moving then, pumping in and out of her in long, deep strokes.

Dear Lord. It felt like Heaven. She whimpered at the pleasure that was flooding her senses. Every muscle in her body was trembling with need to race to that sharp edge of completion, but she wanted it to last, too. She wanted to go slow. And fast. And everywhere in-between. Mac changed his stance and she felt him inside her, touching a place that made her insane with want.

"Oh, God." Her nails raked his shoulders as her body clenched around him. She wanted to be the girl from her fantasies, the one who asked for and got what she wanted. "More."

"Is this what you wanted?" He drove into her over and over, holding onto her and thrusting deep at the same time.

"Yes." She gasped. "This is what I want. You inside me. It's perfect. You're perfect."

His full body shiver told her he liked what she was saying, and he delivered more in spades. She bit her lip, ankles crossed behind his back, thighs desperately clinging to his hips. Her climax took her by surprise. It burst through her like an explosion of light. She cried out, sobbing, pleasure bursting through her as something inside her shattered.

He stilled against her and her fingers dug into the muscles on his back but she no longer had the strength to hold herself up.

She didn't want it to be over. She didn't want him to go.

Disguising the fact that emotions were about to get the better of her, she went with humor. "I hereby declare you a sex god."

He laughed and it rumbled through his chest all the way inside her.

"We're not finished yet," he murmured.

She shivered despite the heat coming off his body. He was like a furnace and she wanted him naked beneath her, behind her, on top of her. She wanted to do everything she'd ever read about with this man. To explore and exploit. Tease and torment. Feel nothing but pleasure. He wouldn't leave her dissatisfied. He'd laugh and give her whatever she wanted. For tonight anyway.

She started to slip and he grabbed her by the ass, walking them into the kitchen.

THE COPS AND FBI agents had all left with the exception of one. What was he still doing here? How many questions could he have? What could ignorant little Tess Fallon be telling the guy that took so *freaking* long?

Poor little Tess had disturbed an intruder. Eddie? She frowned. She wished she knew where he was and why he'd escaped. Was he hoping to steal the glory for himself? After all her years of sacrifice? But then, despite what her father had thought of him, Eddie Hines had always been a bit of an asshole. He'd probably hid in a cupboard while David had fought for his life. David had been planning to get rid of Francis, but had to do it cautiously as the land was in her name.

The bitch had bound him to her with dirt.

She took a chance and sneaked around the back of Tess Fallon's property, avoiding the house with the noisy dog, staying far enough in the shadows not to be seen. There was a light on somewhere in the Fallon house and it filtered through enough for her to find her target with her binoculars. The lenses steamed up.

Her brows rose in time with her smile.

My, my, my, ASAC McKenzie, what big...hands...you have. And he obviously knew what to do with them if the rapturous look on Tess Fallon's face was anything to go by.

This was so perfect it was almost too good to be true. She mulled over the timing as she watched the two animals rut. Let them enjoy the moment. She smiled. Reality was about to crash down all too soon.

Half a block away she pulled out a new burner and dialed

another number she'd memorized. "It's time. You have to do it right now. Right this minute."

She heard him swallow and his uncertainty crackled down the line.

"Okay…"

She frowned. They couldn't afford a mistake. "Can you carry this out, or should I do it?" She wasn't sure she had time, but she'd make time. It was vital to their operation. Getting rid of McKenzie would take the heat off them long enough to get the job done. After that she didn't care what happened.

"I can do it," he said.

She stared up at the stars and thought of her father. What would he have said?

"I know you can. I have faith in you." That was the closest she'd ever come to saying "I love you." She thought about McKenzie and Tess feasting on one another. "You have an hour, maybe two but…" she told him what to do when he got there, then hesitated. What did you say in situations like this? "Don't get caught."

He laughed but there was a bitterness in his tone she hadn't heard before.

"Nothing gets in the way of the mission. Roger that." He'd heard about the old man and was pissed she hadn't called him to commiserate. Embers of anger burned inside her. Sentimentality was for fools and they'd grieve when this was over.

Tess Fallon and Steve McKenzie had somehow been involved in Jessop's demise and she intended to make them pay. She ditched the burner in a trashcan. Tossed the SIM card in the brush.

Now she needed an alibi.

CHAPTER TWENTY-FOUR

"HOW STRONG IS that table of yours?" Mac asked.

Tess shook her head, looking wonderfully mussed and fucked and bewildered. "It's solid oak."

Her last lover had been a jackass. Mac knew they shouldn't be doing this, but he figured if he was going to fuck up, he'd at least do it in style.

He had about three hours to prove she was a sex goddess. Then he'd grab a shower, drink a gallon of coffee and head back to HQ in time for the team meeting.

And it might not be romantic to think about murder and team meetings when he had a naked woman in his arms, but he dare not think about the sweet heat or long legs wrapped around him or else he'd be like the other prick who hadn't been worthy of this beautiful woman.

He pushed aside the nearest chair and the detritus from her purse, and lowered her carefully onto the solid, wood surface. Her eyes widened as the cold hit her back but he didn't give her time to think about it. He drew her knees up and enjoyed the sight of her taking him deep inside her.

Christ, she was beautiful. He'd thought that her face was pretty but the rest of her was spectacular. Hand-sized breasts with perfect, pink nipples he could feast on for days.

As much as he liked this view he knew she was starving for

more. Not just sex, but that notion of sexual daring. He pulled out and flipped her onto her stomach, pulling her thighs on either side of his as he stretched out over her back.

Slowly he guided himself back into her molten heat and gently rocked forward, careful not to crush her against the unforgiving surface. She clung to the table edge. She was completely at his mercy like this, unable to do anything except take what he was giving her and hang on for the ride. He drove her higher and higher again. Heating her blood, wanting to hear those panting cries that had almost driven him over the edge last time.

Backing off again, smiling at her little mewl of frustration, he lowered her feet to the floor and pulled her along his length. Now she was able to brace herself against his thrusts, and the feel of her pushing back, of wanting this as much as he did, made sweat break out on his forehead.

He was officially an animal and he didn't care. He ran one hand over the ridges of her spine. Cupped her breasts and made her moan again. She was perfect. She clenched around his dick and he moved one hand lower, scissoring two fingers around her clit as he did the same with one nipple and drove harder and harder into her. She cried out again, internal muscles squeezing him so hard he gave a roar of triumph as ecstasy rushed over him.

Even as he lay with his cheek pressed to her back, his heartbeat thumping loudly in his ears, the weight of his decision to have sex with Tess Fallon crashed over him.

What the hell had he done?

He squeezed his eyes shut, stroked her skin, warm and pliant beneath his hands. Despite his team's doubts Mac *knew* this woman, knew she had a pure heart. But it was possible she

COLD MALICE

was aware of something she wasn't telling him and he was going to figure out what that was. He couldn't do that by walking away and, fuck, if he was honest, he didn't want to. Not yet.

The Bureau might not approve of his methods but hopefully he'd never have to spell them out on an FD 302.

He withdrew to get rid of the condom and tossed it in the garbage, feeling like a sonofabitch for even thinking of using Tess.

When he turned around she was standing beside the table, her expression happy rather than the vulnerable he'd expected.

Because she isn't in your head, dickhead. She doesn't know you're a douche.

Or maybe he was feeding himself bullshit. Just the sight of her had him growing hard again.

What did it matter if he slept with her? She wasn't the killer. She wasn't actually a suspect, although technically she was involved—why else had someone broken into her home? And if it was Eddie then the more he was around the better chance he had of putting that fucker back in the cage.

She stepped toward him, definitely not able to read his mind as she brushed her body against his and took his insatiable cock in her hands. Within seconds he was unyielding as granite.

"Sex god," she purred against his throat.

"Pretty sure you're having something to do with it," he muttered.

Her head rested against his shoulder. "I want you inside me again."

His fists clenched at the words. He wanted inside her, too. "I don't have any more condoms."

She hesitated, then her breath brushed across his skin. "I'm on birth control. I'm clean. I got tested after Jason cheated on me. You're the only person I've slept with since."

"I'm clean, too." He'd had a full medical when he'd changed jobs. He held her hands. "But I don't do this."

"That's okay. We can do other things." She dropped to her knees.

His stomach contracted as her soft hair brushed against him.

His hands shook at the thought of being inside her again, not that the idea of a blowjob wasn't temptation in the extreme, but, fuck...

The fundamental question was, did he trust her? It wasn't just his life at stake. What about the possibility of a baby? Was it worth the risk getting her pregnant? Unfortunately, the answer was yes and that meant he was about to commit a bigger, more stupendous sin.

He eased her off him and sank to the floor beside her, the wood cold against his bare skin. He lay back and dragged her on top of him. She grinned down at him, so incredibly beautiful in the moonlight his throat closed.

He cupped her cheek. "What do *you* want, Tess?"

A very female smile curved her lips as she wrapped her hand around his throbbing cock. "This."

The way she touched him was earthy and sexy and honest.

"Show me where." His fingers gripped her hips as he let her take control. He knew it was one of the things she craved in a world where her parentage seemed to be the only thing people gave a damn about. She hid her true self from the world—the fear of being judged outweighing the need to really be herself, to be free.

He made himself stay perfectly still as she took him inside her. And his mind was blown. He let her set the pace, let her use his body to arouse, to bring her blood inexorably to the boil while his simmered with need. He played with her beautiful breasts, tweaked the pink crests hard enough to make her buck.

When her eyes closed he took over, gripping her hips, grinding her against him, gathering a handful of her hair in his fist and rearing up, trying to get even deeper inside. And he was the one in charge, in control, right up to the moment she put a twist into the way she rode him and he was gone. She cried out as his world turned black.

TESS LAY ON top of Mac, their limbs entwined, hearts keeping pace with one another as they slowed down and settled back to earth.

She could feel his pulse in the tender flesh between her thighs and the contact was intimate, almost more so than having sex. She licked her dry lips and began to ease away from him, but he grabbed hold of her.

"Hold still. If you move too fast my head's gonna explode."

"Pretty sure it wasn't your head doing all that exploding."

He opened his eyes wide and a slow grin broke out on his face. "You have a dirty side. I guess that explains the books."

The cold air raised gooseflesh on her arms and she shivered. She went to tug away from him, but he rolled them over until he was lying on top of her, staring down at her face.

"It's okay, Tess. It isn't against the law to enjoy sex. If it is I'm a repeat offender."

The reminder he'd had plenty of sexual partners and she was just another notch on the bedpost made something hurt inside. It was dumb. Classic female mistake. She was old enough to know better so she pushed aside the feelings. Tonight was about exploring the sizzling sexual tension that arced between them and appeasing her curiosity about what it would be like to be with this man. And now she knew. She didn't kid herself he'd be back with flowers and chocolates. She considered herself lucky he'd stayed this long.

For some reason, the weight of him felt so right, cradled between her thighs that she wrapped her legs and arms around him and squeezed him, everywhere.

He dropped his forehead to hers with a groan. "I'm not as young as I once was. If you're determined to kill me I'll need a few minutes."

A strand of silver glittered in the moonlight. She reached up and touched it. "You have a gray hair."

"I should have a million by now." He didn't sound like he cared.

"How old are you, anyway?"

He reared back. The question seemed to bother him. "Thirty-nine."

"Ancient." She joked and his lips twitched.

"I can keep up." He rocked his hips to prove the point and her eyes widened. A cell phone rang from the hallway. MC Hammer's "U can't touch this" blared through the quiet of the house. He tensed. It was the irritating ex, who wouldn't leave him alone. She let go as he propped himself on his elbows and swore.

"I'm about ready to smother the woman with a pillow." He pulled away and stalked into the hall. She watched as he grabbed his pants and rifled for his cell. It stopped ringing but pinged with a text.

"Dammit. She says it's an emergency."

She propped herself up on one elbow and brushed her heavy hair back from her face. "Maybe it is?"

He made a noise than wasn't flattering. "The emergency is that her ego was bruised and she wants to screw me to the wall so she can prove she still has someone under her thumb. Heather likes to control men with sex. She probably figures three a.m. is the perfect time to do it."

He pulled on his boxers, then his pants. He didn't seem to notice Tess had stiffened in place.

Is that what he thought she'd tried to do? She had literally and metaphorically nailed him to the wall. Or him her. She wasn't sure the logistics were salient.

He shoved on his shoes, scrubbed a hand through his hair before he did up the buttons of his shirt, which he'd retrieved from near the front door. He pulled on his shoulder holster and checked his sidearm. She lay stretched out on the floor, the stickiness of what they'd done smeared on her thighs, evidence of her immense folly.

She heard his footsteps and opened her eyes. He knelt down, ran a finger over her jaw and fleetingly over her breast. Her body reared up like iron drawn to a magnet.

She made herself smile as he withdrew his hand. She wouldn't be a woman who tried to cling to him. He wasn't hers. She didn't need him. She just wanted him.

"Maybe you need a restraining order," she suggested in a low voice.

He grumbled. "I'd be laughed out of the Bureau."

He leaned down and kissed her on the mouth again.

Didn't appear to know what to say, but this was clearly goodbye. Awkwardness rose up between them as she pulled away and she forced herself to stretch out rather than curl up in a ball and lick her wounds.

"Well, thanks for the ride, cowboy." She grinned as if she wasn't hurting on the inside. "I can now vouch for the sex god status."

He frowned. Then drew back, as if uncertain about what they'd done.

Join the club.

"Tess—"

"Call me if you have any developments with the case." She told him before he made promises he couldn't keep. "Or if anyone tracks down that ass of an older brother of mine."

He smoothed his tie, avoiding eye contact as her heart shriveled. "Sure. Keep the doors locked. I put your Ruger on your bedside table. Ammo in the drawer."

"Thanks." She didn't move from the floor. She was too crippled on the inside. Instead she stretched out, gave him a lazy smile and then let one hand drift down, her fingers stroking over her nipple. As if she were simply a sensual creature who cared nothing about the emotions they'd disturbed like sediment in the water, clouding an issue that should have been crystal clear.

Her body language said she didn't need him to love her. That was for weaker people than her. The sad and the needy. Not the goddess he'd awakened.

"Keep doing that and my ex-wife can forget it." His voice dropped an octave as his eyes followed her hand.

She smiled and didn't stop and he took a half step forward before another text dinged. He groaned with what sounded like genuine frustration.

"Bye, Mac." She smiled, letting a little sadness seep through as he held her gaze.

"We'll talk tomorrow, Tess."

She shrugged like she didn't care. Tension tightened his features. He looked pissed to have to be heading out to talk to his ex. Or maybe it was an act. Maybe he couldn't wait to get out of here and away from the potential conflict of interest that Tess represented. And sex with his ex had once been good enough for a marriage proposal, so who said he wasn't going to the pretty blonde for another round?

She heard him pick up his things off the floor. The front door opened and shut quietly, leaving only the shame of their encounter behind.

Cold washed over her but even as she shivered she didn't get up. She closed her eyes at the realization she'd made another colossal mistake. In her sexual haze, she'd allowed herself to ignore the fact her feelings for this man had deepened. She admired everything about him, his determined search for the truth no matter the cost, his dedication to his job. Combine that with the hot bod, cute dimples and that profound sense of connection she shared only with him, she'd been foolish to assume she could keep her emotions out of this. Her heart was entangled as surely as when she'd been that moonstruck kid watching her idol drive away.

Steve McKenzie was an FBI agent, one who'd saved her life and her soul. Didn't mean he wouldn't sacrifice her now, she realized miserably.

When her teeth started to chatter she figured it was time to move. Tess rolled over on her side and put her hand out to push herself up. Her fingers curled around Cole's data stick.

She didn't remember seeing the drive with her belongings earlier.

Whoever broke in here tonight had been looking for something that wasn't cash, or jewels.

No sign of forced entry...

Cole could *not* be the intruder.

Her brother wasn't that good an actor. Was he?

Her fingers tightened on the hard plastic. She needed to know. Right this minute. She needed to find out if Cole was involved in this mess. She climbed to her feet. She wasn't putting this off any longer. She needed to know the truth and she needed to know now.

CHAPTER TWENTY-FIVE

MAC'S ENTIRE BODY throbbed with well-used satisfaction as he drove down Wisconsin Avenue toward Georgetown. Mixed into it was the growing sense of *"holy-shit what the hell did I just do?"* The justification for having sex with Tess had seemed sound when his body was burning up with lust. Get close, gain her trust, use the attraction he couldn't control to forward the investigation. Be a dedicated FBI agent. Take one for the team.

The fact he was still buzzing from his brain to his balls was a bonus.

Very noble.

The truth was, he'd wanted her so much he hadn't been thinking about the case or the consequences until he'd already been in too deep. He'd fucked her without a goddamned condom because he'd wanted her that much. He'd never had that little self-control before, not even with the woman he'd exchanged vows with. A woman he needed to convince to stop calling him unless she wanted to seriously piss him off.

Except that was bullshit. He'd latched onto Heather's text so goddamned fast he'd almost given himself whiplash. He was running away—not from what he'd done with Tess, but from the emotions that had assaulted him, before, during and after sex. So much for separating the two.

Tess had morphed from quiet, serious tax accountant to uninhibited erotic nymph and had reduced his brain to ashes. But something had shifted at the end, possibly the rising horror at the stupidity of two supposedly intelligent adults having unprotected sex...

Except it hadn't looked like horror, it had been more like she'd turned into his most wanton fantasy, which in any other woman might have been aimed at keeping him around, but with Tess it had seemed like the direct opposite, as if she could take him or leave him—when earlier she'd just been desperate to take him.

He ran his tongue around his teeth. He could still taste her and even that was enough to have him rising to half-mast. He hadn't had this much trouble controlling his dick since he'd been sixteen and had been initiated into the fine art of fellatio by one of his father's girlfriends. Miranda had hooked on the side and given young Stevie a freebie in exchange for the cup of coffee he'd made her. Fact was he'd been happy to talk to someone who didn't want to kick the shit out of him at home. And she'd been happy to receive a simple kindness. Maybe he was now mature enough to admit part of the thrill had been in getting some small-minded revenge against the miserable sonofabitch who'd been passed out in the other room. At sixteen he'd thought he'd died and gone to heaven.

He sure as hell would never forget Miranda Wyatt for what she'd done to him that day in that suffocating little trailer, but what Tess had done with him in her home had been a million times more powerful, a million times more emotional...right up until the moment it hadn't.

It had started off like an inferno. Hell, they hadn't made it up the freaking stairs let alone to bed. They'd spent an hour and a half exploring things neither one of them should have had any business touching and at the time he would have sworn it had been good, honest sex, but…

Thanks for the ride, cowboy?

As if she'd picked him up in a bar and didn't know his name?

Cowboy? *What the fucking fuck?*

He set his teeth and maneuvered toward Georgetown. It was so unlike the woman he thought he knew. He tried to pinpoint when the mood had shifted but the only thing he could think of was Heather's phone call.

Ah, fuck. He hung his head.

That would do it.

How to piss off the naked woman you were literally on top of and possibly inside—by getting a call from your ex that made you drop everything and run.

Goddamn.

His mind drifted to the way she'd touched herself like some sex kitten at the end. He'd almost passed out from sudden blood loss. Now he figured she'd been torturing him for being that *prick* who left to *deal* with his ex. He thought about the other things he'd said although details were blurry. He remembered something about walls, screwing and controlling someone through sex.

What a fucking dumbass.

He shook his head at himself.

He'd hurt Tess and she'd shielded herself in the one way that she'd known would make him think she was fine with it. Not by being clingy and vulnerable, but by being a sexy, confident woman who didn't need anyone. Because as far as she knew he was off for blonde dessert in the 'burbs.

"Shit." He thumped the steering wheel with his fist.

A patrol car put its lights and sirens on in the distance, speeding off to someone else's crisis. Traffic was light at three a.m. There were definite advantages to working the graveyard shift. He pulled into a drive-thru to grab a coffee. He needed to go back and talk to Tess. Apologize for being a coward and refusing to face the fact he had growing feelings for her. Tell her she was important to him and maybe once this case was over they could see where this thing between them might lead.

Another text from Heather dinged. This one said she had something important to tell him about his new girlfriend. What the hell? Did she know about Tess, or was she just fishing?

Was Heather drunk? Did she think she could blackmail him into coming back to her? That was insanity. Should he call the cops? That made more than fifteen messages in twenty minutes. He'd already texted back a less than flattering response. Maybe she'd heard from Lyle's lawyer or discovered that his new girlfriend was younger and prettier than she was.

She was. He'd checked.

One thing was for damned sure, if it was an emergency she'd have called 911.

Divorce meant no contact as far as he was concerned. They didn't have kids. There was no reason for them to ever communicate again. Heather probably had seduction in mind but he'd fulfilled his quota of screw-ups for the day and it wasn't even four a.m.

He debated whether to head back to Tess's, or go to Heather's, but he was sick of being hassled by his ex. It was time to put an end to the insanity.

Mac parked his truck in front of the address Heather had

sent him, a large house on the edge of Georgetown, so close to the Naval Observatory some of the lights from the buildings shone through the trees.

It was a nice place. Near the woods, and not far from where the congressman had been shot. Trettorri was still in a coma. Mac had checked before he'd had mind-blowing sexual relations with someone who might know something regarding the shooter.

He got out of the truck and shut the door calmly despite his anger. The wide, front lawn was sprinkled with dead leaves that rustled as the wind blew in a strong gust.

A light was on upstairs.

Mac needed to convince Heather he'd moved on. That he had someone important in his life now. His mind flashed to Tess and he swallowed.

Regret ate him up inside. He needed to talk to her. Explain... Explain what? That, although he couldn't be in a real relationship with her right now, it was a smart idea for him to stick close to protect her from Eddie? And as they were together anyway maybe they could just fuck like bunnies until this was all over because his dick couldn't get enough of her and his head was having a similar problem?

Just as long as his heart wasn't involved.

But it was. He knew it was. He hadn't had the kind of emotionally derelict sex with Tess that he usually embraced. But he couldn't promise her a damned thing except she'd almost certainly regret getting involved with him and might get hurt in the process. It was another layer of shit added on top of all the other crap she'd had to endure over the years.

He couldn't do that to her. He had to walk away before either of them got in too deep, and maybe it was already too late for one of them, but that was his problem and he'd take it to his grave.

And as for starting something after the case was closed...what was the point? He was a career FBI agent. He wasn't getting out unless it was in a body bag. And Tess Fallon, only surviving daughter of Francis and David Hines did not fit in with that life choice. No matter how unfair that might be.

It was unfair.

It was damn unfair, but he wasn't sure what the hell he could do to change it.

Heather's crazy ex text spree had done them both a favor, he realized as he moved toward the front door, although it hadn't felt like it at the time.

The icy wind dragged its claws over his skin, telling him winter still had a firm grip on this part of the US. A decorative wreath formed a bull's eye on the red, front door of the Georgian mansion. He rolled his eyes at the situation he found himself in. Then he dialed 911 and reported a disturbance at this address. Heather would never be tempted to text him again after this went down.

He climbed the three front steps and pressed the buzzer. No one answered. Another strong gust of wind blasted and the front door moved slightly. Shit, it wasn't even latched properly.

A shiver of unease ran down his spine and he slid his Glock from its cradle.

Heather had gone through a phase when they were married, texting him as if there was some major issue at home, only for him to rush back and find her waiting in bed wearing nothing but sexy lingerie.

It was cute the first couple of times, but then it started to interfere with his job. It wasn't long after he'd started ignoring those text messages that Lyle had started getting a little extra boardroom action. Heather did not like to be ignored.

Mac forced himself to feel a little compassion for his ex's situation. He knew how much it sucked to be cheated on. Heather might have genuinely loved the guy and might be heartbroken, but she needed to realize it wasn't Mac's job to fix that.

He got another text.

"I'm upstairs. Come on up."

He eased the weapon back into the holster but left the clip undone. Even if he'd been stuck on a desert island for the last two years with only his right hand for company, there was no way an hour with his ex would be worth the year of misery that was sure to follow.

He'd risked more than that to be with Tess…

Which was beyond reckless.

Since when had personal relationships been more important than his career? Since *never*.

Impatient with everything that had happened tonight, he pushed the door open. Cops would be here soon.

Dammit, he was in the middle of a multiple murder investigation and was dealing with *women* problems? What the hell was wrong with him? He was about to text Heather back when he realized how ridiculous the whole situation was.

He stepped inside and yelled up the white-painted staircase. "Heather! You better be decent. Cops are on the way!"

The sound of a TV playing loudly came from somewhere on the second floor and drowned out his words. Dammit. He turned on the lights and took the stairs two at a time. The house was beautiful with hardwood floors and framed pictures on the walls. One oil painting was knocked off kilter and he straightened it out of habit. Most of the rooms were dark but light shone from beneath one door.

Shaking his head, he knocked on that door. "Heather. If you want to talk to me you need to come out here with some clothes on. Uniforms are on their way. You said this was an emergency." Again, no answer. Could she even hear him over the racket of the TV?

Part of him wanted to walk away and never to hear from Heather Surrey again. But he'd once pledged his life to the woman and though he despised her for throwing that commitment back in his face, another small part empathized with the fact she was hurting.

"And damned if she doesn't know it," he acknowledged to himself.

This nonsense had to end. He blew out a big breath and reached out for the door handle.

"Heather?" Still no answer.

He stepped hesitantly into the room, which seemed to be a small living room off the master bedroom. The TV showed the news—weird considering Heather's idea of keeping up with current events involved watching *Entertainment Tonight.*

Something felt off. He stopped walking, eased out his Glock.

"Heather," he demanded louder.

Still no reply. He eyed the closed door and made his feet stay firmly planted where they were. He narrowed his gaze thoughtfully, then crept closer and listened for a moment. The TV was too loud to hear a damn thing.

He took hold of the knob, knowing he was going to feel like an idiot if the woman *was* trying to seduce him, but he couldn't shake the sense of unease rattling along his nerves.

He burst into the room, weapon drawn as he cleared the fatal funnel and kept moving left. His heart squeezed as gore rose up his throat.

Heather lay on the bed. Naked. Her arms were restrained above her head by two silk ties, her legs spread eagle. Duct tape covered her mouth. The only other adornment was a thick gold chain around her throat. Blood soaked the sheets from two bullet holes. One to the heart. One to the head.

He strode towards her, gun raised as he searched for a pulse in her throat. Her skin was still warm, but she wasn't breathing and she was way past saving. He glanced around. Was the killer still here?

Had she waited here naked for him, only to be surprised by some opportunistic burglar? Had Mac taken too long to arrive?

Was that a pulse? He pressed harder against her throat, trying to find the carotid.

"Christ." He pulled out his cell, dialed 911 again. "I've found a woman with a gunshot wound to the chest and head." He gave the dispatcher the address.

"Officers are one minute out," she told him.

"Tell them an FBI agent is on the premises. I'm going to search the house for the suspect."

He cleared the en suite and bedroom as efficiently as possible without disturbing potential evidence. He'd worked his way through another three bedrooms by the time the first cops arrived.

"Up here," he yelled. He held his gold shield aloft. "ASAC Steve McKenzie. FBI. Victim's through there." He pointed to Heather's bedroom. "I haven't cleared the whole house yet."

"We've got it."

One guy, a little on the heavy side, gray hair and a buzz-cut, eyed him warily. "You injured?" the guy asked him.

"Nope."

"You know the victim?" asked the other cop, coming out of the room and shaking his head, confirming what Mac already knew.

Mac wiped his jacket sleeve over his forehead. Nodded. "My ex-wife."

"You often visit your ex-wife in the middle of the night?" The cop's eyes narrowed in suspicion.

"I arrived about eight minutes ago," he told the first cop. "Found her like this." He frowned. "She asked me to drop by. Sent me dozens of texts." He held out his cell phone to show the guy.

Where the hell was her cell phone? He started to walk back into the bedroom to look for it, but the guy with the buzz-cut stopped him. "Sorry, sir. You can't go back in there. This isn't your investigation."

Shit.

His stomach hurt and bile tasted bitter in his mouth. "She left the front door ajar, and texted me to come up." He rubbed his forehead. "At least, I assumed she'd done it." The killer must have done that.

Fuck. Had he been played?

He'd definitely been played. Had Lyle set him up to get rid of a woman he no longer wanted?

"You need to call her husband," Mac told them.

"Another one?" the cop asked in surprise.

Mac nodded. "They were having problems, separated at Christmas."

"Those problems have anything to do with you?" the uniform asked.

Mac gave him a hard stare, not liking where this was going. "No. I just got reassigned to HQ in DC a week ago. Heather begged me to meet her for lunch on Tuesday. Before that I hadn't seen her in a couple of years."

"Amicable?"

Mac grimaced. "As a bare-knuckle fight."

He saw the cops exchange a glance, the kind he exchanged with colleagues when he thought the witness might be the bad guy. "Do I need my lawyer, Officer?"

The guy smirked. "Only if you have something to hide."

It was the sort of thing Mac would also say to a suspect to get them to waive their rights. He blinked a couple of times, realizing how this looked. Fuck. He didn't have time for this shit.

Mac walked downstairs to the living room and sat on the couch. Buzz-cut followed. Mac might be a federal agent who'd called emergency services, but he was now the prime suspect in a vicious homicide. He shook his head and covered his face with his hands. Swore. "I have to return to headquarters. I'm leading the task force investigating these DC murders."

"I'm sure you are." The cop nodded sagely, clearly not believing a word. "Weren't they killed by two shots, one to the heart, one to the head? Like the vic upstairs?"

Mac nodded. He wasn't about to go into the differences between the cases, but they couldn't actually believe he'd done this.

"You know as well as I do, we need to question you before you do anything else."

"Then hurry the fuck up," he bit out. Then he closed his

eyes and realized he was being an asshole. Heather had been murdered, and he needed to do everything he could to bring her killer to justice. And if that involved sitting down with a homicide detective for an hour or two to try and sort this mess out, then so be it. "Fine. But I need to call headquarters and tell them where I am."

"You can do that." The uniform gave him the sort of smile that made criminals buckle. "Tell them you're gonna be a while."

TESS DROVE UP to Cole's house in American University Park and parked on the side of the road. The lower half was red brick and the windows had black painted shutters. An addition on the side housed Cole's office, but it was dark. A light shone in the living room. Cole's car wasn't visible but it might be in the garage.

She went around the side to knock on the kitchen door. No one answered so she knocked harder. She didn't want to use her key. The sound of footsteps had her bracing herself.

Dave opened the door. The stocky redhead gave her a puzzled frown and rubbed his eyes. "Tess? Everything okay?"

"I need to talk to Cole. Is he here?" She'd changed into jeans and a red sweater. She hunched inside her coat trying to keep out the frigid wind.

Dave stood back and she brushed past him.

"I don't know. I fell asleep on the couch watching a movie. Last time I saw him he was on his way to your place." He yawned widely and covered his mouth in embarrassment. "You want me to go find out if he's in his room?"

"I'll do it. Thanks. I need to check on something first. Tax stuff." She spoke quietly, not wanting to disturb the other people in the house. She wasn't willing to back down now she'd finally found the courage to confront her baby brother. She took off her boots and left them by the door. The thumb drive was in her jeans' pocket and she wanted to study the look on his face when he saw it.

First, she wanted to see if that black folder had magically reappeared.

She went to his office and started going through each individual file. After a few minutes, she sat back on her heels. Nothing.

Frustrated but determined, she headed upstairs to Cole's bedroom. There were four rooms on this floor: Cole, Zane, Dave and a spare that Joe often used. Tess wasn't sure why the guy didn't move in here, but he claimed to like dorm life too much. Probably appreciated the easy access to the female population, she thought wryly.

She knocked lightly on Cole's door and eased it open. The room was empty. Dammit. She pressed her lips together and took a step inside. The familiar scent of athletic trainers assailed her, but the room was tidy. No dirty laundry on the floor. Bed was made. Tess wondered if he'd turned over a new leaf for this woman he was seeing. Just in case she ever turned up here unexpectedly.

Was that where he was now? Sadness seeped through her. Her lies had driven him away and that left her feeling desolate. But she wasn't compromising her principles again. Not for Cole. Not for anyone.

She closed the door behind her and eyed his bedside table. It was a gross invasion of privacy but she started searching the drawers, ignoring the personal items that were not her focus.

Then she searched his clothes drawers, running her hand beneath the sweaters and t-shirts, across shelves, under jeans. Nothing. She felt beneath his pillow and found the pajama bottoms she'd bought him for Christmas. One of the pictures tacked to the wall above the bed was a photograph of Cole and her when she'd moved into her new house last fall. Another showed him kissing the cheek of a woman, but Tess couldn't make out any distinct features. She stood in the middle of the room with her hands on her hips. Guilt ate at her. She shouldn't be doing this. He'd be furious.

She didn't care.

She turned on her phone's flashlight and knelt beside the bed. The carpet was dusty but aside from two pairs of sneakers and a stray pen there wasn't anything underneath. She frowned as something black caught her gaze through the slats. She heaved up the mattress and there was the file. Her heart knocked against her ribs in a frantic tattoo.

She pulled her gloves out of her pocket and slipped them on. Grabbed the file, and flicked it open. There was the photograph of Judge Thomas. She slipped the folder inside her coat, and held it tight against her side while she did up the zipper. She hadn't imagined it. She put the room back together so no one would know what she'd been doing.

At the door, she met a concerned-looking Dave. "I left him a note," she said to explain the length of time she'd spent in his room, closing the door firmly behind her. Suddenly his confused frown seemed a little sinister. Cole's roommates were just as capable of hiding that file under his mattress as he was.

But what motive would they have?

She smiled brightly. "Sorry I woke you," she whispered.

"Bye."

He shrugged as if coming over in the middle of the night was perfectly normal. "S'okay. See ya at the party?"

"Of course," she lied. A birthday party was the last thing she cared about. She was conscious of his gaze on her back as she jogged down the stairs, holding on to the folder with one forearm. She forced herself to walk not run through the house and pull on her boots rather than bolting barefoot down the street.

She eased out the door, her ears hammering with the sound of fear.

She got into her Mini Cooper and locked herself inside, heart beating frantically. She unzipped her coat and placed the folder on the passenger seat before driving away. Half a mile later, she pulled over. She called Cole, but once again he didn't answer. What was he doing? Spending the night with his lover or plotting how to avenge the deaths of a family he didn't remember?

She glanced at the file and lifted the first page. The paper fought her slippery gloves. Finally, she turned over the first page and her heart solidified into a piece of ice. A picture of Sonja Shiraz, the transgender DJ, was on the second page.

The ice shattered and inside she felt broken. She needed to get this file to Mac.

CHAPTER TWENTY-SIX

COLE FOLDED HIS arms above his head and smiled up at the ceiling. Despite everything, life wasn't so bad. Carolyn swore and then laughed as she searched for the black pumps she wore to work. "I can't see a thing in this mess."

Boxes were stacked everywhere.

"Want me to put the light on?" he asked.

"No. Go on back to sleep. It's early, but we're busy at work and I have to go in. Stay and sleep." She sat on the edge of the bed and leaned over to kiss him on the lips.

She'd called him unexpectedly and for the first time ever begged him to come over and spend the night. Told him she missed him.

Everything else paled into insignificance.

She slipped her hand over his chest as if she couldn't stop touching him. He pulled her toward him for a kiss.

"I was thinking..." She said between tasty bites. "That rather than me moving to that new apartment all alone..." His heart stopped beating at the thought of what she might be about to say.

"We could maybe go to the next level in our relationship."

He pulled away, heart pounding. "You want me to move in with you?"

Her expression, just visible in the glow of the alarm clock, grew uncertain. "Only if you want to. I thought we could try it. See how we fit."

"We fit great."

The timing was terrible. Everything was going to shit, but finally here was something he really wanted, going right. He could make this work in his favor. He drew her up until she was lying over him and then he rolled so she was beneath him, hands pulling her shirt out of the skirt she'd just put on so he could access her breasts. "I would love to move in with you. Hell, if it were up to me I'd take you to the best jeweler in town and—"

She placed two fingers on his lips. "One step at a time, lover." He stopped speaking but his hands never stopped pulling that tight skirt up those delectable thighs.

He grabbed a condom and covered himself. She still wore the black heels and they dug into his ass as he entered her in one hard thrust. They began to move together, her as frantic for this as he was for her.

He wanted to be in her life for as long as possible. He knew the age difference wouldn't be easy but so what? If people didn't like it, fuck them. His secrets were another matter.

He should tell her the truth before she committed for sure but, hell, he'd tell her later when she was as sure about him as he was about her.

He raised her hips so he could thrust deeper and felt her start to lose it as her chin tipped up and she groaned. "I love you…"

He couldn't hear the last thing she said because the blood was rushing through his ears and the tingle in his spine erupted to crash over his body in a tsunami of pleasure. She cried out at the same time and tightened around him, clutching him like he was her lifeline.

"I want us to be together now," she sobbed.

"We are together." He pressed his forehead to hers, their breath mingling, warm and damp on his lips. He didn't want to move though they had to. "What time do you want me to help you move today?"

Her grin was so huge he could see it in the darkness. He hadn't forgotten his promise although she hadn't mentioned it again. He wanted to prove he was serious about her. He wasn't some kid. He listened.

"Trent said he'd drop the truck off this morning and maybe load it up with some boxes before he left."

"Trent has a key?" Unconsciously, Cole's voice deepened.

"No, the super will let him in." She touched his face. "You don't need to be jealous. I love you, not him."

One side of his lips curled. *Epic.* He started to get hard again. Honestly, he loved her so much he physically couldn't get enough.

She pushed at him. "Nope. Get off me. I don't have time. How about we meet here later so my boss doesn't have a fit and you can attend that ethics class you mentioned?"

He laughed. "You're such a rule follower."

She bit his lip.

He reared back and swore, touching the sting. "But don't worry. I won't take it for granted."

She pushed him off her and climbed to her feet. "You'd better not."

He caught her hand. "I love you," he said quietly.

"I love you, too," she said. "Always."

THE HAMMERING ON Tess's door sounded like someone was close to breaking it down. She was jerked out of a deep sleep and scooped up the Ruger from where she'd laid it on the carpet beside the couch.

Easing the drapes aside, she checked the side window. Dawn was skirting the horizon. Shadows blending into dull gray tones. One of the agents from Mac's team, the bald guy she'd met earlier tonight, stood on the stoop. She ran her hand over her hair and gave up on trying to tame it. She had more important things to worry about than her appearance. She placed the Ruger beneath a throw cushion on the couch, then went to the front door and unlocked it. The Fed pushed past her, making her rear back in alarm.

"Can I help you, Agent…?"

He raked her with a hard, blue gaze. "Walsh. We met earlier, remember?"

She set her teeth. She didn't appreciate people thinking she was dumb.

"Agent Walsh." She nodded and gave him a stiff smile.

Hyperaware that the folder she'd found under Cole's mattress was inside a plastic bag on a chest in the living room Tess closed the front door to block out the winter chill. Not taking that information to the nearest police station was no doubt a crime but Mac was the only officer of the law she trusted. She needed to speak to him before Cole discovered it was missing. Mac needed to question him, and fast.

She itched to call Mac again but needed to get rid of this guy. She forced herself to be polite. "What can I do for you, Agent Walsh?"

"What time did ASAC McKenzie leave here last night?"

Why did he want to know? Would Mac be in trouble if his colleagues found out the two of them had had sex? Of course he would. But lying might be worse.

"Why don't you ask him?" she hedged.

"Give me a straight answer, lady," he bit out.

Her head snapped up. *What an asshole.* "He left around three a.m."

"You're sure?"

Her brows rose and her smile was one of reproof. "Yes. I'm sure."

She saw him glance into her kitchen, which she still hadn't tidied after the break-in last night. She'd braced a chair under the handle of the back door and intended to call a security firm today to install an alarm system and new locks. Because the person who'd broken in last night might have a key...

The thought it might be Cole cracked her heart wide open.

Walsh's eyes lingered on items scattered across the floor. Could he tell she and Mac had sex there? Or on the table? Or against the door she was now leaning against? Were her sins like bruises on bone and easy to spot?

"Why are you here, Agent Walsh?" she prompted. Had something happened to Mac? Was that why he wasn't answering his phone? Or did he want her to stop calling him but lacked the nerve to tell her himself? Tess stayed very still, bracing for another dose of reality to smack her in the face. "Did Mac send you?"

Walsh's eye twitched at her use of his boss's name. Hell, she'd known Mac longer than this guy had been in the FBI, but she was supposed to pretend they'd just met?

"Why was he here so long after we left? I thought everything was cleared up?" Walsh's blue eyes were sharp on her face.

A shiver of unease stole over her body and she turned away. She wasn't ashamed of what they'd done but there was no way Mac would want it broadcast to the world and, frankly, neither did she. Their time together was private.

Was it illegal to lie? Or was it immoral to ask?

"We were talking about Eddie, trying to figure out who he might have gone to for help. Why are you here?"

Walsh watched her critically. "Can you confirm the time he left again?"

She didn't understand. "I thought I just did?"

"Did something precipitate his leaving?" he pushed.

God, the guy was being an ass.

"He got a series of texts. Said it was his ex-wife and he needed to go and sort something out." She crossed her arms as that familiar sense of awkwardness swept up her neck and into her cheeks. She doubted Mac would want her talking about this either.

"Was he angry?" asked Walsh.

She blinked in surprise. "No. I mean, he was irritated. Said she kept texting him and he wanted her to stop. He wasn't angry." He'd had too much mind-blowing sex to be truly angry. "He seemed frustrated and eager to do something about the fact she was texting him." Too eager.

Walsh watched her face so avidly it was like he was scanning her micro-expressions for deceit. "Where were you?"

She frowned in confusion. "What do you mean, where was I? I was here. Obviously." She opened her palms to indicate her home.

"Did you go out at all?"

Unease did a little somersault in her stomach. "I went to my brother's house after Mac left, but Cole wasn't there."

"So no witnesses?" His tone said, *how convenient.*

"I didn't say that. One of his roommates let me in. Dave... God. I forget his surname."

"Address?" he pulled out his phone and eyed her expectantly.

Her mouth went dry as the Gobi Desert. Her nails bit into her arms through the wool of her sweater. Had someone else been murdered? Was their name in that file? Might she have saved them if she'd gone straight to the police? A terrifying thought occurred to her. "Please tell me Mac wasn't shot?"

"He wasn't shot."

Relief wasn't as enormous as it should have been. Walsh's expression was too fierce and unamused. She was missing something. "What is this about, Agent Walsh?"

"Mac's ex-wife was found murdered in the early hours of this morning," he said without inflection. "Cops think he did it."

"What? There is no way he killed her." She clenched her fists. "He isn't that sort of person."

"I never said I thought he did it. That's not my job." Walsh's eyes were like lasers cutting into her and she wanted to take a step back. "I'll give it to you straight, *Tess*, as Mac seems to have a weakness for you."

Weakness?

"I don't care what happens to you"—*holy crap*—"but Steve McKenzie is a fine man and a helluva well-respected agent. He's dedicated his life to law enforcement and now his career is going to be destroyed because he got involved with you."

A rush of humiliation engulfed Tess. This was why she'd

changed her name and concealed her background. Her truth had the power to destroy—and not just her own life but also the people who cared about her. Which wasn't fair. None of this was fair.

Anger unfurled and took hold.

"Because he got involved with *me*? If he didn't do it, he didn't do it and his," she tripped over the words, "*association* with me should be irrelevant. I thought *you* were supposed to protect the innocent, Agent Walsh?" She took a step toward him and his mouth tightened. She remembered shoving Mac into a wall earlier this morning and how that had ended. She stopped moving. The file sitting on the chest taunted her. Maybe she wasn't as innocent as she wanted to believe. "Why are the cops even considering a man like ASAC McKenzie for murder?"

Walsh's face went blank. "I can't reveal the details of a case to you."

Her mouth opened and closed in confusion. "Details? How can there be details if Mac didn't do anything?"

He remained closed-mouthed and she stood in her hallway feeling impotent and alone. She had to talk to Mac. She didn't know who else she could trust, certainly not Walsh. But she couldn't give that file to Mac either. He was probably off the case and she was his alibi for another murder.

"How can I help?" she said finally.

She half expected him to tell her to keep away from his boss, but he didn't.

"Get dressed and I'll escort you to the PD to make a statement."

She blew out a long breath. She could do that.

"Bring your cell phone."

She nodded.

"Anyone see you and Mac between the time I left and the time you say Mac left?"

She shook her head.

"Pity." He pinched his lips together.

She begged to differ.

"Corroboration would be useful."

Her upper lip drew back. "My word isn't good enough to count as an airtight alibi?"

His huffed out a dry laugh. "You ever heard of the word *accomplice*, Ms. Fallon?"

Her eyes bugged. *What the hell?* "You think *I* might be involved in the murder of a woman I've never met?" Her voice came out high-pitched and loud. What a nightmare.

He jerked his chin. "It's not my case so I don't think anything. But you might want to think very carefully about what you tell them, and I suggest sticking closely to the truth."

As if she made a habit of lying?

Anger stained her cheeks and she glanced at the file folder on the side table. Guilt and shame warred within her. But logic won. "Did you ever stop to wonder why Mac's ex-wife was killed now? Was he relieved of duty? Taken off the task force? Do you actually believe this is a coincidence? How about you really do your job, Agent Walsh?"

He stared at her without blinking and she knew she was supposed to be intimidated. But she didn't scare easy. Never had.

All she actually wanted was to be left alone, but the world wasn't letting that happen. So she'd deal.

She pushed past Walsh and grabbed her laptop and purse off the table. She placed the thumb drive and file folder inside, too. He eyed her with curiosity but she didn't trust him enough to confide. She didn't trust him at all.

No way Mac had killed his ex. Hell, she'd known he was honorable from the moment she'd first met him and she'd been ten. That hadn't changed despite everything they'd been through together. She'd help get him out of jail, and then give this information to the FBI…but who?

She didn't know. Her heart sank. What if Cole *was* involved? Could Mac save the boy she loved or was it already too late?

WHAT SEEMED LIKE an eternity later, Mac was still being questioned by local cops. He'd surrendered his service weapon, his backup, his cell phone, not to mention his goddamned pride because he wanted this over with. He wanted the cops to verify what he was telling them so they could move on and catch the real killer and he could go back to work. Apparently, they liked the color of his motive.

The young, female detective who'd been pushing him hard for the last hour shifted her chair to the side of the table, rather than sitting across from him—invading his personal space in a move designed to make him uncomfortable.

"So, you think the suspect was still in the house when you got there?" she asked.

With her attitude, he half expected her to pop gum. She reminded him of Dunbar, but Dunbar had a heart and a brain rather just a hard-on for some federal ass.

"Not necessarily in the house. I told you, I got a text telling me to come in when I was standing on the doorstep. The sonofabitch was watching me from somewhere."

"But you didn't see anyone?"

"No."

"You didn't touch anything?" the male cop asked. He appeared near retirement. Old enough to be the female detective's father. Hell, Mac was theoretically old enough to be her father.

"I straightened a picture in the hallway outside the upstairs living room. It was crooked." The killer had probably knocked it askew. "I touched the doorbell, possibly the knob of her bedroom. And I checked Heather for a pulse." He wanted to scrub the whole thing from his brain. No one deserved to die like that.

"You didn't touch any evidence?"

"I'm not an idiot." This wasn't his first rodeo.

"You don't seem that cut up about her death." The woman detective tipped her head to one side.

Man, he hoped he got to grill her on federal charges one day. He could not wait.

"I mean, you're not exactly shedding tears. The uniforms who picked you up said you didn't appear that cut up to them either."

Mac stiffened at the expression "picked you up." He hadn't been *picked up*, he'd called the cops, come in voluntarily for questioning. But he didn't say anything. He was a trained professional. People reacted in different ways to this kind of event and sometimes how they acted made them look guilty. If these two were any good at their jobs they'd know that.

"And you say you went over there to just talk to her?" the older detective said with a tired expression.

"I told you before." He was beginning to realize how annoying repetitive questioning could be though he understood the reason for it—being an experienced federal fucking agent he appreciated all the ways cops tried to trip suspects. "The last few days she wouldn't stop calling me. When I started getting texts tonight I'd had enough. I decided to go over there to persuade her that we would never get back together and that I didn't want to hear from her again."

"Persuade her?" the old guy asked.

"As in *tell her* I wasn't interested."

"I'm thinking your ex wouldn't like the sound of that." The female detective's brown eyes gleamed like he'd given away something vital.

Mac leaned forward and spoke slowly in case they were both a little dense. "She never found out, guys. She was already dead when I got there."

"Where were you again? Before you say you went over to Mrs. Surrey's house?"

He eyed her. Her detective shield must be brand spanking new given her age and enthusiasm. That or she hated Feds. "I was in Bethesda, at a suspected break-in tied to my current task force investigation."

She checked her notes. "I spoke to Agent Walsh. He said they all left that house around one. How come you were still there at three?"

No way was he admitting to having sex with Tess. Not even to save his career. Hell, he wasn't sure which the Bureau would frown on more, murder or inappropriate relations with someone involved in a case.

"I had more questions for her."

"I bet you did." The young detective's smirk was a work of art. "We'll be checking that out with Ms. Fallon."

Mac forced himself not to tense up when they mentioned Tess's name. Of course they knew about her. This was a murder investigation.

The older guy took his turn. "Why'd your ex suddenly start calling you this week if you hadn't seen her in two years?"

Mac rubbed his eyes, wishing to hell he'd handled this whole thing differently. Maybe Heather would still be alive then. But why was she dead? Who'd killed her? And why the hell were the cops still questioning him? "Heather's pride was bruised from her new hubby screwing around on her and I just transferred to FBI HQ. She probably figured she'd be able to manipulate me into having an affair."

"Manipulate, how?" asked the older guy, adjusting the belt that rested beneath his gut.

He gave the man a look. "How'd you think?"

"You thought she was going to use sex to snare you?" The female detective gave him a cynical sneer.

"Actually." He leaned forward across the table, holding her gaze. "I think she was hoping to use sex with me to somehow get back at her current husband. Maybe make him jealous? Heather got most of her relationship pointers out of *Cosmo*. You questioning her actual husband this hard?"

She ignored that. "Did you have sex tonight?"

"I haven't had sex with Heather since eight months before our divorce." Fuck. How to not answer the question. He did not want to be in this fucking room. His sex life was not their business and if she pushed it he was getting a lawyer.

He stared at an ink spot on the table. Why had this happened now? Why two gunshots?

"Someone had sex with her tonight."

Mac's stomach lurched. Had Heather been raped? He

blinked away the sharpness of tears. He'd learned young, never show weakness.

Funny, Tess had learned the same thing.

"Your ex cheat on you?"

He wanted to roll his eyes. "Yes, she did, with the guy she then married—Lyle Surrey. So if I'd been going to kill anyone it would have been him."

The detective's eyes gleamed brighter. "So you thought about it?"

Mac had meant it as a joke. "Why? Is he dead?"

Homicide cops usually had a dark sense of humor but these guys seemed like they both had a bad case of irritable bowel syndrome. He'd thought this was routine but things weren't adding up. Like the fact it was nearly seven a.m. and they still hadn't let him leave yet.

Damn.

"No. I didn't think about killing Lyle. I thought about punching him in the mouth a time or two just to teach him some manners, but once I found out Heather cheated on me I wasn't really interested anymore. He was welcome to her."

"Not the forgiving type?" Detective teenybopper's tone was snide.

"I don't like liars, Detective." He raised his gaze towards the mirrored glass where somebody important was bound to be staring back at him. He hoped to hell it wasn't his boss. "And if I had decided to kill Heather I wouldn't have been caught at the murder scene and you would never have found her body." They'd taken his clothes for gunshot residue analysis. Thankfully they'd allowed him to grab clean stuff out of his go-bag so he wasn't wearing jailbird stripes.

"Maybe it happened in the heat of the moment. You guys

go at it for old times' sake and then she says something to piss you off—"

"So I *shoot* her?" he said incredulously.

"Did you?"

"No. I did not shoot her. I did not have sex with her. I did not inflict any harm upon her person and nor would I want anyone else to harm her." Was that clear enough for them? He scrubbed his fingers through his short hair. He bet he had more than one gray hair now. "Look, I'm in the middle of a big investigation that I need to get back to. When Heather's texts started arriving in the middle of the night I decided I'd talk to her face-to-face and make it clear that she had to stop causing me grief."

"Trust me," the female detective told him. "Her texting you is not going to be your biggest problem anymore."

"Cute."

The detective leaned back in her chair and stretched her booted feet out to the side. "You have a temper, Steve?" She flipped the top page of her notes over the top of her clipboard. "Says here you punched a US marshal in the jaw last year, during that investigation into the mall attack in Minneapolis."

Mac rolled his eyes extravagantly and crossed his arms over his chest. The guy had swung at him first. "Okay, I take it we're done here? I told you everything that happened last night, including the fact that if you didn't find her phone at the house the killer likely still has it and you need to track that shit the fuck down." He stood. "So unless you're gonna charge me, I'm outta here."

"I don't know why you're in such a hurry to leave, ASAC McKenzie." The detective's mouth curved the exact same degree as her elegantly winged eyebrows. "They've already

342

taken you off the case."

"What?" He sat back down. Fuck. "Why the hell would they do that?"

She admired her manicure. "Press has gone nuts about this whole murder thing. I spoke to your boss about an hour ago. He said that while you have the full support of the Bureau, blah, blah, blah, you'd been assigned desk duty until this murder investigation is concluded."

"Is this a joke?" Mac closed his eyes for a moment. But he knew it wasn't. "You've got nothing on me. The cell phone GPS data will confirm when I left Bethesda. No way did I have time to set up the text messages and kill Heather. Did the ME give you time of death yet?"

The detective's mouth tightened. "Maybe you had an accomplice."

His eyes widened. The idea that Tess might be dragged into this mess made his chest ache. After him being so sure she'd be the one to ruin his career, instead he was going to destroy her life.

"Anyway." She gave her fingers a jaunty tap on the table. "We don't need the cell tower information when we have solid proof you killed her. You should save us all a lot of trouble and just confess, Steve."

He stared at her dumbfounded. *What the fuck*?

She leaned forward, mimicking and mocking him. "I guess you thought you'd committed the perfect crime to get rid of the annoying ex, huh? Set it up like one of these other murders going on around DC to confuse the issue, huh? Or maybe so you'd be in charge of that investigation, too?"

If she said "huh" one more time he was going to punch the wall.

"Only you're not as smart as you think, ASAC McKenzie, because you forgot one of the most basic pieces of forensic evidence." She stood up. "Your fingerprints were on the shell casings found at the scene. On the bullet casings next to your ex-wife's dead body. So tell us again you didn't touch any evidence or murder Heather Surrey."

CHAPTER TWENTY-SEVEN

M AC MADE HIS phone call and hoped Frazer remembered to contact a lawyer on top of the other things he'd asked him to do.

The interview room door opened. Walsh stepped in. "What the hell is going on?"

Mac sat at the bolted down table. In front of him was a notepad and pen they'd left so he could make a statement. He'd written everything out in excruciating detail, excluding the hot and heavy encounter with Tess. It wasn't just because it might not look good to his bosses. It was none of their goddamned business and he didn't want that negative attention focused on Tess. She didn't deserve it.

Mac raised his brow. "I'd ask how the investigation's going, but apparently I'm a murder suspect so I won't bother."

They hadn't booked or charged him yet. Fuck. He'd been arrested on suspicion. He was hoping evidence would be enough to clear him before things went any further but the detectives were getting off on the fingerprint bullshit—as if he'd got his gold shield in a Cracker Jack box. To say he was pissed was a massive understatement but he knew how the system worked so he kept his mouth shut.

"What the hell happened after I left you in Bethesda?" Walsh's shaved scalp shone under the hot lights. "I mean

Bethesda for Christ's sake, how much trouble can you get into in that neighborhood?"

Mac winced. A lot, apparently.

He'd spent the last hour or so mulling things over and the more he deliberated, the blacker it looked. Someone had gone to a lot of effort to set him up.

"Cops here are suggesting I tried to stage Heather's murder to look like another one of the string of murders happening in DC." Grasping at straws to make their square peg of evidence squeeze into the round-shaped hole. "The detective also intimated Heather was sexually assaulted before she was shot."

Mac's stomach hurt to think about it. Heather had been immature and demanding and annoying but she had not deserved this.

"They think you're a sexual predator who is this inept at staging a murder?" Walsh leaned against the wall and crossed his arms and legs in a relaxed pose.

Mac met Walsh's gaze. "They claim to have my fingerprints on the shell casings. Sounds like a slam-dunk to me."

"Obviously, they have a low appreciation of your brain capacity." Walsh's mouth twisted.

Mac contemplated his former second-in-command. Did the guy think he'd done it? Walsh hadn't asked him outright.

"Could your ex have any of your ammunition from when you were married?"

"No." Heather hadn't liked guns. He rubbed his hands across the scruff on his jaw. There was only one place those casings could have realistically come from—an FBI gun range. Either Quantico, or headquarters.

And that meant David Hines's crazy dream of getting a

ghost skin working for the Feds might have been realized. And the traitor had gone after Mac for several reasons.

Revenge. They were punishing him for his role in the Pioneers' downfall. Maybe they'd just discovered the truth about Kenny Travers, in which case, retribution had been swift and brutal. Or maybe it was payback for Jessop's trip into eternal hellfire and they wanted Mac to join him there.

Or, Mac and his team were getting close enough to this SOB to have him worried.

So why did Mac feel like he'd never been further from solving this thing? Not a lot he could do sitting in an interview room—which was probably the goddamned point.

They'd gotten rid of him by discrediting him and ruining his reputation. So much for making SAC by forty. He'd be lucky to be drawing a pension.

Was there only one of them? Or more?

The measures the FBI had in place to combat this sort of bigoted bullshit were rigorous. He found it hard to believe more than one of these bastards had slipped past all the safeguards.

What was the next step in their plan?

David Hines's manifesto had involved a series of murders followed by a bombing, which would be a call-to-arms for all the boneheads who felt the same way Hines did. It was to have been a declaration of war on the government.

Mac wasn't about to let them get away with it. As much as each individual murder caused him pain, he was not about to forget about the big picture here, and that big picture involved a lot of fear, a lot of noise, a lot of media attention.

Fear. Instability. War.

"You need to increase security at all federal buildings,"

Mac told Walsh.

"What? Why?" Walsh looked confused.

"I think," Mac said deliberately, "that whoever is behind these murders is ready to move on to the next phase of the plot. They got rid of me as I know what David Hines's dream was. You read my notes yet?"

Walsh scowled. "I started but I've been busy."

With this bullshit. Mac wanted to ask about DNA from Trettorri's fingernails and how the congressman was doing. Whether the guy had woken up yet. He couldn't. Walsh couldn't keep him informed of the investigation now he was on the outside. Not just on the outside, but on the wrong side.

Walsh narrowed his gaze. "Why'd you stay at Tess Fallon's so long last night after we left?"

Mac eyed him. "We were talking."

"Give me a break, Mac," Walsh shot back impatiently. "I wasn't born yesterday. I saw the way you were looking at her."

Mac pressed his lips closed over the words he wanted to say. Leaned back in his chair. "How exactly was I looking at her?"

Walsh threw his hands up. "Like she's an attractive woman. Shit, a blind man would get a hard-on looking at her, especially when everyone in the neighborhood could see the outline of her tits through her flimsy nightshirt." The man's eyes blazed in line with Mac's temper. "Ever occur to you she might have been wearing that get-up on purpose?"

"You mean her pajamas?" Mac ground his teeth together, knowing his former buddy was trying to rile him for some reason. "Most people who have an intruder don't worry about what they're wearing when they call the cops." Tess hadn't put herself on display on purpose. She'd been frightened. "What's your point? The fact Tess Fallon is an attractive woman means nothing—"

"Did it ever occur to you that she might be in league with whoever is committing these murders?" Walsh got in his face. "That maybe she's in league with whoever killed your ex-wife and deliberately kept you at her house to set you up?" Walsh's voice grew louder. "If you hadn't been '*talking*' to her you'd have been back at HQ and your alibi would have been rock solid. Now, even if evidence shows you didn't kill Heather, your career is still in the toilet because you were 'talking' which I think means 'screwing' Tess Fallon, David Hines's daughter. At a time when David Hines's Pioneers are the prime suspects in a major crime spree in the nations' capitol."

Mac forced down his rage. Losing his temper would make him look like an asshole who couldn't control himself. Ironic, considering Walsh was the one who was yelling.

Mac looked away. He had considered the fact Tess might have been using him, tricking him, manipulating him with sex. It made him hate himself because they had a connection and he didn't just mean sex. She meant something to him. Hell, she meant a lot.

"What did Tess say?"

Walsh gave him a look.

"She tell you we were fucking?" Mac never took his eyes off the other guy's expression.

Walsh finally blew out a sigh. "No. She said you were 'talking', too. Like I believe that shit."

What Walsh believed was irrelevant unless he was the ghost skin undermining the task force's operation. And that was the real dilemma. Sure, Tess could have been involved, but if she had been she would have fed him to the wolves when the cops questioned her about his alibi.

The fact he'd been suspicious of her made him feel like a douche—again. But someone knew he'd been alone with Tess last night, rather than being at HQ or with another agent. They'd no doubt spied on him and Tess before they killed Heather. The idea made him sick.

It could have been Walsh. It could have been anyone.

"Agents in Coeur d'Alene track down Brandy Jordan yet?" Mac asked.

Walsh's lips tightened. He gave a slight shake of his head.

Mac's fingers clenched. Who else would remember whether or not David Hines had a girlfriend?

"Tess Fallon says she went to see her brother, Cole, after you left last night. I'm about to go talk to his roommates and verify she was there when she says she was. The brother wasn't home."

Mac filed that information away with all the other facts spinning in his brain. "You should bring Cole in for questioning."

Walsh nodded. It was no longer Mac's business so he shut up.

"As soon as the ME estimates time of death and corroborates my truck's GPS, my cell, and every traffic cam between Bethesda and Georgetown, cops can establish that I couldn't have gotten to Heather's house in time to assault and murder her." Poor Heather, even in death she was causing him grief. "They should lose their boner for me and I'll be released." To desk duty. "You get back to work and solve the murders before anyone else dies. And send out those security alerts. Whoever's doing this is dead serious about their cause. They're trying to start a goddamn revolution and we need to be prepared."

He sounded like a freaking paranoid delusional maniac, but stats said people in the US were seven times more likely to die from a domestic terrorist event than a Muslim one. He took *all* threats seriously, but knew which threat worried cops most—and it wasn't the Islamists.

Hate crimes had started popping up all over the US. As if the murders in DC were the signal these lunatics had been waiting for. The FBI needed to quash this killer's agenda and make sure others understood they'd be caught, tried and convicted if they supported it.

Adios, freedom. Hello, penitentiary.

Walsh rubbed his eye sockets. "Like we don't have enough to worry about."

"No kidding," Mac agreed.

"Want me to call your lawyer?" Walsh asked.

"It's being taken care of." He hoped. "You can do me one favor though."

Walsh lifted his chin in question.

"Put a protective detail outside Tess Fallon's house. Eddie is still on the loose and Heather's murder is pretty much what he threatened to do to Tess." Mac's throat closed. Eddie could have killed Heather. He had no doubt the guy would have enjoyed it.

Walsh didn't comment, but hopefully he'd tail Tess if only because he thought she was guilty of something more insidious than being an attractive woman.

"Talk to the marshals and see what the latest is. Eddie Hines would love to be seen as a driving force behind these attacks, but he isn't. He has the brain capacity of a sugared almond."

One way or another Mac knew he was the reason Heather

351

had been targeted and he'd carry that guilt with him for the rest of his life. He thought of her parents, weak-willed and doting. They were going to be crushed.

Shit.

At least putting a detail on Tess's home should keep her safe. The coincidence of her disturbing an intruder and then his ex-wife being murdered was too big to be put down to random chance.

Maybe Tess had been the initial target but had scared them off with her Ruger.

Thank Christ.

"Keep your pecker up. You'll be out of here soon," Walsh told him, grabbing the handle and opening the door to leave. Something Mac was well aware he wasn't allowed to do.

Mac's lip curled. "Go nail this bastard." He was gonna have to sit here with his thumb up his ass until the Toy Town cops figured out he was being set up.

———————

TESS WALKED OUT of the squat, brown building that housed the Washington DC Police Department, feeling as if she'd gone walking in Pamplona the day they let loose the bulls.

She'd given a statement, but the look on the detectives' faces suggested they didn't believe a word she said. Great. If her career as an accountant tanked—and at this rate it might— she could always start writing fiction. She heard her name called and looked up. A camera flash blinded her. Her vision danced with black spots.

The media.

She shielded her face, put her head down and kept walking, but was suddenly surrounded by a crowd of people, invading her space, sticking oversized lenses and sound booms next to her face.

"What's your relationship with ASAC Steve McKenzie?"

"Is it true you're living under a false identity and you're actually the only surviving daughter of David Hines?"

She flinched and tried to keep moving but several people blocked her path and prevented her from heading to where she'd parked her car on, aptly enough, Idaho Avenue.

Someone from the police or FBI must have leaked her name to the press. Her stomach clenched. Had they tracked down Cole yet? She hadn't told the detectives what she'd found in his house last night, what she carried in her purse. She desperately needed to talk to Mac but the cops refused to tell her where he was.

"Did you help McKenzie murder his ex-wife last night?"

She gaped, shocked beyond measure someone would suggest that. She whirled, looking for an escape through the crowd but finding none. Someone took her by the arm and herded her toward a big, black Lexus waiting at the curb.

She opened her mouth to ask who the man was and where he was taking her but she was already inside the vehicle, the stranger climbing in behind her and making her slide across the butter leather of the back seat. Then the door yanked shut and the car pulled away.

"Who are you? Where are you taking me?" Fear entered her voice when she realized she'd effectively been kidnapped.

The man who'd hustled her through the crowd smiled. "Sorry for the lack of introduction. You appeared to need help." The man had silver eyes and the sort of self-deprecating smile that turned women into fools.

"Who are you?" she repeated. She looked around. They'd passed her Mini. "I need my car."

The driver turned around the block and immediately pulled up on the side of the road, out of sight of the reporters.

"Which one is it? Give me the keys and I'll pick it up," the man with the silver eyes offered.

She dipped her hands into her pocket before she realized what she was doing. "I don't even know you. Why would I give you my car keys?"

He tilted his head to the side. "Why would you climb into a car with me?"

"Alex, don't scare the woman," the driver admonished. "I'm ASAC Lincoln Frazer, ma'am."

Ma'am? She didn't know whether to be insulted or turned on.

"I'm a friend of Mac's."

The ASAC in the driver's seat was classically handsome with blond hair, a chiseled jaw and a piercing blue gaze that examined her thoroughly in the rearview. She eyed him warily and then turned to the man at her side. "Why did you help me back there? FBI agents are not generally big fans of mine."

Alex grinned. "I'm not FBI."

She frowned in confusion.

"He's just a consultant," the man called Lincoln Frazer said dryly. "Like I said, Steve McKenzie is a friend of mine. He didn't kill his ex-wife and I don't believe in guilt by association so I'm not going to torture you just because of who your parents were."

An unexpected surge of emotion welled up inside her, revealing just how vulnerable she was today. They were probably playing her and she was lapping it up. "The detectives I spoke with think I had motive for setting Mac up."

"Did you?" the man next to her asked.

"Revenge for the police killing my hateful family? I was there, remember? They committed suicide by cop and tried to take me with them. Why would I think they were worth avenging?"

"So that's a no?" Frazer questioned.

"No! What is wrong with you people?"

"Too many things to mention." The man next to her held out his hand. "I'm Alex Parker. I consult with the FBI on matters of cybersecurity and other things. Pleasure to meet you, Tess."

Tess took his hand, his grip firm and warm. This whole week had been bizarre. "So you examined Henry Jessop's hard drive?"

He gave her a nod.

"Did you identify the person doing this?"

He waited a moment, then gave a slight shake of his head. Maybe he wasn't allowed to tell her.

She hugged her bag close to her chest. Should she trust these people with the file? She had no idea if they were telling the truth or just trying to gain her trust and set her up.

"I believe in you, Tess," Alex said in a low voice.

He must have seen her hesitancy. "Why?"

Alex grinned and she was struck by how handsome he was. Not as hot and built as Mac, but handsome and lean with a mysterious edge that suggested he was just as capable of being tough as he was of being a gentleman.

Mac looked like exactly what he was—a dedicated officer of the law who wasn't afraid to take on the bad guys. Despite his undercover work, Mac had no real artifice, no Machiavellian streak—but he had used her. She looked down at her hands. Wished she could figure out exactly who she should trust.

"Alex believes in you because he's scrutinized every facet of your life and background, including email, internet, financial and phone records, and found no red flags," Frazer said from the front seat.

A scar dissected one of Alex Parker's pale brows. "She also has kind eyes."

She gave a sharp laugh and hugged her purse tighter to her breast. "You're crazy. I have my mother's eyes and she made serial killers look warm and fuzzy."

"You're probably right on the former." Alex put his warm hand on top of hers and she realized how tense she was. Tense and terrified and paranoid. He squeezed gently. "But just because you have the same eye shape, doesn't mean they look the same. Eyes are the window to the soul, remember?"

"And she didn't have one," inserted Frazer.

Tess blinked rapidly at a sudden onslaught of emotion slaying her ability to speak. Why would these strangers' words nearly bring her to tears? Her adoptive mother had always said kindness was one of the most underrated human acts and, after the last few days, Tess was poorly in need of some compassion.

"Can we save the rest of the touchy-feely crap for later?" Frazer suggested smoothly. "Or do we need a group hug?"

Tess burst out laughing and Alex grinned. His pocket buzzed and he checked his cell. "He's out. Do you want your car or not, Ms. Fallon?"

Who was out? Mac? She opened and closed her mouth.

"It should be safe enough where it is for now. Pick it up later, when the press has gone home." Parker answered his own question, correctly assuming she was incapable of making a decision. She wanted to see Mac. Make sure he was okay.

Frazer circled the block and they pulled up next to the curb outside the police station again and she watched as Mac strode through the throng of reporters and opened the front door and climbed in.

He looked frustrated and angry as he slammed the door. "Let's make like shepherds and get the flock out of here."

Tess laughed, but was grateful for the tinted windows as cameras flashed against the glass.

Frazer screeched away and she was pushed back against the seat. Mac turned around and his gaze hooked her like a fish. "What are you doing here?"

He didn't look pleased to see her.

She shriveled a little on the inside.

"Rescued her from paparazzi hell after she left the police department," Parker told him.

"Vultures," said Mac without heat.

"I had to make a statement about last night." How did she tell him that she hadn't told the police they'd slept together without revealing the truth to Frazer and Parker, or making it look like they both had something to hide?

"Sorry I dragged you into this mess." The blue-green of his eyes was vivid against the tan of his skin. His full lips were pressed into a stern, uncompromising line.

She smiled wryly. "I think that's my line. They let you go?"

She'd been so worried about what would happen to him, but he was out. That had to be a positive sign, right?

"For now. They haven't charged me. Yet. They checked my cell data and found me on several traffic cams heading across town before I called nine-one-one. Twice. But they kept my badge and gun and are basically hoping to rush DNA so they can finish the job of nailing my ass to a cross."

"Except you're innocent."

His smile was a thin slice of mean. "Exactly."

He pulled out his cell and popped his SIM card.

"What are you doing?" she asked in surprise.

"Where should we drop you?" Mac didn't answer her question.

She froze and felt the two men do the same.

"I, ah…" She hadn't thought that far ahead. Her home would likely be engulfed by reporters. She couldn't go there.

And suddenly she knew she couldn't keep quiet any longer about what she'd found at her brother's house even if it meant telling Frazer and Parker as well as Mac. She couldn't believe Cole was involved, but she couldn't keep quiet if people might be in danger. If he was guilty she was already complicit—the thought was horrifying.

She cleared her throat as Frazer negotiated traffic. "I have something to tell you. You aren't going to like it." Guilt oozed from every pore, so thick she was sure they could smell it. "On Monday, when the judge and his wife were murdered?"

Mac stared at her over his shoulder like a law enforcement officer rather than a lover. Surely he'd understand why she hadn't mentioned this before?

"I went to Cole's house that morning. He was supposed to meet me to go over his tax forms but I assumed he forgot. So I went through some of his drawers to get the information I needed." The whole car held its breath.

Her mouth turned into sand. She rubbed her left arm. "I found a piece of paper with a picture of the dead judge on it."

The silence in the car sounded like a sonic boom.

"I didn't mention it because I know my brother. He would never be involved in this sort of thing—"

"We don't always know people the way we think we do," Parker said quietly.

"Ain't that the truth," Mac stared at her like he'd discovered she was an alien.

"I went back the next day. With Cole. I figured I could confront him with the file and see whether or not he was lying to me, but the file was gone."

She reached into her purse and pulled out a thumb drive.

"What's that?" Mac asked.

"This was in the same file folder in my brother's file cabinet. It was lying on the bottom of the filing cabinet when I went back for a second look. I took it. I don't know why I took it." Mac raised his brows in a "really" motion. She tried to ease the dryness in her throat but no amount of swallowing helped. "There's nothing on it except porn movies."

Alex plucked it from her fingers and examined it closely. "Let's head to my apartment where we can check it out—not the porn." His grin was pure mischief.

Frazer nodded.

"You didn't think this was worth mentioning?" Mac's voice was deceptively soft. She knew him well enough to realize he was furious.

Tess shrank back against the seat. "You don't understand. Cole isn't like that. He's not a violent person. He's a pacifist."

"Where is he now?" Mac demanded.

"I have no idea," she snapped back.

"You know his schedule?"

She nodded. "He has a lecture on a Friday morning at nine-fifteen. He's free after that." Those eyes of his darkened to a turbulent green. She'd screwed up.

"Did it ever occur to you," he said very slowly, like she was slow-witted, and maybe she was, she certainly felt stupid. "That data stick might be what your intruder was looking for last night?"

"It's just porn—"

"You're a computer expert now? Like your brother is?" Mac's lips curled. And she shut up.

"If you'd told investigators we could have combed Cole's house and maybe saved a life. Maybe saved Heather's life. Did you think of that?"

Her chest split wide open. No. She hadn't. "Cole isn't a violent person."

"And if you'd truly believed that you would have told me about the file when I turned up at your house." Mac turned away from her and despair tried to swallow her whole.

Protecting her brother had been something she'd done since she was a little girl, since the raid that had left them orphans against the world.

"I didn't even know Kenny Travers survived the gunfight until Tuesday, but I was supposed to blindly trust you when you show up with a different identity twenty years later?"

As angry as she was she still needed to finish this. "There's something else."

"What?" The impatience and anger in Mac's tone made her flinch.

"I went to Cole's house after you left last night."

His eyes flashed to hers and she glared back. She'd kept their dirty secret. She was beginning to think she'd been the biggest fool imaginable for sleeping with him and that she was a complete failure when it came to judging people.

"I decided to confront him about what I'd seen on Monday. But he wasn't there, so I searched his bedroom. The paper file was hidden under his mattress." She took a deep breath and pulled the plastic bag from her purse and handed it to Mac, careful not to touch him. "I called you several times but you didn't answer." She twisted her hands together. "I took it. I didn't know what else to do. I didn't know who else to trust."

Mac's eyes were wide. Then he took the latex gloves Frazer offered him and turned his attention to the printed pages. He started swearing and looked up. "We need to obtain protection for everyone on this list."

She turned to stare out the window as the streets of DC rushed past. Her lack of trust might have gotten people killed and she wasn't sure she'd be able to live with herself if that was true.

Frazer took an incoming call. After he hung up he told them, "Eddie Hines was just arrested in a remote cabin belonging to a female prison guard. In northern Idaho."

So who had been her intruder last night? Cole? Had her brother shot at her? Had Cole murdered Mac's ex-wife and tried to frame him?

Ice formed in her veins, jagged shards that ripped through her flesh. Her teeth chattered so much she huddled deeper into her jacket. How could she have been so foolish? How could she have made such a stupid mistake? Mac met her gaze and she knew he was thinking the exact same thing.

CHAPTER TWENTY-EIGHT

"W HAT DO YOU want to do?" Frazer asked Mac.

Mac had left angry far behind and moved on to combustible, molten rage. He was reeling from the fact Tess had lied to him from the start. He closed his eyes and breathed deeply to quiet the fury, but it was like something volatile beneath his skin and once it ignited it wasn't going out until it burned down to the bone.

He'd been on the verge of contemplating how they might make a relationship between them work after this whole debacle was over.

How had he allowed himself to trust her on the basis of who she'd been as a kid? What sort of idiot did that?

His sort, apparently.

Except his feelings for who'd she'd been as a kid had nothing to do with what had happened last night. That was strictly eighteen-plus.

"Do we call the task force and have them send a team to Cole Fallon's house?" Frazer asked.

"No." Mac was working on the assumption that the ghost skin might be inside the task force. "But we need to track him down and arrange warrants."

"I'll find him." Parker pulled out his cell and made a call.

They needed to talk and Mac needed a clear head to figure

this shit out. But regardless of what had happened over the last ten hours he was still an FBI agent and FBI agents did not discuss cases in front of uncleared witnesses, especially those linked to the case. He shifted uncomfortably in his seat.

"What about DNA? Any results back?" asked Parker.

"We can't talk in front of a civilian," Mac said tersely.

"He's not an FBI agent." Tess pointed at Parker. Her face was pale but there were two bright spots of color on her cheeks. She was pissed. Excellent. That made them even.

"Parker's a consultant," Mac bit out. "He has security clearance."

Tess's eyes glistened and she reached for the door handle. "Stop the car and let me out."

"Not gonna happen, sweetheart."

"Are you saying I'm your prisoner?" Her voice vibrated with anger. "Or perhaps you haven't finished using me to further your career yet? That's what you've been doing every step of the way. At the prison, at the compound, every time you came to my house."

Tension in the car ramped up until it felt like a garrote wrapped around his throat.

"I'm saying," he tried to be rational, "that I don't want you to warn your brother that we're onto him."

"Then I should remind *you* that I'm the one who brought you the information!"

"She has a point," said Parker.

Mac's eye twitched. "She's a little late coming forward with this."

"I would have come to you last night but you didn't answer your phone."

"I was a little busy getting arrested," he snarled.

363

"And that wasn't my fault!" she snapped. Then her anger seemed to crumple and she put her hand over her mouth and closed her eyes. "I'm sorry about your wife."

"Ex," Mac said sharply and meaning it. "*Ex*-wife." Despite what Tess probably thought when he'd left her lying naked on the kitchen floor, he hadn't had feelings for Heather. His ex had killed their relationship with her betrayal and deception. He really wasn't the forgiving type. It didn't mean it hadn't hurt to see her brutalized.

Where did that leave him and Tess? It left them exactly nowhere, where they'd always been. But he needed to be diplomatic. Unless he wanted to have to forcibly manhandle Tess and make her do what he wanted, he needed to convince her to come with them voluntarily. And she was right. He had used her. He had put her in danger. It didn't mean he didn't care about her. He just couldn't trust her. Not anymore. Not ever again.

"The FBI will no doubt have more questions for you. It would be better if they knew where to find you rather than wasting their time running around the city looking for you. Plus, it will look better that you surrendered yourself."

"Surrendered? I just gave you your goddamned alibi." Her lips clamped down and she retreated into herself.

"The FBI planned to put a protection detail on you and now the news has broken about your identity the media will be all over your home. Where precisely are you planning on going?"

Her mouth tightened. "I don't know."

She stared fixedly out the window and looked so isolated something inside his chest snapped.

He didn't believe she was involved in murder, but she'd

concealed information. Now she'd have to pay the price. So would he.

Parker interrupted. "You can get some rest at my apartment while we try to figure this out, Tess. I have a spare room. No reporters. And no one would think to look for you there. You'll be safe."

Mac met Parker's gaze, grateful but unable to voice it. Parker seemed to understand.

"I'm worried about Cole," Tess said quietly.

"You're not his mother, Tess."

Her eyes flashed red hot. "I'm all he has. You saw to that."

Ouch.

"I swore to protect him the day I curled over his body in that small cramped closet as bullets whizzed above our heads. Since the day we were taken into foster care and people wanted to separate us because I was damaged goods. He's my little brother and I love him. Obviously, that's an emotion you can't comprehend."

He flinched but kept his mouth shut. No one said another word but she didn't try to defend Cole again.

He leafed through the file on his lap, trying to get his breathing under control. It contained details on all of the victims and several other potential targets. They needed to warn these people, which meant he was going to have to contact HQ soon. But he needed to figure out who the ghost skin was before he gave away the fact he was on to them. They couldn't risk this person going to ground.

So—who to trust?

ASC Gerald? The color of his skin made him the safest bet. And if that was racial profiling people could go fuck themselves. Antigovernment types weren't always racists, and racists weren't always antigovernment. However, Gerald was unlikely to have connections with the Pioneers.

Hopefully the thumb drive contained details of their other planned attacks and they'd be stopped before being carried out. It wasn't looking good for young Cole.

Mac glanced at Tess. From the angle of her chin as she gazed fixedly out the window she was pissed, but she was also upset.

He'd hurt her. Again. This time, it was her own damn fault.

"Make sure we don't have anyone following us," Mac told Frazer. He didn't want the ghost skin finding out where they were or whom he was talking to. The wheels of justice were renowned for turning slowly, but in this instance, they needed to act fast.

"Give me your phone." He addressed Tess.

She handed it over reluctantly and he popped the SIM card.

No one asked questions.

They got to an apartment near the Watergate Building and Frazer parked in the underground garage. They took the elevator up to Parker's pad. Mac knew he and Rooney were buying a house nearer Quantico, but this place was pretty swish, too.

Parker showed Tess into a spare bedroom. "Grab a shower. Get some rest. You're safe here." Mac didn't like the quiver of guilt that wriggled inside him. He was the one who should be reassuring her, but he couldn't bring himself to risk it. Tess was his weakness and she'd brought this on herself by lying to him.

Except...given the circumstances he couldn't blame her

for being reluctant to trust anyone.

Hell, she hadn't known he was still alive until he'd turned up on her doorstep Tuesday night. If someone stepped out of his past after a twenty-year absence would he tell them his deep, dark secrets? The answer was hell no, but he didn't have time to forgive Tess right now.

Lives were at stake. And he was still so furious she'd conned him he didn't trust himself to behave judiciously.

Chances were his career had been blown to smithereens. Maybe if he helped expose the ghost skin, and proved someone was trying to set him up for murder he'd be forgiven, but this wouldn't look good no matter what color he painted it.

He followed Frazer into the fancy kitchen with its wide, marble countertops and shaker cabinets.

Mac peered out the window. The place had a great view of the Watergate complex. "As ironic as it sounds given the view, I need to know that what I'm about to say cannot be overheard."

Parker eyed him solemnly and pulled out a keychain. "I swept for bugs yesterday." He pressed a button on the fob and a small red light appeared on his keychain. "This will stop electronic ears in the immediate area and I have some other anti-listening devices installed." Parker looked pointedly at the windows.

Mac blinked at the guy. He'd briefly forgotten Parker was in the security business.

"We're as safe from eavesdroppers as any human can be, although I can't guarantee flapping ears." Parker inclined his head in the direction of the bedroom where he'd left Tess. He then pulled out his laptop and inserted the thumb drive.

Mac kept his voice low. "I think the killer is one of us."

"Us?" Parker cocked his brow.

"You mean FBI?" Frazer said.

Panting sounds started coming from Parker's computer. Mac went around the island to look. Two men and a girl were being creative in a car wash.

Mac blew out a frustrated breath. "Is Tess right? Is this her brother's porn collection?"

Parker frowned. "Maybe...but," he pointed at the screen, "Looky here."

Mac saw a list in a directory with faded file names.

"Hidden files." Parker clicked on one. "Encrypted."

"You think it's related to the murders?"

Parker shrugged. "I have no idea. Could be gardening tips." He cracked his knuckles. "But I intend to find out."

"What makes you think they have a mole inside of the FBI?" Frazer asked while Parker did his thing.

Mac helped himself to a glass of water from the tap. He could still taste the sour scent of jail on his tongue.

"I should have thought of it from the beginning. David Hines was a smart fucker and always had his eye on the long game. He—along with other white supremacist groups—urged some of their followers to keep quiet about their racist or antigovernment beliefs and sign up for law enforcement. Told 'em to rise through the ranks and find other like-minded souls and secretly influence policy from within. Act as early warning systems for groups like the Pioneers and be ready to rise up when called upon. It's the latter part that worries me now."

This could damage the FBI's reputation irreparably, particularly coming close on the heels of ASAC Guy Clarkson being uncovered as a Russian spy who'd framed one of his best friends to take the fall. Richard Stone had almost died in ADX Florence, reviled as one of the most hated men in FBI history. Frazer and Parker had been involved in overturning that miscarriage of justice, too. They were good people. People he could trust. Unlike Tess.

"It's not that easy to fool all the background checks," said Frazer.

Parker cocked his head thoughtfully as he worked. "Not impossible either, as we both know. Also, they don't need to be an agent to gain access. They might be tech support."

"So what do we know for sure?" Frazer grabbed a stack of post-it notes and a pen from beside Parker's phone. He made a list of the victims. Seeing Heather's name gave Mac a kick in the gut. It still didn't seem real that she'd been murdered.

"How's Trettorri doing?" he asked.

"Hanging in there. Docs think he'll recover but it'll take time."

Which this investigation didn't have.

"They run the DNA from his fingernails yet?" Mac asked.

"I'll call and check. Let's get our priorities straight first." Frazer wrote a note and stuck it on one side of the butcher's block.

DNA.

Mac thought about all the evidence they'd collected and were sifting through. The evidence would eventually nail the bad guys, but by then it might be too late.

"Someone got hold of my bullet casings from the gun range." Mac ran his fingers through his hair. "Could only have been Quantico or HQ."

"They've been planning this for a long time, but information about your undercover work at Kodiak Compound only surfaced this week and the task force was only formed on Tuesday." Frazer frowned. "I'm thinking the casings had to come from HQ."

Mac felt a lump in his throat. "What makes you guys so sure I didn't kill my ex?"

"Only a moron would use his own gun to shoot his ex-wife, leave the bullet casings with his prints on them, and then call the cops," Parker muttered. "Twice."

Mac's lips twitched. "So not for my sterling character traits and moral fortitude? Good to know." He put his hands on his hips. "Pisses me off cops think I'm an idiot."

Frazer smiled sadly. "The fact someone targeted you should piss you off. A lot of innocent people have died this week, including your ex-wife."

Frazer wrote "Bullet Casings" on another post-it and slapped it on the counter. "You've more than likely seen this UNSUB's face," he said quietly.

Mac nodded. "But I've seen a lot of faces this week. Jessop was involved and knew who it was." He added the name to Frazer's list. "Once he found out I was a Fed, he burned his house to the ground rather than reveal any clues that might give them away."

Parker nodded. "I've run into a bit of a brick wall when it comes to Jessop."

"I thought you could find anything online," Frazer mocked.

Parker raised his hands in a *what-can-you-do* motion. "Not when it's been completely scrubbed from the records. The FBI might need to go check out original paper files in Idaho."

"That's another indication it's someone on the inside. They've backtracked and removed the links to Jessop. They didn't even have to lie about him when they joined the FBI. Just erase the connection after the fact."

"So we can assume they have computer skills." Frazer wrote more notes.

Mac added the fact the murder weapon was likely from Kodiak Compound and the date of the first murder coincided with David Hines's birthday.

"I think it's a woman," Mac said quietly, staring at the brightly colored squares of paper. "I was thinking it over while I was sitting in that interview room. I think this ghost skin is Jessop's daughter. She joined the Bureau and has been silently planning this for years. Targeted me after Tess and I helped get her daddy killed."

"You think she's at HQ now?"

Mac nodded.

Frazer nodded thoughtfully. "That knocks out a lot of suspects. It's still a lot of people but we'll have a ball park age of what, thirty?"

"Jessop was seventy. His daughter could be anything from mid-fifties to mid-twenties." Mac shrugged.

"Why would she have sacrificed her whole life for David Hines's cause? A man she'd never met? Especially now her father is dead?"

"Who said she'd never met David Hines?" Mac vocalized more of his thoughts. Suddenly Tess's idea that her father had had a girlfriend coalesced into that lightbulb moment he usually got on the gun range. "Hines was a good-looking guy—charismatic, charming. Tess mentioned she thought he had a girlfriend. Hines died twenty years ago this August so we'll assume any girlfriend was at least sixteen back then. Makes her mid to late thirties at the youngest."

Frazer's phone rang.

"It's Harm." Frazer told them as he answered. "The Washington Police Department sent him the casings and your service weapon last night to try and tie you to the DC murders."

Mac rolled his eyes. "My alibi for most of the murders is being inside FBI HQ when they occurred."

Frazer answered and listened to his cell for a moment and then grinned. "That's official then? I owe you."

Frazer hung up. "You're off the hook. Harm worked through the night. Conclusively matched the casings found at your ex-wife's murder scene to your service weapon."

"That's not good news." Parker was still typing and didn't bother to look up.

Mac crossed his arms over his chest.

Frazer continued. "Harm ran the residue from inside the casing through a gas chromatograph. The casings from the crime scene originally contained frangible bullets."

Which might sting if they hit someone but probably wouldn't kill anyone. They disintegrated upon impact.

Mac grinned. "I owe him a beer."

"You owe him a case of beer," Parker corrected.

"So now we can confirm the casings came from HQ as the instructors there were using up frangible ammo before everyone gets switched over to the new nine-millimeters. Am I back on the task force?" Mac asked, putting his cell back together and looking for messages.

Nothing.

Officially Mac was still on desk duty. *Shit.*

Frazer shrugged. "Harm didn't know. Just said that he'd told MPD you were being set up as those bullets might have blinded someone but they wouldn't have caused the wounds seen on your ex-wife."

Mac closed his eyes as he allowed himself to think about poor Heather. All she'd really wanted was to be someone's center of attention. He thought about Tess in the other room. She'd never wanted to be the center of attention. The two women couldn't be more different.

Parker swore. "This is gonna take more computing power than I have here," he admitted, closing his laptop. "Can I email it to one of my guys? My team can devote more resources to it, hopefully figure out who compiled it."

"I'm more concerned about preventing a terrorist attack than prosecuting a court case at this point," Mac said. Although DOJ wouldn't see it that way.

Frazer must have decided the same thing. "As long as it's secure."

Parker gave him a look.

The evidence had been removed from Cole's house by Tess and was tainted when it came to being used in court to convict Cole Fallon. The only person it could really be used against was Tess herself. Maybe she knew that. Maybe that was why she'd taken it. Protecting someone who didn't deserve it.

After a few moments Parker ejected the drive and tossed it to Frazer who stuck it in his pocket.

"Your *wunderkind* have any luck on the users of the One-Drop-2-Many site?"

"Nope, but he's working on it. He's got a real knack for this stuff. We'll track the IDs down, but it won't happen overnight."

The site had been shut down. Someone had realized Jessop was compromised.

"From the screen captures we obtained before they took it down I think it's the main networking tool of this group. It'll be a goldmine of information when we untangle the details."

"We already have a shit-load of evidence being processed. It's only a matter of time before we narrow it down to the right person." Mac rubbed the back of his neck. He couldn't stop that feeling of impending doom hovering over his shoulder.

"They got rid of the team leader in an effort to slow law enforcement down and throw the investigation into chaos." Frazer frowned.

Mac checked the time and stared out the window at the concrete edifice of one of Washington's biggest scandals. "It's nearly the weekend. If you want to make a statement against the government you do it before four o'clock on a Friday."

"Otherwise nobody's there," agreed Parker.

It was nearly eleven a.m. Mac slid Tess's file across the marble surface. "You need to call ASC Gerald and ask him to warn anyone listed here that they might be a target. Don't tell him where you got the information. Not yet."

Frazer leafed through the names.

"Do you want to bring Cole Fallon in for questioning?" Parker asked, checking his gun in a way that made Mac have no doubt he knew how to use it.

Mac shook his head. "If the inside man or woman finds out I've been released and we're onto them, he-or-she might bolt. I want to figure out their identity first. Let's stake out Fallon. Where's Cole now?"

Parker opened a piece of software, then eyed him warily. "Does the FBI have a warrant for this information or is this our little secret?"

Mac held his hands up and turned away. "I didn't see anything."

He had to go speak to Tess before he left. Because last night they'd made a massive mistake and as much as he'd enjoyed it there was no future for them. Not after the lies she'd told him. The rusted, corroded feeling around his heart was regret for crossing that line and making that mistake.

Sure.

But it was still possible she was in cahoots with these people and had seduced him on purpose. He needed to talk to her but he needed to think of her not as a woman he had feelings for, but as a suspect. He couldn't afford any more stupid mistakes when it came to Tess Fallon.

CHAPTER TWENTY-NINE

C OLE WALKED OUT of his lecture and searched for Joseph but the guy hadn't turned up today. Probably gotten lucky again. Cole knew the feeling. He grinned.

"Hey, dude."

Cole spotted Dave heading toward him, weaving through the throngs of students leaving class.

"What's up?"

"You need to start talking to your sister, man." Dave rubbed his eyes and yawned. "She came over in the middle of the night, upset but pretending not to be." Dave's eyes were dragged away from Cole's face by a passing blonde wearing short-shorts.

Cole scrubbed his hand through his hair. Tess needed to butt out of his life. Right now, he needed a little space. They started walking, Dave following the blonde, Cole heading to the metro. "I'll talk to her."

Dave nodded. "You pick up the booze for Joe's party tomorrow?"

Fuck. Cole had completely forgotten about the party they were hosting. He nodded. His fake ID was better than some real ones. "I'll pick it up tomorrow morning."

Dave grinned. "Gonna bring your new girlfriend?"

Cole rolled his eyes. Bring a beautiful, mature woman to a

student party? Hell, no. He shrugged. It was easier to lie. "Maybe. You got a date?"

Dave eyed the blonde. "Not yet. About to change that though. Just wanted to tell you your sister was freaking out and to remind you about the beer."

"No worries." Cole added a reminder to his calendar. Worst case scenario was he ordered a bulk delivery from the liquor store using Tess's credit card. He'd pay her back. "Later."

He wondered exactly when he'd outgrown his friends. He'd break the news he was moving out next week. He didn't want to ruin Joseph's birthday.

It wasn't like he'd never see them again, but things would be different. He'd outgrown the party scene. He wasn't even sure why he was trying to get a degree when he could earn plenty of money writing software.

His cell rang and he grinned. "What can I do for you, gorgeous?"

"I wish." She laughed. "You got through your ethics class?"

"I would rather have been in bed with you."

"Yeah, welcome to reality." Her voice changed, got deeper. "Although I might be able to squeeze you in over lunch."

His cock jerked to attention.

"My friend Trent phoned me five minutes ago," she added.

Cole hated this mysterious "Trent" with a passion.

"The truck's in my parking garage with the keys in it. I'll be done for lunch in about an hour and planned on taking the first load over to the new place—"

"I'll help you."

"I don't want to put you out."

"You will never put me out. Shall I meet you at the apartment?"

"Hmm…" That low noise stroked over his senses like a confident hand. "Why don't you go grab the truck and pick me up from work? Then I don't have to walk back to the apartment in these stupid heels."

"I love those heels." He could still feel their imprint on his ass.

She'd asked him to pick her up from work. She was finally starting to believe in him. In them.

"Park by the visitor's entrance and send me a text when you get there. I'll make it worth your while, promise. I have to go. Love you," she said so faintly he barely heard her.

"Love you, too," he whispered.

He hopped on the escalator to take him to the metro line.

TESS SAT ON the edge of the double bed and stared at the door. She'd grabbed a super-fast shower. Washed away the evidence of her torrid encounter with Mac even if she couldn't erase the memory of her colossal mistake. Her braided hair fell in a thick rope down her back, making the red wool of her sweater itch. She ignored the cold, uncomfortable feeling that seeped along her spine.

She needed to know what was going on. Despite the fact Alex Parker had treated her with consideration she felt like a prisoner here. Why couldn't she have fallen for a nice guy like Parker, rather than the smooth-voiced, irritating ass from Montana?

Her one hand was strangling the other and she made

herself relax her grip and smooth her fingers along her thighs. She knew she'd made a mistake in not telling Mac about the files earlier. Her reasons had felt justified at the time, but she'd been wrong.

But she still didn't believe Cole was a killer.

The door opened and Mac walked in. She eyed him warily. His usually iridescent blue-green gaze was guarded. She started to open her mouth to say how sorry she was, but he cut her off.

"Is there anything else you haven't told me?" He didn't look at her when he spoke. As if he couldn't bring himself to. As if he was also ashamed of what they'd done.

She gritted her teeth and lifted her chin. "No."

"Anything about Cole I should know?"

He was casually dressed in jeans and a navy sweater but the Federal Agent was back in full force. No more friend or lover.

"Does he carry a weapon?"

She blinked rapidly, then stood and walked to the window, looking out at the cars driving below, the people going about their normal daily lives. Her life was in ruins. Her concerns about her business were nothing compared to her worry that her brother might die or the fact her heart was splitting like dry wood under a heavy axe.

Her finger traced a line in the sill. "Cole doesn't like firearms. I don't think he's ever fired a gun, let alone owned one." She pressed a hand to her stomach. The Feds were going to go after her baby brother with guns drawn. They believed he was involved in these murders.

Mac came farther into the room, not closing the door behind him.

TONI ANDERSON

Ironic that she was the one with trust issues.

She sneered in contempt as she looked at him over her shoulder. "You actually think *I* might be involved with these people. Don't you?" Her voice cracked, giving away how close she was to breaking.

A flicker of uncertainty crossed his features. He avoided her gaze, not denying it.

"What possible motive could I have?" she demanded. "You know how I felt about my family."

"I can't discuss an ongoing investigation."

"A little late to play by the rules now, isn't it?"

His eyes narrowed and she watched the play of light across his features. The broad forehead and stubborn chin. Stubble sprinkled his jaw and neck. Part of her wanted to touch the rough skin, to run her palm across the scratchy flesh. To feel it between her thighs.

But those thoughts would have to be consigned to memory and filed under "once in a lifetime experiences."

She returned her attention to the view out of the window. Heavy clouds gathered against the blue of the sky. Teardrops of rain hit the glass.

Her emotions wanted to crush her but she refused to let them. She was not showing weakness. Not to Steve McKenzie. Not to the world in general. She wasn't going to reveal just how much he'd hurt her.

"I didn't tell the police we had sex, by the way. Just so you know. Not that your less than polite pal Agent Walsh believed me."

He frowned as they watched each other in the reflection of the glass.

"I told them you were asking me for more details about Eddie and where he might be hiding." She forced down the tightness in her throat that wanted to choke her. "So your job is safe, unless you confessed your sins, which I very much doubt."

His mouth tightened.

She smiled grimly. She could tell from his expression he hadn't breathed a word. He probably thought she was going to blackmail him with the information at some point in the future.

"So what happened between us is our dirty little secret and I won't ever be admitting I made such an enormous error in judgment."

Hurt flickered across his features and then it was gone. Was he upset she no longer viewed him as her hero? He'd be more upset if she told him the really ugly truth—the fact she'd fallen in love with him.

Below her a cab cut off a limo and blared its horn. Life going on as normal as her world split open and exposed every secret and pain she held within her fragile heart. Well, the world wasn't having that one.

A muscle in his jaw flexed. "I never asked you to lie for me."

She laughed, a nasty, bitter sound. "I'm aware."

"My job is important to me." Now he sounded defensive.

"Trust me, if there's one person in the world who knows that you are defined by the letters on your badge, it's me."

"Last night was a mistake."

The words hit her like a shotgun blast and she put her hand on the windowsill to steady herself as she struggled to keep her mask in place. It hurt.

She hadn't realized how much she'd let her shields down for him. And what she was feeling now felt a thousand times worse than Jason and Julie's betrayal. This time she'd been stupid enough to start to trust Mac, not just with her body and her secrets, but with her heart.

She didn't believe in love. Not anymore. That cheap illusion was for suckers and fools and unicorn chasers. It was a myth. A fraud. A Disney marketing ploy.

She made herself face him. Raised a bored brow. "Yes, it was. I realized the moment you left me naked on the kitchen floor as soon as your ex-wife snapped her fingers. Anything else?"

He lifted his chin, eyes narrowed and glittering. But, really, what could he say that he hadn't already said?

"Have a nice life, ASAC McKenzie. Hope your promotion is worth it. And don't you dare hurt my brother."

MAC STRODE OUT of the bedroom. Apparently, the only thing Tess gave a damn about was her worthless brother.

He didn't know why he was feeling quite so pissed—oh, yeah, someone had murdered his ex-wife and tried to frame him for it, and he'd almost terminally fucked up his career by sleeping with a woman he shouldn't have gone within a mile of. Never mind the fact that someone was going around town shooting people based on color, creed and sexuality, and likely had more atrocities planned.

The look of betrayal on Tess's face destroyed him, but that was his own stupid fault for letting her get to him. He wasn't some naïve teenager. He'd been through the relationship wringer more than once, which was why he'd sworn off them for so long. Should have learned his lesson by now. Maybe a letter of censure would be the kick in the balls he needed to finally get his head on straight. His heart should be impenetrable, but apparently, a beautiful brunette with pi tattooed around her arm, had managed to sneak past his guard.

But his job was the only thing that truly mattered in his life. The only thing that had allowed him to feel a measure of pride and importance—that what he did mattered. That what he'd done with his life mattered.

Fidelity. Bravery. Integrity.

Yeah… About that.

In the FBI, perception was everything. Rules were king.

There was a high chance Tess's brother was about to be arrested for conspiracy to murder and one of the few things that might save Mac's career was bringing Cole Fallon in before anyone else died and rounding up everyone involved.

Tess really wasn't going to be very happy about that. Shit, she might be looking at obstruction of justice charges for not telling them about that file earlier. And that was assuming she was innocent.

He met Frazer in the hallway. "Ready?"

The other man nodded. "Got a location on Cole Fallon's cell phone. Heading east toward Capitol Hill."

Jesus.

Parker joined them and handed Mac a Glock-22. Mac nodded his appreciation as he checked the weapon.

"What about her?" Mac inclined his head toward the bedroom.

"Tess?" Frazer asked nonchalantly. He was the master of being an asshole using just one word.

"Yes," Mac gritted. "*Tess.*"

"I'm coming with you."

"Over my dead body." Mac didn't even turn to face her.

"She can ride with me," Parker suggested. "Taking two cars is a useful idea in case we need to split up. After we locate Cole, I can drop Tess at her car. Assuming the press has dispersed."

Mac met Parker's gaze. He needed her contained. He needed her safe. But nobody gave a fuck what he needed.

"I won't get in the way. I won't put your operation in jeopardy but I might be able to help. With Cole." Tears glistened in her eyes.

Mac felt his upper lip curl.

The goddamned baby brother again. When was she going to see Cole was an adult, responsible for his own actions? Mac turned without saying anything and led the way back to the parking garage. Maybe this was what it would take to convince Tess that Cole wasn't some innocent, little kid anymore. And maybe it was exactly what was needed to draw a line between the two of them. Arresting her baby brother was not something she'd forgive him for.

But he did not like the idea of her being in the crossfire. Not again.

He didn't look at her as he got into Frazer's Lexus and they drove away. The distance between them grew exponentially with every second of this investigation, with every word he left unspoken. And that's what he needed to do even though what he really wanted was to take her in his arms and tell her everything was going to be okay.

It wasn't.

Time to get his head on straight and prove where his true loyalty lay. Time to keep the vows he'd made when he'd sworn fealty to the United States of America and take these bastards down. Time to forget everything he was feeling for Tess.

CHAPTER THIRTY

TESS CLIMBED INTO a low-slung Audi and sat back in the seat. She couldn't bring herself to even look at Mac as he drove away in the Lexus with the other agent.

Alex Parker placed his phone in a holder on the dash, the screen displaying a map with a red dot on it. That red dot was Cole.

Tess's heart pounded like prey scenting a predator even though Cole was the one they were hunting.

Parker slipped a laptop behind her seat. "You, okay?"

"Only if the feeling of incipient vomiting is normal? You have family, Mr. Parker?"

His grip was loose but competent on the steering wheel. He took his time heading up the ramp onto the street. He was giving her space from Mac. Space she desperately needed.

"I didn't for many years…" He looked at her with a smile she couldn't read. "I do now."

The acknowledgement that family was everything flashed in his eyes.

The panic inside her kept growing and threatened to choke her. "With the exception of my adoptive mother who died last year, Cole is the only real family I've had since I was ten years old." She rubbed her hands together, trying to generate some heat. "I've dedicated my life to taking care of him."

"He's all grown up now."

"I know. And I know he's responsible for his own actions. If he's involved in these murders or in some crazy plot then he needs to be held accountable." She sucked in a deep breath. "He needs to go to prison."

"But you don't believe he's involved." Parker eased through traffic, one eye on the dot. Tess tensed as she watched it, too. Would Cole resist arrest? Probably. He was a belligerent young male. Would they shoot him? Her stomach roiled at the thought.

He was about a mile away. This time on a Friday morning traffic was quiet.

"You don't think Cole would shoot anyone?" he asked.

She bit her thumbnail down to the quick and winced at the sharp burst of pain. "I know he wouldn't."

"Sometimes people have secrets."

Tess wanted to laugh. She knew all about keeping secrets.

"They hide who they really are even from the people they love." Parker was quiet for a moment. "It's not unusual to be resistant to the idea someone might be guilty of killing another human being—"

"I'm not naïve, Mr. Parker. I grew up in a white supremacist compound with a daddy who wanted to murder innocent people and blow up the government for funzies. They beat up and possibly killed anyone who didn't agree with their ideals, and married their daughters off to perverts to hide sex crimes. I am not one of those females who see the world through rose-colored glasses, or if I do, the roses are blood-red and thorny as hell."

Parker gave her another considering look. "Call me Alex.

And whether Cole is guilty or not, custody might be the safest place for him, right now." He paused, considering. "If someone is using your father's doctrine to try and start a war with the federal government then who's to say they wouldn't use you or your brother to further their cause—with or without your consent?"

She hadn't thought of it that way. She frowned as she read the names of the streets they were passing, a memory tugging at her subconscious. "It's weird the fact I live here now. The only books I was allowed to read growing up were *The Bible* and *The Turner Diaries* which is partly set in DC. You ever read it?"

Parker shook his head.

Her mouth went suddenly dry and her heart beat thundered. "It's hate-filled garbage. The so-called heroes of the book attack FBI HQ."

Alex held her stare for a full second and she thought they were going to crash. Then he put his foot flat on the accelerator.

Tess held on tight. He started driving so fast she was terrified she was going to die in a head-on collision as he sped down the wrong side of the wide avenue named for the great state of Pennsylvania. The Capitol Building stood like a sentinel in the distance.

She saw it at exactly the same moment Parker did.

"Shit." He applied the handbrake and managed to screech his car to a halt sideways across the road, blocking two lanes of the four lanes of north bound traffic. He leapt out and ran to a patrol cop, yelling at him to stop traffic. Tess jumped out of the passenger seat and, while Parker had his back turned, she started sprinting toward the white van that was parked outside the visitor entrance of the FBI.

––––––––––––––––––

MAC AND FRAZER had just turned from Ninth onto Pennsylvania Avenue, hoping to get eyes on Cole Fallon when every molecule of saliva evaporated from Mac's mouth.

A white moving van sat smack outside the south entrance of the J. Edgar Hoover Building. The red dot of Cole's cell phone flashed on Frazer's screen in that exact position. Mac called Walsh at SIOC. "Possible truck bomb at FBI HQ. Penn Ave. Tell security and get the bomb squad down here ASAP and move people to the north of the building." Frazer was on the phone to Parker saying something about getting signal jammers in place. Mac got out of the Lexus and looked around. Tourists dotted the sidewalk. It wasn't packed, but enough people were around to make a bloody statement. Headquarters had been designed to withstand a bomb blast, but with enough explosives, a McVeigh-wannabe could inflict some serious damage.

It was OKBOMB all over again. In *The Turner Diaries*, the cocksucker hero attacked this very building. Copying that cancerous narrative was the perfect way for these assholes to try to start their revolution.

He should have guessed.

A flash of red had his heart stopping. Tess was running toward the vehicle. For a split-second he wondered if he'd been wrong the entire time about her being involved. Then he stopped thinking and started running.

Frazer was at his shoulder, both had weapons drawn and civilians scattered and fled. Tess was screaming her brother's name. Then, when she got about twenty yards away from the truck, Parker tackled her. She was still well within blast range.

Sweat poured off Mac and his mouth felt dry as a furnace. The idea of Tess being hurt or dying was enough to slam terror straight to his marrow.

She was crying out her brother's name, begging him not to do anything stupid. That train had left the station long ago.

Parker tossed Mac his keychain and he caught it one-handed. The red light was on and Mac remembered what the guy had said about it blocking electronic signals within a small radius. Mac placed the fob on the rear bumper and said a little prayer as he and Frazer approached the driver's side door.

Didn't matter your religion or how much training you'd received when faced with a potential IED—you still said a few prayers to the man upstairs.

He pointed his gun at the driver. An open-mouthed Cole Fallon gaped at him. Only the fact Mac could see both hands stopped him putting a bullet straight between the young man's eyes.

Mac opened the door and hauled him from his seat. Thankfully there was no detonator in sight. But the cold sweat of fear didn't ease up.

If the explosives were on a timer they all were still fucked.

"Cole, what have you done!" Tess screamed.

Parker pulled Tess to her feet and dragged her backwards, away from the danger. Mac didn't dare look at her.

Frazer cuffed Cole while Mac held a weapon on him. Then they yanked Cole to his feet.

"What the hell are you doing?" Cole yelled.

"Like you don't know," Mac muttered.

"I'm going to have you charged with police brutality.

People are filming this."

Mac glanced around. Sure enough, there were tourists filming the show without a thought to the danger they might be in. Shit. The Feds needed to get a handle on this now. Clear the streets. Shut down the news reports. Contain it.

First, they needed to make sure the bomb was deactivated.

Frazer grabbed the guy's cell and the keys from his pocket. Then Mac pushed Cole so they moved to the back of the truck. Bomb squad techs came rushing out of the building. He wouldn't do their job for all the money in the Federal Reserve.

"We have reason to believe there's a bomb inside," Mac told the tech.

Cole's jaw dropped.

"A security expert set up a signal jammer. Open her up. We want to see what's inside so we know what we're dealing with," Frazer said impatiently.

"And let's get a move on in case it's on a timer," Mac added.

The bomb tech shot Mac and Frazer a withering glance. "Yeah. That's how we all die. Move back to a safe distance and I'll look inside."

Mac wanted to argue but wasn't given a choice. He moved back and dragged Cole with him. Tess was evacuated in the opposite direction and every foot between them seemed like a black hole opening up.

"You guys are going to feel like fucking morons when that guy opens that truck. It's full of my girlfriend's furniture. Call her. Carolyn Martin. She works here. I was about to text her that I was here to pick her up." Cole was laughing, but his voice was high and strained. "Hope the press caught your humiliation on film, assholes."

The guy sounded like he believed what he was saying. If Mac didn't know what he knew, he might have believed Cole.

Mac and Frazer took cover behind Frazer's car and drew Cole down beside them. After a few minutes, the tech slowly opened up the back of the truck and whistled.

They all peeked around the edge of the vehicle and Mac's heart stopped beating. There were enough barrels of fuel and fertilizer packed into the cargo area to bring down an entire city block. Enough to kill and maim anyone close by.

"What the...?" Cole whispered. His skin took on a milky glow. He swayed.

Mac stared at Tess's brother and knew they were both about to break her heart. But at least she was alive. At least this fucker hadn't detonated that truck and her along with it. Mac's gut clenched at the idea of Tess being caught up in something like that. He wanted to punch Cole in the face for throwing away all the advantages he'd been raised with, but instead he did something better.

"Cole Fallon, I'm arresting you on possession of a weapon of mass destruction..."

CHAPTER THIRTY-ONE

S HE CHECKED HER watch and looked up nervously from her computer terminal. It was eleven-fifty a.m. Where was Cole? He should have texted her by now. Then she heard a murmur of excitement race through the building.

"What's happening?" she asked a tech who was passing behind her.

"Conflicting reports of a possible bomb threat on the street."

"Bomb threat?"

"Truck bomb."

Shit. "Should we evacuate?"

"We've been told to shelter in place. SIOC was designed to withstand that sort of blast. We should be fine."

A tremor of excitement ran through her. She reached into the pocket in her fancy leather satchel to retrieve her newest burner phone. Reverently, she punched in the numbers of the cell attached to the five-thousand pounds of explosives packed into the back of that truck—the exact same amount McVeigh had used in Oklahoma. She waited for the call to connect, bracing herself for the blast even though she should be safe. She'd never intended to die for the cause. She couldn't lead from the grave—or from a jail cell for that matter.

She regretted Cole would die, but it turned out his resemblance to his father didn't extend beyond his good looks. Cole had been corrupted by the impure. But he'd die honoring his father, the man she truly loved.

Her lips tightened and she dialed the number again. She kept expecting to feel a boom but nothing happened. Dammit. She called a third time. Again. Nothing.

Had the idiot fucked up making the bomb? Trent was a farmer out in Virginia who was all for the reinstitution of slavery. He wasn't the brightest bulb in the box. She should have known he was the weak link in the chain, but how hard could it be? She put the cell back in her bag and closed it. If you wanted something done, do it yourself.

"Excitement's over," their section chief shouted across the room. "Bomb has been disarmed."

She clapped like every other mindless drone.

"Who's responsible?" someone yelled back.

"Some young guy. Related to that white nationalist group, the Pioneers."

"They shoot him?"

"Nah, pulled him from the cab and arrested his skinny ass. He's being brought in for questioning."

Ah, crap. That sealed it.

She'd failed.

Everything she'd done. Everything she'd worked for. All for nothing.

She climbed to her feet and stretched out her back. Cole might not know her real name, but it was only a matter of time before he was shown photographs and identified her as his lover. She had to disappear before they found her.

A commotion started near the main door. The Director of the FBI and the US Attorney General headed into their briefing room. She checked her watch. They were later than usual, but maybe they were here because of the bomb threat. Excitement fizzled through her blood and almost made her dizzy.

Their bomb plot might have failed, but maybe this would be better. Killing the FBI Director and the AG in the heart of the Hoover Building would send a message that would ring through the centuries.

On the screens in the media room she could see newsfeeds of the van out front. The news hounds would be baying and snarling for more information, for a story. Her fellow patriots all over the country were waiting, ready to rise up and take action just as soon as they saw a definitive sign that the revolution had started.

This would work.

She started walking toward the meeting room where some of the aides mingled. Her hand slid to her weapon. Everyone was talking excitedly. No one noticed her. Then the director and AG went into the small private briefing room and firmly shut the door. The man who stood in front of the door caught her eye and stared hard. Her hand dropped away from her weapon. She carried on walking and veered right, heading into the outside corridor. She went to the ladies' room to regroup.

Patience, she told herself. She'd already waited nearly twenty years. She could wait a few more minutes.

———

SHUDDERS WRACKED HER body so violently Tess couldn't stand up. She huddled in Parker's Audi, numbed by the enormity of what she'd just witnessed.

Her little brother had been dragged out of a van that was apparently full of explosives. Seeing Cole in that truck had made her feel equal parts terrified and ashamed. What was wrong with her family's DNA? Why did they feel the need to hate and destroy?

The idea that Cole and Mac could both have been killed made her want to curl into a ball and stay there. It would have been all her fault. The revelation that she loved the federal agent had hit her with renewed ferocity when faced with the possibility of his imminent death.

She should have trusted him with the information she had on her brother. The FBI could have arrested Cole without putting so many lives in danger.

She kept picturing Mac running up to that truck and pulling her brother out onto the road. She loved Cole. But she also loved Steve McKenzie. He was annoying and aggravating and brave and courageous. She had the horrible feeling she'd always loved him and would always love him. She couldn't hide from her feelings anymore, but so what? There was no future for them. No redemption from this disaster.

Parker slipped into the driver's seat beside her.

"Was it really a bomb?" she asked him quietly.

He nodded, looking completely unfazed. "Bomb techs made it safe."

Her heart twisted. Her brother was a domestic terrorist. But…it still didn't feel right. "You'll think I'm crazy, but I grew up with these kinds of people." She rubbed her chilled arms. "My brother just doesn't fit in with those characters."

Parker's gaze grew quizzical. "You still doubt he's involved?"

"Didn't they try to frame Mac for his ex-wife's murder?"

she argued. "Why is it out of the realm of possibility to think someone framed Cole for this?"

"Hmm...he drove a truck bomb to FBI HQ and was caught in the act?"

"But he was just sitting there! Cole isn't stupid and he isn't suicidal. Look." It was starting to make sense to her now. "He recently started dating a woman significantly older than he is. He's been very secretive about her, refused to introduce us. I followed him on Tuesday and he met with her for lunch not far from this very spot. Could she be involved? Could she have tricked him?"

Alex's eyes shot to the huge FBI building and he frowned. "You're talking about a pretty complex deception."

"They've been planning this for twenty years, Alex. I think they've had time to think it through."

His gaze got even sharper.

"No one's going to believe me if I say anything. Especially Mac."

Someone opened her door and squatted beside her. She braced herself to confront Mac, but it was Agent Walsh. Her stomach resumed its awful churning.

"I need you to come inside and make a statement." Walsh started to drag her out the car and she cried out as he gripped her arm hard enough to hurt.

"Hey. Careful." Mac was suddenly beside her, elbowing the guy aside.

Mac extended his hand and Tess took his reluctantly. His fingers squeezed but there was no matching reassurance in his eyes.

She pulled away as soon as she was standing on the pavement, and crossed her arms. Whatever her feelings for the man she couldn't afford to let her guard down. The only thing she had left was her dignity and that was shredded.

"I need to take her in for questioning," Walsh insisted.

"You mean to make a statement?" Mac furrowed his brows.

Walsh rolled his eyes on a heavy sigh. "She could be involved, Mac. You have to see that?"

"She's not part of this," Mac said adamantly. "I've been with her for most of the past week." He didn't mention the files and Tess found herself watching his face trying to figure out when that piece of information was going to drop on her head and explode. "We've had people analyze her internet activity and email and phone calls."

That reality finally registered, even though Parker had mentioned it earlier. Mac had used their mutual attraction to get closer to her while they checked her background. She hadn't made it difficult for him. Another reason to despise him and herself.

"There is nothing to suggest she had anything to do with these murders or this plot. I'll stake my career on it."

"What career?" someone muttered.

Tess jerked her head up. What did that mean? Her eyes searched Mac's face, but he wouldn't meet her gaze.

"I need to do my job, Mac," said Walsh. "You're off the case, remember?"

"You did hear they cleared me of killing my ex-wife, right?" Mac said impatiently.

"And that's why I'm letting you walk Cole Fallon in for questioning."

She felt sick. "Did you ever stop to think that maybe they're setting up Cole the same way they set you up?" She held Mac's stare though the doubt she saw stung.

Nothing she said was going to make a difference. She took a deep breath. "Let's just get this over with." She held out her wrists.

Walsh fished his handcuffs out of his pocket.

"You're kidding me," Mac fumed.

"It's a little late for chivalry," she bit out. "You've been investigating me from the start, don't pretend you haven't. All those trips down memory lane trying to figure how much I knew? Hopefully you found all the information you needed."

His brows lifted at that. That's not what had happened between them. Tess was giving him a way out and she hoped he was smart enough to take it. Her life here was ruined. She needed to start over. But at least she could repair his career.

Mac glared at her, those blue-green eyes of his dark with annoyance. "Trust me, chivalry is the last thing I'm feeling right now."

He looked ready to kill someone.

Parker bent toward her ear and whispered, "Don't say a word about anything in the interview room. I'm calling my lawyer. He's the best in DC."

"I can't afford him, Alex. Don't waste his time."

"Let me worry about the cost." His fingers squeezed her shoulder. "Mac is just doing his job. Don't blame him for that either."

She didn't. She really didn't. Tess nodded, but she felt miserable.

"Tell him what I told you about the girlfriend," she insisted to Parker. No way would anyone listen to her now.

Walsh snapped on the hard metal bracelets and the man she'd gone and fallen in love with stood by and watched. It felt like the night of the raid again when Mac had left her to survive on her own. Then she was walking across the wide avenue, surrounded by a group of agents all looking like they'd caught one of the FBI's Most Wanted.

She couldn't believe she was being escorted into FBI HQ, handcuffed like a common criminal. Her parents would be so proud.

MAC HEADED BACK inside the FBI building where Frazer was waiting for him. He took Cole by the arm and ushered him along a different route from the one Walsh would take Tess. "I checked. There's no one by the name of Carolyn Martin working here. You need a better story, kid."

Mac was worried. He needed to catch this ghost skin, but he also needed to keep other agents safe.

"That's ridiculous. You're wrong. She works here. Check my cell."

"Oh, we're checking your cell, sunshine." Mac had passed it to Alex without anyone seeing.

"Stop treating me like a fucking kid," Cole yelled.

An FBI security guard moved toward them, concerned, but Mac waved him away. Frazer shadowed him as they headed across the courtyard and into the elevators.

"Then stop telling stories." Mac tried not to think about Walsh leading Tess away in cuffs. He closed his eyes for a moment. When he'd seen her running toward that van it had felt like someone had ripped the ground right from under his feet, and just now she'd tried to protect him. Telling the onlookers he'd gotten close to her to use her—which he

399

thought he had at the time, but now knew he was lying to himself.

He'd gotten close because he couldn't stay away. He'd had sex with her because he couldn't have walked away if his life depended on it.

"What's she look like, this supposed girlfriend of yours?" Mac pushed.

Cole clammed up.

"You do realize if what you're saying is true, she set you up? Right?" Mac taunted. He crowded Cole into the elevator, let his disbelief shine through. "She left you sitting on enough fertilizer to bring down a city block. You think there'd be anything left of you to even identify?" He got in Cole's face. "You'd have been a fucking aerosol, dickhead, and yet, I'm supposed to believe you're dumb enough to protect her?"

Cole's eyes narrowed.

"Now you really look like your daddy. Like father like son, huh? What was the plan? You wanted to be a martyr for the cause?"

Cole shook his head and looked away. "I don't know what's going on. I don't have a cause." He went to raise his hands but the cuffs stopped him. He frowned at them like an alien had taken over his body. "Carolyn asked me to help her move today. She said her friend Trent packed the moving van with the first load of boxes and suggested I grab the truck and come pick her up from work so we could drop off the first load." Cole's face lit up with hope. "It's this guy Trent you're looking for. He must have known she worked here and set her up."

Bullshit. "What does she look like?" Mac repeated.

"Slim. Straight brown hair. Blue eyes."

"Got a photo?" Mac asked.

"She didn't like having her picture taken," Cole insisted. He sounded less sure of himself now. "She's older than I am and said photographs reminded her of the fact. But she doesn't look older. She's hot." His explanation lacked conviction, as if he was starting to see the holes in his story.

"Yeah, if she's who I think she is she's old enough to have been screwing your real daddy, too." Mac gauged Cole's reaction to that information. "I bet she got a real thrill out of nailing you when you look just like David."

Cole appeared to sag in defeat. "I don't believe any of this."

"You better believe it, and if you ever want to see the outside of a jail cell you better help us find her."

Tears filled Cole's eyes and ran down his cheeks. "This isn't happening." Then he pinned Mac with a glare. "Why did they cuff Tess? Is she in trouble?"

Mac gave him a tight smile. "I get to ask the questions." Except he didn't, not really. He had until he got this guy up to SIOC and the task force would take over. He'd be sidelined. The murder of his ex and his involvement with Tess meant there were too many conflicts of interest. Dammit. He needed to find the mole ASAP. Cole may or may not be telling the truth, but Mac was sure someone was working the inside.

They exited the elevator, but the hallway was empty. Thank God.

"So this Carolyn woman told you she was an FBI agent?"

"Yes."

"And you believed her," Mac jeered.

"She had a gun, a badge. Why wouldn't I believe her?"

"Why'd you have a file of the murder victims under your mattress?"

Cole scrunched up his face. "What the hell are you talking about?"

The confusion seemed genuine. Mac exchanged a look with Frazer.

"You thinking what I'm thinking?" Frazer asked.

That maybe Tess was right. Maybe the kid had been set up the same way Mac had been. He tilted his head. "It's possible."

"If he's telling the truth you're gonna have to grovel so hard to Tess you'll be spitting dirt for a week," Frazer told him.

Cole jerked around. "What do you mean?"

Frazer laughed and Mac glared. "This guy is in love with your sister."

"Don't be a fucking asshole," Mac muttered but it felt like someone had wrapped claws around his heart and squeezed. Of course he was in love with Tess. And he'd arrested the person she cared most about in the world. The only person she cared about. She hated him now.

Even if he didn't lose his career over this mess she would never be accepted by his colleagues, and the FBI was a family first and foremost.

None of it mattered right now. He needed to figure out who the traitor might be. He suddenly remembered something and pulled out his cell to make a call.

"Miki? Run a search for me on FBI agents and support staff who were based in all the field offices where the murders with similar MO's occurred and call me back." He hung up.

"You think she's still here?" Frazer asked skeptically.

Mac gritted his teeth in frustration. "I doubt it. Pretty sure we just scuppered her plans of a big demonstration of antigovernment sentiment. She knows we're onto her. She's gonna be pissed."

CHAPTER THIRTY-TWO

WALSH WASN'T ROUGH or unkind as he walked Tess along miles of bright white corridors.

"Am I under arrest?" she asked him.

"Not yet." He didn't sound friendly or approachable.

"You think I'm involved."

"I don't know if you're involved or not, which is why I want you to answer some questions." He grunted. "I do think you messed up the career of a really great federal agent and good friend of mine."

"He didn't do anything wrong. He renewed an old acquaintance in order to further the investigation. I would have thought he'd get a commendation."

Walsh clenched his jaw.

"What's going to happen to my brother?"

"Lots and lots of questions. Then I'm guessing life without parole. You?" His gaze traveled up and down her, eyes glinting in contempt. "I guess we'll find out."

She shivered. All these years she'd run from her past and it had still led to this. Handcuffed by the FBI. It must have been pre-ordained at birth. She raised her chin and pressed her lips together. She would do well to remember Parker's advice and keep her mouth closed until his lawyer arrived. She did not want to end up in prison.

They came to a door and Walsh used his ID to get them inside.

They stepped inside a small crowded conference room and Tess came face to face with her worst nightmare.

In front of them, Mac and Frazer flanked Cole, who was wearing handcuffs just like she was.

A large, black man pointed to the side of the room with a hard stare. "Wait there until a secure room is made available."

She wanted to speak to her brother, but knew in doing so she'd only make things worse.

Mac looked over his shoulder as if sensing her presence and their eyes locked. That short moment of silent communication held every ounce of regret and guilt.

The main door behind them opened, and at the same time another door opened off to the right. A small trail of men and women in suits poured out of a meeting.

Walsh pulled her back against the wall.

Cole glanced over his shoulder. He caught her eye and his expression was so confused and miserable her heart clenched for him. Then his eyes widened and Tess turned to see what he was staring at. A woman held a clipboard in front of her, but from Tess's side-on vantage, she spotted a weapon. The woman raised it to aim at the people leaving the meeting room.

No time for a verbal warning. Tess did a snap-kick that knocked the woman's aim off target, but the bitch didn't drop her weapon.

"She went for my gun!" the woman screamed.

"Carolyn!" Cole shouted across the room.

Everyone started moving at once.

Walsh tried to restrain Tess, but she knew the other woman was lying. She also knew this must be Cole's "girlfriend" who'd led her brother on, set him up, and tried to kill him.

The gun was still in play and Tess saw the agents react almost in slow motion. She knew they'd think *she* was the threat and by the time they figured out the truth someone could be dead. She didn't intend it to be Mac or Cole.

Eighteen years of martial arts training had Tess twisting out of Walsh's grip. The cuffs got in the way of her efforts to block, but she batted the clipboard away so the woman's hands were no longer hidden. Everyone was still a split-second behind her in reaction time and Tess didn't think, she just acted. She rushed the woman, crowding her against the wall. The blast of a handgun exploded through the chaos and fire seared her side like a white-hot poker sinking into her flesh.

———

PAULA SCREAMED IN frustration as Cole's traitorous bitch of a sister ruined her plans of revenge. Twenty years of planning and preparation destroyed and for what?

She'd had the director in her sites. She inched the weapon out from under Tess's weight and fired off another shot, but the director and AG were back in their protective bubble, while her colleagues scrambled, trying to figure out what the hell was going on.

Fools. Idiots. Imbeciles!

Paula held Tess up with her left arm and put the Smith and Wesson that David had given her against his daughter's forehead.

The room went silent and Tess tensed even as she leaned heavily on Paula. One wrong move and she would happily put another bullet in the bitch.

Agent Walsh was down on the ground, bleeding.

"Paula?" ASAC Steve McKenzie approached with his weapon drawn, his eyes never leaving her face even though she knew he was seeing everything around him, from his pal Walsh bleeding out on the floor, to Tess, her human shield.

"Do you love her, McKenzie?" Her voice came out ragged. "Or did you just fuck her to get information?"

"I love her." Mac's words surprised her in their honesty. She hadn't thought him capable of even that much truth. "If you ever truly loved David, you'll let his daughter go."

She smiled bitterly. Steve McKenzie was the last person who should be allowed to even utter David's name. He was the reason the man she loved was dead.

And then it struck her. There was still some revenge she could salvage from this mess. "I watched you two going at it like sex-starved rabbits. Figured you'd be busy on that kitchen table for long enough for me to murder your pesky ex. The cops were stupid enough to fall for it and the FBI obediently followed suit."

Tess tried to struggle but Paula tightened her grip. The people around them didn't seem to realize Tess had taken a bullet and was slowly bleeding out. "Stay still if you want your brother to live," she hissed into Tess's ear.

Paula looked at Cole, who was white-faced with shock. Poor kid. He'd never stood a chance being brought up in such a tainted environment.

"Carolyn?" Cole swallowed noisily. "What are you doing?"

She pursed her lips and shook her head. "Not Carolyn, lover. Paula. Carolyn was an undercover identity I used occasionally." She watched his forehead crease in confusion. "I was doing what your daddy wanted me to, Cole. Didn't mean I didn't love you."

Tess was leaning heavily against her now. Paula felt the hot, slick slide of blood seeping into her suit.

Mac edged closer. Paula knew he was capable with a pistol. She'd studied him avidly at the gun range. She intended to make him use the weapon to give her the spectacular ending she deserved. She just hoped to delay that inevitable long enough to take the woman he loved with her.

"You're Henry Jessop's daughter?" he asked.

A fresh wave of hatred rushed over her but the longer she stretched this out, the more chance she had of making Steve McKenzie weep.

She knew exactly how hard it was to lose the person you loved.

He cocked his head to the side. "I don't remember seeing you at the compound."

"David's bitch of a wife suspected us so I never came over to the compound. We used to meet at the old cabin or in town." Memories made Paula's throat clog.

"You were friends with Brandy Jordan?" he asked.

Paula smirked. "Yeah, I heard you were looking for her. She wouldn't have told you anything." Finally, she was free of the lies and deception. She didn't have to pretend to be some little, drone bitch. "Brandy dragged me to the bar one day to meet Eddie and his brother. David was there, too." It had been fate—beautiful and capricious. Despite all the pain and misery that followed, she wouldn't swap that one magical year for anything.

"You were young and impressionable. He used you for sex, but he would never have left Francis for you." Mac's eyes held pity and she wanted to pull the trigger and obliterate Tess Fallon's skull just for that. To witness the destruction of all Mac's hopes and dreams. But this was better. The classic negotiator's tactic of slowing everything down and getting the hostage-taker to talk was gonna cost Tess her life. Paula was smarter than he was. She was smarter than them all.

"He *was* gonna leave her but then she got pregnant with Cole." Her eyes lifted to the young man she'd seduced. "Your mother really was a bitch."

Mac ignored her. "So you married some guy called Rice or is that another false identity?"

She shrugged and settled Tess's heavy weight against her chest. Didn't matter now. "He was one of Dad's ranch hands. I paid him for the privilege of being my husband and then paid him off a few years later. He was harmless." She hadn't even slept with him. The only man she'd slept with since David was Cole. Their relationship hadn't been about the sex. It had been about love.

"What happened to your son, Paula?"

Icy cold washed over her. How did he know she'd had a child? "Henry raised him, but he…" Her voice cracked. "He died in an accident on the farm when he was fifteen."

Mac was moving to her right where she was more open. How long before he spotted the blood on Tess's side? But he didn't drop his gaze from her eyes.

"It's over, Paula. Let Tess go and you can have your day in court. You can gloat about how easy it was to make us look like fools. You can brag about all you accomplished. How you infiltrated the FBI."

"Nah." Paula kept her shield in place. It was tempting, but prison wasn't her idea of infamy. "You guys are going to be too busy fighting to prosecute anyone. The courts won't even exist anymore."

He laughed. "You think your fellow antigovernment nut jobs are gonna come out of the woodwork and rise up now? Because you parked a truck out front? Give me a break."

"It's already happening and you know it," she hissed.

Tess went completely limp in her arms. Paula struggled to hold her upright but never took her finger off the trigger. Was the bitch dead yet? Or just passed out? Paula took a step along the wall. There was nowhere to go. "They'll see the truck bomb on the news—"

"We already spun it as a training exercise," Mac cut her off. Another man discounting her opinions, her value.

"The media knows better," she ground out. "So do the others who think the same way I do."

Mac laughed scornfully "They won't do a damned thing and you know it. They're chickenshit. You wasted your whole life on some fruitless exercise in revenge and when we round them up, they'll squeal like babies and head straight to prison."

"You'll never find them all. They're everywhere." She smiled evilly. "In every facet of law enforcement, in every government department. Even elected officials. The revolution just began and you can't stop it. Not anymore."

Mac was shaking his head like he knew more than she did. God, she hated him. Hated his supercilious arrogance and smug over-confidence while his girl died in her arms.

"We have their names and IP addresses from the One-Drop-2-Many site."

"Liar." No way could they decrypt that information.

"High school grad hacked the site. Feds are knocking on doors as we speak." Mac grinned and she swung the gun toward him, determined to wipe the smirk off his handsome face.

———————

MAC LINED UP his sites between Paula Rice's navy blue eyes and smoothly squeezed the trigger.

She crumpled to the floor, no more revolutionary bullshit oozing from her lips. Tess dropped like a deadweight on top of her. He hadn't hit her—thank God. What was wrong? Had she passed out?

Other agents moved in, blocking his view, kicking Paula's weapon away from her body. Someone lifted Tess and laid her on the floor. Three agents were attending to Walsh who was in bad shape. Mac pushed past Eban Winters who was checking Paula's pulse.

"She's dead," he declared, catching Mac's eye. "Nice shot."

Nice shot, an inch to the left of Tess's skull with a gun he'd never fired before. He'd put his trust in Alex Parker's professionalism.

God. He felt sick. Why wasn't Tess moving? What was wrong?

He knelt beside her on the floor. Moved the hair off her face. "Did she faint?" He felt for her pulse. Then he glanced lower and saw a pool of blood staining the top of her jeans. He ripped up her crimson sweater and saw a bullet hole just above her hip. "Get the medics over here!" he roared.

"Apply pressure to the wound," Eban ordered, coming in beside him.

Sweat burst out of his pores as Mac ripped off his sweater and folded it several times, and pressed it over the wound.

Eban checked her pulse again. Frazer was giving Walsh CPR. Fuck. How had Rice got this far?

"Is she breathing?" Mac asked Eban, holding back a scream of fear and frustration.

"Tess?" Cole's anguished cry came from behind him. He didn't want to imagine what the kid was going through. He'd been in love with a woman who didn't exist, who'd used him and maybe gotten his sister killed.

"Don't die on me, Tess. Don't you dare die on me. I've got a lot of making up to do."

"She's not breathing. Pulse is thready." Eban started blowing into her lungs and Mac felt hope draining out of him with every drop of Tess's blood that seeped into the carpet.

"Where are the fucking medics!" he yelled.

He felt a hand on his shoulder and looked up with a glare. It was the director.

"Is there any evidence to suggest she's involved in this plot?" the director asked.

"No, sir. We've checked all her banking activity, online communications, all her known associates. There is no proof she is involved."

"Then take those handcuffs off."

Eban obeyed. Mac wasn't removing his hands from Tess's injury for anything or anyone.

Finally, he heard running feet and medics burst into the room.

Cole dropped to his knees beside his sister. Tess's face was blueish-white and last time Mac had seen someone that pale they'd been in the morgue.

The paramedics pushed him out of the way and started pulling Tess's clothing aside. Cole swore when he saw the small bullet hole was still seeping blood.

Mac wanted to scream and rage but needed to focus.

"We're going to find every last one of the people who thought they could attack us in the heart of the FBI." The director was talking to him but Mac's gaze was on Tess. "Frazer, I want you and ASAC McKenzie to nail down every piece of information we have on these people. Stamp out any signs of this so-called uprising."

Mac nodded. Yes. Law enforcement needed to make sure they rounded up all the crazies involved in this mess before anyone else had any lightbulb moments. The paramedics eased Tess onto a stretcher and lifted it. Started running out the doors.

The director strode off to deal with the fallout.

Frazer squeezed his arm. "This is one of those moments that defines us for the rest of our lives."

Mac snapped out of his fugue state. He started walking. Then he started running. No way was he letting Tess out of his sight. His job suddenly seemed irrelevant compared to the concept of losing her. The paramedics were about to close the door of the ambulance when he swung up beside them.

"You can't come in here," one guy said.

He sat down on the end of Tess's stretcher and squeezed her foot. "Just try and stop me."

CHAPTER THIRTY-THREE

M AC WORE A groove in the waiting room floor.
A young man paced in another room across the
corridor. Tears streamed down his face. Mac wondered who
he was here to see.

Agent Makimi had taken over the task force and confirmed that Paula Rice had been assigned to each of the field
offices where similar hate crimes had been committed.

Agents had gone to her apartment with a bomb squad but
there had been no explosives. Her workstation, home, vehicle
were being examined in minute detail. Carter had left a
message saying they'd found the original copy of David
Hines's manifesto in her desk drawer. Alex Parker had told
him his people had identified the IP addresses of over a
hundred users of the One-Drop-2-Many chat group. Law
enforcement were checking every address and shaking down
anyone they could get their hands on.

The news cycle kept repeating the footage of the truck
being parked outside FBI HQ and showed him and Frazer
pulling Cole out of the van and taking him down. Mac was
pretty sure Cole was innocent, but they'd need to question him
extensively and tear his place and computer apart to make sure
they didn't miss anything.

If Mac concentrated on the case he didn't have to remember the sound of Tess flat-lining in the ambulance or the shouts of the doctors saying they were losing her again as they rushed her through those wide, double doors. He didn't have to remember seeing one of his best friends lying pale and bleeding on the stretcher as he was wheeled into the adjacent OR.

Frazer entered the waiting room holding hands with a woman with strawberry blonde hair. Mac didn't recognize her.

She nodded to him and then disengaged her hand and went to sit in an empty chair.

Tess had no one besides Cole to contact. He stared around the empty room and it hit him just how alone she was, how alone she had always been because of her damn family.

The lump in his throat grew when Frazer pulled him into a rough embrace. Frazer wasn't the huggy, feeling type. Mac hadn't realized he'd been crying.

"Did you see her go after an armed woman in a room full of trained federal agents? Wearing handcuffs?"

Frazer nodded.

"She's never gonna forgive me."

Frazer gave his arm a squeeze before letting go. "Do you love her?"

Mac closed his eyes. "Yeah. I do."

"Then grovel and beg until she does. Hell, if she lives, tell her you'll change and be a better man even though it isn't true."

Mac held tight to his ragged emotions. "You want to introduce me to your lady friend?"

"That's Izzy. But let's not do proper introductions," said Frazer. "Not today. Not here."

Mac nodded.

"Any news?" Frazer asked.

"Not yet."

The doors opened and a man in green scrubs started looking around. He opened the door to the waiting room and as anxious as Mac was to hear how Tess was, another part of him wanted to run. If she was dead Mac knew he'd never recover.

Was this why his father had drunk himself to death? Grief? Mac had never appreciated it before, but maybe his father had died the same day his mother had, it had just taken longer. For the first time ever, Mac felt a sliver of sympathy for his old man.

"How are they doing, Doc?"

"I'm looking for Mr. Walsh's family—"

"His parents are on their way. About two hours out. I'm his ASAC. Is he gonna make it?" Mac asked.

"The bullet nicked Mr. Walsh's spleen and we had to remove it. There was a lot of bleeding but I think we got it under control. It was touch and go."

Mac was aware of Izzy coming to stand beside him.

"And Tess?" Frazer asked because every time Mac tried to open his mouth his tongue refused to work.

The surgeon drew in a ragged breath and gave his head a little shake. Mac's knees started to go and he felt an arm grip his waist. Frazer's girlfriend seemed to be holding him up.

"She's alive but..." The surgeon searched around as if expecting someone else. "Are you family?"

Mac stood straighter. "Yes. I'm her fiancé."

It didn't feel like a lie.

The surgeon nodded. "The bullet hit her pelvis and fragmented. The real damage was to her ovaries." His lips turned down. "I'm afraid we had to perform an emergency unilateral salpingo-oophorectomy."

"It's where they remove a single ovary with its fallopian tube," Izzy explained in English.

"You're a doctor?" the surgeon asked her.

She nodded and they spoke gibberish for another minute.

Then she squeezed Mac's arm again. "She's been through a lot and will have a long recuperation. She can probably still have kids if she wants but her fertility may be affected."

Mac kept swallowing and swallowing, but he'd lost the ability to speak.

"But she's alive? Any other damage?" Frazer asked.

The surgeon nodded. "Her pelvis was broken and we had to put a plate and screws in to fix it. Both patients are very lucky to be alive. They're in the ICU. I'll send a nurse down as soon as you can see them."

Mac drew in a deep breath as the surgeon left. The guy walked across the corridor and started talking to the young man there. The OR must be hellish busy on a Friday night.

"I have to get back to HQ," Frazer told him. "The director gave me an order so I figure I better see it through even though it's not my task force." Frazer loved being involved, though. He was just like Mac in that regard. "We figured out Rice knew each of the victims through her work as an agent. She'd given testimony in Judge Thomas's court, spoke to Sonja Shiraz and Rabbi Zingel on the phone when they made complaints. Not sure if she knew Trettorri personally or just chose him because of his prominence. He's upstairs in a private room, recovering. We'll interview him when he's feeling better."

Mac nodded.

The director had given him an order, too. But if he had to

choose between his job and Tess he was going to choose Tess. For once in her life she deserved to be someone's priority and not an afterthought. What happened when she woke up was up for debate though. Earning forgiveness wasn't going to be easy and she might never absolve him of his sins. But he'd rather risk everything trying to make her love him, than turn his back on her again.

─────────────

TESS OPENED HER eyelids a tiny slit and scanned the dim shadows. She knew she was in the hospital, but she couldn't remember why.

Her lips were ragged and cracked, mouth dry, throat sore. Beeps sounded from nearby, dragging her further out of the darkness. Constant. Reassuringly steady. Her heartbeat.

She remembered feeling Mac's pulse after they'd made love. The strong, steady rhythm. The heat of his flesh. The smell of his skin. Then she remembered everything that happened afterwards and the cadence stuttered.

She swallowed tightly. So that's what a broken heart sounded like.

She tried to move and pain streaked through her body as more details rushed back. She'd been shot. What had happened to the rogue agent in the FBI building? Was Mac safe? Was Cole? Had the bad guys succeeded with their crazy plan?

A shadowy figure moved around the bed and she blinked, trying to clear her vision.

"Joseph? What are you doing here?" Her voice was gravelly.

He sat heavily on a chair beside her bed and took her hand in his. He'd been crying, she realized.

Her heart gave a little flutter. "Is it Cole?"

Was he okay? Was he alive?

Joseph squeezed her hand, but accidentally snagged the IV line and it hurt.

She sucked in a sharp breath. He looked up and something changed in his eyes. He deliberately moved the IV, the needle stabbing into her arm.

"Ouch! Joseph, what are you doing?"

He released her hand and dragged his fingers through his hair. "Sorry. I don't know what I'm doing anymore."

He stood and moved out of sight, staring at her heart rate monitor as if fascinated.

"It's my birthday tomorrow," he said.

She crinkled her brow in confusion. Why was he telling her this? She'd been shot. She wasn't up for a party. "I know. I'm sorry Cole won't be there to help you celebrate. I'm sure he'll make it up to you afterwards."

The Feds would have to release him, wouldn't they? But he had driven a bomb to headquarters even if he hadn't realized it. What would happen if they didn't believe he was innocent?

"Birthdays have always been a bit weird. I was actually born on February twenty-ninth so most years I never know whether to celebrate on the twenty-eighth or the first. I ever tell you about my parents?"

"No." She wished she could have a drink of water. She peered around for the call button. She didn't even know why Joseph was here.

"I never knew my daddy." He reached up to press a button on the machine and the beeping got quieter.

"I'm sorry." She tried to shift position. Pain shot through her again, as if she'd been struck by lightning. Sweat broke out on her brow. She was okay as long as she didn't move, but not moving was proving tough.

"Does it hurt?" He came back to the bed and sat beside her.

She nodded. Where was Mac? She wanted to know what had happened. She couldn't remember much after she'd been shot. Why was Joseph here? Why had the nurses let him in? "Did you speak to Cole?"

He shook his head. "I was on the phone with Zane when the FBI showed up at the house. I heard them arrest Zane and Dave. What happened?" he asked.

She rolled her head on the pillow as the discomfort intensified. "Some crazy bitch shot me."

He nodded quietly, as if people got shot every day. She supposed they did, but it didn't make it less traumatic or painful.

She glanced at him as he inserted a SIM card into a phone followed by the battery. "I don't think you're allowed to use cell phones in here, Joseph."

He nodded as if considering her words, then dialed a number and put the phone on a shelf beside her bed. "Did I ever tell you about where I grew up, Tess? Or maybe I should call you Theresa Jane?"

Her eyes bugged. Her heart stalled.

"I think you know the area. In fact, I think you met my grandpa in Idaho this week?" He smacked his lips appreciatively. "I sure do miss his cooking."

Tess's lips felt wooden. "Henry Jessop was your grandpa?" She knew it was true even as fear crawled up her spine and along every frayed nerve. She was completely powerless lying here in this bed. Something else snapped into place. "It was you in my house last night. You used Cole's spare key."

"Cole's not real good with security. You might have noticed." Joseph gave a smile that didn't reach his dark blue eyes. "I was looking for a thumb drive of mine—did you take it?"

Her mouth opened in shock.

Then he shrugged. "Doesn't matter anymore. The grand plans all went to shit. I tried to tell them it wouldn't work, that we should concentrate on sabotaging them via cyber warfare, but they wanted blood. I think my mother just wanted revenge for the Feds killing her beloved David." His eyes locked onto hers. "Did you know the name 'Joseph' means 'son of David'?"

And the final piece clicked into place.

His lips tipped. Her father's lips. "Have you figured it out yet, darling Tess?"

"You're my half-brother..." Oh, God. "You came on to me!"

"My mother always said the MacAfee's were inbred, but I think it was the Hines who were the perverts."

Tess's mother had been a MacAfee before she'd gotten married.

"But I'd have totally done you if I'd had the chance." Joseph smiled sadly.

Tess refused to believe there was a gene for incest. She thought about Cole and herself. They were both decent people. "Joseph, you don't have to be like them..."

An ugly laugh escaped his lips. "Too late for that." Another tear escaped and this one dripped off his chin.

"You can go to the cops. Explain how you were brainwashed."

He hung his head. "I've committed too many crimes to ever walk free."

"Give them the names of the others involved. They might swap the information for immunity." Where the hell was the call button for the nurse? Where was everyone?

She watched him remove the heart-beat monitor from her finger and slip it onto his own.

"That might have worked for conspiracy but not for pulling the trigger." His bottom lip wobbled. "What's that saying? You can pick your friends but you can't pick your family? Sorry, Tess. Not sure you're going to be able to hide from fate this time around."

Her heart was pounding so fast it didn't even speed up when he slipped the pillow from behind her head.

"That crazy bitch who shot you today? That was my mother." Joseph pressed the spongy pillow gently over her face.

Tess tried to struggle, but the pain in her pelvis was so bad it almost made her pass out. The inability to draw in breath had panic running rampant along every neuron. Lack of oxygen made her lungs scream. Surely someone would rescue her? But none of the alarms had gone off, so why would they?

The pillow pressed tighter around her face, the cool cotton at odds with the dense suffocating material. As she gasped and struggled to inhale, the stitches in her abdomen tore and started to bleed. Black spots danced in her vision and the abyss screamed at her to just give up and fall. No more pain. No more suffering. No more hate.

FRAZER AND IZZY left with the promise they'd return later.

Mac headed to the cafeteria to buy some coffee to try and keep his eyes open for the next few hours. He hadn't slept last night. Apart from that night in the motel with Tess he'd barely slept this week.

He closed his eyes. Twelve hours ago he'd been making love to Tess. Now she lay in a hospital bed with a gunshot wound.

She'd never forgive him for what he'd done to her brother. Never. But he needed to tell her that he loved her, even if she could never bring herself to love him back. He had to give her that truth, that honesty. He had to tell her he didn't care about her past or her family or the secrets she'd kept from him this week. He got it. He understood. She loved her brother, and she was probably right about him being innocent in all this. And he hadn't believed her. Trust was her big issue. Demonstrating he was a good FBI agent was his. So maybe instead of trying so hard to be a good FBI agent, Mac would just concentrate on being a better man.

He wasn't that trailer trash kid anymore. He didn't have anything left to prove.

And if she didn't want him?

He shook his head at himself. Why the hell would she want him after this fiasco? This wasn't just a slight misunderstanding. This was life and death.

His phone rang. Makimi. He wanted to ignore the call, but she was on this task force because he'd requested her. He owed her.

"McKenzie."

"We just got the DNA back from Trettorri's fingernails."

"Okay." Mac nodded. He should visit Trettorri, see if the guy was awake and remembered anything else from the shooting.

"We also got the results back from your ex's murder scene."

"Were they a match to Paula Rice?"

"Her DNA hasn't been run yet so it's too early to tell. The weapon she pulled at SIOC today was a match for the make of the one used in the rabbi's murder and Trettorri's shooting, but…"

He wanted her to just spit it out, but she'd been working non-stop for days, too. He couldn't let his impatience affect how he treated the people he worked with.

"Here's the thing, the DNA from the two crimes wasn't a complete match."

"What do you mean?" His brain wasn't working.

"The DNA found at your ex-wife's murder was not the same as the DNA from the Trettorri shooting, but there was a link through maternal DNA. Another interesting thing popped up in the results. David Hines was likely the father of whoever killed your ex."

Mac gripped the nape of his neck as he processed the science. "So Paula Rice lied about her son being dead. She was protecting him."

"Probably. Sorry I don't have more."

"Thanks, Miki. I appreciate it. You're the best. The kid's probably gone to ground."

"Yeah, I know. I just wanted to tell you. I'd want to know," she said softly. So much for her sharp corners. Makimi had a heart of gold.

"Any luck rounding up these so-called revolutionaries?" he asked her.

She snorted. "FBI is picking people up but being careful to

avoid any hostage situations. So far everyone is denying everything. There are a couple of people we're going to sit on and watch. People in interesting places."

"DOJ better put these assholes away."

They said goodbye and he hung up. He turned and saw Tess's surgeon waiting in line for coffee.

The man nodded to him. "I just spoke with Tess's brother and told him he could sit with her for a while."

Mac frowned in confusion. "Her brother?"

"Yeah, he was in the other waiting room. Don't you guys know each other?" The surgeon seemed confused.

Mac's heart stopped. "That wasn't Tess's brother." *Oh, shit.* "Which way to the ICU?" he asked, hand on his weapon.

The surgeon seemed to realize it was an emergency. "Follow me."

Then Mac's cell phone started ringing with the MC Hammer tune, and he felt like he'd been buried alive in a Montana blizzard.

MAC'S TRAINING KICKED in just as they reached the ICU. Even though every fiber of his being screamed for him to rush in there and save Tess, he knew he had to think. He forced his breathing to calm and grabbed the surgeon's arm before the man crashed headlong into Tess's room.

Paula Rice's bastard was expecting him. Mac didn't intend to be a sacrificial feeb.

"Is there another way into the room?"

The doc nodded and backtracked into the room next-door. Walsh was asleep in the bed and Mac hoped to hell no one else got shot today.

Mac pressed his ear to an adjoining door, suddenly reminded of Tess trying to listen to the threesome in that motel in Salt Lake City.

The thought of losing her scrambled what little was left of his brain.

It was quiet except for the beeps of Walsh's monitors. With hand signals, Mac indicated the surgeon clear the area. If anyone else got injured he'd never forgive himself, but he didn't have time to wait for backup. Tess was in danger.

He opened the door and rushed inside the dimly lit room. A young man sat in the chair beside the bed. Mac frowned. He didn't see a weapon. The guy just sat there, smiling.

Tess lay in the hospital bed unmoving. Then Mac realized what was wrong with the room. The quiet. Unlike Walsh's room next door, there were no telltale beeps or other intrusive sounds.

Tess lay inert on the bed. No rise and fall of the bedsheets.

He grabbed the kid and had him on the floor, knee in the center of his back as he slapped on the cuffs.

"Doc!" Mac yelled. "Get in here! It's safe."

He hoped to hell it was safe. There was a scramble of footsteps and the slide of feet.

Mac couldn't even bring himself to look at Tess.

This frat boy, hell, he was virtually still a kid, had probably murdered Mac's ex last night. And he'd done more than just kill Heather, he'd gotten off on it. The guy was sick and proved it by laughing his ass off.

If he'd killed Tess, too, Mac would put a bullet in this piece of shit. Career or no career.

Mac glanced up at the doctor and nurse trying to revive

the woman he loved. All he wanted was to be with her but, once again, because of his job, he couldn't go to her. He was stuck guarding the trash.

The utter stillness of Tess's form and the electronic inertia of those fucking machines were driving stakes through his heart in perfect time to his own heartbeat.

Then suddenly there was a solitary, lonely beep, then another, and another.

"We have her back," the surgeon yelled. "Get me some adhesive to seal her incision." The doc grinned across at him. "She tore some stitches. She's gonna be fine."

Mac jerked the scumbag who'd tried to kill Tess to his feet and turned him to face the woman who lay in the bed, still fighting, still resisting the evil that infected so many of her relatives. She was a shining light of goodness. This guy was slime.

"Mac?" She opened her eyes and croaked.

Mac kept a firm hold of the young psychopath who'd finally stopped laughing and instead swore furiously.

Mac caught Tess's gaze. "Yes, sweetheart?"

Her voice was thin and crackly, but the sheer strength of her will shone through. "I love you, Mac."

Relief punched him in the gut.

"I love you, too. Be a good girl now and get some sleep until I get back. No more excitement, 'kay? I need to get this guy booked so we can get on with the rest of our lives."

A life that was categorically going to involve Tess.

CHAPTER THIRTY-FOUR

MAC PACKED UP his desk and figured there was no avoiding it any longer. He hefted the heavy bag that contained all his paperwork and headed upstairs to SIOC. He bumped into Libby Hernandez outside ASC Gerald's office.

"Going somewhere?" she asked.

"Today's my last day."

"Ha, good one!" She put her hand on her heart. "You almost had me for a moment."

Mac remembered the date. "Yeah. I know it's April Fool's Day but I'm not actually kidding."

The file she held in her hand crinkled as her grip tightened. "But you only just started here." She appeared upset, which was more than he'd expected.

Truth was he felt like he'd been here a thousand years already. Tess was getting out of the hospital this week. It had been a month since she'd been shot and almost died. They hadn't spoken about the future, but he had a ring burning a hole in his pocket and he intended to be there for her every step of the way.

Libby appeared genuinely horrified. "But you can't go now—"

"Hernandez!" She was cut off by Gerald who opened his door.

ASC Gerald was the only person here who knew of Mac's decision and he'd asked Gerald to keep it from the others.

Frazer and Parker knew. Parker had offered him a position if he wanted it, but Mac hadn't figured out the future yet. He just wanted Tess.

The investigation into Paula Rice's infiltration of the FBI and how much damage she'd caused was ongoing. Makimi was doing a hell of a job weeding out the right-wing extremists who'd colluded in acts of sedition against the US government, not to mention murder. A couple of the lucky ones had flipped like breaching humpbacks and the whole stack of cards had come tumbling down in the resultant tsunami.

Makimi was going to go far and Mac was thrilled for her.

Gerald stepped out of his room to shake Mac's hand. "The director wants to say something to you…"

The director stepped out of Gerald's office and Mac blinked in surprise. Mac didn't want any speeches. He shifted uncomfortably. He should have slipped out without anyone noticing.

The director held out his hand. "You did great work on HQBOMB, McKenzie."

HQBOMB was the name of the investigation into the events leading up to and surrounding the attempt to bomb headquarters. The FBI did love its acronyms and this one seemed appropriate.

Mac smiled politely. "Not really, sir."

The man held onto his hand and pressed a little harder. "I think you forgot the part where you and ASAC Frazer raced to a vehicle you suspected was laden with explosives, detained the suspect, and managed to neutralize the threat without anyone getting hurt."

"We still missed the main culprit."

Cole Fallon had been released and Mac had spent a lot of time with the kid lately as they'd kept Tess company. Cole was young and pliable, but seemed like a good guy who'd been through hell. He'd discovered the woman he loved had set him up to take the fall for an act of terrorism. He'd also watched that same woman shoot his sister before Mac put a bullet between her eyes.

Paula Rice had deserved to die. At the time of the raid twenty years ago, Paula had been three months pregnant with her son, Joseph.

It had been a tough time, but Cole had rallied around his sister and cooperated in every facet of the investigation. He'd had no idea one of his best friends was actually his half-brother, or that he was sleeping with Joseph's mother. He'd been targeted and used by them both.

"You saved lives that day. Possibly mine." The director's brown eyes were intent on his.

"Tess saved lives. We got lucky." Mac didn't like to think what could have happened if that bomb had gone off, or if Tess hadn't stopped Paula. It was bad enough Walsh and Tess had both taken bullets.

"Good training and keen instincts help people get lucky." The director stepped back. "I have a proposition for you."

"Sorry." Mac shook his head.

"You don't know what it is yet." The director laughed. "The Special Agent in Charge of the WFO is retiring due to ill health. I want you to take the job."

Emotion crowded Mac's throat and he couldn't speak. It was everything he'd ever wanted, but he wanted Tess more.

"I'm truly honored by the offer, sir. The FBI has been my

whole life." He swallowed roughly. "But I'm hoping I can persuade Tess Fallon to be my wife just as soon as she's walking again."

"I don't see why those things are mutually exclusive." The director lifted his chin and angled his face towards Gerald's office. "Ms. Fallon. What do you think?"

Mac's eyes widened as Frazer opened Gerald's door wide, and there was Tess. Finally standing up again. The curly, brown hair, which annoyed her so much, was pulled back in a loose braid. She wore a pretty wraparound dress because pants were too much effort to get on.

Her eyes were smiling, her skin pale, but there was a little color in her cheeks. Frazer was holding her arm.

"You had something to ask the lady?" Frazer prompted when Mac stood there like a dummy.

It was an ambush but there was Tess—standing, smiling—and he didn't care.

He put his bags down on the secretary's desk and stepped past Gerald and the director. Maybe now, she'd finally understand what she meant to him.

He dropped to one knee in front of her. "Tess Fallon, would you do the very great honor of letting this sad, lonely, former FBI agent become your husband?"

"No." She crossed her arms and blinked rapidly. "Being an FBI agent isn't just a job for you, Mac, it's who you are. If you quit because of me, eventually you'll hate me for it."

"No, I won't."

She huffed. "Yes, you will."

"First domestic," the director intoned quietly to Gerald.

"Better get used to it and just do as she tells him," Gerald agreed.

Mac glared at the interrupters.

Frazer sighed. "If you'd really screwed up the investigation I'd agree with you resigning, Mac. But no one blames you for Paula Rice. The entire FBI missed the signs. We all messed up to the same degree. Without you we wouldn't have solved this thing until a lot more people had been murdered and a lot more agents had died."

Frazer put a good spin on it, but it was Tess who Mac was watching. He was trying to read those clear, hazel eyes and that full, mobile mouth.

He assessed her carefully. "So, would you consider marrying a sad and lonely, *employed* FBI agent?"

She grinned. "Yes."

Tears sparkled in her eyes when he pulled a ring out of his pocket.

"Boy scout," Frazer muttered, clearly disgusted.

"Always prepared," Mac muttered back.

"Not always," Tess said softly.

Mac's cheeks heated at that and Frazer coughed into his fist.

Mac slipped the pink diamond set in platinum onto her finger, happy that it fit. "We can change it if you like." He'd chosen it because it was delicate and feminine, but also strong and durable. And the pink stone reminded him of her lips.

She stared at the ring for a long moment and then at him. "I don't want to change it. It's perfect. Thank you."

Mac rose to his feet and reverently cupped her cheek, and leaned down very slowly to kiss her. She kissed him back, her hands rising to his shoulders and holding on tight.

He pulled back, letting her rest her head on his chest. Tess was recovering well, but she'd suffered a terrible injury and she'd done it to protect a bunch of heavily armed, highly trained people who'd previously vilified her.

He glanced over his shoulder. "Maybe I'd like to reconsider my resignation."

Gerald grimaced. "Just as well I never put in the paperwork then."

"Seriously?" Mac put his arm around Tess's back, supporting her, and turned to face his boss. Tess leaned against him, already tired from her exertions. "What were you going to do if I left today?"

Gerald looked embarrassed. "Donate my vacation days and hope my wife didn't notice."

Mac's mouth went dry at that. "I appreciate your confidence, sir." Mac turned his attention to the director. "As much as I would love the WFO post, I don't feel I've earned it—yet. I'd like to stay on in my position here if possible. There's still plenty to do. Plenty to learn."

"Is this penance for any mistakes you think you made?" the director queried. "You have more than earned this posting."

"I appreciate that." Mac wished he could talk to Tess alone. "This whole time I was chasing the wrong dream. I was looking at the destination and not concentrating on the journey." He kissed the top of Tess's hair and she rested her hand on his heart. "I want to enjoy the journey for a little longer."

The director nodded. "Fine." Then he came and grasped Mac's hand. "Glad you changed your mind, and congratulations." He leaned down and kissed Tess on the cheek. "Thank you again, Tess. You saved lives that day and will always be welcome here." The director winked. "And I expect an invitation. My wife loves weddings."

Gerald held the door. "I'm gonna give you two some privacy for a few minutes."

Frazer removed himself from the side of the room. "That's my cue to leave, too. Let me know if you need to buy a new tux. I have connections." He grinned hugely. "Congratulations."

Finally, it was just Mac and Tess.

He stroked an unruly strand of her hair and hooked it behind her ear. "You tired?"

She denied it, but the white around her mouth gave her away.

He steered her to a seat and knelt in front of her.

She smiled as she examined her ring. "So I get to change my name again, huh?"

Mac rested his hands along the outside of her thighs. "If you want to."

"I do." She drew in a big breath. "I want a fresh start. New home. New name."

"As long as I'm the one constant in your life I don't give a damn about the rest. We'll start house hunting as soon as you're feeling stronger."

"When I was a little girl I used to dream about marrying you." She stared into her lap shyly. "Is it crazy that it's coming true?"

"Nope. Not crazy at all. But it seems like a million years ago."

She seemed pensive.

"What is it?"

"I figured out a few things."

He knew she'd been doing a lot of thinking.

"I want to write a book about my experiences. I want to donate the proceeds in Ellie's honor to an organization that's fighting to end child marriage in America."

Mac's voice was rough. "I think that's a great idea."

"And I spoke to Cole. We want to donate the land to a good cause, but we haven't figured out which one yet." She shuddered. "I want to be free of all those old ties."

Mac nodded. "What's Cole gonna do now?"

Mac hadn't revealed the existence of the file and thumb drive. Parker had examined it and sure enough their plans were encrypted on the drive, but the documents had belonged to Joseph. The plan had been to frame Cole so he and his mother could get away with murder and start their revolution. Cole had been nothing but a pawn. Joseph was in jail awaiting trial. Chances were he'd die in prison. Eddie was locked up again and the prison guard who'd helped him escape was up on charges.

Mac hoped Eddie enjoyed the reduced privileges of maximum security.

Tess smiled and Mac touched the gentle curve of her lips. "He told me he was going to take some criminal justice courses at the university. Said the good guys needed more geeks."

Mac couldn't agree more and didn't mention it had been his suggestion.

"I might also want children. One day." Her gaze turned pensive. "There's nothing like being told you might not be able to have kids to make you reassess that priority."

Mac drew in a deep breath. The idea of starting a family with Tess made a lump form in his throat. "Let's give it some time. If you still want kids we can try in the future. Or we can adopt." He stared deep into her eyes. "Plenty of kids around in need of a good home."

Tears welled and her hands started to shake.

"I need to get you back to bed," said Mac.

She huffed. "I wish."

"Doctor said no sex for another month." He smoothed a hand over her cheek. "Doesn't mean we can't get inventive in the meantime."

She blushed and brushed her thumb over his bottom lip. "Sex god."

"Damn right. Let's go home and get started on that, shall we? I think I've earned a day off." He pulled her carefully to her feet and bent down to lift her into his arms.

He opened the door and stopped short as a whole crowd of people started cheering. His throat closed with emotion. *Crap.*

"Surprise," Tess whispered in his ear.

"Does this mean I'm going to have to wait to get you in bed again?" he whispered back.

"Patience. We have all the time in the world now."

He carefully eased Tess back onto her feet and Frazer pushed over a wheelchair he must have brought from the hospital. Tess wasn't happy to be sitting in it but Mac didn't leave her side.

Everyone from SIOC had come to celebrate their engagement and to make Tess feel their love and gratitude. Walsh was there in a matching wheelchair. He was as frustrated as Tess at the slowness of their convalescence. They'd been competing with each other as to whom recovered the fastest. Like everyone else who spent any time with Tess, Walsh had fallen completely in love with her.

"Tired?" Mac asked her after thirty minutes of cake,

champagne and congratulations. Everyone there had needed a little light relief after what they'd been through. They were celebrating one of the few good things to come out of a difficult period.

She grinned. "I never imagined I'd be here, at FBI HQ, getting engaged to someone as wonderful as you are. I'm so lucky."

Mac frowned down at her. "You've got it all wrong, sweetheart. I'm the lucky one." He smoothed away a tear that had slipped down her cheek. "And I'm smart enough to know it."

"Fidelity. Bravery. Integrity." She sniffed.

"Or Fucking Bunch of Idiots, depending on who you talk to."

"I prefer my version," she told him quietly. But her lips were pinched and she looked like it was time for her next painkiller.

He took the handles of the wheelchair and headed for the door. "Say goodbye to the inmates. Time to go home."

She reached up and touched his hand. "I like the sound of that."

"Me, too, sweetheart. Me, too."

USEFUL ACRONYM DEFINITIONS FOR TONI'S BOOKS

AG: Attorney General

ASAC: Assistant Special-Agent-in-Charge

ATF: Alcohol, Tobacco, and Firearms

BAU: Behavioral Analysis Unit

BOLO: Be on the Lookout

BUCAR: Bureau Car.

CIRG: Critical Incident Response Group

CMU: Crisis Management Unit

CN: Crisis Negotiator

CNU: Crisis Negotiation Unit

CODIS: Combined DNA Index System

CP: Command Post

DEA: Drug Enforcement Administration

DOB: Date of Birth

DOJ: Department of Justice

EMT: Emergency Medical Technician

ERT: Evidence Response Team

FOA: First-Office Assignment

FBI: Federal Bureau of Investigation

FO: Field Office

IC: Incident Commander

HRT: Hostage Rescue Team

HT: Hostage-Taker

LAPD: Los Angeles Police Department

LEO: Law Enforcement Officer

ME: Medical Examiner

MO: Modus Operandi

NAT: New Agent Trainee

NCIC: National Crime Information Center

NYFO: New York Field Office

OC: Organized Crime

OCU: Organized Crime Unit

OPR: Office of Professional Responsibility

POTUS: President of the United States

RA: Resident Agency

SA: Special Agent

SAC: Special Agent-in-Charge

SAS: Special Air Squadron (British Special Forces unit)

SIOC: Strategic Information & Operations

SSA: Supervisory Special Agent

SWAT: Special Weapons and Tactics

TC: Tactical Commander

TOD: Time of Death

UNSUB: Unknown Subject

ViCAP: Violent Criminal Apprehension Program

WFO: Washington Field Office

COLD JUSTICE SERIES OVERVIEW

A Cold Dark Place (Book #1)
Cold Pursuit (Book #2)
Cold Light of Day (Book #3)
Cold Fear (Book #4)
Cold In The Shadows (Book #5)
Cold Hearted (Book #6)
Cold Secrets (Book #7)
Cold Malice (Book #8)
A Cold Dark Promise (Book #9~A Wedding Novella)
Cold Blooded (Book #10)

COLD JUSTICE – CROSSFIRE
Cold & Deadly (Book #1)
Colder Than Sin (Book #2) Coming 2019

Cold Justice Series books are also available as audiobooks narrated by Eric Dove. See Toni Anderson's website for details (www.toniandersonauthor.com)

ACKNOWLEDGMENTS

Thanks, as always, to my wonderful critique partner, Kathy Altman, who reads the early, really crap versions of the stories and continues to believe in me regardless. And thanks to Rachel Grant who did a great beta read on this manuscript and helped me fix a few issues with my hero.

Thanks to my editors, Alicia Dean, and Joan Turner at JRT Editing, for the extra layers of polish. And Paul Salvette (BB eBooks) who formats my ebooks with such care, and the guys at Createspace who take care of the print book interiors.

Special thanks goes to Angela Bell of the FBI's Office of Public Affairs for arranging an inspiring tour of the Strategic Information and Operations Center (SIOC) at FBI Headquarters in Washington DC, and for answering a long string of odd questions. Bless you. Sorry for the ending! Any mistakes in this book are down to me, and the ever-forgiving concept of artistic license.

Mostly, I want to thank my husband for being the love of my life, and my kids for being awesome.

ABOUT THE AUTHOR

Toni Anderson is a *New York Times* and *USA Today* bestselling author, RITA® finalist, science nerd, professional tourist, dog lover, gardener, mom. Originally from a small town in England, Toni studied Marine Biology at University of Liverpool (B.Sc.) and University of St. Andrews (Ph.D.) with the intention she'd never be far from the ocean. Well, that plan backfired and she ended up in the Canadian prairies with her biology professor husband, two kids, a rescue dog, and one chilled leopard gecko. Her greatest achievements are mastering the Tokyo subway, climbing Ben Lomond, snorkelling the Great Barrier Reef, and surviving fourteen Winnipeg winters. She loves to travel for research purposes and was lucky enough to visit the Strategic Information and Operations Center inside FBI Headquarters in Washington, D.C. in 2016, and she also got to shove another car off the road during pursuit training at the Writer's Police Academy in Wisconsin. Watch out world!

Sign up for Toni Anderson's newsletter:
www.toniandersonauthor.com/newsletter-signup

Like Toni Anderson on Facebook:
facebook.com/toniannanderson

See Toni Anderson's current book list:
www.toniandersonauthor.com/books-2

Follow Toni Anderson on Instagram:
instagram.com/toni_anderson_author

Printed in Great Britain
by Amazon